DIRTY

BLOOD

DIRTY
BLOOD

HEATHER HILDENBRAND

ISBN 9781461065715

CHAPTER ONE

"C'MON, Tara, you didn't even give tonight a fair chance," George said, his blue eyes a mixture of pleading and irritation.

I returned the pool stick to the wall rack and tried to think of a fair answer before turning to face him again. I was careful to keep my voice down; the tiny pool hall was crowded for a Tuesday night. The smoky haze, a permanent fixture in the dimly lit room, gave the illusion of privacy around our corner table, but the couple next to us was already glancing over, trying to look as if they weren't listening.

"George, you were an hour late picking me up because you were working on a press release with your agent." I stepped closer. "Your agent," I repeated, shaking my head. "Seriously. You haven't even graduated yet, much less secured a scholarship. Why do you even need an agent?"

He ran a hand through his hair, evidence of his impatience, though he was careful to keep his tone light, in an attempt to win me to his way of thinking. "I told you already, my dad set it up. And a lot of the pros got one early, especially the big timers. And I'm sorry I was late, but I'm here now and I'm focused on us." His expression became accusing and he added, "More than I can say for you."

I rubbed at my temples, trying in vain to massage away the

stress headache that had become a trademark of our relationship.

"I'm sorry, George, but I'm not the one who messed things up. And I don't fault you for a change in priorities. Football is important to you. That's fine, but it's pushing out everything else, including me. It would make it easier for you to just admit it."

"You're wrong, I can do both," he insisted, shaking his head vigorously. His loose blond hair shook with it.

"You've cancelled on me three times in the last week," I argued. "Not to mention standing me up two nights ago."

"Tay-" he began, using his nickname for me.

I put my hand up to silence him. I couldn't do this anymore. "Just stop, George. Stop with all the excuses. It's just not going to work. You should go. I'll find my own ride home."

George stared back at me and I waited for him to argue some more. The tone of regret in my voice had been obvious, but so was the finality of my words. Finally he sighed.

"I'm going to find a way to fix this," he said quietly.

I didn't answer. There was nothing to say. Reluctantly, he grabbed his jacket and left. I watched him until the door swung shut behind him and then turned back to our half-finished game. I went to the wall and retrieved my stick, as if the breakup I'd just initiated didn't bother me one bit, and lined up my next shot.

I ignored the curious looks from the nosy couple beside me and focused on sinking the three ball. Only a small twinge of regret ate at me while I finished the game. I hadn't wanted things to end with George. We'd known each other since sixth grade, and in a lot of ways, he was my best friend. I cared about him. But he'd changed in the past few months. At first, it was so slow I'd barely noticed. We'd go two days without talking—a record for us at the time—which gradually turned into a missed date or a last-minute change of plans. Then he got an agent, and it was only downhill from there. And while I hated thinking I was throwing away everything we'd ever been to each other, I wasn't going to be a "back burner" girlfriend, either. A girl had to have some self-respect.

With the game finished, and my pride still somewhat intact over letting a pool hall full of strangers witness my breakup, I called my friend Angela for a ride home.

"Hello?"

"Ang, you busy?" I asked, doubting she was.

There was a second of hesitation and then, "Um, Dave and I are having dinner."

"Dave? That guy from pre-calculus?" I knew my surprise came through, maybe a little too loud and clear and I felt bad for the way it sounded. "That's great," I hastily added. And it was great. Angela had been harboring a crush on this guy for months. And it wasn't that she couldn't get a date; she was really pretty with her long dark hair and sexy-librarian-style glasses, but she was mortifyingly shy.

"Thanks. We just ordered, so ... Is everything okay? Are you already home from your date?"

"Oh, yeah, I'm fine. Never mind." I decided against interrupting her. "I'll talk to you tomorrow. And I want details."

Angela giggled and I pulled the phone away from my head to stare at it like maybe it had just morphed into another life form. Angela never *giggled*.

We disconnected and I dialed Sam. Even if she was out, I wouldn't feel nearly as bad interrupting her. Sam was always "out." Unfortunately, it went straight to voice mail. Darn. I hung up without leaving a message. No point. She rarely checked it anyway.

The only option left was to call my mom but I quickly dismissed that. No doubt she'd have questions as to why I'd gotten myself stranded in the first place. Which would lead to what happened with George, which was something that, even though I loved her, I didn't really feel like discussing with my mother. It wasn't that she wouldn't listen. The problem was, she'd listen too eagerly. My mother was a classic worrier, and because of that, she hovered. She always wanted to know every single detail of my day, down to what I'd had for lunch and who did I stand next to in gym. And it seemed like the older I got, the worse her worrying became. No way I was calling her.

With all my transportation options exhausted, I sort of regretted letting George leave. Only sort of, though. If he'd driven me, it would've extended the argument or his pleading attempts to change my mind, which in the end would've pissed me off. And I was still hoping to maybe salvage our friendship.

I turned in my rack of balls to the bar attendant and walked to the door. I stood there, staring out the foggy glass of the front window, and considered my last resort. There was a bus stop a few blocks away. Not ideal in the middle of February in northern Virginia but it was all I had. I yanked my arms into my coat sleeves and headed for the back hall, past the restrooms, to the back door to head through the alley. This shortcut would shave at least five minutes off my travel time, which was five fewer minutes I'd have to stand in the cold. I despised the cold.

I slipped out the metal door and pushed it closed behind me, making sure it clicked. A few yards to my right, a streetlamp cast a yellow beam onto the asphalt, but I turned left, toward the bus stop, and into the darkness. My eyes were slow to adjust, but the dark didn't bother me. I'd made this shortcut dozens of times. I passed the free parking lot on the right, wishing I'd driven separately so that my hand-me-down Honda—and its wonderful heater—would've been waiting for me instead of the drafty city bus. Matter of fact, I wished I hadn't come at all. George's tardiness would've been the perfect excuse to change my mind. Especially when we both knew our relationship already hung in the balance, precariously leaning toward breakup before we'd even made it out tonight.

It was quiet and my boots thudded loudly against the sidewalk. I hurried to reach the bus shelter, hating the bite of the cold air, and glad that the surrounding buildings were high enough to keep the wind to a minimum. I drew my coat tighter around my neck against the chill that seeped its way into my skin, giving me goosebumps from head to toe.

I hated goosebumps because it meant the hair on your legs grew back twice as fast. And yet they were a chronic issue secondary to some weird cold chill that would come over me. Even in the summer, when everyone else was wearing shorts and bathing suits and thus shaved legs was sort of a priority. When I was younger, I complained to my mom about it a few times and she would always say that Godfreys were thin-blooded and easily chilled. Then she would stare at me, an odd expression on her face, and disappear, either into the backyard to weed the flowerbeds or to the pantry to reorganize the canned goods.

The tingling of the goosebumps subsided and my thoughts wandered back to George, and all the history between us. Like in sixth grade, when he'd tried growing his hair out, saying he wanted a surfer look, but really, I'd had no choice but to tell him he just looked ... grungy. Back when grungy was NOT "in." And seventh grade, when he'd shaved it all off again, after we'd watched a video on career day about the army. He'd talked about joining for months afterward, talking about how cool it would be to shoot guns for a living. In eighth grade, we'd each had our first kiss, though not with each other.

George had fallen hard for the girl until her family had moved away. She was military and her dad had gotten re-stationed. George changed his mind about enlisting after that. Ninth grade, he'd gone out for football, and made junior varsity MVP. He changed a lot that year, gaining a self-confidence that hadn't been there before. By the end of sophomore year, I'd started to notice him as more than just a friend. Last summer had been awkward between us. I'd spent the entire time stressing over the uncharted territory of having feelings for him, and whether he might have feelings for me.

I'd never questioned being with George. It felt natural and right. He was my best friend for so long that the only thing dating had really changed was adding kissing into the mix. Not bad, as perks go.

Up ahead, a movement caught my eye, pulling me out of my thoughts. I stopped short and felt my pulse jump at the unexpected company. I didn't usually see anyone else in this part of the cut-through, but just past the next Dumpster, a girl with long blond hair and pointy-heeled boots stood in the center of the alley, shaking uncontrollably. I took a step towards her, wanting to help in some way, and then stopped again when I saw her face. She was glaring at me with a look of hatred so raw, it sent a shiver down my back.

"Um, are you okay?" I called out, still trying to understand why she was basically convulsing. Was she having a seizure? But she was managing to stay on her feet. Her gloved hands were balled into fists at her sides, and she was breathing heavily now. I tried again. "Do you need some help?" Something about the way she looked at me made my skin tingle.

I shivered again.

"Help," she repeated, through clenched teeth. "Right." Her words dripped with sarcasm and unconcealed malice.

Then, before I could think of something to say to that, her shaking reached its crescendo and then she ... exploded. There was really no other word for it. With a harsh ripping sound, her clothes disappeared, scattering into the air in tiny pieces. In the same second, her body seemed to waver and then morph, leaving in its place the largest wolf I'd ever seen. My jaw dropped. Was I crazy, or had that girl just turned into a giant dog?

I had a split second to stare at her before she charged. The brown fur became nothing more than a blur as she rushed forward, teeth bared, claws extended. In that moment, I was completely sure that I was going to die. I didn't even have time to be afraid; it would all be over too quickly.

Then, somehow, though my conscious brain had nothing to do with it, my body reacted. Just before impact, I twisted aside, dodging her. Using my body's momentum, I brought my hand around and swung. I hadn't even realized I'd made a fist, but my knuckles connected and I heard the crack of bone as my hand slammed into the wolf's cheek. The hit drove it—her?—back a few paces, but then she straightened and seemed to right herself. Her yellow eyes locked onto mine and she came again. I shed my jacket, and let it fall next to me on the concrete; some hidden part of me knew I needed better use of my limbs.

Three more times I managed to dodge the wolf as she lunged. On the fourth, her claws caught on my shirt and raked down my abdomen on either side, driving me back. I stumbled and fell. My back slammed onto the pavement with a hard thud. Again, I accepted my inevitable death. I watched as she continued to come at me, slower and more confident now that I was on the ground.

All I could see were razor canines aimed straight for my throat. I cringed and turned away, unable to look into those bright yellow eyes, knowing what was coming. When I turned, a glint of slivered moonlight caught a piece of piping nearby, probably meant for the dumpster but somehow had landed here.

Again, subconscious reasoning took over and I felt myself reaching for it, my hand closing around the cold steel. With a grunt, I swung out.

I hadn't expected to actually land the blow or for the crack to be quite so loud. I felt the vibrations from it all the way up my arm but managed to hold onto the pipe until I felt the wolf's weight go slack. She crumpled in a heap, half on top of me. I pushed her aside, which wasn't easy, and scrambled to my feet. I stood, staring down at the giant mass of fur, wondering how in the world no one else had noticed what just happened.

As I stared, the wolf's form began to shake and then shimmer around the edges, going hazy, and then finally, it was the girl again. Her long hair covered her face in stringy waves, matting to her head on the side where the pipe had made contact. Blood seeped slow and steady from the wound to the pavement.

Her body was naked and curled together, almost fetal, except for her knee wedged at an unnatural angle. I could see that her eyes were open and staring vacantly but I didn't linger on that. I couldn't.

Shock and disbelief surged through me as I gaped at her crumpled form, struggling to accept what I was seeing. No way. It was impossible. People couldn't be ... wolves. That was a myth. A way for Hollywood to cash in.

But there was no mistaking it. The girl lying in a heap in front of me was definitely the same girl as before. And she smelled, distinctly, of animal.

I kept hoping she'd move, or at least groan, from the pain of the head trauma. Ignoring the feminine details of her bare body, I stared hard at her shoulders and chest, looking for any sign that might indicate breathing. I didn't see any. And I knew, deep down, that I wouldn't.

My hands began to shake. Maybe from the cold, but I was too

numb to feel the temperature against my skin. I took a step back and stumbled.

Hands closed around me, keeping me upright. I jolted and tried to jerk away from the unexpected contact. A strangled scream escaped my lips as the hands whirled me around to face my attacker.

"Whoa, it's okay. I'm not going to hurt you," he said.

I didn't answer. My ability to speak coherently had been momentarily lost; any sound would've been a scream, anyway. My breath came in uneven gasps and he waited until I got myself under control.

There was concern in his eyes but that didn't go very far with me. I noticed vaguely that his eyes were the same exact color as his hair, a sort of bronzed brown. The color was fascinating: unlike anything I'd ever seen, and they seemed to hold some dark edge that hinted at danger, no matter how gentle they got. The rest of him wasn't bad, either. His face matched his eyes, rugged and hard edges from his cheekbones to his jaw. When he'd spun me around, I'd grabbed out to steady myself and even now my hands still rested on his shoulders, where I'd first gripped. Underneath my fingers, and the leather of his jacket, was solid muscle.

The fact that I was actually checking him out—just moments after killing a girl—was my first clue I was in shock.

"Are you all right?" His gaze swept over me without waiting for an answer, critically inspecting the rest of my body, not unlike the once-over I'd just given him.

It dawned on me that he was trying to help, and thankfully, that dialed back my panic enough for me to find my voice.

Then again, now that my brain was convinced the danger had truly passed, some switch seemed to release, giving me permission to officially freak out. "I think so," I answered automatically, without really knowing if I was or not. I felt numb and strange inside my own skin.

"Did she bite you?"

His voice seemed to come from inside a tunnel. I blinked to try and clear the fog. "What?"

"Did she bite you?" His voice was firmer now and his hands

pressed down on my shoulders, trying to keep my attention.

"No," I answered, finding it easier to concentrate if I stared into his unwavering, gold-flecked eyes.

"Good." A look of genuine relief passed over his features before his eyebrows arched downward with new worry. "Are you alone out here? Do you have a way home?"

"I—" I struggled to remember and kept my eyes fixed on his while I waited for the answer to come. "I was taking the bus. My ride left earlier."

His brows curved deeper and he shot an almost imperceptible glance at the exposed body lying behind me. His hands finally dropped away from my shoulders. "Well, I'm not going to just leave you here," he mumbled, almost to himself. He seemed to debate something a moment longer and then pulled a phone out of his pocket, hitting a single button.

"It's me. We've got a situation. Liliana's dead." There was a pause as he listened to whomever was on the other end. Then, "No, it wasn't like that. It was a girl but it's … confusing. I can't get a read on her at all." Another pause and then, "I'm in the alley behind Fleet Street. She'll be in the Dumpster until you get here … No, not the girl, Liliana."

I blanched and felt new panic rising as he finished his call. Whatever else he said didn't make it past the warning bell ringing in my ears. He must've seen the look on my face, though, because he quickly put his hands, palms up, in front of him, and spoke soothingly. "I meant her— the girl you fought with. I didn't mean you."

I nodded, inhaling deeply to wash away the adrenaline coursing through me. I really needed to get a handle on myself. This was ridiculous. I probably looked and sounded like a moron, and the fact that I was shivering didn't help.

It reminded me of the way the girl had been shaking, right before she—

"What's your name?"

His voice snapped me out of it, cutting off the imminent replay in my brain. "Tara," I answered in a voice that sounded much weaker than I'd intended. "Tara Godfrey," I repeated, louder.

"Tara, I'm Wes and I'm going to help you, if you'll let me. Can I give you a ride home?"

"A ride? Seriously?" I gaped at him. "I just killed that girl. We need to call the police, a coroner, somebody."

"I made a call and someone is on his way to take care of it."

I shook my head. "Yeah, that didn't exactly sound official. And you called her by name. Liliana. You know her? What's going on?"

"Look, obviously you saw what's going on," he said, a little impatient. "That girl wasn't human. And I don't think either of us wants to answer the questions that would come with admitting that to the police. Not that they would believe you in the first place. So, I'm taking care of it—discreetly. And unless you want to end up in a padded room, you'll do the same."

Okay, he had a point, especially about the padded room part. I mean, I saw it with my own eyes and I was still having a hard time with it. I could guess how it would sound, trying to explain it to police or doctors.

It didn't feel good, lying about something like this, though. I'd just killed a girl—or dog—or whatever. But, maybe I'd be willing to deal with it if I had some answers about what the hell was actually happening.

"Fine, I'll do it your way. But you have to give me something in return," I said.

He eyed me, wary. "What?"

"Answers. An explanation. I mean, seriously, this kind of stuff isn't real. Or isn't supposed to be, but here it is. And you seem to know a lot about it."

He sighed in response but didn't argue my demand. Maybe he'd been expecting it. "I'll tell you in the car. For now, we've gotta get out of this alley before someone sees us. Come on."

"No way. We talk here and then I'll take the bus, like I planned."

He glanced down at my shirt with a wry half smile. "I don't think that would be wise. You would draw a considerable amount of ... attention."

I glanced down, too, and noticed for the first time that my

shirt was all but destroyed. It hung off me like a rag, long slash marks running up both sides of my abdomen, along my ribs. Underneath the fabric, I could see shallow slash marks on my skin. The wounds were raised and red and looked like I'd faced off with a cat. Oh, wait. A dog.

I reached down to zip my jacket and remembered I wasn't wearing it.

"Here," he said, holding it out to me.

"Thanks." I put it on, fully preparing to just zip it up to cover the damage. No such luck. The zipper wasn't just broken; it was completely gone, as was a huge chunk of my sleeve, near my wrist. Apparently the she-wolf had gotten closer with her teeth than I thought.

"Crap," I sighed, long and loud, letting him know exactly how I felt about this idea. "Fine, you can take me home."

"Let's go."

He turned and started walking, slowing his pace to match mine and blocking my view of the girl as we passed by on our way back down the alley. We ended up in the public parking lot. The lot was lit with yellow-bulbed street lights at each corner and down the middle, like glaring spotlights compared to the pitch darkness of the alley. My senses kicked into overdrive. Something in me snapped. Maybe I was finally coming out of the shock—or maybe I'd hit a new level of freaking out. Either way, at the sight of the lights, I froze.

I tried putting one foot in front of the other but it just wouldn't happen. I was shaking badly now, enough to make my teeth chatter, though I felt weirdly numb and unaffected by the cold. I didn't even have stupid goosebumps anymore. My heart pounded, echoing loudly in my ears. Behind that was a rushing sound that made me lightheaded.

"Tara?" I heard Wes calling my name. I hadn't even noticed him standing there.

"Tara, we need to go. My car's over here." His hand closed over my arm and sent me over the edge.

I jumped away, startling both of us, and stared back at him in panic. This was all just too much.

"Tara," Wes's voice was low and soothing. "I know you're scared but I'm not going to hurt you. I'm trying to help you. Let me help you." He took a step closer.

Some closed-off part of my brain was yelling at me, telling me to shake it off and stop acting like a complete lunatic. But I couldn't seem to calm down.

"I can see that you're in shock," Wes said, still edging closer while I fought the urge to bolt. "I can't afford to take you somewhere to be treated, so I'm going to do something for you. I'm going to help you forget—just for now. It should wear off in the morning, and if not, I'll help you remember. But for right now, it's better if you just forget for a while. Okay?"

I didn't answer. Partly because I was scared if I tried to talk, I'd scream like a banshee, and partly because not a single thing he'd just said made any kind of sense.

Apparently he took my silence as agreement because he nodded and said, "Good, now just relax." He was using that same patronizing tone, the one meant to be soothing. But he was looking at me like I was some wild animal, ready to run. And he kept his distance. "Now just keep your eyes on mine. That's right. Just focus on me ..." He murmured reassurances and somewhere around the third or fourth one, I felt myself being drawn in. I looked down but my body hadn't moved. It was my mind, something inside me, that seemed to pull closer and closer until I felt like I could reach up and touch him. "Right here, Tara. Just look here, in my eyes. It's going to be okay." I looked up and our eyes locked. His held a piercing stare that stabbed all the way through me and out the other side.

Then, it all disappeared.

CHAPTER TWO

"TARA? Time to wake up."

Reluctantly, I cracked an eye against the cheery sunlight filtering through my window. My mother stood at my open bedroom door, like a sentry. We both knew I wasn't a morning person, and we also both knew she wouldn't walk away until she was convinced I was really up and about.

"C'mon, get moving," she said, slightly more impatient, as she watched my slow progress.

I rolled over and groaned, just awake enough to be aware of my body—and it was aching and creaking in protest of having to move. "Mom." My voice came out a croak. "I don't feel so good."

"What's wrong?" My mom's impatience turned to concern. I might not be an early riser but I rarely ever stayed down or got sick.

"I ache, all over." My head pounded like a bass drum with every syllable.

She crossed to my bed and laid a hand on my forehead. "Hmm...you're pretty warm." Her fingers stroked my cheek. "You probably caught that bug that's going around. I guess you're spending the day in bed. I'll call school and let them know."

"'Kay," I managed. Her fingers felt deliciously cool against my skin.

"Do you want me to stay home with you?" she asked, suddenly looking torn.

I looked back at her, into a pair of blue eyes that perfectly matched my own, and shook my head, not willing to worry her. "There's no need. I'm just going to sleep."

"I told you not to go out in that weather last night," she said sternly, making a smooth switch from nurturer to lecturer.

"What weather?" I tried to remember last night.

"That brutal wind that whipped through," she said. "Obviously. I told you that last night, too. It was just brittle out there and there's this flu bug going around." She gestured to me, like I was the official carrier or something.

I stared blankly back at her, trying to figure out what she was talking about. I knew being sick could make my brain fuzzy, but I had no idea what she was talking about. I hadn't gone anywhere last night. I opened my mouth to tell her that, but she just kept talking.

"Anyway, I hope George doesn't get this, too. He doesn't need this slowing him down. Not with those recruiters coming around." She turned back to me, eyes studying. "He is okay though, right? I noticed it wasn't him who dropped you off. Is he sick, too?"

"I—I don't think so."

"So who did drop you off?"

"Um ..." Okay, obviously I should remember this; my mom was certainly sure that it'd happened. But I just had no idea. Everything was fuzzy, from the time I'd gotten home from school until—well, now, basically. I kept my mouth shut. I was afraid that if I mentioned that, my mom would whisk me away to the closest emergency room. I looked back at her expectant face; I still hadn't answered. "Um, Angela."

She nodded and rose, looking halfway satisfied. "Well, I need to get going. Julie has the morning off and I need to water everything before we open."

Mom owned a flower shop in the tiny scrap of land that was known as downtown, though Frederick Falls' version of downtown wasn't very impressive. We didn't even have our own mall. You had to drive to the next county over for that. Still, she did okay here—her passion and talent for all things botanical had apparently skipped a generation with me—and as confused and achy as I might be, I didn't want to keep her from it. Nor did I want her hovering.

"Are you sure you're going to be okay?"

I nodded and settled back against the pillow in an effort to give my achy muscles some relief.

"I'll make sure I'm home for dinner," she said, heading for the door.

"Okay. Hey, Mom," I called. "What time did I come in last night?"

She gave me a strange look. "Ten thirty. Right on time for curfew. Why?"

"Just wondering. Have a good day." I forced a smile.

She smiled back, still with a question in her eyes, and disappeared down the hall. A few minutes later I heard the front door open and close and the key slide in the lock. Then, silence.

For the next hour I lay in my bed and tried, without success, to remember the details of last night. Mom had said I'd gone out with George, and I remembered making plans with him at school but the details were still hazy. I squinted with the effort of recalling the conversation we'd had after last bell ...

"Tay, look, I know things have been rough on you. My schedule and the team and my weekends away ... I get it. But at least give me the chance to work it out," George had said.

I'd tapped my foot impatiently at that. "George, it's not really about any of those things. It's about you, or the new you, I guess. You've changed and I just don't think I can do this anymore."

"My life has changed," he argued. "Football has always been a part of me, though, and deep down, I'm still the same person."

I raised an eyebrow at him. "You blew me off two days in a row to do an interview for the school paper. Half the front page is your picture."

"Social networking is necessary at this point." It was his voice but the words were that of a stranger, a new George who I just couldn't connect with, try as I might. I tried to think of a nice way to just say it and get it over with. But I'd never been good at endings.

George took advantage of my silence and pressed on. "Tay, we've been friends since middle school. Do you really want to throw all that away?" His eyes were soft and pleading, reminiscent of the old George. It was a look that normally would've made me cave or breathe faster or something.

But I'd been down this road already and given him plenty of second chances. "George, look—"

He cut me off. "Let's go out tonight, just you and me. Do something fun. It'll remind you of the real me. The real *us*."

"George—" I rubbed a fingertip in circles on my forehead, trying to smooth out the tension.

"Please, Tay. We can shoot some pool."

Okay, my weakness for pool aside, the offer was tempting. Some part of me felt like I owed George this much. Like he said, we'd been friends for a long time. And I could feel my resolve wavering. I hated feeling ... mean. "Fine. Pool tonight. Then I decide, and you don't argue."

"Deal." George grinned and I could tell he viewed this as a victory.

"George," Eddie, George's best friend, waved and called to him from down the hall where he stood with half the football team. George glanced over and then turned back to me with a guilty expression that I'd come to recognize over the past couple of months.

"Crap. I made plans with Eddie to go over some of the unedited footage from our last game. His dad said we could view it in their media room on the big screen." He must've seen the disappointment in my expression and rushed on before I could respond. "It's the first team we'll face in playoffs, and we need to learn their signals. I'll be done in plenty of time, though, promise. I'll pick you up at six." Then he flashed me a brilliant smile and strode away ...

My memory went fuzzy after that and I let the images fade away. I couldn't even remember leaving school. What bug could've erased my memory of an entire evening? I wasn't even sure the flu could cause something like this. But what else could it be? Nothing like this had ever happened before. Not even the night of my friend Sam's sixteenth birthday party. I'd had way too much to drink that night, some fruity concoction that had smelled like strawberries on alcoholic steroids. The highlight had been when I'd fallen into the pool and almost drowned. George had jumped in and "saved me" by pulling until I realized it was only four feet of water. Even then, I'd remembered most of it the next day, unfortunately, which was why I'd vowed never to drink again. But this felt different.

I was starting to worry.

I sighed and rolled over, ignoring the ache it caused in my shifting muscles. Random pieces of clothing littered the carpet in my room—evidence of my tendency toward laundry procrastination. Nearest to my bed, a scrap of bright red fabric caught my eye. A silk V-neck blouse, my favorite, lay in a heap, under a still- damp towel. I reached down and yanked it free, trying to remember when I'd last worn it. I thought it was still in my closet. Then I looked closer. The shirt was torn in several places, the silky fabric hanging by threads. S I stared at it, an uneasy feeling washed over me. A picture flashed in my mind: me, staring at my reflection in the bathroom mirror, hair disheveled and sticking out, the tattered shirt hanging off my shoulders and exposing my ribs on either side. Bloody scratches showed through the tears in the fabric.

I dropped the shirt, and sucked in a sharp breath. Hesitantly, I pushed the covers away and lifted up my pajama tee. In several places along my ribs were jagged scratches running down my torso. They were clean, and shallow, like I'd been in a fight with a cat. Only problem, I didn't have a cat.

"What the ...?" I said to the empty room.

"Could've been worse," a male voice answered.

My head snapped up. A boy with bronzed brown hair and eyes to match leaned against the frame of my bedroom door.

I gripped the covers, my knuckles white. "Who are you? What are you doing in here?" Despite my voice's earlier croaking, I managed a shriek just fine.

"Calm down, Tara, I'm not going to hurt you," he said.

His tone was calm and a little patronizing, but he'd said my name with familiarity. That surprised me enough to block out the fear for a moment. "How do you know me?"

"The same way you know me. We met last night. I'm Wes."

"I don't know who you are, but you need to leave, or I'm calling the police." I grabbed my cell phone off the nightstand without breaking eye contact. I held it up in the air, like a weapon.

He pushed off from the doorway and took a step into the room. The black leather of his jacket crinkled as he moved. "Look, I don't want to hurt you any more than you already are, but I'm not leaving, either, so you might as well put the phone down. Besides, you agreed to 'discreet,' remember?"

I stared at him with wide eyes. "What do you mean, hurt me more than I already am? Did you do this to me? Did we—?" Oh, God. Visions of after-school specials and date rape warnings from health class danced in my head.

Halfway across the room, he turned and grabbed my desk chair, spinning it around to face the bed before sitting down. "No, I didn't." His lips twitched. "And no, we didn't."

I breathed a silent prayer of thanks and then returned to glaring at him. "But you know who did this to me?"

"Yes."

I waited, and then realized he wasn't going to say more. "Well? Are you going to tell me who it was?"

"I haven't decided."

I threw my hands up in frustration. "Then why are you here? What do you want?"

"I told you, I want to talk to you."

Something about the tone of his voice, the cadence of his words, unnerved me. It was familiar, but it wasn't. I stared at him for a full minute, waiting for some memory to fall into place about where we might've met. Nothing came, but I got that same uneasy feeling I'd had when the torn shirt had been in my hands, something unfamiliar and unlike anything I'd ever experienced. I know it probably sounded silly because I'd only been around him for a few minutes, but I got the distinct feeling he was nothing like anyone I'd ever met before. Not even close.

I squared my shoulders. "So talk," I said, trying to sound tough.

But he didn't, not right away. He just continued to watch me with cool, studying eyes. They roamed my face and arms, and then glanced speculatively at the comforter I still held up to my chin.

"Strong, amazingly strong," he said quietly, almost to himself.

"What?"

"What do you remember about last night?" he asked abruptly.

His eyes found mine and I was struck by their unique color. Last summer, I'd taken a trip to California to visit my grandmother. She and I had hiked to the top of a bluff that overlooked a forest, thick with redwoods, and picnicked there, just the two of us. His eyes reminded me of the redwoods—a swirling mixture of tawny brown.

I blinked, trying to remember the question. "Nothing, actually. Which is pretty frustrating. Are you finally going to tell me where these scratches came from?"

"Like I said, it wasn't me. I just happened to come along at the right time."

"What does that mean?"

My cell phone rang, cutting off his response. I looked around, only to remember I still held it in my hand. I loosened my grip and glanced at the screen.

"Go ahead," Wes said, gesturing toward the ringing phone. "I'll wait."

I flipped open the phone. "Hello?"

"Tara?"

"George. Hey."

"Are you okay? Angela was in the office and heard that your mom called and said you were sick."

I hesitated. I'd fully intended to disclose my situation, a.k.a. scream for help, to the first person who called and then wait to be rescued from Wes, the crazy bedroom stalker. I glanced over at him, wondering why he'd even let me answer the phone at all. If he was going to hurt me, he could've done it already—and he definitely wouldn't have let me take this call. His eyes glinted back at me in a silent challenge. He was willing to risk me telling someone? Why? What exactly was going on here?

"Yeah, I'm sick," I said finally. "The flu, I think."

"Listen, Tay, about last night. I really think we should talk about this."

As soon as I realized where this was going, my head began pounding in time to George's voice. "George, I don't feel good. Now's not a good time."

"Okay, I get it." I could almost hear his shoulders slumping. "Can I call you later?"

I hesitated. "Yeah, sure."

We hung up and I found Wes watching me. "You didn't scream for help."

I met his eyes. Yep, definitely a challenge there. "I want to know what's going on. What happened to me last night?"

"You were attacked."

I nodded. His answer wasn't all that surprising. I had figured as much, after seeing the scratches on my abdomen. I just hoped that "attack" didn't mean ... I wouldn't think about that. "Attacked by whom?"

"Her name was Liliana."

"I was attacked by a *girl*?" Okay, I know that probably sounds sexist, but I'd fully expected my attacker to be male. I mean, I'm a seventeen-year-old high school student, apparently out alone, in the dark.

Wes ran a hand through his hair, further tousling it, and shifted in the chair. "What do you remember?"

"Nothing." Then I added, "Actually I remembered one thing, a flash of something, really. Of looking at myself in the mirror, bloody and bruised. But that's it."

"Hmm. It must've worked better than I thought." He was staring at a spot on the wall; he seemed to be talking to himself again.

His reticence was getting annoying. "Would you just spit it out already? Why was I attacked?"

"Fine. I don't know what started it. I wasn't there for that part. By the time I got there, Liliana was already on the ground."

"On the ground? You mean, I hurt her?"

"Yes, which was definitely a surprise to me and why I'm here now. But what you need to know is that Liliana was more than just some girl. She was a Werewolf."

Wes might've kept talking after that, but all sound and movement suddenly ceased for me. I was still stuck on that last word: Werewolf. I would've laughed out loud, but there was no denying Wes was serious. He absolutely believed that this Liliana girl was a Werewolf and the look on his face told me arguing wouldn't change a thing. This just figured. The hottest guy I'd ever seen, alone with me in my room, and he was completely whacked.

I abruptly cut off whatever he was saying. "You seriously just said Werewolf, didn't you?"

He stopped, midsentence, and his shoulders sagged a little. "Yeah."

"Do I need to explain how crazy that sounds?" I decided my wording might be better than "you're crazy," which was what I was thinking.

"What I don't get is what *you* are," he said, basically ignoring my question.

"Hello? Are you listening to me?"

"Yeah, just trying to figure this out," he said, distractedly.

"That makes two of us."

He sighed, like he was getting impatient. "This will be easier for you when you remember. Close your eyes."

"What?"

"Close your eyes."

"Why?"

"I'm going to help you remember."

I stared at him, waiting for him to explain more, but he didn't. "What are you going to do?" I asked, trying to sound more confident than I felt. I was beginning to wonder if I'd made a mistake in not telling George about this.

"I'm not going to hurt you. I won't even move from my chair. If you hear me get up or move at all, you can open your eyes, scream, call the police—whatever you want."

I eyed him suspiciously but I could feel my curiosity winning out over my fear. I really, really wanted to know what had happened to me last night. "Fine." I closed my eyes and waited.

"Now relax and clear your mind."

I tried not to think how much he sounded like my mother's yoga video. I took a deep breath and let it out as slowly as I could, imitating what I'd seen my mother do when she tried meditating, which really seemed like a rip-off of sleeping. Then I waited.

A moment later, I felt something. Not a physical feeling, but rather a mental one—a weird tickling sensation in my mind, like when you try really hard to recall an old memory. I jumped and started to open my eyes.

"Keep your eyes closed. I'm almost done."

I fidgeted with the comforter but kept my eyelids clamped shut. Black and blue bursts of light danced behind my closed lids, swirling into abstract pictures that reminded me of ink blobs a psychiatrist might use on a patient. A moment later, the tingling receded, and then I jerked in surprise as images flooded into my mind.

My eyes snapped open and I found Wes watching me. His lips were pressed together in a tight line. All I could manage was to stare back at him with a slack jaw, as the images played over and over in my head. What I saw was almost too much. Impossible, really.

"Did it work? Do you remember?" he asked, though it was pretty clear that he knew I did.

I answered anyway. "Yes," I breathed.

The memories flooded back and then replayed over and over like a video simultaneously stuck on fast forward and repeat. I could feel Wes's eyes on me, taking in my reaction. I wanted to say something, to ask him what he'd done and how he'd done it, but the images in my mind were too overwhelming to push aside.

First, an image of me in the kitchen. The clock above the stove read six forty-five. George was late. No surprise there. Then, the replay of my attempt at one last date with him, at Moe's, my favorite pool hall. The arguing. Him talking on the phone to his dad or agent through half a game of nine ball. The inevitable break-up. Then, me cutting through the alley to get to the bus stop.

I let the image fade away, already knowing what came next.

How was any of this possible? More than the memory of the night was the knowledge. Somehow I'd known what to do, to fight that ... creature. But how? What kind of person was strong enough to fight—and defeat—a Werewolf? Not a normal human, that's for sure. And how could Werewolves exist and no one even know it? And why, out of everyone who could've gotten pulled into something like this, did it have to be me?

The questions went on and on and finally I had to shut them out to think straight. I hoped Wes could answer some of them, but I honestly couldn't even figure out where to start. Instead I focused on what I did know: Werewolves were, in fact, very real. And Wes had somehow manipulated my memories. Twice.

CHAPTER THREE

I looked over at Wes, focusing first on the whole memory-erasing thing, since that was actually easier than discussing the reality of Werewolves. He'd been watching me intently the whole time the images had played back inside my mind, and I could tell he was waiting for me to say something. "I can't believe I killed something," I whispered.

Wes's eyes narrowed, and for the first time, he seemed suspicious. "You've really never done this before?"

"Should I have?"

"Considering how easily you took down Liliana, I'd say yes. But based on your reaction, I'm not so sure."

"I've really never done this before," I assured him. I shook my head. "Seriously, this can't be real. I mean, I know it is, but... wow. Werewolves? Okay, so what about vampires? And goblins? And fairies? Is all of that real, too?"

Wes rolled his eyes. "Nope. It's just us wolves."

"Us?" I repeated, my eyebrows lifting. Did he mean ...?

He shifted in the chair. I got the impression he hadn't meant to say that last part. "Yes. I'm a Werewolf."

I pulled the comforter up tighter and felt my eyes widen. I hadn't meant to show fear but I couldn't help it. There was a Werewolf sitting three feet away. And if my first impression was any indication, three feet was dangerously close. Still, once I had a moment to think about it, I realized I wasn't actually afraid. At least, not like I had been last night. Crap, I'd been a mess last night. A big, fat, convulsing mess—especially near the end. A small amount of embarrassment washed over me at what a complete moron I'd been. Logically, I knew Wes was right. I'd been in medical shock. But still, I must've seemed like a total wimp.

Besides that, Wes had been the one to help me get it together after the attack. He'd given me a ride and helped me sneak past my mom and, as far as the memory removal thing, I had to admit, it'd certainly been necessary. I couldn't really be mad at him for it. And most importantly, he had answers, which was something I still wanted. So, rather than call attention to my reaction, I changed the subject. "How did you do it?"

"Do what?"

"Mess with my head like that. How did you make me forget everything?"

"I thought you remembered."

"I do. I mean, I remember you telling me you were going to do it and I remember agreeing. I closed my eyes. One minute the memories were there and the next minute they were gone. I want to know how."

He shrugged. "It's a gift. Some of us are gifted with special ... skills. Altering memories is one of mine."

"What, like a superpower or something?"

"Or something."

"So, do all Werewolves have extra gifts, or just you?"

"Most Werewolves can manipulate memory on some level. It helps us keep our secret."

"But how do you do it?" I pressed.

"Shouldn't you be more concerned with your role in all of this?" he snapped.

I blinked, trying to figure out what I'd said to make him suddenly so irritated. "I guess I hadn't gotten to that part yet."

He spread his arms wide. "Well, here we are."

My eyes narrowed. I was tired of his attitude and instead of feeling guilty for having somehow caused it, it was making me angry. "No, here *I* am. Thanks for helping me last night, but I'm fine. You don't still have to be here."

"Actually I do," he argued.

"And why is that?"

"To determine what kind of threat you are."

"Threat? To who?"

"Werewolves, of course."

"But she came after me. I was defending myself."

"Still, only a Hunter would've had that kind of strength. Which means, it could happen again. It's only a matter of time before you figure yourself out and when that happens, I need to know whose side you'll be on."

I was trying to follow what he was saying, but none of it was making any sense. "There are sides?"

"Yes."

He didn't elaborate. I tried to keep the irritation out of my voice. "Okay, well, we won't know which side I'm on until I understand all of this, so how about you fill me in, from the beginning."

He frowned and I was sure he was going to refuse, so it surprised me when he started talking. "Liliana was in town for the night and said she wanted to meet up. We'd been ... working on something together. I was running late so I cut through the alley, which is the only reason I found you. By then, Liliana was already down, and you looked like you were going into shock. I couldn't have you running back inside and bringing humans into it, so I decided to help you."

I hadn't missed the way he'd hesitated over why he'd been meeting Liliana. Was it possible they'd been a couple? If so, no wonder he seemed pissed. I didn't ask about it, though. Something told me it would end the conversation, and there was still plenty more I wanted to know. "You called me a Hunter."

He nodded. "You must be. It's the only possible way you'd have the strength to kill one of us." He gave me a strange look before continuing. "The thing is, I don't even get a feeling from you, or—I do, but it's not like a normal Hunter would feel. It's ... I don't know. Which definitely makes no sense. Added to that, you obviously have zero training and no weapons so you can understand why I'm more than a little curious about you."

"Why didn't you tell me any of this last night?"

He gave me a pointed look. "You were pretty shaken up. I don't think it would've gone over well."

"I'm fine now," I said, lifting my chin a little.

He raised an eyebrow. "Are you?"

"Okay, whatever, I lost it. Anyone would have, in my situation. But I'm dealing with it now and I'm not going to freak out. That won't happen again."

"Yes, it will." He cut me off before I could argue. "Not you freaking out—at least I hope not—but the attack, killing a Werewolf. That part will happen again. If one found you, so can others, and even though I can't sense 'Hunter' on you, I can only assume Liliana did. Which means they will, too, and they'll attack as soon as they feel it."

"You're just trying to scare me."

He didn't respond but the look he gave left no question that he was serious.

Knowing he was right did weird things to my gut. It was scary, once you got over the hump and believed it all. Who wanted to spend their lives looking over their shoulders for angry Werewolves? But, if this was all real—and I was slowly starting to recognize that it was—then I needed to be prepared. I needed to face it. The truth was always better than a lie, no matter how scary it might be. "All right, then, so what do I do?" I asked.

"First off, we need to figure out if you really are a Hunter."

"How do we do that?"

"The best way is to get you around some others who can maybe sense you better. Are you sure you've recovered from the shock, though?"

An image popped into my head, of seeing my reflection in the bathroom mirror—after. The look on my face was one of shock and underneath it, pure terror. "I think I must've been afraid of myself a little," I admitted. "But yes, I'm fine now. Promise."

He nodded, his expression hedging on understanding. He studied me a minute longer. "C'mon," he finally said, rising from my desk chair. "Get dressed."

"What? Why?"

"I'm going to take you to see someone. Try to figure this thing out." He put the chair back and took up his original position, leaning against the doorframe.

I didn't move from the bed. "Who?"

"Friends. Like I said, maybe they can get a read on you."

I had no idea what he meant by "a read on" me, but I was interested in answers. Still, I didn't know where he might take me, or to whom. It could be dangerous, some kind of trap.

"I'm not going to hurt you, and neither will anyone else," Wes added quietly, seeing my hesitation.

"Promise?"

"Promise."

I had no idea why I was making him guarantee something I didn't understand. I still didn't know if I could fully trust him, but right now he was my only shot at discovering what was truly going on. Scary as it was, I needed clarity; I needed to know the truth. Some things were just too big to brush under the rug.

I flung the covers aside and hopped up, making my way towards the bathroom. I felt Wes's eyes on me, and my cheeks heated up in automatic response. His gaze lingered on my abdomen, and only then did I remember my shirt was short enough to reveal the ends of the scratches along my ribs. Then, my neck and ears ignited as I realized he hadn't been checking me out in the way I'd assumed. I turned away, hoping he hadn't noticed my embarrassment, and booked it to the bathroom. On the way, I scooped up a pair of jeans and a fresh shirt from the laundry basket.

I threw on the clothes, ran a brush through my tangled hair, added some light makeup. Dark circles ringed my eyes, and I did my best to cover them. Satisfied, I reached for the door, and paused. I really had no idea where Wes was taking me, or who—or what—I'd be meeting. Maybe this dangerous stranger would be mad that I'd killed Liliana.

I needed a weapon—something I could conceal on my body but access easily, if needed. I looked around the tiny bathroom.

The choices were limited.

I didn't think my razor would do much good, unless my attacker stopped and demanded a haircut.

Makeup brushes and bottles of foundation littered the counter, along with my toothbrush. Again, no good.

My eyes landed on the plunger tucked behind the toilet. I grabbed it and held one end of the wooden handle in each hand.

Using my knee as a brace, I brought it down hard, and had the satisfaction of watching it break off at the bottom. I snapped the wood again, so I now held a piece in each hand, and stuffed them into my back pockets, using my shirt to cover them up. I threw the rubber end into the cabinet to hide it from my mom. It would have to do.

Chapter Four

"READY," I announced, stepping back into my bedroom.

"What was that noise?" Wes asked immediately. He looked more curious than suspicious, though.

I hadn't doubted Wes would have heard me and my reply was dismissive. "Oh, nothing, I dropped my compact in the sink," I said, smoothly. "Eye-shadow everywhere. It's going to take forever to clean that up."

He raised an eyebrow and shrugged. "Let's go."

I thought about scribbling a note for my mom, but then decided against it. I had my cell if she tried to call, and I planned on being back before her, anyway. Her rules said that if you were too sick to go to school, you were too sick to hang out with friends. And even though I didn't feel like Wes was exactly a friend, I didn't think she'd see it my way. Nor was I ready to explain it to her. I closed the door and locked it behind me. Turning the key in the deadbolt made me think of something. "Hey, how'd you get in if the door was locked before ...?" I trailed off as I turned.

Wes was standing at the edge of the yard, next to what I could only assume was his car. I guess I hadn't thought about how we'd travel. Perhaps learning what I had about mythical creatures I assumed we'd run, or fly, or something equally magical.

Instead, he stood holding the passenger door of the nicest and most expensive car I'd ever seen. The memories I'd regained of last night hadn't included this and I could only assume I'd been too out of it to notice it then.

It was silver and sleek, and screamed speed. Beyond that, I had no idea of its make or model, but I gawked anyway. "What is that?"

"A car," he said, obviously amused.

I walked toward it, still staring at the car's sexy lines. We just didn't have cars like this in Frederick Falls. "I know that. What kind?"

"Aston Martin, Volante."

I'd heard of the first but not the second. At his gesture I climbed in and he shut the door. I took a hearty inhale of the dreamy new-car scent and reached for my seat belt as he slid into the driver's seat.

"How old are you?" I asked.

"Old enough to drive," he replied. The engine purred to life; even the sound of it was silken, like a cat's purr.

"Is this your dad's car?"

He looked offended. "No, it's mine."

I shifted in my seat. "Did you go to school around here?"

"Homeschooled."

For some reason, that was all it took to raise my suspicions about myths and legends and gory B movies. "How old are you?" I repeated, my head cocked to one side.

"Nineteen."

It was too much to resist. "And how long have you been nineteen?"

He looked at me like I had a screw loose. "Since I haven't been eighteen?"

"So, you've been on this planet for nineteen years?"

"That's usually what an age implies." I knew I sounded crazy but there was that one movie franchise and even though I couldn't say it aloud ... I couldn't let it go either.

"What's with the twenty questions?"

I didn't really want to admit what I'd just been thinking, so I said, "I've just never seen such a nice car, especially driven by someone my age."

"Trust fund," he said, keeping his eyes on the road.

The ride was smooth and quiet and made me feel like the tires were floating over the ground. Maybe there was magic involved after all. Or maybe this car was amazing. He turned on the heat and then pressed another small button near my seat. "This is your seat warmer. You can turn it off if it gets too hot."

I nodded. Seat warmer? Wow, my mom's Taurus had two vents on my side of the car, and I thought *that* was luxury.

He navigated through my neighborhood and then turned us onto Route 1, away from town. Light traffic turned into almost no traffic as we got farther out. Wes increased our speed and the other cars dropped away. As leafless trees and winter-deadened scenery rushed by faster and faster, I glanced at the speedometer and gasped.

"Slow down!"

He looked over at me with a wicked grin. "Scared?"

"No, but you're going to get a ticket if you keep it up."

He shook his head. "I don't think so."

"How do you know?"

He didn't answer, but I saw the speedometer creep down by a few degrees. I relaxed my death grip on the armrest by a few inches.

"Where are we going?" I asked a few minutes later. We'd turned off the highway a couple miles back and had taken a series of turns onto various back roads. Sad to say, I didn't even know where we were anymore.

"I told you. To see a friend."

The back road we were following now had sections of open fields interspersed with even larger sections of woods in between. I'd long since realized this "friend" didn't live nearby, but I was starting to wonder exactly how far out we were going. Rather than ask again—since I was pretty sure he'd said all he would about our destination—I decided to use the time to learn all I could about the new me. "You mentioned something about needing to know what side I'd be on. What does that mean?"

"It means there's a chance I could wind up at the wrong end of your stake. And I'd prefer to know that ahead of time, if you don't mind."

My eyes widened. "You think I'd kill you?"

His lips curved into a wry smile. "You could try. Then again, with no training it's unlikely you'd make it that far. Something you should think about."

"Training? Why?"

"Liliana wasn't looking for you. She found you by accident. It's just a matter of time until it happens again."

"So you think I should train to fight … them?" I couldn't bring myself to put Wes into the same category as Liliana. "Who would train me?"

"Your parents—" he began.

I shook my head. "My mom is not an option. I don't even want to think about what she would say if I tried telling her a story like this."

"Your dad, then."

"My dad died when I was a baby. House fire."

Wes didn't answer right away. He seemed to be struggling with his next words and I tensed, waiting for him to ask me more about it, but he didn't. "I might know someone else."

"Uh-huh, and how exactly does one train to kill a Werewolf?"

"Simulated fights, a lot like the one you had last night. Running. Exercise. Staying in shape. Conditioning." He shrugged. "Think of it as UFC training."

"Great. It sounds …"

"Useful?"

"Time consuming. I wouldn't be able to explain something like that to people. Besides—" My phone beeped with a new text. I flipped it open. It was Angela, checking up on me. I typed a response that I was sleepy and knocked out on cold medicine, hoping it would keep her from calling, or worse, showing up at my house. The last thing I needed was for her to realize something was up. I clicked send and snapped the phone shut again.

Through the windshield I could see we were coming up on a section of woods again and I tried to push back the unease that was growing within me. The area was remote and unfamiliar to me. I didn't want to think about how I'd get home if I had to leave in a hurry. I shifted in my chair, trying to relieve the pressure that was turning painful from the plunger handles against my back.

Without warning, Wes's foot stomped down on the brake, throwing me forward against my seat belt. My head jerked up to see what had made him stop so suddenly. A massive black wolf stood in the middle of the road several yards away; even from this distance, I could see that its head would easily reach my shoulders, maybe higher. It stared back at us with yellow, unblinking eyes, and it made no attempt to move out of our way as the car finally skidded to a halt.

"What the heck?" I shrieked, clutching at the dashboard against the momentum of the brakes.

Wes didn't answer. The wolf was staring straight at him. It didn't even seem to notice me. Their eyes remained locked for a long moment and then, abruptly, the wolf turned and bolted into the trees. When it was gone, Wes put the car into drive again and we eased forward.

"What was that?" I demanded. My heart thudded heavily in my chest, and I had to concentrate on taking a couple of deep breaths to calm the flow of adrenaline shooting through my veins.

Wes glanced over at me with a look of concern. It made me wonder how much showed on my face. "Sorry if I startled you. Nothing to worry about. He was a friend."

I gaped at him. "That was your friend?" I asked, in disbelief.

"Yes."

"Why didn't he move out of the way? We could've hit him."

Wes rolled his eyes. "Tara, we stopped in plenty of time."

"Okay, but you guys didn't even speak. Why did he run off?"

"I'll be sure to ask him when we get there. Here we are," he added, before I could respond.

CHAPTER FIVE

WE turned onto a gravel road, surrounded by thick fir trees on either side. Up ahead, the road curved and I watched as a weathered house came gradually into view. It was two stories, probably painted blue at one time, though now it had faded to a peeling gray. One of the shutters hung crooked, and looked like all it needed was a strong wind to finish it off. Wes pulled the car to a stop directly in front, where the grass edged down to meet the gravel. Leading the way to the door was a path of flat stepping stones, all of them cracked. The grass was yellowed and dead from the season, though I wondered if it would make the house look worse or better, to have a lush green lawn.

Wes shut off the engine and came around to get my door. I let him open it for me and then fell into step behind him, not wanting to be the first one up the path. Everything was so quiet here, giving the whole place an eeriness to it, even in the cheery sunlight.

There was no doorbell, only a tarnished brass knocker. Wes rapped twice and then we stood in silence, shoulder to shoulder. I listened for movement on the other side of the door, but heard nothing. A minute passed.

Maybe nobody's home.

"They're home. Give it a minute," said Wes, startling me. Had I said that out loud?

Before I could ask, or wonder further about his strange response, there was the sound of a lock being turned from within and the door was thrown wide open. I balled my hands into fists to resist the urge to reach for a piece of the plunger from my back pocket. At the same time, a strange tingling sensation sent a shiver down my back and over my arms.

A man stood in the doorway, though he was bigger than any human I'd ever seen. He reminded me of a bear, with his broad chest and huge shoulders. A bushy beard gone gray covered most of his face and the same brown-gray color covered his head in bushy tufts. He took in the two of us and startled me by breaking into a wide smile.

"Wes, my boy! How the hell are ya?" He grabbed Wes into a hug and patted his back hard enough to rival the Heimlich.

Wes was smiling as he pulled away. "Could be worse, I guess. And you?"

"Just relieved it's you, and not some nosy local. Would've hated to have to kill somebody this early in the day." He smiled again and then his eyes flicked to me. "And who's this?"

Wes stepped back so he was standing next to me again. "This is Tara Godfrey. Tara, this is Jack."

Jack stuck his hand out and I took it, automatically, still reeling a little from Jack's comment about killing someone. I was pretty sure he'd been joking but who knew?

"Pleased to meet you, Tara. Any friend of Wes's is a friend of mine, even if she is a Hunter," he added with a wink. "Come on in." He stepped back to let us enter.

"Thanks," I mumbled, unsure how to respond. There was that word again, but how did he know? Especially when Wes seemed so confused by it? I glanced at Wes but he wore a hard expression. From his profile, I could see his jaw muscles flex back and forth.

I wandered farther inside and blinked a few times to let my eyes adjust to the much dimmer lighting. When the room came into focus, I was surprised to see how nice it was. The floors were hardwood, a deep mahogany, and the walls just a shade lighter than that. The end tables and chairs were all varying shades of brown, giving the room an earthy feel. The biggest splash of color was a cherry red couch and matching chairs in the center of the room. The lamps provided soft white light and the roaring fire in the stone fireplace gave off enough heat to make it all cozy. After seeing the rough exterior, this was a pleasant surprise.

At the sound of hushed voices, I turned. Wes and Jack stood huddled just inside the door, heads together and voices lowered. I caught only pieces of what they said.

"... confirmed it. She was working for the other side," Jack was saying.

"I know. I heard you earlier," said Wes. "I knew there was something going on with her." He glanced over at me. I shifted but it was too late; they both realized I'd become aware of them.

Jack stepped away and strode into the room, his expression transforming to friendly and blank. "Have a seat and then you can tell me what this is all about."

I sank down into one of the oversized chairs opposite the sofa and shrugged out of my jacket. Partly because the room was overly warm and partly so I could reach my plunger handles easier if it came to that. What had Wes meant when he said he'd heard Jack earlier? I would've assumed it meant a phone call or maybe he'd been here before me, but something about the way he'd said it made me feel as though I'd missed something. Kind of like the way Wes had almost answered my thoughts, out on the porch. And who was working for the other side?

I was still on edge and the weird tingling feeling had intensified since we'd walked inside. It was starting to make me itch; I rubbed absently at my arms. Wes took a spot on the sofa and leaned forward, looking tense and distracted. He wouldn't meet my eyes.

Jack took the other chair, his massive body filling every inch of cushion. "So, what's this all about?"

"It's about Tara," Wes told him, nodding at me. "She's the one I told you about last night. I think she could use your help. She's a Hunter," he said, though the last part came out more like a question.

Jack looked over at me with open interest and a gleam in his eye. "She's the one who killed Liliana?" His voice lowered and became thoughtful. I could practically see the wheels turning in his mind. I just wished I had some idea of what he was thinking.

"Knocked her head in with a piece of piping from the garbage," Wes said.

Darn it, I thought. Could he be any more blunt? I glared at him and prayed Jack and Liliana were not BFFs, because if the gleam in his eye was any indication, Jack was definitely interested in this piece of information. I noticed he didn't look very sad or put out over the news, though he did shoot a hard look at Wes, who shook his head almost imperceptibly, before turning back to me.

"Metal?" asked Jack. Wes nodded. "Impressive. Especially for her age. Where did you train?" Jack asked me.

"I didn't."

Jack blinked at me in confusion. "You've never trained?"

I shook my head. "I didn't know what I was until last night, or I guess, this morning. It just sort of happened."

Jack sent Wes a look that I couldn't read. "Without training, she's pretty inexperienced to be able to help The Cause."

"No," Wes hissed. "I didn't bring her here for that. She needs help, someone to explain it to her, and I thought—" He broke off, looking uncertain.

I was itching to know what "cause" Jack had meant, but I didn't interrupt.

Jack's brows knitted together. "What answers can I give her that you can't?"

"Let me ask you something. How did you know she was a Hunter when we walked in?"

"I felt it, of course."

"Huh." Wes leaned back on the couch, staring at a spot on the floorboard.

"Why do you ask?" Jack pressed.

Wes shook himself from his thoughts and looked back at Jack. "Because I can't sense her, at least not as a Hunter."

Jack sat back. "At all?"

"There's something ... but it's like nothing I've ever felt."

"Describe it."

Wes paused, obviously concentrating on pinpointing what he wanted to convey. "Well, scientifically speaking, instead of repelling, it sort of attracts, like a magnet."

"Really." Jack rubbed his beard, his eyes glinting with fascination as he looked back and forth between us.

At Wes's description, my heart made a couple extra hard thuds in my chest, but I ignored it and told myself that in no way did he mean anything resembling a physical attraction. Still, something about his explanation seemed to fit how I'd felt about him that first moment I'd seen him in my room, and part of it—at least for me—was definitely physical attraction. I noticed the two of them had fallen back into some sort of silent eye communication. I thought only girls could do that. "Hello? You guys are talking about me like I'm not even here. Can somebody please fill me in?"

Both of them glanced at me but Jack was the one who spoke. "Tara, how do you feel right now?"

"Uh, fine, I guess. Confused."

Jack smiled. "I meant physically. Do you feel anything ... different happening to your body?"

"Just a little cold," I said.

"Nothing else?"

"Goosebumps."

"Tell me about that."

I raised my eyebrows as if to say, "are you sure" and "this is weird" all at once. He just nodded for me to answer. "Um. My skin sort of tingles and itches all at the same time. Like I have ants crawling on me or something." I shrugged. "It happens sometimes."

Jack looked back at Wes who was watching me with narrowed eyes. Then he faced me again. "And when did that start, exactly? When you saw Wes? In the car? At my house?"

"When we came inside, I think."

Jack rubbed his beard. "Have you felt this way any other time?"

I thought about it. "Yes. Last night with ... Liliana." I had to struggle to say her name out loud. Mostly, I didn't want to remind

Jack of it until I knew for sure that he wasn't going to try to take a bite out of me in revenge. "And maybe other times. Like I said, I get goosebumps a lot." I watched him and Wes exchange another cryptic look. "Why? What does it mean?" I glanced at Wes again who was looking less angry and more perplexed by the moment. Jack cleared his throat.

"The feeling you have right now is something every Hunter feels when a Werewolf is nearby, so you aren't caught off guard," Jack explained. "Werewolves have something similar."

"So, you're saying the goosebumps are like an alarm system for Werewolves?" It was an anomaly that I'd always dismissed as a weird personal tic or something. Now Jack was telling me that every time I'd ever felt chilled, there'd been a Werewolf nearby?

"Yep." Jack sat back in his chair and propped his feet on the coffee table, completely at ease. He looked like he'd just accomplished a full day's work, and was happy to be done. But I had even more questions now than when I got here.

I looked at Wes, the wheels slowly turning, putting things together. "And it's a big deal to you, because you can't sense me."

"And apparently you can't sense me, either." He watched me, and I knew he was waiting for me to disagree, or at least admit I felt the magnet thing with him, too, but I kept my mouth shut. No way was I admitting, out loud, to this boy that I was attracted to him, even if he did think it was scientific. When I didn't respond, he turned back to Jack. "Have you ever heard of this?"

"No, I haven't," Jack admitted. "Interesting, though ..." He hooked his hands behind his head, and then leaned back, staring up at the ceiling. "Especially considering you."

We all fell silent after that. A thousand thoughts and questions and unbelievable answers flitted through my mind. It seemed the more I learned, the more questions I had. By now I figured it was safe to assume I was definitely a Hunter. And that a Hunter was someone who could kill a Werewolf. Basically with their bare hands. I looked down at my own hands in wonder. It amazed me that inside my tiny, and, shall we say less than athletic, body lay superhuman strength. And what was this deal with Wes and me not sensing each other? Or at least not in the "normal" way, as he put it. It didn't seem that big a deal to me until Jack said he'd never heard of it before. And apparently I was sensing Jack just fine. I rubbed my arms, trying to lessen the tingles.

I turned my attention back to Jack and Wes. They were locked in quiet conversation. Wes had scooted over to the far side of the couch and both of them were leaning forward, so their heads were only inches apart. They were whispering pretty low but every once in a while, Wes's response would turn to more of a hiss. I strained to hear without being obvious that I was paying attention.

"I could train her," said Jack. When Wes nodded, he continued, "You know we could use another Hunter, a young one, for our side."

"No!" Wes hissed. "I don't want her dragged into all of our politics. She's too young and inexperienced. And it's too dangerous."

Jack put a hand up. "All right, calm down, it'll just be training." His expression looked thoughtful. "You know as well as I do that once this door is opened, you can't close it again. More will come for her."

"I know."

Wes's whispered reply was grim and his expression matched.

Something about it gave me a sinking feeling in my chest, though yet again, I had no idea what half of it meant.

The parts I did know were the ones that worried me. Like the fact that both of them were convinced my run in with Liliana—a Werewolf—would not be an isolated incident. Despite the fact that it had been seventeen years in the making. With all of the explanations and half answers I'd been given, it felt like I was coming up on the edge of something. I just couldn't figure out what it was.

Their conversation seemed to be over, so I averted my gaze like I hadn't noticed them. I could feel their eyes on me, so I kept my face down and absently played with a lock of my hair, twirling the brown strands into endless loops. A nervous habit.

"Tara?" Wes called.

I glanced up, keeping my expression blank.

"What do you think?"

"About what?"

Wes sighed. "Don't pretend you didn't hear us. About training. It would be a good idea to learn how to defend yourself."

"I don't know."

"Look, you need to be prepared for what happened last night to happen again. It will. It's just a matter of time. So knowing how to properly defend yourself is a good idea. Jack can help you."

Before I could answer, the tingling under my skin suddenly intensified. I shivered and looked down. The hair on my arms stood on end. Footsteps approached behind me. I twisted in my chair, knowing what this feeling meant. Another Werewolf was coming. I thought about grabbing for the plunger handles still lodged in my back pockets. My heart pounded with sudden adrenaline and I braced for the threat.

When the "threat" appeared, I felt my jaw swing open in surprise. A beautiful blond woman stood in the doorway. She carried a pitcher and four glasses on a tray and her hair swung softly around her face as she moved. She was dressed comfortably in jeans and a white sweater, but more than the relaxed look she wore, it was something about *her* that made me feel instantly at ease.

"Tara, this is my wife, Fee," said Jack.

"Hello, Tara, it's nice to meet you," she said, smiling in a way that reached her pale eyes and let you know that she meant it.

"You too." I could feel the adrenaline draining out of me. I was really glad I hadn't gone for the plunger handle. Though the tingling remained, the sense of anxiety and danger had passed as soon as Fee had spoken. She obviously wasn't a threat and I actually felt guilty for considering a defensive maneuver.

I watched as she perched on the edge of the couch and poured liquid into each cup. Her movements were fluid and graceful, and something told me she made a beautiful wolf.

"Tea?" she asked, offering one to Jack. He took a cup and downed it in one long gulp. "Wes." She handed him a cup. "Nice to see you, as always." She leaned over and kissed his cheek when he reached for the glass. He smiled affectionately at her. Then she turned to me. "Any friend of Wes's is a friend of ours. Tea?" she asked, holding it out.

"Yes. Thank you."

Jack set his empty glass on the table and smacked his lips together, appreciatively. "Tara's that Hunter, Fee. The one Wes found last night. We were just talking about the possibility of training her. What do you think? Are you up for it?"

"It's been a while since we took on a new student," mused Fee. She turned to me. "Jack's known for being kind of a hard teacher but I think we balance each other out. Besides, it's all just an act with him anyway. He's really a big softie," she said with a chuckle. "Oh, and it would be so much fun to have another girl around."

Jack stroked his beard again, either ignoring or not disagreeing with her description of him. "It would be a lot of work, of course, but from what I'm hearing, you've got enough raw talent that I think we could make up for lost time."

"Okay, wait." I set my glass down and put my hand up. "Slow down. I never agreed to any training."

Jack looked surprised. "I assumed that was why Wes brought you here."

"It may have been. But I didn't get a vote in that plan," I said, throwing a warning look at Wes. "Mainly, I just wanted answers. Which I still don't feel like I've gotten."

Fee gave Jack a scolding look and then turned back to me. "Let me guess, he made you tell him everything he wanted to know, and hasn't offered anything in return?"

"I was about to," Jack said, defensively.

Fee rolled her eyes at him and then turned to me. "Come with me," she said. She stood up and strode away without waiting for an answer. I glanced at Wes and then got up and hurried after her.

She led me down the narrow hall and stopped in front of a scarred wooden door with a brass knob. She fished a small key out of her pocket and turned it in the lock and then stepped back to let me enter. I did so cautiously—half expecting to find a torture chamber or something equally horrifying—but stopped after a few steps, relieved and surprised at what I found. The room was old and worn, as was everything in it. It smelled of dust and old paper but no hint of violence or torture jumped out at me. Unless you counted heavy reading as torture, which I didn't.

Bookshelves lined the walls, interrupted only by hefty, ornate wall sconces that served as dim lighting. Antique chairs were scattered around, in front of the bookshelves. In the center of the room sat a wooden table scarred with age and use. The room, and everything in it, was charming in an ancient, classic sort of way; I felt like I'd stepped into a castle.

Behind me, Fee hit a switch, flooding everything with bright overhead lighting that added a touch of modern, and then went straight to the back wall and retrieved a worn leather-bound book from the middle shelf. She brought it to the table and gestured for me to pull up a chair.

"This book is called the *Draven*," she said, using a hand to wipe the dust from the cover and then wiping her hands on her jeans.

Dust bunnies flew in every direction, and tiny particles danced in the light above our heads. The book's cover bore a symbol etched into the leather that I didn't recognize, even with the dust removed.

"It contains the history of the Hunter race." She opened to a bookmarked page, revealing thick cursive. "Hunters begin training usually around age five, just like you would start grade school. It's mostly informational at that point and a lot of it comes from this book. I won't bore you by going through it page by page but you should read it in your spare time. It will answer a lot of your questions about where you come from."

She flipped through a few pages and I saw that it was broken down into topics and categories and even had a few rudimentary pictures portraying various weapons and fighting techniques.

I scanned the pages for a few minutes, taking it all in. "So, if I'd known what I was, I'd be carrying this thing around instead of my world history book?"

"Well, not this exact one. This one was a gift from a good friend, years ago. It's an original print. Few Hunter families have an original print anymore."

"Are you sure you want to loan it out, then?" I asked, worried.

"Yes, I'm sure." She smiled at me reassuringly, and I was

struck again by how open and honest her expression was. It made me trust her on a level I couldn't really explain, but I decided to go with my gut, mainly because it felt good to trust someone right now.

"Thank you," I said. Then Fee's first comment suddenly dawned on me. "How do the parents know? That their kid is a Hunter, I mean. You said they start training at five, but how do the parents know?"

Fee hesitated and there was something unreadable in her usually open gaze. "Well, to answer your question simply, it's in the genes. Your gift is passed down in your blood, as it will be in your children's blood, also."

I blinked. "So, one of my parents was a Hunter?"

"Yes." She watched me with a look of understanding and then just waited while I let that sink in.

My thoughts jumped back and forth, first of my mother. She was the exact opposite of everything I imagined a Hunter to be. (I got my slim, not exactly muscular build from her.) She was the least violent person I'd ever met; she didn't even like fight scenes in movies, for goodness' sake. Then I thought of my dad. Maybe it was him. He'd died when I was so young; there was no way I would've really known. And what if he'd kept it from my mom, too? She might have no idea, either. Which meant she would never believe me if I told her now.

"Just read through the book when you get a chance, and we'll talk more after that," Fee said finally.

I nodded, still reeling. Fee started to rise from her chair and that snapped me out of it. There was still so much more I didn't know. "Wait, I have another question," I said. "What is the point? I mean, why do Hunters train to fight or even exist for that matter? What's the purpose?"

"Well, the quick version is this: Werewolves and Hunters are enemies, and have been for centuries. There are many legends as to how both races came to be, but no one knows for sure anymore. What we do know is that Hunters are here to protect humans from Werewolves. A lot of Werewolves aren't ... friendly to humans. That's when a Hunter steps in. They train to fight from the time they are very young in order to perfect their speed and strength because without training, and even with a Hunter's added physical attributes, it's nearly impossible to win against an angry Were."

"You mean like with me and Liliana," I said.

Fee nodded. "Yes, you were lucky to have survived. Which is why Jack and I want to help you. Without training, you're an easy target."

"But I've never met any other Werewolves. Maybe I won't."

"It's possible that you're right—but not likely. The main thing to know, whether you choose to train or not, is that they can sense you. And they will attack if they think they can beat you. Now, as a Hunter, you've got extra strength and speed on your side, but you're also susceptible to their venom."

"Werewolves have venom?"

Fee nodded again and her expression turned serious. "Don't forget that. It's the most important part. A Werewolf's bite is like poison to a Hunter. One bite, if left untreated, can kill you in the span of just a few hours."

"What about their nails?" I asked, remembering the scratches hidden under my shirt.

Fee shook her head. "They'll burn like crazy at the time, and you'll feel sore, but they'll heal on their own. The poison is in their saliva, which is why the bites are dangerous."

"So what about humans? Isn't a Werewolf bite just as dangerous for them?" I asked.

"Not in the same way. All you need to be infected is their teeth to break your skin. A human is not affected that way. But their bodies are more fragile than ours, and they won't be a physical match for a Werewolf trying to attack them. Instead, they'll die from blood loss or organ damage."

I shuddered. "Oh."

"What I'm trying to say, Tara, is that by choosing not to train, you could be putting yourself in more danger. If they sense you, a Werewolf *will* attack. And you may or may not be able to fight back."

"I did just fine last night," I said stubbornly.

"You did," she agreed. "But are you willing to take that chance the next time?"

I didn't answer. I couldn't. Training to fight Werewolves? Because of some age-old promise to protect the human race? This was not happening to me. It was ridiculous, and far-fetched, and impossible. And even if I believed it, which I didn't want to admit that I did, I couldn't just run off and train for hours each day. I wasn't the Karate Kid. And my mom and my friends would definitely know something was up—not that I could explain it to them, and not that they would believe me even if I tried. It took seeing it—up close and personal—for *me* to believe me.

And even now, there were two thoughts that were so clear, they felt branded into my mind: One, Werewolves <u>do</u> exist, and two, I was born to kill them.

Chapter Six

I looked back at Fee, apologetically. "Look, I appreciate the offer, but I need some time. This is all a little too much, too fast. Sorry."

"I understand," Fee assured me. And I could tell by the way she looked at me that she really did. "Let's get back out there, shall we?"

I hefted the book up and tucked it underneath my arm as I followed her out. Fee locked the room again and we made our way back to the living room.

"Well?" Jack boomed.

Fee answered for me. "She needs time."

Jack nodded but I could see his disappointment. "Of course."

Wes just shook his head, like he'd given up arguing.

I gathered my jacket around me, preparing to leave. I still needed to make it back before my mom.

Fee stopped me at the door and squeezed my arm. "Take some time and let it all sink in. Even if you decide not to train, Jack and I are here if you need anything."

"Thanks," I said, managing a smile.

"They were really nice," I said when Wes and I were in the car.

He didn't answer but I purposely ignored his lack of response.

I told myself it was just normal behavior for him and I pressed on. "I'm surprised, though. Fee made it sound like all Werewolves are bloodthirsty killers and will attack me on sight. Yet, you three haven't tried to hurt me at all. If anything, you've helped more than you needed to."

"Not all Werewolves are like us," he said.

Not as detailed an explanation as I'd been hoping for but better than nothing. "How do you know them?"

"They raised me after my parents died."

"Oh. I didn't know. I'm sorry. How did they die?"

He hesitated. "Werewolves."

His lips pressed into a hard line and a muscle in his jaw flexed. There was malice in that one word, and disgust, and I finally understood his earlier comment. "That's what you meant by different sides?"

"Yes."

Finally, I felt like I was getting somewhere. "Does this have anything to do with that cause Jack mentioned?"

"Forget about that, okay? It's not for you."

"Shouldn't that be up to me, just like choosing whichever side I want to be on?"

He gave me a hard look. "No."

I huffed in frustration. The boy was a walking contradiction. I tried another tactic. "What's your favorite color?"

The corner of his mouth twitched. "Why?"

"Because you want me to choose a side but you still haven't told me enough to make me decide whether I can trust you."

"I've told you plenty."

I shook my head. "No, Jack and Fee told me plenty. You've told me nothing." I saw he was about to argue and continued. "Giving me my memories back doesn't count. They were already mine."

"Okay, but how does knowing my favorite color help you trust me?"

"You can tell a lot by a person's favorite color," I insisted. "For instance, mine is blue because I love the ocean and the sky."

"Okay, then, green." He raised a brow. "What do you get from that?"

"Well, could be for money, but I don't think so," I mused. "The forest, I think."

"Could be for envy, too, you know," he said, his voice taking on a teasing quality that surprised and confused me. Just moments ago he'd been clipped and silent, to the point of rude.

"You seem in a better mood," I said carefully.

Wes made the turn into my neighborhood and paused at the stop sign before answering. "Tara, it's impossible to be in a bad mood around you."

I looked back at him in surprise, unsure of what to say. It was easily the nicest thing he'd said to me since we'd met. "Thanks?" His lips twitched, making me wish I knew the meaning behind his cryptic compliment. "Are you always so hard to read?" I asked, finally.

"Are you always this difficult about taking compliments?"

"I'm still trying to figure out if it was one."

"It was."

Something about the way he said those two words made my face and arms heat up. The air in the car thickened into something almost tangible and I remembered what he'd said to Jack, about the magnet. It was definitely happening now, a pull or polarity between us. It was unnerving and enjoyable all at the same time, and I shifted in my seat, trying to get comfortable in my own skin. I wondered if he felt it too, but when I glanced over, his brows were arched down, in either deep thought or confusion.

In much less time than it would've taken a normal person—or normal car—we pulled up in front of my house, and he cut the engine. I didn't wait for him to come around and open my door. I needed a minute to clear my head, but the blast of cold air that greeted me when I stepped out was sadly not enough, though at least I could breathe easier out here in the chilly open space of my front yard. I was pretty sure—unless Werewolf customs were totally different—that Wes had just been flirting with me.

The problem was that I'd felt myself react to it. My pulse raced and my stomach fluttered. I felt like one look at my face and he'd know all those things. So I made sure to stay ahead of him as he followed me to the door. I fumbled with the key, ridiculously nervous all of a sudden. Wes waited patiently without comment as I finally slid the lock aside and wrestled the key out again. When I couldn't avoid it any longer, I turned to him.

"I don't really know what to say for everything you've done, but thanks," I told him.

"Wow, sounds like a brush-off."

"No!" My reply came out a little more forceful than I'd intended, and then I felt my face go red at the humor I spotted in his expression; he'd only been joking. "I meant, you didn't have to do all this, and I appreciate it."

He reached out, like he was about to take my hand, and then stopped. Instead, he shoved his hands into his pockets and stared at the ground. "Tara, there's something-"

A very nearby car door slammed shut and Wes broke off. We both looked over at the same time and I groaned at the figure fast approaching my doorstep. Beside me, I could feel the tension in Wes as he eyed our visitor suspiciously.

"George," I called with fake calm, mostly so Wes would realize he wasn't a threat. I didn't really feel him relax, though.

"Hey, babe." George's smile faltered at the sight of Wes and his eyes narrowed slightly.

I looked back at George, desperately trying to figure out how to explain this in a way that didn't involve the truth. "George, Wes. Wes, George." I gestured back and forth between them and paused. Neither spoke. Wes watched George intensely. It wasn't menacing, necessarily, but it held a challenge that I didn't like. George eyed Wes back and sort of grunted a hello at him. I felt my patience thinning at their show of testosterone. "George, what are you doing here?"

He finally tore his eyes from Wes's, breaking whatever macho stare-down they were locked in and looked back at me. "I figured since you were out sick, I'd come over and see if you needed anything. Maybe take care of you." His expression hardened a little. "But it looks like maybe you're not so sick after all."

"I was sick, George. I mean, I am sick."

George ignored me. His eyes swung back over to Wes. "Who are you, anyway?"

I tensed. Out of the corner of my eye, I could see Wes standing still as a statue.

"I'm a friend," Wes answered, finally. His tone was not very friendly, however.

George's eyes narrowed even further. "I know all of Tara's friends and I don't know you."

"Then I guess you don't know all of Tara's friends," Wes replied.

I exhaled loudly, hoping to let it be known how little patience I had left for all of this. "George, Wes is a friend from out of town. I didn't know he was coming. Either way, it's none of your business. You and I are not together anymore."

It seemed to take George a minute to accept this, but eventually, he seemed to get it. He stuffed his hands into his pockets and mumbled something about still caring about me. He shot a glance at Wes again and then stepped over and planted a very deliberate kiss on my cheek. "I'll see you, Tay," he said and headed to his car. I watched him go, wondering whose benefit the kiss had been for: mine or Wes's.

I waited until George had driven off before whirling at Wes. "What was that?" I hissed.

His eyes were sparkling. "What was what?"

"You were baiting him."

He shrugged. "I don't like him very much."

I gave him a look.

"Your mom will be home soon," he said.

"Crap. I forgot about that. You better get going." I hesitated and then added, "Will I see you again?"

He pulled a small card out of his pocket and handed it to me. "Here, take this. It's mine and Jack's numbers. Just in case."

"Thanks, I guess I'll ... see you around," I said, hoping to mask my biting disappointment. His lips curved up on one side. "Probably."

Then he left.

CHAPTER SEVEN

THE next morning, Angela was waiting for me at my locker. "Feeling better?" she asked.

"Much. Guess all the cold meds knocked it out of me."

"So?" she prompted, raising a dark eyebrow behind her glasses. I looked blankly back at her. "What happened with you and George? The one time I saw him yesterday, he was moping like a little boy who'd lost his puppy."

I grimaced and rummaged inside my locker for my English book. "We broke up."

"I figured that much. What happened?"

I straightened and stuffed my book into my bag before facing her. "You mean, besides the fact that his head has grown too big for his body? Nothing."

She gave me a sympathetic look. "Are you okay?"

"I am, actually. I thought I'd be more upset but mostly I just feel bad that it might've ruined our friendship, you know?"

"Well, I'm glad you're feeling better. I was worried you were just upset about the breakup. I almost came over after school to check on you."

I tried not to seem relieved that she hadn't, so I shrugged. "I was probably sleeping it off."

Angela's reference to the previous day did weird things to my stomach, but I tried to ignore it and fell into step next to her, headed to class. I'd spent the entire night basically wide awake and fending off crazy thoughts, like visions of training with a Werewolf to learn how to fight Werewolves. Or of not training, and being attacked by a pack of them in an alley somewhere.

And of course, Wes. The way he'd looked at me when I'd gotten out of bed and the comments that might or might not have been evidence of his interest in me. And then there was the inexplicable pull between us that only seemed to intensify when his eyes held mine for a particularly long moment. Was I actually attracted to him? Or was it all a product of simply feeling his animal presence?

The more I thought about it, the more I decided there was no way he'd been flirting. Making fun of me? Likely. Flirting? Not so much. I was pretty sure he'd been somehow involved with Liliana. Which, of course, brought me back to the fact that I'd killed somebody. The fact that the "somebody" was also a "something" made it a little easier to process but part of me felt guilty enough to march right into the police station and hold out my wrists for cuffs. All of it just added up to complete, impossible, surreal weirdness; I had no idea what to do about it.

"Tara, did you hear anything I just said?" Angela asked.

We were standing outside the English room now. I forced myself to pay attention under Angela's scrutiny. "Sorry, I guess I'm still a little out of it." I would've felt badly for the lie I kept perpetuating about being sick, but the statement I'd just made was actually the complete truth. I definitely felt … out of it.

"I said, Sam was asking if we wanted to go to the mall and get dresses for the dance next weekend," Angela said, a little impatiently.

As if the mention of her name had summoned her, Sam waved at us from across the sea of bodies that crowded the hallway and began weaving toward us. "Hey, guys." Without waiting for a response, she rushed on. "You would not believe what Cindy Adams wore to school yesterday." The first bell rang and Sam ignored it. "Ohmygosh, it was this plaid homemade thing. Hilarious. I have a picture on my phone. Look."

"You weren't even here yesterday," said Angela.

Sam shrugged. "I know, but Jenny Slater was, and she has homeroom with Cindy so she sent it to me. I laughed for, like, twenty minutes."

"You weren't here, either?" I asked.

Sam winked. "My Tuesday night was sort of draining."

I shook my head. "Your social calendar makes me tired."

"Which is exactly why I'm entitled to a day of recuperating," she said, flipping her hair. "Plus, Macy's had buy one, get one on the eye shadow I love."

I rolled my eyes and at her prompting, glanced at the phone she was holding out. It was pretty bad. "Wow, nice," I said with a laugh.

To be fair, Cindy Adams was the closest thing I had to an arch nemesis. When we were in sixth grade, she and I had run against each other for student body president. I hadn't even wanted to do it, but the teacher didn't give us a choice; our office had been assigned to us. Cindy couldn't have been happier. She'd wished me luck and then thrown herself into campaigning, making elaborate signs and even preparing a speech to give on the morning announcements.

Unfortunately for Cindy, in sixth grade it's all about who you know, and Cindy's circle of friends was considerably smaller than mine. When she saw that everyone was going to vote for me, she started playing dirty, spreading rumors and lies to bolster her chances.

Several different rumors flew around, the nicest being that she'd found me in a compromising position with her cat during the last sleepover we'd had. Yeah, you've got to be pretty twisted to come up with the stuff she did. Needless to say, that was the end of whatever friendship or civility we might have had. She won the election, which would've been fine by me, except now I couldn't stand her. So, we've enjoyed a quiet, though vicious, rivalry ever since.

As a result, seeing her in an outfit like this sort of made my day. "Where did she get this and why does she think it's cute?" I asked as Sam pocketed her phone.

"I don't know. Maybe she doesn't have a friend to tell her how bad it is." Sam flashed an evil smile. "Maybe we should be those friends."

"Maybe we should," I agreed.

The warning bell rang, and we all scattered to make it to class.

"Find me at lunch," Sam called, sailing down the quickly emptying hall, her dark hair billowing out behind her.

CHAPTER EIGHT

"THIS dress would be perfect for my date with Ryan," Sam said, holding up a black mini with a sequined waist.

"I thought the dress you bought at the last store was for your date with Ryan," Angela said.

"No, that was for my date with Chad," Sam corrected.

Angela laughed. "I can't keep up anymore."

"Feel free to pick up my slack anytime, Ang," Sam said, smiling and wiggling her eyebrows.

"No thank you. Besides, once you go out with these boys, they're hooked. They follow you around like you're the Pied Piper."

"I know. Poor things," Sam sighed dramatically.

Angela and I grinned and kept browsing. We were at the mall, dress shopping for the dance I was thinking more and more of not attending. George would've insisted, for social standing, if nothing else. But I was actually free to decide for myself, and the thought of going alone just didn't appeal.

"I'm going to try this black one on," said Sam. "Tara, can you hold my bags?"

"Sure." I took the four bags from her, set them on the floor nearby, and plopped into a chair. This could be a while. Sam was a serious shopper—no such thing as browsing. Everything about Sam was that way. Impulsive, indulgent, and fun—always fun.

"Hey, Ang, you never told me how your date with Dave went," I said.

"It was really great," Angela said, her smile turning a little dreamy. It was sort of fun to watch; Angela never looked dreamy.

"Are you going out again?" I asked.

"Yeah, he asked me to the dance."

"Oh. My. Goodness. Did I just hear that Angela the Librarian has a date? Like a real date with a real guy?" Sam called from the dressing room.

"Ha-ha, Sam," said Angela.

"Well, hot damn, how exciting is this! Is he a good kisser?" she called back, in a loud voice.

Angela's face turned red, and she glanced around the store, adjusting her glasses. "Can you be any louder, Sam?"

"Probably." The latch unhinged and Sam stepped out, the little black dress hugging her like a glove. "Okay, what do you think?"

I whistled. "Wow."

Angela nodded in agreement. "Definitely a show-stopper. How short is that thing?"

Sam twirled slowly, inspecting herself in the small mirror. "Short enough, I'd say. You wanna borrow it, Ang?"

Angela's cheeks reddened a little. "I'm good, thanks."

"I'm getting it," said Sam. "What about you, Tara? You haven't even tried anything on."

"I don't think I'm going."

"What? Why?"

I realized I'd forgotten to tell her. "George and I broke up."

She leaned down and put her arms around me. "I'm so sorry, Tay. Are you okay?" She pulled back and looked down at me sympathetically.

"Yeah, I'm fine. I think it was the right thing. But he doesn't agree—or seem to be accepting it."

"Okay, that's it. You have to get something new," Sam declared. "If you're going to be boring and not get a new dress, at least get a new pair of jeans. You know, the ones that squeeze your butt like a vise and you have to lay down to zip." She wiggled an eyebrow. "It'll make you feel better."

I laughed. "I do not want a pair of jeans that cut off my air supply. And if I change my mind, I'll be sure to borrow them from you."

"Fine. But I'm going to change and then we ARE going to find you something new. It's a rule. After a breakup, you have to buy new clothes."

"Fine," I agreed.

We waited while Sam changed and then spread out and wandered through the racks.

"Tara, this is cute, come see," called Angela a moment later.

I wandered over for a closer look and froze. It was a hoodie, with the face of a wolf on the front. Even worse, its face was split in two, one half on each side of the zipper. I tried to keep my expression neutral while I mentally cringed. "I think I'll pass." I moved away as quick as I could.

"What about this one?" Angela called again, this time holding up another. This one was a myriad of different shades of a single color: green.

"Perfect," I said, taking it out of her hands.

"It doesn't have anything on it," Sam argued.

"Which means it'll go with everything," I argued back.

Sam rolled her eyes.

By the time we reached the food court, I realized I was in a good mood and the most relaxed I'd been in days. Normalcy agreed with me, something I'd seriously taken for granted up until forty-eight hours ago. Maybe, despite everything that had happened, nothing needed to change for me after all. Maybe nothing like it would ever happen again, which also meant I'd probably never see Wes again. And just like that, my good mood evaporated.

On the way out to the car, I saw that clouds had rolled in, painting the sky a dismal shade of winter gray. A dampness in the air made the chill feel heavier. I pulled my coat tight around me and kept my head down.

We'd almost made it to the car when I felt it. My skin prickled and tingled in warning, giving me the feeling of something crawling on me. I shivered and spun around, fully expecting to see a wolf lurking somewhere between the parked cars, but when I turned, there was nothing there. I kept searching, spinning a full circle, as my eyes looked for any movement, furry or otherwise. Nothing.

I thought of my broken plunger handles, still under the bathroom sink where I'd stashed them last night. I should probably carry them around with me, just in case.

"Tara? Are you okay?" Angela asked.

Out of the corner of my eye I saw her and Sam watching me with confused expressions, but I ignored them and continued to scan the lot. "Yeah, I'm fine ... just thought I saw something," I finally said, giving up and turning back to face them.

"Like what?" Angela pressed. The look on her face told me I was coming off crazy.

"A bird, I guess," I said lamely. I shrugged and climbed into the backseat.

"Maybe the breakup is bothering you more than you thought," said Sam as she pulled the car onto the road.

I didn't answer. I was focused on the creepy-crawlies I was still feeling. Thankfully, the feeling faded as we turned into traffic. I sighed in relief.

"Or maybe you aren't as recovered as you thought, from whatever bug you had," suggested Angela.

"I'm just distracted, guys. I've got a lot on my mind."

"See, I told you it's the breakup," said Sam.

"It's not the breakup," I argued.

"You don't have anything else going on, though. Unless ... there's someone else." Sam stole a glance at me in the rearview. When I didn't answer, her eyes went wide. "Ohmygosh, there is someone else. Who is he? Does he go to our school? Do we know him?"

Angela turned and eyed me. "Is Sam right? Come on, Tara, you can tell us."

I hesitated, debating how to answer. If I didn't tell them, they'd never let it go and would eventually get suspicious as to why I wasn't talking. On the other hand, if I did tell them, choosing my words carefully, I wouldn't feel so secretive. And it would feel good to have my girls to talk to about it. At least the parts I *could* talk about. "Okay, yes, Sam is right. I met someone. Sort of. It's kind of complicated, though."

Sam hopped around in the driver's seat, somehow remembering to keep her hands on the wheel. "I knew it. This is so exciting. Tell us everything."

"His name is Wes. We met two nights ago, at the pool hall. It was after George left. We talked and ... hung out and then he gave me a ride home."

Angela twisted in her seat so she could look at me. "Are you going to see him again?"

"Well ... he came over yesterday."

"And?" Sam demanded. "What happened? Did you guys—?"

I didn't have to see her to know she was wiggling her eyebrows—her code for sex. "No, Sam, we did not. We didn't even kiss. I was sick, remember?"

"So he took care of you?" Angela asked softly. I could hear the romantic wheels turning inside her head.

"I guess. We talked and just hung out. But, I don't know if I'm going to see him again."

"Why not?" Angela asked.

"Because he didn't say anything about it. Everything he says is so ... cryptic," I sighed. "He did give me his number, though." I didn't add that I'd stared at the card so many times, I'd memorized it.

"Call him!" both girls shouted together.

I smiled. Despite the vague details I'd given, it felt really good to have someone to talk to. "Maybe. It feels weird being the one to call."

Sam shook her head. "Guys like a girl who takes the initiative. You should call him. Tonight."

Angela twisted in her chair again. "For once, I agree with Sam. You should take the first step and call him. He wouldn't have given you his number if he didn't want you to."

I didn't answer. The problem was he'd made it sound like I should only call if I needed him. Like, if I came across another angry Werewolf or something. But I couldn't exactly divulge that detail.

Sam pulled the car into my driveway and turned. "Call him. We'll be waiting to hear what happens, so call us tomorrow. No excuses."

I smiled again. "Okay," I agreed, on a deep breath. "Thanks, guys. See you tomorrow."

Inside, I tried to slip by my mom with minimal questions. She'd been looking at me kind of weird since yesterday morning. I think she suspected something was up when I'd acted so confused over where I'd been the night I'd ... fought Liliana. (I still didn't want to say *killed*, even to myself.) So, I'd been trying to steer clear until I was convinced I could play it off effectively. Or until she forgot about it.

"Mom, I'm home," I called out, dumping my jacket in the front closet.

"In here." Her voice floated out from the back of the house.

I found her in the sunroom, bent over a flat of herbs she was planting. She looked up and smiled when I came in and I noticed a streak of dirt smudged across her forehead. Her hands were black with soil, seed packets spread out on the table beside her.

"Did you have fun?" she asked.

"Yeah, the girls got dresses for the dance next week and I got a new sweatshirt."

She frowned. "You didn't get a dress, too?"

"I don't think I'm going." I took a deep breath. "George and I broke up."

She eyed me curiously. "Is that good or bad?"

I laughed at that. "Is this an 'if you hate him, I'll hate him' scenario?"

She shrugged. "Not exactly, but I don't want to tell you how sorry I am unless you're sorry."

I leaned against the doorpost and then straightened again when I realized who it reminded me of. "No, I'm not sorry. I feel okay about it. Like maybe we're better off as friends."

She nodded. "Good. I agree."

I raised my eyebrows. "You do?"

"Yes. I see how you look when you talk about it or when he's around. Or how you don't look, I should say."

"And how do I look?"

She tapped a dirty finger against her chin. "Friendly affection is how I'd describe it, I think."

"Oh," I said, staring at the flat of potting soil.

"I'm glad you told me about George," she said, pulling me back to the conversation. "You know you can talk to me about anything, right?"

"I know. Thanks, Mom." I started to turn away but her voice stopped me.

"I mean it, Tara. Anything. You can always come to me." Her tone was more forceful than it had been a moment ago.

I searched her face, trying to unlock any hidden meaning behind the words. Did she know something about what was going on after all? Was this my chance to tell her?

Then she blinked and her gaze became unassuming. "Anyway, you should get some sleep. You're probably still recovering from that bug."

"Yeah, I guess. I'm pretty tired." I picked up my bag and started edging toward the door, still confused.

"You do feel better, right?" she asked, eyeing me with scrutiny.

"Much."

"Hmm. I expected it to last longer with how out of it you were yesterday morning."

I shrugged. "Sam was home with something, too, and she felt better today, so it must've been a twenty-four-hour thing."

"Apparently," she agreed, though she still looked a little unconvinced.

"Well, good night." I turned for the door before she could say more.

"Good night."

In my room, I sat on my bed with Wes's card in one hand and my cell phone in the other. My heart was already pounding in my ears. I took a deep breath and tried to calm myself. This was ridiculous. Why was I so nervous? He was just a guy. And I was a badass Werewolf slayer. This should be a piece of cake. I repeated that to myself over and over until I was at least breathing normally again. Then, before I could change my mind—or hyperventilate—I punched in the number and held the phone to my ear.

He answered on the first ring. "Hello?"

My breath caught in my chest and I had to struggle to make my voice sound calm and casual. "Hey, Wes. It's Tara."

On the other end, there was a long pause. Then, "Is everything okay?"

"Yeah, everything's fine. I was just—" Well, crap, now what did I say? He seemed all business, driving home my original assumption that he'd only given me this number in case of emergency. But I was in it now and there was no turning back. "I was just calling to say hi, I guess. And thanks again for all your help." Okay, I chickened out.

"No problem. Have you thought any more about training?"

"Um, I'm still thinking about it."

Another pause. "Okay, well, I'm kind of in the middle of something, so I need to hang up."

I tried to keep the disappointment out of my voice. "Right, sorry. I'll talk to you later."

"Are you sure you're okay?"

"I'm fine."

"I'll talk to you later, then."

"Bye." I disconnected and fell back on the bed, feeling like an idiot. I stared up at the ceiling, replaying the conversation a million times until I was convinced I was more than an idiot. I was inept. I'd never had a problem talking to guys before, but apparently that was just warm-ups. This was the big leagues now, and apparently, I sucked. I wished briefly I could be more like Sam, with her confident, self-assured attitude.

Under normal circumstances, I probably wouldn't have felt so unsure of myself, but my life was hardly normal circumstances, anymore. Everything was changing so fast; it made me dizzy. It felt like someone had come along and pulled my legs out from under me. I didn't even know if being a Werewolf Hunter was something I wanted. Then again, it's not like I had a choice.

I rolled over and my eyes landed on a flash of red. My tattered silk shirt was still on the floor below me. I grabbed it and balled it up, swooshing it into the trashcan. Then I closed my eyes and waited for sleep.

Chapter Nine

"I'LL probably be out late tonight," my mom said. "There's chicken in the fridge. All you have to do is microwave it."

I sat at the table with a bowl of cereal, watching her gather her purse and keys. "Why do you have to stay late? It's Sunday."

"Inventory and ordering night, remember? I told you about it a couple of days ago."

"Oh, right, I forgot," I said.

Inventory night happened once every three months, for my über-organized mother. She and Julie—her one employee—would stay late and go through everything in the stockroom to make sure it matched up to her many spreadsheets. I couldn't think of a single thing more boring but it made my mom happy to check things off lists.

She eyed me. "You okay? You seem distracted. Are you still feeling sick?"

I shifted under her stare. "I'm fine. I just forgot."

She didn't look convinced. "You didn't even go out yesterday, just sat in your room all day. Maybe I should make a doctor's appointment for you."

"Really, Mom, I'm fine. I just needed some more rest. You know being sick always wears a person out."

I *had* spent all of Saturday in my room, just not for the

reasons she thought. After the weird feeling I'd gotten in the mall parking lot, I'd decided it was definitely time to do something. And after my botched phone call with Wes, I'd decided maybe I'd be better off doing it on my own, so I'd spent most of Saturday reading through the book Fee had given me—the *Draven*.

Most of it was reminiscent of my high school English book, in that it was completely boring and irrelevant. But the section on basic fighting techniques had been helpful. I'd even practiced some of the stances to get a feel for them. And there was a section on weapons, too, that made me feel slightly better about my own homemade ones.

Apparently, the weapon of choice for most Hunters was a wooden stake. The whole silver bullet thing was a myth and besides, guns couldn't get through most security and really tended to draw attention. So, I still had my plunger handles in my backpack because despite being rudimentary, they were better than nothing.

The *Draven* had taught me something else, too. The more I read, the more I realized that Hunters were serious about the whole "born and bred to kill" thing. It made me understand what Wes had said about picking a side; if I was going to be true to my nature, it would mean killing first, and asking questions later. No wonder he needed to know where I stood. Not that I could ever raise a hand—or stake—to him. I still felt nauseated whenever I thought about what I'd done to Liliana.

But the thing that kept bugging me the most was that the book kept coming back to the fact that being a Hunter was a bloodline thing. You got it from your parents, or parent, but usually both, since marrying outside your race is apparently frowned upon—and since my mother still showed no sign of carrying around some knowledge of a secret identity, I still hadn't decided what to do about that.

My mom was eyeing me, though, and critically. Careful to keep my face blank, I returned her gaze as innocently as I could. Finally, she nodded. "Okay, well, I'll see you later. Call me if you need me."

"I will. Love you." I forced a smile and kissed her cheek as she left.

I finished my cereal and set the bowl on the counter before heading back to my room. There'd be plenty of time to wash the dishes later. It's not like I had any plans. Sam and Angela had three-way called me yesterday, demanding to know how the phone call to Wes had gone. I'd filled them in and noticed how they both went conspicuously silent after. It hadn't cheered me. Then they'd both let loose with the usual "he probably really was busy" and "his loss" sentiments. That hadn't helped, either. So, I'd told them I was helping my mom at the store and would see them Monday. I just couldn't take any more sympathy right now. I was feeling sorry for myself just fine.

In my room, I sat in my desk chair and tried to come up with something to pass the day. I contemplated the merits of using the time to finish my English paper that was due in two weeks. Okay, maybe I wasn't that desperate yet. I flipped my computer on and surfed Internet news, reading national headlines first, then local. Near the bottom, one in particular caught my eye: "Animal Attack in Mountainview. Two Dead."

I clicked on it and scanned the story: "Two local college students were found dead in the woods last night. Their throats had been ripped open and their bodies covered in cat-like scratches. No witnesses have been found, and the police have no leads on a suspect as of yet. Empty beer cans were found scattered around the scene as well as the remains of a small fire. Police are assuming the couple had camped out for the night when they were brutally attacked. Both were students at Frederick Falls Community College. Their names will be released after the families have been properly notified."

I sat back and stared at the screen. A sinking feeling consumed me. Based on the sketchy details, I had a pretty good idea who—or what—had caused these deaths. For the first time, I felt a little less guilty over killing Liliana. If her kind did stuff like this, maybe they deserved it.

"I see you've heard."

I swiveled in my chair, recognizing the voice even before I turned. Wes stood in my bedroom doorway, leaning against the frame. His jacket, jeans, and boots were of the same variety and color he always seemed to wear and his hair was just as stylishly disheveled. Something fluttered in my chest and landed in my stomach. "You have a knack for the unexpected entrance."

He shrugged. "It's a gift." He nodded to the computer screen. "You saw the article."

"It's awful." I didn't follow his glance to the computer. I couldn't bring myself to take my eyes off him. I stared up at him, trying to somehow read his thoughts through his expression, and overcome with relief and excitement at seeing him again. "But what
are you doing here?" I blurted.

He raised an eyebrow.

"I mean, you made it sound like you'd only be back if it was an emergency and you didn't sound thrilled to hear from me the other night." I couldn't help the note of accusation that crept into my voice.

A look of regret passed over his features. "Sorry about that. I was involved in something that made it … difficult to talk on the phone just then. I was glad that you called, though."

"Oh." My insides soared with that one single comment, my brain already trying to dissect what it really meant.

He watched my expression for a moment and then sighed. "Actually, I am here for a reason, though. There's something I need to tell you."

"What is it?"

"That attack, the one you just read about," he said, slowly, "There's something else that wasn't in the papers."

Something twisted in my chest. I had a feeling I wouldn't like where this was going. "What?"

He hesitated, shooting me a worried look. "There was a message, of sorts, left at the scene. It was addressed to you."

"What do you mean a message? What did it say?"

He handed me a photograph of some words written in red lettering, painted across some sort of black tarp. A tent, maybe? It read: "Dear Tara, Consider this a preview. See you soon."

"I took it before I cleaned it up last night. This was their tent. I disposed of it before the police got there," he explained.

"And the red lettering?"

"Blood. Probably theirs."

I swallowed hard and looked away from the picture. I could feel his eyes on me, scrutinizing, and my temper flared. "I'm not going to freak out, if that's what you're waiting for," I snapped.

"Good." His expression lightened only barely. "My memory altering skills are slightly tapped at the moment."

"I'm fine," I assured him. No way was I letting him remove my memories again. I'd been in the dark long enough, and even if I wasn't sure where I stood, or if I truly wanted this life, I'd still rather live with it than live a lie. "Wait a second. Last night?"

He nodded.

"So you knew about it when I called and you didn't tell me? That's why you acted so weird on the phone?" I asked.

"I didn't want to scare you or push you too hard, too fast. The other day, when I saw how you reacted, I knew telling you this would only make it worse. It would be better if you stayed away from it all, anyway."

His keeping things from me, which I was quickly learning was his chosen approach, was irritating, but I didn't want to end what seemed like the most honest conversation we'd had so far. I tried to keep my emotions out of my voice. "Why? Why are you even bothering? You don't even know me."

"And you don't know me, but you don't scream for help no matter how many times I show up in your bedroom, uninvited."

He had a point. "That still doesn't really answer my question."

When he answered, all traces of humor or sarcasm were gone, replaced by something that resembled compassion. "Because I know what it's like to try and figure out what you are, with everything coming at you at once. And because no one should have to do that alone."

"Thanks," I said, unsure of how else to respond now that he wasn't teasing or dancing around a question. I decided to take a chance that my luck—and his mood—would hold. "Why did you have to do it alone? Didn't you have Jack and Fee?"

"Yes, and they've been great, putting up with me when they

shouldn't. I was the one who made it a solitary experience."

"Losing your parents made it harder, I'm sure."

"I don't remember much about them. I was only two when it happened." Despite his words, there was evidence of old pain in the way he spoke. I decided to let it drop for now, especially knowing how much I hated when people asked about my dad.

"So, you want to help me figure things out?" I asked, changing directions.

He shrugged. "If I can."

"Then maybe you can answer some questions for me."

He nodded, so I got up and went to my bed and retrieved the Draven. I opened to a marked page to a drawing that depicted a drawing of a Werewolf fighting a Hunter; the Werewolf lunged with clawed feet and the Hunter wielded a wooden stake. "I've been reading through this book and it just doesn't make sense, based on what I've seen of you and Jack and Fee. All it talks about is how much Werewolves and Hunters hate each other."

Wes stepped closer and eyed the picture for a brief moment, before retreating to the desk chair. He settled into it with the stiff crunch of leather.

"You can take that off, you know," I said, eyeing his jacket. He looked at me and I felt my cheeks heat up as I realized the invitation he could've mistaken it for.

"I know," he said, without removing the jacket. He cleared his throat before going back to my question. "So the Draven is right, in that aspect. Weres and Hunters are mortal enemies, as a general rule. Most will attack each other on sight, while some are willing to wait until provoked. But mostly, yes, they hate each other."

"So, what it says, that Werewolves can't be trusted and that a friendship between a Werewolf and a Hunter is basically unheard of, that's true?"

"The Draven is old and was written only from a Hunter's perspective. Times have changed."

"Then it's more common now?" I asked, confused.

"No, not common, exactly," he said. He seemed to be choosing his words carefully. "It's complicated."

"Explain it to me, then, because I don't understand. This book tells me that you're supposed to be my enemy—and I'm yours."

"I told you, that book is outdated. It has a narrow view of things. It doesn't give you the current ... politics of our world. A lot has happened between the two races since it was written."

"Like what?"

He settled back in his chair, like whatever story he was about to tell was a long one. "Up until about thirty years ago, the two sides were separate and distinct. Each side saw the other as an enemy and fought to the death to destroy each other. The Hunters were aggressive and relentless, sending search parties out; they made a serious dent in Werewolf population for a while. All of this I'm sure you read."

He nodded toward the open book in my lap. "But then something new began to happen. Werewolves starting forming groups—combining packs—which was unheard of for our kind. Before that, they had never been able to exist in packs larger than three or four without fighting for the alpha spot and destroying each other in the process. In this case, their common purpose united them, though, and they began seeking out the Hunter settlements, ambushing them. They focused mainly on the children, knowing it would diminish the rising ranks and future generations of Hunters."

"Oh my gosh. That's awful. Children?"

He nodded, grim with some memory that he was too young to have experienced himself. It made me wonder what he was leaving unsaid. "After that, the Hunters went into hiding. They scattered from the settlements—bought houses, got jobs, paid taxes. They hoped to stay hidden long enough to raise their children and teach them to fight properly before the packs could find them again."

"Did it work?"

"Mostly. They were a lot more secluded from each other that way, so there wasn't any real way to know when an attack might be coming. Because of that, they formed bases—boarding schools of sorts—for Hunter kids. It provided a safe haven and the illusion that their numbers really had been depleted. The kids went to school there and learned to fight from the best Hunter warriors available. Because of that, the next generation of Hunters was even more skilled and vicious than the last. It changed the way the war between the two was fought. Hunters continued to send out search parties, but they were stealthier, more discreet, and more successful.

"Some of the new generation of Hunters began believing times had changed enough to try a new approach. Peace. They formed a group, calling themselves The Cause, and began seeking out Weres with the sole purpose of preaching to them. They fought only when they needed to defend themselves and avoided killing, only injure and retreat, hoping to win others to their side."

"What happened? Did they bring peace?" I leaned forward, completely wrapped up in his story. There was nothing like this in the *Draven*. Between that, and the earnest way Wes spoke, I knew there was something very important about this particular bit of history.

He continued, without really answering my question, as if he'd told this story many times, without deviating from the script. "There was a man during that time. His name was Sebastian Saint John and he was a Hunter. He befriended a Werewolf named Audrey and they formed an alliance. When others of their kind heard, they were angry, but Sebastian had a way with words and Aubrey was gentle. They spoke of peace to anyone who would listen. Many came around to their way of thinking despite their controversial message and a council was formed—six Werewolves and six Hunters—to govern relations between the two races and form a treaty."

He got up and went to the window, no longer facing me. I knew without seeing his face that he was somehow no longer in this room, but far away, wherever this Sebastian was.

"It probably would have worked, but those who didn't want it were loud and began recruiting for their side. In the end, a group of thirty Werewolves came and attacked the council in the middle of the night. All twelve of the council were killed. Negotiations fell apart after that. The families and friends of the dead council members came together, and the Werewolves responsible for the killings were hunted down and destroyed. That was the last act performed as a joint effort by the two races."

He continued to stare out the window when he'd finished. I wished he'd turn so I could read his expression; something about his tone suggested that the story he told was more personal than he let on.

"How did you know them?"

"What?"

"How did you know them?" I repeated. "I can tell this story means something to you, so how did you know the people who died?"

It took him a long time to answer. So long that I wondered if he even remembered the question. Finally, he did, in a voice so low I almost didn't hear. "I guess I didn't. Not really."

I waited, but he didn't say more. I wanted to press it, but I didn't. I knew better. There was something else, though I didn't know how it related to now. "But that makes it sound even more like we shouldn't be friends," I said, finally.

"It explains the risk of it, though. Which is something you should consider before spending more time with me or Jack or any of us."

"I'll take it under advisement."

It didn't take a rocket scientist to hear the warning in his words, but it was too late. I was involved in this world, in a big way, like it or not. And even though I knew next to nothing about it, I *wanted* to be involved. This "Cause" that Wes spoke of was a way to be who I was and still do some good. I wanted that.

He turned from the window, irritation flashing in his eyes. "I'm serious," he snapped. "You're a walking target if you're with us."

"What happened to picking a side?" I shot back. "You made it sound like it was either you or them. Do you want me to choose them? Would that be safer?"

He regarded me and then his shoulders deflated almost imperceptibly. "You're safer with us," he agreed quietly.

"Besides, it sounds like someone's already put me on their radar, even before I decided whether I was going to use my powers for good or evil. So, it sounds like I don't have much of a choice, except to be good." I shrugged. "So that's what The Cause is for? They want to bring peace?"

When he turned to face me, his expression was clear of the heavy emotion that had colored his tone before, but he didn't move away from the window. "There are a few, from both races, who still believe in the possibility of it." He shrugged, like it was as simple as that.

But I knew it wasn't that cut and dried. There was more. I could hear it in his voice when he'd told the story. It had lingered in his eyes when he'd turned, if only for a second. Sadness. And pain.

"Let's go somewhere," I said, letting the book fall shut. It made a snapping sound that only crisp, dried paper could make.

"Go somewhere?"

"Get out of the house, do something fun."

"I don't think that's a good idea, with what happened last night. That note—"

"Was vague and nondescript. Besides, I'll be with you."

"So you trust me now?"

I thought about his question, and the many meanings it could hold. Something about the intense way his dark eyes held mine told me to choose my answer carefully. "To keep me alive, yes."

"Where do you want to go?"

I shrugged and then went to the closet to find my boots. "I don't know. Anywhere. What do you like to do for fun?"

"Fun," he repeated, the word sounding almost foreign and unused on his lips. "I don't know. There's not a lot of time for that."

"There's time now," I pointed out, and suddenly I was determined to do something fun and unimportant with him, if for no other reason than to see if he was capable.

"What do you like to do?" he asked.

"I like pool," I said, then cringed when I remembered what had happened the last time. "But it's probably not a good idea to show my face in Moe's for a while," I added.

"I know a place."

Chapter Ten

THE pool hall Wes took me to turned out to be a dive bar in the middle of nowhere. The crooked sign out front said Fred's Place, in dirty letters, and there were only two cars in the gravel lot besides ours. Both were old enough to be antiques, and not in the classy, expensive sense of the word. One had a bag taped over the passenger side window in place of the glass. Wes parked the car, and I raised my eyebrows at him.

"What?" he asked.

"Is this place safe?"

Wes laughed. "You managed to slay an angry Werewolf in a dark alley with barely a scratch and you want to know if the drunks inside Fred's are going to bother you?"

I didn't answer.

He sighed. "Safe enough," he answered. "And out of the way. Besides, Fred will make sure the regulars leave us alone."

I reluctantly got out of the car and followed Wes to the entrance.

I stopped, just inside, to let my eyes adjust. The lighting was dim and hazy with smoke so thick you could taste it in the back of your throat, even with your mouth closed. To my right was the bar, scarred and chipped. A bald man in a flannel shirt stood behind it and nodded to Wes before going back to washing dishes. Two men

occupied bar stools, their hands clamped protectively around half
-filled glasses. Neither one looked up. One of them tapped his foot
against the stool, in time with the static-filled radio that droned
with the sounds of country music. Other than that, the place was
empty, and I remembered it was noon on a Sunday. To my left
were three pool tables spanning the length of the small lounge
area. Wes pointed to the table in the far corner.

"Meet you over there. I'm going to grab us some sodas," he
said, wandering up to the bar.

I went to the table and began to rack. A moment later, Wes
appeared with two drinks. He set them on the table, and I handed
him a stick.

"You break," I said.

"Ladies first," he said, pushing the stick back at me.

I took it and leaned down, lining up to break. The cue ball hit
with a satisfying crack, sending balls spinning in all four
directions. A striped one sank in the far left pocket and I turned to
Wes with a smirk.

"You're solids," I said. I turned back to the table to work out
my next shot. Wes slid into a chair nearby and waited. Neither of
us spoke as I lined up and sank two more shots. I missed the next
one by a centimeter and stepped back to let Wes shoot. He did a
lap around the table, eyeing the setup, and then bent over to line it
up. His stick glanced off the side of the cue ball, sending it
spinning in the opposite direction of his target. He straightened
and frowned at the table, before returning to his chair.

"So, how'd you find this place, anyway?" I asked, leaning
down to line up my shot. The ball glanced off the corner pocket,
barely missing the hole.

"Someone brought me here," he finally said.

"Like, on a date?"

"Not quite." He rose, shot, and missed. "I met someone here,
on Cause business, a few times. He had information, but he didn't
want to be seen giving it to me."

I looked around the sad little bar. "I guess it's a good place to
go unnoticed." I wondered what sort of covert missions went along
with being a part of this Cause.

"Your turn," Wes said, interrupting my thoughts.

"Oh, right." I slid out of my chair and sank another ball but missed the next. "I have another question about Werewolves," I said, settling back in my chair. "What is your favorite food?"

The hint of a smile ghosted his features. "Cheeseburgers."

"I had a feeling it would be some kind of meat. You do like them cooked, though, right?"

"Funny." He got up to take his next shot. "What's yours?" he asked, returning a minute later after missing, again.

"Sushi," I said.

"Interesting."

I took my shot, and the next, and the next, finally ending the game. "You rack," I said, sitting back when I was done.

Wes complied, and we started a new game. "Keeping on the 'favorites' topic, I've got one for you," Wes said. He was standing at the front of the table, fumbling with the ball placement in the rack. I tried not to laugh. "Month of the year?"

"Month of the year? That's a little off the wall."

He used my own argument against me. "You can tell a lot about someone by their favorite month."

"Well, then, I'd have to say June, for my birthday, and because it's finally not cold anymore. You?"

He finished racking and walked back to the chair, sliding into his with a swish of leather. His eyes found mine and instantly, there was a heavy undercurrent of tension. "February," he said, quietly.

I held his gaze, wanting to ask why he'd chosen the current month, but within seconds I couldn't even remember the conversation. My face began to heat up as I realized I was just staring at him, wide eyed and open mouthed, with no real sense of exactly how long I'd been doing that. I looked away and tried to collect my hazy thoughts.

"Favorite holiday," I said, finally.

"Thanksgiving. You?"

"New Year's."

"Seriously? Why?"

"It's a fresh start, anything is possible, and everyone tries to put their best foot forward, you know, with resolutions and stuff. I think it brings out the best in people."

"And you like it better than Christmas? Or your birthday?" he asked.

I shrugged. "Those are nice, too. But for Christmas, we usually just go to my Grandma's, and it's just the three of us, so it's not really that big of a deal. New Year's is a big deal—without the pressure of presents—and everyone is different because of it, at least for a little while."

"What?" I asked, taking in his slanted brows and thoughtful expression.

"Nothing," he finally answered. His gaze flicked to the pool table behind us. "Is it my turn?"

"No, it's mine," I said. I got up and picked my shot, and missed, which wasn't like me. But Wes's eyes had a way of making my extremities feel like Jell-O. Wes took his turn and actually sunk a ball this time, only it was mine. He returned to his seat, smiling at his own mistake.

"See, this is what fun looks like," I said.

By the end of our third game, I couldn't pretend I wasn't totally kicking his butt. "Have you ever played pool before?" I asked, trying not to sound like I was enjoying myself too much. It was fun knowing I was actually better than him at something.

"I'm better at sports," was his reply.

I gave him an offended look. "Pool is a sport."

"Whatever."

"People make a lot of money competing at pool," I said, icily.

Wes rolled his eyes. "The potential for making money doesn't make it a sport."

"You're being a sore loser."

I hopped out of my chair and did a lap around the table, sizing up my choices. I picked my angle, and leaned over to line up the shot. As I did, a prickly feeling began on the back of my neck, raising the hair. I jerked and straightened, already scanning the room.

"Do you see it?" Wes asked, already beside me.

"No."

I tried to see through the haze in the air. The two men were still at the bar, looking bored and half drunk. The bartender was wiping glasses with a towel, not paying attention to the rest of the room. I dismissed all three of them as the source. They'd been here the entire time, but the creepy crawlies had just started.

As I scanned, I realized there were two places I couldn't fully see from where I stood. A door behind the bar, leading to what must've been the kitchen, and a hallway to my left, a faded restroom sign hanging on the wall above it.

Instinctively, I took a step toward the hallway and felt Wes's hand on my arm, pulling me back. I turned to snap at him to let go but his expression stopped me. His gaze was fixed on the back hallway, too, a dangerous glint in his eye.

"Stay behind me," he said.

I nodded, glad he hadn't told me to wait here, and we made our way toward the darkened hallway. The tingling grew stronger as we got closer, raising goosebumps on my arms and legs. When we reached the opening, a door slammed at the other end, from around the corner.

Wes took off toward it, and I ran after him. I rounded the corner and was out the door a split second behind Wes. I blinked into the sudden glare of the afternoon sun and scanned the gravel lot. It was empty. And the creepy-crawlies had dissipated.

"It's gone," Wes said, turning back to me.

"Who do you think it was?"

"I don't know, but we should assume it wasn't friendly. Are you okay?" He looked down at me, brows creasing with worry.

"I'm fine," I said, before turning to head back inside.

He grabbed me by the elbow and stopped me. "You're sure? I mean, I would understand if you're shaken up." His eyes seemed to be searching for something, and it took me a minute to realize what it was.

"I'm not going to freak out," I said, in a firm, slightly frosty voice. I removed my elbow from his grip and headed for the door. "But I'm definitely ready to go." Two pool halls ruined. That sucked.

"Give me a second, okay?" He pulled out his phone, without

waiting for an answer, and pushed a button. I stopped and waited, tapping my foot against gravel. It wasn't that I was that impatient, but I felt like I should do everything possible to prove I wasn't going to have another nervous breakdown. Which was obviously what he kept expecting. It irritated me.

A minute later I heard a faint male voice answer on the other end of the phone. "Jack, it's Wes. Listen, I need a favor." They talked for less than a minute. Wes filled him in on our unidentified visitor and then listened while Jack responded and then they disconnected. "Okay, let's go," he said to me, sliding his phone back into his pocket.

"What was that about?"

"Jack's going to come and try to get a trail, so I can get you out of here."

We passed back into the bar and no one even glanced up. Apparently, the entire episode had gone unnoticed. Our jackets were still on the hook by the door. I pulled mine on quickly and followed Wes out to the car.

We were backing out of the lot when I felt a buzzing in my jeans. I jumped, sure I was tingling again, but it was just my phone. I pulled it out and checked the screen. My mother. Crap. I motioned for Wes to be quiet with a finger to my lips and then pressed the talk button.

"Hello?"

"Tara?" My mother's voice was strained. It sounded like she was close to tears.

My anxiety kicked in, and I gripped the phone tighter. "Mom? What's wrong?"

"I just got a call from Julie's father. She was camping last night." My mother paused to take a deep breath, to brace herself for what she was about to tell me. "She and her boyfriend. They were attacked by an animal. She's dead." Her voice cracked on the last word.

"Mom, I'm so sorry," I said, my eyes blurring with tears. The article, the dead college kids. That had been Julie? "Are you okay?"

She sniffled. "I think so. There's nothing to be done, really. I'm going to stay and do inventory, anyway. It'll keep my mind off

... things. I just wanted you to know because they haven't caught the animal responsible, and I want you to be careful. No going into the woods. And keep the alarm on, okay?"

"Okay," I agreed. What good would the alarm do if it was some wild animal, assumedly without opposable thumbs? I didn't ask. I was starting to think Mom knew more than she was letting on, and I just couldn't handle that conversation right now. Mostly, I didn't want to bring it up and then find out I was wrong. That would be hard to talk my way out of; a one-way trip to a padded room.

I was sad for Julie and her boyfriend. I'd only met her a couple of times, but she was nice and friendly and hadn't talked down to me, like an adult might. She'd treated me like I was her peer, and I'd appreciated that. She and my mother had spent a lot of time together, though, and I could only imagine how hard this was for Mom.

"Okay, I'm going to hang up and get some work done," she said. "I'll see you later."

I wanted to say something to make her feel better, but I was drawing a blank. "Okay, um, love you. Bye."

We hung up, and I could feel Wes watching me. I shoved the phone back into my pocket and stared down at my jeans, trying to blink the tears away before I met his eyes. He surprised me by taking my hand and gently squeezing it.

"Did you know her well?" he asked, quietly.

Now, I did look up. "You heard that?"

He nodded. "Wolves have excellent hearing."

"Right." I let out a deep breath, wishing all of the stress would go with it. "I didn't really know her. She worked for my mother, at the flower shop."

"I see." He frowned and his gaze settled on something beyond me.

"What is it?"

"Well, whoever left you that note obviously picked someone you knew."

"You think they did that on purpose?"

"Probably. What are the odds?"

"So, the message about this being a preview, you think that means they'll do it again, with someone else I know?"

His gaze swung back to me, and he squeezed my hand again. "We'll make sure they don't."

I felt the air in the car begin to change as I stared back at him. It felt warm and thick, like a humid, post-rain summer day. And even though we were already touching, palm to palm, I suddenly had an intense desire to be closer to him, pressed to him. My muscles ached with it and I had to restrain myself from scooting across the seat, and wrapping my arms around his shoulders, and burying my face in his neck.

The image wouldn't remove itself from my mind and I finally had to wrench my gaze from his to keep from acting on the impulse. I was breathing heavier, partly because of the thickness in the air and partly from wanting to touch him. I wondered if he was affected, too, but I couldn't look at him again or I wouldn't be able to stop myself.

His hand slid free from mine, and he started the car and busied himself with checking the rearview and easing us out of the lot. I pressed the button for the window, letting in a gust of cold air. For once, I didn't curse the cold, and was relieved when I felt the tension melt away.

When we were on the road, Wes cleared his throat. "Well, that was ..."

I lifted my head from where I'd been leaning closer to the open window and looked over at him. He was running a hand through his hair, still searching for a word to describe what had happened. He'd noticed it, too. "Different," I finished.

He sent me a half smile. "Yeah. Definitely that."

My phone buzzed again. Not my mother this time, but a text, from George. "Babe, miss you. Call me." I typed out an excuse and hit send, hoping it would be enough to keep him from stopping by this time, and shoved the phone back into my pocket.

"Who was that?" Wes asked.

"George," I answered, after only a few seconds hesitation.

Wes made a noise, like he was about to speak but then he stopped. I looked over at him. His lips were pressed together in a frown.

"What?" I asked.

"I just don't understand why you chose him."

"We broke up," I said, like that was somehow answering his question.

"I know. I mean, initially."

I tried to think of an acceptable answer. I'd never had to put it into words before, especially not to another guy. And not just any guy, but my human magnet. "Well, we've known each other for a long time. Sort of grew up together, I guess, and I know him better than almost anyone."

"That's not a reason," Wes pointed out.

"I know. It's not just that, though ... We have a lot in common, and I can tell him anything," I finished.

"Anything, huh," Wes repeated.

"Well, I used to be able to tell him anything."

"And that's important to you?"

"Very." I might've said more, but we'd already pulled up in front of my house.

"I'm going to park around the corner," said Wes. "No point in drawing attention. And whoever's doing this might show themselves if they think you're alone."

I got out, and he pulled away to park.

CHAPTER ELEVEN

"SO, now what?" I asked. We were back in my room, after scarfing the chicken my mother had left in the fridge. Jack had just called back to say the search had been a dead end. There wasn't even a trail to follow.

"Now, we keep looking, and you don't go anywhere alone." Wes was sitting in his usual spot, in my desk chair, twirling back and forth in half circles with his feet.

"That doesn't sound like much of a plan. We have no idea who's doing this."

"We have a few ideas worth exploring."

"We?"

"The group."

"And does this group include me? Or do I get left in the dark about everything?"

Wes stopped spinning and sighed. "It might include you. If you want."

"You're going to let me meet them?" I asked, surprised.

"I probably shouldn't," he admitted, "but Jack asked me to. He's called a Cause meeting for later, and you're invited to come."

"Do you want me to?" I had to ask, because even though he'd extended the invitation, his tone seemed like he was hoping I'd say no.

"I don't know."

I let out a frustrated breath. "I still don't get why you're here, if you don't want me to be a part of your world," I said, putting emphasis on the last two words. Because even though it was obvious that our worlds were connected, it seemed like he was determined to make sure they stayed separate.

Wes slid out of his chair and came over to sit by me on the bed. He looked into my face with a gaze that seemed to penetrate straight through me, and I found myself holding my breath. "You intrigue me. I've never met anyone like you." He paused, and then added, "It's probably a bad idea to involve you, but I don't think I have a choice anymore. And Jack thinks it's best if you know what's going on."

The way he looked at me suddenly made it very important for me to know his motive for including me. "You're only inviting me because Jack told you to."

His gaze deepened and he leaned closer. "Why do you keep pushing me, Tara?" he asked, quietly. "I'm trying to keep you safe."

I squared my shoulders and gave him an even look, refusing to be drawn into the spell of his eyes. "Well, you can stop. I just needed time to process everything. But I'm not scared. And Jack's right. I have a right to know who is threatening me."

"I don't think you're scared. I think you don't know what you're getting yourself into. But like I said, I don't have a choice. If I hadn't come, Jack would have."

Irritation flickered in me. Every word out of Wes's mouth was like a rejection while the entire time, he looked at me like ... well, like he wanted a whole lot more than conversation. Or maybe I was imagining it. The whole thing was becoming beyond frustrating to interpret. "Well, maybe I'd be better off dealing with Jack then. You can save yourself the trouble." I started to get up, but his hands shot out and grabbed my arms, holding me in place.

His face was only inches from mine now, and he was staring at me with that same blazing intensity that made me think he was feeling something besides just "protective responsibility." I stared back stubbornly, trying to remain unaffected. It wasn't working.

Slowly, he raised a hand from where it still rested on my arm and traced his fingertips down my cheek and into my hair. My entire body reacted by going pleasantly numb. I inhaled the scent of crisp leather, from where his arm hung in the air by my face, mixed with a dried-leaf and pine smell that could only ever be Wes and made me think of sunshine on bare skin. His fingers moved from my hair back to my face, and that tiny gesture was all it took to awaken that polar pull between us.

I wasn't even sure who leaned in first, but by the time our lips met, it was completely mutual. His kiss was soft at first but his touch brought with it a heat that I'd never felt before. It radiated out and spread into the rest of my body, like wildfire. He tasted like apple cider and the woods in summer, and I knew I'd never tasted anything so delicious, nor would I ever again. The kiss only lasted a few seconds, and I tried to hide my disappointment when he pulled away so quickly. He gazed back at me, his lips curved into a small smile.

"Does this mean you've officially chosen a side?" he asked, quietly.

"Probably," I mumbled.

His grin widened. "Are you okay? You look kind of distracted."

"I didn't exactly see that coming," I admitted.

"Me neither."

"Does this mean you're okay with me coming today?"

"Probably."

We sat that way for a few minutes, and I waited to see if he'd kiss me again, but he didn't. He smiled and got up, holding his hand out to me. "Ready?"

I nodded, still reeling from the kiss and the weight of his eyes, and let him pull me toward the door. "So there's going to be others at this meeting? Like other Werewolves?"

"Yes, some." He raised his eyebrow in a challenge. "I thought you said you weren't scared."

"I'm not. I just—what if some of them aren't happy with me about Liliana?"

"Tara, no one's mad at you. They all understand it wasn't your fault. You had no choice. Besides, we're pretty sure Liliana was a double agent."

"Like I have any idea what that means," I mumbled.

"You don't have to do this, you know. Get involved, I mean. We'll still protect you."

His tone was gentle and meant to be reassuring but I bristled at what he was suggesting. "So, just stay home and hide out while somebody out there takes a shot at everyone I care about? Let a pack of strangers fight my battles for me?"

"That's not what I meant."

"I said I wouldn't freak out again, and I meant it. I'm going to do whatever it takes to find this guy and stop him from hurting people."

He nodded, something unreadable in his eyes. "Okay, then."

I stopped short, throwing a glance at my closet. "Can I have a minute to change?"

"I'll be downstairs."

I listened to the sound of his footsteps on the stairs, already feeling bad for snapping at him. I hated my temper, and I hated when it got the better of me even more. But he'd started it, with suggesting I stick my head in the sand. That just wasn't me.

When I was sure he wasn't going to pop his head back in, I took the plunger pieces out of my backpack and stuffed them into my back jeans pockets. Like before, I pulled my shirt down to hide them. Then I pulled on my boots, grabbed my sweatshirt, and headed downstairs. Wes was waiting for me at the door.

"I'm going to pull the car around. Wait here," he said.

I nodded, and he slipped around the side of the house. I turned the key in the lock on the front door and then dropped my keys into my bag. As I did, a familiar tingly feeling hit me, and crawled along my skin, underneath my jacket. My head came up, and I scanned my yard, looking for the source.

Just like earlier, I saw no one, but I wasn't going to let it go so easily this time. I flattened myself against the house and crept to the corner, but when I peeked around, it was empty. The quiet purr of an engine broke the silence, and I saw the Aston Martin coming down the street, sleek and silver. The tingly feeling abruptly disappeared. I hurried down to the curb.

Wes pulled to a stop, and I climbed in, grateful that he'd already been blasting the heat. I held my hands up to the vents as he pulled away.

"When you picked me up just now, did you feel anything?" I asked, as we curved through the neighborhood.

He glanced over, sharply. "No—did you?"

"I don't know. I think so …"

Wes slammed his foot on the brake, and the car jerked to a stop. I felt myself slam forward, and then the seat belt caught and held me in place. Wes swerved the car onto the shoulder, and a spray of gravel flew up behind us as we came to a halt. "What did you feel?"

"The same feeling I got at the pool hall. A Werewolf."

Wes responded by flooring the gas and jerking the wheel hard to the left. We spun around in a U-turn and sped back through my neighborhood. A second later the car lurched to another stop. Wes threw his door open and then he was out of the car, striding quickly across my front lawn, scanning the yard as he went.

I reluctantly followed, carefully aware of my body's nerve endings but there was no trace of tingles this time. I waited on the lawn while Wes did a circle of the house. When he walked back over to me, the disapproval was plain on his face.

"You should have told me right away," he said.

"It was already gone by the time you pulled up," I said defensively. "Besides, I figured I was just being paranoid, like the other day."

His eyes immediately narrowed, making me regret the admission.

"What do you mean 'like the other day'?"

"I got the same feeling in the mall parking lot on Friday night." I shrugged like it was no big deal. "It went away, though, and I didn't see anything suspicious so I figured it was nothing, maybe an aftershock of my encounter with Liliana or something."

A muscle in his jaw flexed. "Hunters don't have aftershocks."

"Oh."

He squeezed his eyes shut and ran a hand over his face. "Next time, tell me immediately, okay?"

"Okay," I agreed.

"You do realize that someone is possibly trying to kill you, right?"

"Yes," I said, my voice icy. I crossed my arms in front of me.

"You're impossible," he said, throwing his arms up.

"And you're overprotective."

Wes looked down at me like he was about to launch into another lecture. Instead, he shook his head and got back in the car. And just like that, the feeling of connection that had lingered since our kiss evaporated.

Chapter Twelve

JACK'S house looked only slightly less deserted this time around, mainly because of the shiny black Lexus sitting out front. The lustrous paint glinted off the filtering sunlight and contrasted sharply with what looked like brown leather interior. I noticed the engine was creaking, like it was still warm. I eyed it in much the same way I had Wes's car.

"Whose car is that?" I asked.

"Miles. He's a friend."

"And a Werewolf?"

"No, he's a Hunter."

Wes led me to the front door and I waited while he knocked. Fee answered. Before she could even speak, my skin hummed and tingled. I pushed it aside as best I could.

She broke into an immediate smile when she spotted Wes and pulled him into a quick hug before stepping back to let us enter.

"Tara, I'm so glad you decided to join us today," she told me, squeezing my hand. "Jack's in the clearing, already building the fire with Miles. We're going to have close to a full group today." She seemed excited by the prospect. Meanwhile, I wondered exactly how many Werewolves made up a "full group."

"I'll go help him, then," said Wes, already heading for the back door before I could object.

"Come on in, Tara," said Fee, leading the way through a doorway opposite the living room.

I followed her and found myself in a wide, brightly lit kitchen that, again, contrasted sharply with the outside of the house. White marble countertops shone brightly against the light and spanned the room on three sides, broken up by stainless steel appliances that gleamed like new. In the center was a marble-topped island with three barstools. Fee stopped at the island and began stirring the contents of a bowl.

I followed and perched on one of the stools. "What are you making?" I asked, unsure if I really wanted to know but trying to make conversation. I mean, who knew what they served at Werewolf parties?

"Brownies," she answered. "Listen, Tara, I'm really glad you decided to come today. Jack said he knew you would but I wasn't so sure. And Wes, well, he didn't think you should. But I'm glad you did."

"Wes and I disagree on a lot of things," I said.

Fee gave me a knowing look.

"Good for you. Have you had a chance to read through the *Draven* yet?"

"A little. Mostly the stuff about fighting. The history is kind of heavy," I admitted.

"It is. But it might help you understand a little better what it is we're doing here with The Cause."

"From what I gather, it's completely opposite of the current way of thinking, for both races," I said.

She nodded. "It is. Which is why we have to work so hard to get people to listen."

"How does it work?"

"Well, as for what will happen today, a meeting is probably the best way to describe it. Other Weres who we've partnered with will come and report on whatever assignment they've been working on. Any problems will be discussed and new assignments given."

"Assignments for what?"

"For furthering The Cause."

"What sort of things will be assigned?"

She stopped stirring and blinked at me. "Wes didn't tell you much, did he?"

I thought about telling her what I knew, but I held back, wanting to see how her version would match up with the one Wes had given me. I shook my head, and she continued.

"I'll give you the short version since that's about all we have time for now." She went back to stirring while she talked. "The Cause is made up of a group of volunteers, a mix of Werewolves and Hunters who work together toward a common goal. It's been around for years, mostly underground to avoid violence by the opposition, and progress has been slow because of it. We keep our circle tight and are very selective about newcomers as a matter of safety, so you should feel honored that you've been invited to be included."

"What's the common goal?"

"To peacefully unite Hunters and Werewolves."

"What's so hard about that?"

"Our races have always been enemies, for longer than anyone can remember. Trust is not easy after so many centuries of war. On top of that, the opposition is big and loud and quick to stamp out our message. So it's been difficult to change people's minds, on either side. Our group has dwindled over the years but we're hoping that changes soon." She stopped, abruptly, and bit her lip, giving me the impression she thought she'd said too much.

"Why has the group dwindled?" I asked, wondering about the way she looked at me now.

Her expression lightened, and she looked almost relieved by my question. "I guess we never really recovered after that first attack. Times were different when Jack and I met. It was a time of open-mindedness, for both races. We got involved with a group that thought maybe there was a chance for peace and we pursued that possibility. We campaigned and traveled around, speaking out about it, hoping to make others realize the benefits of coming together. Our kind had been so close-minded and one way about the two races for so long, it was hard to convince people it could be different, it could be better.

"For a while, though, it looked like it might be possible. Our numbers grew and everyone seemed to be really listening to us. Then, word got out about the marriages."

"Marriages?"

She gave me a wry smile. "You've never seen political scandal like that before, believe me. It was rocky at first but in the end, it made people listen even harder, and it made them think. The Council was formed and talk of a treaty began. Then the babies came and everything changed. The attack happened not long after. Most of the founding leaders of our group were killed and the rest scattered. All progress was lost."

"I don't understand. Why would marriage and babies make people so angry?"

"They were intermarriages. A Hunter and a Werewolf as husband and wife. Which wouldn't have been so bad, until they had children. After that, people were scared and even more closed off than before to the idea of peace. Fear of the unknown does that."

"So the babies were a mixed race?" I was starting to understand the reason for the controversy, though it seemed a little impossible to me.

"Yes. It scared people that we had no idea how they would turn out. And people don't like change."

"Did you know all of the leaders who were killed?"

Fee nodded and her eyes misted. Her smile was sad. "Some better than others, but yes, we were all good friends."

I hesitated only briefly before my next question. I had a feeling it would give away my real reason for asking, but I was hoping she would answer, anyway. "Did you know a man named Sebastian St. John?"

Fee looked surprised by that. "Wes told you about his parents?"

"His ... Oh, yeah." I tried to recover quickly and not give myself away, but my shock made it hard. I swallowed. "He told me about him and Audrey being a part of the Council and then the attack happened."

She looked at me with an odd expression. "Not just a part of the council. Sebastian was the leader, well, for the Hunter side, anyway. He started the whole movement, won a lot of people over, too, even after his marriage to Audrey. Her father was the alpha in the pack and after Sebastian won him over, it brought a lot more Weres to their side."

"Yeah, he said that," I mumbled, my mind still reeling and putting the facts together. No wonder Wes had been so upset about their deaths. Did he remember anything? Was that another reason that made it hard to talk about? And the biggest mind boggler of all: Wes was half-Werewolf, half-Hunter? I looked back at Fee and spoke carefully. "Wes didn't go into this very much and I was just wondering, how is it possible? To be half... of each, I mean."

"We don't know," she admitted. "Or at least we didn't at the time. None of us ever imagined it would be possible for a couple made up of each race to conceive. But it happened. When Wes was born, Sebastian took blood from Audrey and from Wes, to have it analyzed and try to understand. The biggest question was what he would be, obviously. Coming from one of each race, well, we all wondered what that would mean for him."

"How did they figure out he was a Werewolf instead of a Hunter?"

"Wes was two. He was in the middle of some temper tantrum with Audrey, and he just shifted. Soon after that, the blood samples came back and it was determined he had both genes, but for whatever reason, the Werewolf gene was dominant. Sebastian was determined to learn all he could about it, and spent a lot of time researching the blood samples and Wes himself. But then, he and Audrey were killed, along with the rest of them, before any more answers could be discovered."

"Is that why you took Wes in?" I asked, imagining the story from Wes's perspective, trying to understand what it would be like for a baby born of both blood lines.

"Yes." Her eyes clouded at some memory, a soft smile on her lips. "Audrey and I were very close and I knew it was what she would've wanted. And now, I couldn't imagine loving him any more if he were my own."

We were both silent for a minute. I didn't want to interrupt whatever memory she was reliving, but I couldn't hold back my questions for long. "So the Werewolves who were against the peace treaty—they knew about Wes?"

"Yes. That was part of the problem, I think. It sparked more controversy and debate, when news surfaced there was a 'half-breed' running around. That's what the Hunter community called it. The Werewolf clans called him 'dirty blood.' They said it was a disgrace to their kind. I think it's what finally led to the attack."

"Must be hard to know you're part of the reason for a war," I mused quietly.

Fee nodded. "He had a rough time for a while. Jack and I tried to help as best we could but there was bitterness in him, probably still is. But he believes in The Cause so that's something ... Anyway, listen to me rambling on when it's not even my story to tell. I'll leave the rest for him and I hope I haven't spoken out of turn."

"No," I assured her. "Most of what you told me, I already knew." She didn't need to know that, indeed, she was the one who had pieced it all together and spilled the most important secret of all.

Fee turned to slide the brownies into the oven. As she straightened, the back door opened and closed. Footsteps sounded against the hardwood, coming closer, and a man appeared in the kitchen doorway. He strode in, wearing a wide smile aimed at Fee. His dark hair was just long enough to be wavy around the edges and melted perfectly into his tanned skin.

"Hey, Miles. You guys all done?" Fee asked.

The man stepped forward to kiss Fee on the cheek. "Just about. People are starting to arrive. Is this her?"

"Oh, yes. Miles, Tara Godfrey. Tara, Miles Ducati."

"Nice to meet you," I said, taking his outstretched hand.

Miles smiled at me, looking charming and devilish all at once. "My pleasure. I've heard a lot about you."

"Great," I mumbled, my anxiety level rising a few degrees as I tried to decide what he could've heard and how bad it made me look.

Miles laughed. "Relax. Nothing too bad. Though, we'll all have to be sure not to leave any metal piping nearby with you around."

He winked and I felt myself flush, partly from the teasing and partly because, for an older guy, Miles was pretty handsome, in a suave and too-charming sort of way. Everything about him screamed smooth and polished, from his black slacks and jacket to his shiny black hair that didn't seem to need product to make it stay exactly in place. It made me feel self-conscious about my loose, and probably unruly hair, and casual attire.

"Miles," Fee scolded. "Quit teasing the girl before she changes her mind and goes home. Get outside and round everyone up. We'll be right behind you."

"I'm going, I'm going," he said, striding out, still smiling.

"Don't worry about him," Fee said when he was gone. "Miles likes to give new people a hard time. Okay, he likes to give everyone a hard time. He likes seeing the reaction, so just don't give him one. You ready?"

I nodded that I was and slid off my stool. I waited until Fee was in front of me before checking on the plunger handles in my back pockets.

CHAPTER THIRTEEN

I followed Fee out the back door and the moment the door opened in front of me, my body's warning system kicked into overdrive. The dull tingle becoming harsh pinpricks and goosebumps rose so fast, it felt like ants crawling over me. Instinctively, I searched for the source. My eyes landed on something unexpected.

At the edge of the yard, through the bare branches of trees that lined the dead grass, a roaring bonfire was visible. Yellow and orange flames rose several feet into the air and the branches piled high underneath crackled and popped, sending sparks and ash overhead. But the thing that got my attention was the bodies that surrounded it. Half a dozen human forms ringed the fire and interspersed between them were at least as many Werewolves, all in wolf form. I faltered.

"Tara, they're all friends," Fee said, gently.

I glanced down and found Fee waiting patiently at the bottom of the steps.

"Right," I said, with way more confidence than I felt. Mechanically, I descended the small porch and fell into step beside Fee. As we grew closer to the trees, my anxiety doubled. My heart thudded loudly, ringing in my ears, and in response to some instinctive protective part of my brain, I realized my fingers itched to draw my weapons. I ignored it at first, but then we passed into the small clearing and the group noticed us approaching. Every single pair of eyes—human and otherwise—turned to stare at me. I felt my shallow breaths edging toward hyperventilation. My skin crawled and the hairs on the back of my neck stood up.

Then a familiar figure broke away from the group and strode toward me.

Wes lowered his head and spoke low into my ear. "You're doing great." He took my arm and fell into step beside me, leading me around the group, to the far side of the fire, with plenty of breathing room between me and them.

When we stopped, I stood in between Fee and Wes. I didn't look up to see if everyone was still watching me. I just stared at the fire and tried to keep my expression blank, or at least clear of any expression that said, "A big part of me wants to kill you right now."

"Looks like most everyone's here, so let's get started."

I followed the sound of Jack's voice and did a double take. His voice sounded exactly the same as I remembered: burly and booming. But it was coming out of the body of a great brown wolf. The biggest wolf I'd ever seen, easily the biggest one here. His fur ruffled in the slight breeze and I wondered if half his size didn't come from that alone, as thick as it was. I knew I was openly staring, but I didn't care.

He was magnificent and beautiful. Even standing still, there was a gracefulness in him that would've been impossible to achieve in human form. Especially Jack's human form. And in a way, this was the first time I'd really seen a wolf up close. With Liliana, there hadn't exactly been time to stand back and admire. So, I watched in fascination as Jack the wolf shifted on his paws—which were probably twice the size of my feet—and shot sharp glances at some who still hadn't ended their hushed conversations.

"First, I'll go ahead and properly introduce our guest," he said, when the group had quieted. "Everyone, this is Tara Godfrey, a Hunter. Tara, this is our group. They've all given permission for you to be present today, so just watch and listen. If you have any questions about what you hear, I'm sure any one of them would be happy to answer them for you. We're all glad you're here."

I could feel everyone watching me again, so I nodded and kept my eyes on Jack. I managed to stay relatively calm this time, though, with Wes beside me.

"Updates," Jack said, shifting on his paws to look at someone across the fire. "Derek, how'd it go with the clan in the Outer Banks?"

A lanky wolf, with fur the color of mud and eyes to match, spoke up. His voice was gravelly and sounded young, close to my age, but it was impossible to tell from his wolf form. "Not great, Jack. They've had a problem with newbie Hunters lately." His eyes flicked to me and then back to Jack. "The Hunters attacked without provocation and managed to take down a couple of the pack, including the alpha's teenaged son. Emotions are running high and I wouldn't be surprised if they retaliate. Not much hope of diplomacy there, at least not now."

"Damn. Did you identify the Hunters?" asked Jack.

"No. New graduates from what they can gather. Glory seekers. Vigilantes. You know how it goes." Derek's eyes flicked back to me again.

"All right," said Jack. "I'm going to draw up a letter for you to deliver to Gabe, their alpha. You up for a second trip?"

"Sure." Derek dipped his head and hunched his fur, giving an odd impression of shrugging shoulders.

Jack made a noise deep in his throat, something between a sigh and a growl, and then his eyes flicked down the line. "Cord? What have you got?"

Next to Derek, a blond-haired girl stepped forward. Her hair was perfectly combed, her long bangs swept to the side and covering part of her face. She wore black leggings and boots. I thought she looked mysterious and gorgeous—until she spoke. "Jonah's still sending out new initiates with nothing more than a stake and delusions of grandeur." Her voice was nothing like her appearance. It was hard and biting, and all business.

While she spoke, her eyes flicked to me, like Derek's had, but the message in them was much more brittle. I shifted and looked away, with the unmistakable feeling of being sized up.

"How many of them?" asked Jack.

Cord turned her attention back to him. "Three for now. The

next group doesn't graduate until June and then we'll have probably ten or twelve on our hands."

"Where were they headed?"

"The mountains. Near Shenandoah. They're camping to stay under the radar. All cocky confidence, too. They'd be easy to find again, though, trust me." She rolled her eyes.

"We'd better follow them and make sure they don't do any damage. Kelsey's pack is just on the other side of those mountains and they've recently decided to ally with us. I don't want anything messing that up," said Jack.

"No problem," she said. And I knew just from looking at her that it wouldn't be.

"Take Miles with you," Jack added.

Cord's expression hardened at that but she nodded. "Fine."

Jack continued down the line, calling on Bailey, a smaller Werewolf the color of vanilla ice cream. Jack asked him for an update on someone named Xavier, but Bailey said he hadn't made any more progress, whatever that meant. He sounded really young, younger than me, when he spoke.

Jack moved on again, this time to a Hunter named Jill who reported about some piece of land she'd been sent to check on. Most of it was passing right over my head, but from what I gathered, these assignments were all pieces of a puzzle that Jack oversaw, a part of a bigger picture—and the thing that got me was that it was, above all, a peaceful picture. That appealed to me. These people didn't go around killing each other. They found a way to defend themselves and others without violence. It was something to consider.

"That wraps up all the works in progress we have at the moment," said Jack after Jill completed her report. "I know it's not as many irons in the fire as we would like, but we have to be patient. We're trying to reverse hundreds of years of a certain way of thinking." He paused and then in a brisk voice added, "New business. Miles, what have you got?"

Miles, the man I'd met in the kitchen, cleared his throat. "We tracked Liliana's last forty-eight hours to a motel outside of Warrenton. The clerk remembered her and said she came in with a guy but couldn't describe him. Probably he was too busy watching her to notice. They stayed the night, and he says she left alone the next morning. That would've been the same day she called you." He nodded to Wes and I got a sinking feeling in my gut.

"Any leads on where she went that day? Or the guy at the motel?" Jack asked.

"Not yet. Still working on it," said Miles.

Jack shook his head. "No, I need you to go with Cord in case any of those frat boys get carried away." He shot a look at Cord. "No killing."

She rolled her eyes.

"Fee can look into the Liliana situation while you're gone. Vera can help, which may be easier than the usual channels," said Jack, turning to a woman directly on his left.

She was tall and willow thin and even though she wore a pant suit and low heels, there was a regal authority about her that made you stop and take notice. I'd been glancing her way since the beginning of the meeting, unsure what someone like her was doing here, in front of a bonfire with a bunch of wolves.

"Of course," she answered. Her voice was just as polished and regal as the rest of her.

Jack nodded and then addressed the rest of the group. "Okay, last order of business today is the situation with Tara."

At the sound of my name, everyone looked over at me. The woman, Vera, met my eyes. (I must've still been staring at her without realizing it.) Her gaze was sharp and penetrating and made me feel like she was waiting for something. I looked away and stared back into the fire.

Why were they talking about me? Oh God, this was it. I was going to be called out for killing Liliana. Maybe even punished. So much for a jury of my peers. I squared my shoulders and braced myself. At my sides, my fingers twitched, ready to grab for my weapons. I wasn't going to go easily.

"All of you know about the campers that were killed. It was in the paper. What you don't know is the message that was left at the scene. Wes, pass that picture around, will you?"

Wes reached inside his jacket and pulled out the photograph

he'd shown me earlier, with the bloody lettering. He passed it around me, to Fee. She barely glanced at it and passed it on. As much as that picture disgusted me, at this moment, I was beyond relieved to see it. This was why Jack had brought me up. Not because I killed one of theirs. I breathed out slowly and forced my hands to relax at my sides.

"The words are written in the victim's blood on the side of the tent," Jack explained, as the picture circulated. The humans all made sure whatever wolf was beside them got a look before passing it to the next outstretched hand. "Wes got there first, as he was on call that night. He snapped this before he disposed of the evidence. We need to find out what it means and who it was. Tara may not be an official member of our group, but she's still one of us and she's been thrown into this without any warning. She needs our help, so we need to figure out what's next."

"This would've taken some time," said Miles as he studied the photo. "They would've had to change back to do the writing. They're patient." He examined it like a slide under a microscope; I wondered how he could be so detached about the gore.

"They're sick is what they are," said Cord, with obvious disgust.

"How do they know Tara? Why do they want to scare her?" asked Bailey.

"We don't know. Tara doesn't have any enemies," answered Jack.

"Everyone has enemies," muttered Cord.

"She knew them," Wes said. "The girl was an employee in her mother's store. We should assume that he picked his victim because of her connection to Tara."

Murmurs went around the group and Jack silenced them with his booming voice. "Tara knows nothing of what she is or of our world and how it works, which means our group has a better chance of finding who's responsible, knowing what we know. So here's what we need to do: Surveillance. Use your contacts. Find out if anyone new has come into the area recently. Especially Weres but not exclusively. It could be a frame. Anything is possible until we know more." A few more whispers went around and then

Jack wrapped up. "I think that's about it for today. We'll reconvene in one week, same time, to share what we've learned."

"Jack," Wes interrupted. Everyone stopped and waited. So did I. It was the first time he'd spoken during the entire meeting. He paused, seeming to second-guess his words. I caught Vera looking at him. Their eyes met and she nodded. "I think it might be wise to widen the scope of our watches to include a regular patrol around Tara's house until this thing is figured out."

Jack nodded. "I agree. Good idea, Wes."

"I also think it might be wise to keep a close watch on her, personally, at all times. Whoever did this, if they come after her again, won't be expecting one of us. We'll have the advantage, and be able to ID him better if it's one of us who sees his face."

"I agree with that, too. But it's a pretty time consuming job. We don't really have the manpower for that—"

"I'll do it," said Wes.

Excitement speared through me. I really wanted to look up at him, to see the expression on his face but I couldn't. If I did, my own emotion would show through and I could still feel everyone looking at me. Instead, I kept my expression as blank as I could and remained fixed on the fire. So, Wes would be with me all day, every day? The logical side of me knew that it was strictly for my safety, but I couldn't help the wild fluttering that had taken over in my stomach.

For some reason, Jack didn't seem surprised, at all, by Wes volunteering. "Okay, then. We'll take you off the patrol schedule as much as we can spare you. I'll get you the list so you'll know who to call for backup."

Wes nodded, and Jack ended the meeting. Wes and Fee stayed close to my side as everyone wandered off in different directions. Most of the wolves left the circle, cutting deeper into the woods in groups of twos and threes. The Hunters all turned toward the house.

"Where are they going?" I asked, gesturing to the wolves.

"Home," said Wes.

"Through the woods?"

"It's less conspicuous than parking fifty cars in Jack's yard. So they run," he explained.

"What did you think?" Fee asked, with a smile.

"It was um ... interesting," I finally said.

Fee smiled wider. "Yes, that's a good word for our group. Do you have any questions?"

"Many," I admitted. "I didn't really understand much of what was going on, but from the little bit I did understand, I think what you guys are doing here is great."

Fee's eyes lit up, and Wes pressed a hand between my shoulders, guiding me away.

"I'll be inside," Fee called, obviously confused but unwilling to intervene.

I managed a wave and then had to turn to keep from tripping over leaves and dead branches. Wes led me back into the yard and around the side of the house.

"What are you doing?" I demanded, jerking my elbow free of his grasp and taking a step back.

"Saving you."

"From what? There was no danger."

"From yourself. I could see the look in your eyes when you were talking to Fee."

"What look in my eyes?"

"The look that said you want to hear more, maybe even get involved somehow. But that's not going to happen. This is way more dangerous than what it looks like out in front of a big pretty fire. It's not for you."

I crossed my arms. "You're just trying to scare me. Besides, it's not up to you."

His eyes widened, and his voice grew louder. "Trying to scare you? Are you serious? If anything, I haven't scared you enough. I've sugar-coated it or not been honest enough. I've been trying to protect you, keep you out of it. But apparently, you're too stubborn to be grateful for that."

"Apparently," I agreed through clenched teeth.

His glare sharpened, and he actually bared his teeth at me. I could see his temper boiling but I didn't care. I had a temper of my own, just as big, to go with it, and I wasn't going to sit on it just because he was a good kisser. Okay, a great kisser.

"Fine," he said. "Then here's the truth. We spend most of our time doing one of two things: sitting for hours, staking out a Werewolf or Hunter, so we can learn how best to kill them, or actually killing them. It's a war, plain and simple. One that you've only made worse by what you did to Liliana."

I blanched. I felt my temper flare, like the fire we'd just left behind. "What I did? She attacked me!" I shrieked, letting my voice rise to drown out his.

He shifted his weight and smirked, apparently satisfied that he'd gotten to me. "Doesn't change the fact that we have to do damage control."

"Look, I get that you're mad. I killed your little girlfriend, mistress, whatever she was. But I didn't start it. So whatever damage control issues you've got are because of her, not me. Probably whoever she was holed up with, in that motel, is who's after me now."

Wes's eyes widened in genuine surprise, momentarily drowning out the anger. "Liliana wasn't—we weren't together."

"But you said—"

"I said we were working on something ... for The Cause ..." He trailed off like he was waiting for me to finally get it.

"Oh." I did feel stupid then, for not figuring out the connection sooner, but I was mad now, and I wasn't about to let him win. "Well, how was I supposed to know that? It's not like you made it clear. Just like everything else, you only told me half the story." I crossed my arms.

His eyes narrowed and when he spoke, his voice was lower. Dangerously low, actually. I could see I'd gotten to him. "What are you talking about?"

"Everything," I said, with a sweep of my arm. "Like, for starters, the fact that Sebastian St. John was your father."

"Oh." His expression cleared, and he actually looked relieved.

"Oh? That's all you have to say?"

"I just thought—" He ran a hand through his hair and exhaled. "I tell you what you need to know to be safe. There are things you still don't understand about The Cause. I get that you would be drawn to something like this. Our group, the idea of it—it probably seems exciting and noble. But it's also dangerous and bloody and violent. People don't always want to listen to reason and some of them don't even want to talk to begin with. They figure out what message you're spewing, and they attack you twice as hard. That's not exciting or noble, and it's not something you can just jump into with no experience."

"I get that. But you can't keep trying to push me out of it all, either. I'm a part of this world too, apparently. And I have to figure out for myself where and how I fit into it all. And I can't do that if the one person who has promised to help me is keeping secrets or always ordering me around."

"Fine. I won't order you, but I will insist, at least for now, that you do what you can to protect yourself and stay out of danger. Which means, staying on the sidelines of our little group."

"Whatever," I mumbled, with absolutely no intention of heeding his wishes. It wasn't that I'd already decided to join, but I didn't like being told I couldn't, either.

"And since you don't have the ability to protect yourself, I'm going to also insist on guarding you, like we discussed at the meeting." His eyes flashed, challenging me to argue.

Suddenly, the idea of him spending every waking hour with me didn't sound so good. Especially if he was just going to act like my mother the entire time, lecturing and telling me what I could and couldn't do. "I managed just fine with Liliana."

"And what about next time? Metal piping going to become your weapon of choice?"

His mocking tone was meant to make me feel like an idiot, but I was too angry to give in. I didn't need him. I could handle myself. Probably.

"Next time I'll be ready," I shot back. "I have weapons. See." In a swift move, I reached behind me and yanked out the plunger handles, angling them downward in my palm, in what I hoped was a stance that made me look battle ready.

Wes's eyes widened in surprise. I got a certain satisfaction out of that. Then his eyes narrowed as he got a closer look at my makeshift weapons. "Where the heck did you get these?"

"I made them."

"Out of what?" He was still staring at the splintered ends, obviously trying to figure out what it had been before.

I hesitated, already regretting showing them to him. Finally, I sighed. "A plunger."

Wes bit down on his lip.

I glared at him. "Well, I had to protect myself somehow," I hissed, "especially that first day. I had no idea where you were taking me or how Jack and Fee would react to me." I knew I was rambling but I kept talking, hoping the sound of my voice would drown out the laugh I could see building. When I was done, I shoved the wood pieces back in my pockets to get them out of sight.

Wes snickered, and looked like he was trying to hold in something louder. He managed to keep mostly quiet, probably from the murderous look on my face. "Okay, so help me understand," he said, a little breathlessly. "You've actually been carrying these around since last week?"

"Every day."

"Wow. That's actually kind of impressive in a strange, disgusting, unexpected sort of way."

"Whatever. Laugh it up. But I can protect myself."

Wes's face turned red from the pressure of holding his breath. Finally, it whooshed out of him, along with loud, knee-slapping laughter. I glared at him a second longer, wondering if now might be a good time to test out the durability of my plunger handles, and then abruptly turned on my heel and strode away.

Chapter Fourteen

IN the end—after Wes stopped laughing—I had no choice but agree to him serving as my babysitter. I could've said no, but he would've done it anyway. It was going to take a few hours for him to help Jack switch the patrol schedule around, given that they were short-handed as it was. But Jack said they'd make it work and Wes promised to be at my house after school. Whether I liked it or not.

The next morning, I stood in my kitchen eating a muffin while the car warmed, and the windshield defrosted. Every night, I'd tell myself to get up early and start the car so it would be warm and clear by the time I needed to leave. And every morning, I'd forget until it was too late and then I'd end up running late. Vicious cycle.

Luckily, the roads were clear. No precipitation to go with the cold. It snowed in Frederick Falls only about three or four times a winter; usually the last good covering happened at the end of February or beginning of March. Just when you thought spring might have sprung, a snowstorm would blow through and crush that dream underneath six inches of powdery white. I figured we were due for that anytime.

I took the back roads to avoid traffic, and police, and sped my way to school. Screeching into a space, I slammed my car door and hurried toward the side entrance before the final bell made me officially late. Once inside, I skipped my locker and began weaving in and out of bodies. There was still time to avoid the tardy bell—and hopefully George.

He'd texted me last night, more than once, to remind me that he wasn't giving up on "us." The last one had come at one in the morning. And even though sleep eluded me, it had nothing to do with our breakup. I didn't respond to any of his attempts, and I had a feeling there'd be even more today. I felt kind of guilty that I'd given so little thought to the relationship ending. The truth was I really did care about George. We'd known each other forever and had a lot of shared history and what you might call growing pains, but none of that made up for his behavior these past few months, or the way he'd become totally engrossed in himself.

And none of that was enough to hold my attention when you compared it with the double life I was now leading.

Or the kiss.

Dang that had been a good kiss. I'd never felt like that when George kissed me, not once. I'd never even known it existed, that kind of heat. Now that I did, I wasn't sure if I could go back to "comfortable" and "nice." Because what I felt for Wes couldn't be described as either of those things.

I dodged a group of kids huddled outside my English classroom waiting until the very last second to dart into their assigned classes, and managed to slide into my seat with a total of three seconds to spare. I peeled off my jacket and shook out my still damp hair.

"Seriously?" came a shrill voice from directly beside me.

I glanced over and then away again in disgust. "Cindy," I muttered.

"Keep your slimy hair in your own space," she snarled.

I rolled my eyes and did my best to ignore her. It helped that I was now very aware that with one punch, I could probably knock her nose a few inches further into her face. It helped a lot.

Mr. Knowles walked in and launched right into his lecture, so any further comments were halted. It was probably a good thing, too. I'd never been prone to fighting but the more I thought about it—and the longer Cindy glared at me—the more tempting it was to shut he up once and for all. The idea must've plastered a pretty smug grin on my face because Cindy's look of disdain turned into a heated glare.

"What are you looking at, troll?" she hissed, when Mr. Knowles turned his back to write on the white board.

My smile turned hard around the edges and I pulled my lips back, baring my teeth at her in a way that reminded me of my argument with Wes, and the way he'd basically snarled at me. I wondered if it made me look as wolfish as it had him. "Cindy, I'm getting seriously irritated with your snarky little comments. If I were you, I'd shut it. Now. Before I ruin that slutty, charcoaled eye shadow of yours with my fist."

Cindy stared at me open-mouthed for a few seconds, clearly in shock that I'd actually stood up to her. Up until now, I'd mumbled retorts and exchanged dirty look for dirty look but nothing like this. I watched her glance around, for witnesses, no doubt. Plenty of people were staring. Okay, pretty much the whole class was staring, but no one was willing to admit they were listening; in other words, none of them came to Cindy's aid.

Cindy looked back at me and snapped her jaw closed. Her glare leveled into a wary stare but she didn't offer a retort of her own and finally turned back to the front of the room. I could practically see her wheels turning as she thought of new and twisted ways to get back at me for telling her off.

I tried turning my attention back to Mr. Knowles, but I couldn't concentrate. The entire lecture went in one ear and out the other. I couldn't believe it. This was great. I'd never have to deal with Cindy's crap ever again. Or anyone else's for that matter. I could feel some of the other kids glancing over from time to time, probably just as shocked as Cindy about what I'd said, but I ignored them and spent the rest of class enjoying the fact that Cindy didn't so much as look at me after that. This Hunter thing might just have its perks after all.

By the end of my next class, word had obviously spread. Sam was waiting for me at my locker, tapping her foot impatiently. Angela stood next to her, looking just as antsy.

"What the hell?" Sam demanded, as soon as I got close

enough in the sea of bodies. "I heard you went ape shit on Cindy this morning."

I grinned. I couldn't help it. "Maybe."

"How are you not suspended or something?" Angela put in.

"Suspended? For what?" My smile disappeared, replaced by confusion.

"You punched her in the face, in the middle of class," said Sam.

"What? No, I didn't. I told her to shut her trap or I'd replace her charcoal eye shadow with a black eye."

"Damn. High school gossip does it again," Sam muttered. "Still," she said, grinning, "That's pretty badass. What happened? Did you finally snap under the strain of her bad haircuts and horrible fashion sense?"

"I guess you could say that."

The warning bell rang, and we scattered to class. I caught a glimpse of George rounding the far corner as I walked away, and I increased my pace to keep him from catching up to me. I really didn't want to deal with that right now.

I spent the rest of the day dodging George and enjoying the fifteen minutes of fame that came with telling Cindy off. Everywhere I went, kids kept stopping me to ask me about it. Mostly, though, I was enjoying this new sense of power and confidence. I felt like I could take on anybody or anything and it felt good.

By last period, though, I was itching for the bell. Wes would be waiting when I got home and at some point during my "conquer the world" day, I'd decided it was time to do something about him—and whatever it was that he wasn't telling me. Which, I was sure, was plenty.

So, when the final bell sounded, I skipped my locker, this time avoiding more than just George, and sprinted for my car. Just as I'd hoped, I was among the first to the lot. I threw my bag over the seat and hopped in, going as fast as I dared through the school-zone flashing lights and then hitting the gas for home.

Just like this morning, I took the back roads, which were actually faster than Route One. I'd learned the curves so well that I barely had to brake as my tires hugged the corners.

I cranked the volume on the stereo and sang at the top of my lungs to an old Britney Spears song, my possession and enjoyment of which, I hoped, would remain a secret between me and my car.

When I was about halfway home, I rounded a sharp curve on Ramoth Church Road and gasped. Standing directly in the middle of my lane was a Werewolf. I slammed my foot against the brake pedal and resisted my body's reflex to swerve. That's what sent people on a one-way trip over the guardrail. The brakes screeched and screamed as the car slid closer and closer to the wolf. I was close enough to see not only the color of its fur, which was storm-cloud gray, but its eyes as well; they were an eerie, glowing yellow and as big as golf balls. As the car slid toward it, the wolf didn't flinch. He stood his ground and bared pointy teeth in an obviously open display of malice. I barely noticed the tingling on my skin through the panic. I wasn't going to stop in time.

The crash was more of a giant, echoing thud, as my bumper made contact with the wolf's flesh. The impact was enough to finally halt my wheels, and my car jerked to a stop, shooting me forward before my seatbelt caught me and hurled me back again. My head hit the headrest with a muted thump.

Outside, the wolf bounced off the bumper and slid up onto the hood, before slumping back off again. Everything went silent and sort of froze for a minute. I stared out the windshield, which was somehow still in one piece, at the pile of gray fur on the road in front of me. It didn't move.

My skin still tingled, so I knew it wasn't dead, but it didn't seem to be in a position to do any damage. I clicked the seatbelt's release and climbed out, still eyeing the pile of fur. Blood matted the fur in a couple places, and still it didn't move. I was just about to step forward, see if it was conscious, when its head lifted and two yellow eyes focused on me. Before I could react, it was up, standing firmly on all fours, a low growl emanating from deep within its throat.

I made a lunge for my open car door, but the wolf was quicker and already anticipating that move. It shot forward, and hurled itself at the door, slamming it shut with the force of its shoulder.

Now, nothing but open space separated us. It growled again and stepped forward. Reflexively I stepped back.

"Isn't this a treat? I hadn't expected you to come along this road, or to find me so soon," he said, in a silky-smooth voice. It sounded almost funny coming from his weathered wolf form. Almost. Because, hidden in the words was definitely a threat.

"Who are you?" I asked, though I had a feeling I already knew.

It was him, the one leaving me bloody messages.

"That's right. I know you, but you don't know me. Well, not personally, anyway. My name is Leonardo DeLuca. You can call me Leo. Liliana did."

I clenched my jaw, more angry than afraid, at his egotistical attitude. A part of me knew I should be running or calling for help, but the new me, the one who'd told Cindy off, insisted I could handle this. Then again, it would help if my plunger handles weren't in my backpack, which was in the car. "And I'm Tara, but you can call me 'the girl who knocked you out with her car,'" I said, with way more confidence than I felt.

You know how in books or movies, the killer always leaves himself open for that extra few seconds, giving the heroine time to counter? Well, this wasn't like that at all. Without warning, Leo sprang at me, and I threw my hands up, going on instinct, like I had with Liliana. I managed to block him and throw him to the side at the last second, but not before I felt his nails rake my arms. I ignored the burning and stepped out of reach, lowering into a crouch.

Leo came at me again, this time grabbing my sleeve with his teeth. I heard fabric tear and rammed my fist into the side of his head. The blow drove him back, and he released his hold.

His teeth snapped forward again and caught on my skin, tearing a gash into my arm where the nails had already drawn a thin line of blood. Without meaning to, I screamed at the burning it left behind.

My body seemed to go on autopilot after that, maybe from the pain. No longer did I have to tell my brain what to do with my limbs, or any other part of my body. It just sort of knew. We circled each other for a while and I could feel myself tiring out.

My hair had come loose from the bun held in place by a pencil. The pencil! I reached up and pulled it loose, taking a few strands of hair with it in my haste. I gripped the pencil, pointy side up, and fell back into a crouch.

This time, Leo came at me in a leap, his paws and teeth arcing down from above. At the last second, I twisted my shoulders and angled my body away from the impact and awkwardly shoved the pencil into his left shoulder.

I felt it give against flesh and muscle, and shoved harder, one more time, before jumping clear. I dropped and rolled to the side, rising quickly and struggling to stay alert against the searing pain where Leo had bitten me.

Leo was advancing on me again, a little slower this time. I could see the pencil protruding from underneath his fur, and the look in his eyes every time he stepped on his front paw said it wasn't a comfortable feeling. A small stain of red was just beginning to show around the edge of the "2" on the pencil shaft. Leo ignored it and lunged at me, but it was sloppy and I managed to dodge him easily enough by stepping back. When he turned, I saw that his front paw was held slightly off the ground, and he leaned a little to the right, shifting his weight. I must've hit a muscle or something. Despite the damage I'd caused him, there was no sign of giving up.

I tensed, ready for another attack, knowing I was moving slower each time. I was still doing my best to ignore the burning in my arm, though the fire had already intensified by several degrees; it was getting harder and harder to block out. Knowing I didn't have much time, I lunged, feinting to the left and then going right. Leo blocked me and we went back to circling each other.

"You're the one I keep feeling nearby," I said, through labored breaths.

"Just testing your reflexes. Your instincts aren't bad, for someone so new at this."

"Why? I never did anything to you. I don't even know you."

"Therein lies the tragedy. You should've known me, though I

guess it's not your fault that you don't. Nonetheless, I cannot allow you to become a Hunter."

Maybe it was from the adrenaline finally beginning to cool in my system, but suddenly the wound left by Leo's teeth reared up and screamed in my head. Black dots danced around the edges of my vision, and I swayed slightly. Leo's keen senses noticed my falter, and his eyes sharpened.

"So, the poison affects you after all," Leo said. Then he growled, low and deep, and crouched, ready to spring.

I stood there, having no idea of the meaning behind his words but really too exhausted and in too much pain to care. I knew Leo was about to charge, and I also knew I probably didn't have it in me to stop him.

A howl broke the silence. It came from the woods behind us but it was close. Neither of us looked toward the sound, both unwilling to let our guards down.

I tensed, ready for Leo's spring, even accepting it. A part of me welcomed it if it would stop the flames licking underneath my skin.

The howl came again, and I knew the other wolf was almost upon us. I groaned. Seriously? I couldn't handle another one right now. No way I'd be able to take on two at once, not with my arm burning like the fires of hell.

I backed up and repositioned myself so I could keep my eyes on Leo, but not leave my back exposed to the new wolf.

Dead branches and leaves crunched lightly, signaling the newcomer's approach. It was almost to the road. Finally, unable to help himself, Leo's eyes cut toward the newcomer. I allowed a split second of the same, and saw a wolf, bigger than Leo, with reddish-brown fur, hurtling toward us. I cut my eyes back to Leo, but he continued to watch the new wolf, instead of me. They didn't look happy to see each other.

I watched in confusion as Leo tensed. His yellow eyes cut back and forth between the new wolf and me before settling back on the wolf again. His lips were pulled back over his teeth in a silent snarl, and I knew then that this new wolf was not a friend of his. The red wolf howled again, the wail morphing into a growl as he

116

took the final leap and surprised me by landing directly in between Leo and me—eyes on Leo.

"You're not needed here, Dirty Blood," growled Leo.

"You've got it backwards. You're the one not needed," growled the red wolf.

I recognized him as soon as he spoke. Wes.

As if I'd called his name out loud, he turned. Two seconds. That was it, but it was enough for me to fully see him, in his changed form. He was magnificent. His fur was a zillion different shades of brown and red, all mixed together, and it glinted in the sunlight, shiny and sleek. Even the coarse hairs that ran down his back looked soft and beautiful, especially next to Leo's mangy coat.

And his eyes.

They were the same tawny brown as those of his human form. When they flashed to me, the sharpness dulled to gentle, and then steel and power flashed through them again as he turned back to Leo.

Even as a wolf, his moods were infinite and ever-changing.

"She brought it upon herself," Leo hissed, "when she decided to step back into our world."

"Forget her. It's me and you." Wes leaned toward Leo, baring his teeth in a guttural snarl.

"You're a traitor, a disgrace to your kind. Stay out of this, or there'll be consequences. I'll do more than just take her life. I think I've already made that clear." Despite the threat, Leo backed up a step. Blood seeped from his shoulder, leaving a dotted trail on the pavement.

Wes didn't answer. Instead, he rushed at Leo, launching himself into the air, and taking Leo to the ground in a blur of fur and fangs. I stood there, a little dazed by the speed with which Wes had moved. I'd never seen anything like it. Liliana hadn't moved like that; neither had Leo, for that matter.

Pain licked its way through my body. I faltered, torn between searching for cover and wanting to give in and sink to my knees right here, let the darkness take me under. I blinked, but it did no good. Blackness encroached. I swayed.

Grunts and snarls sounded, but I couldn't tell which of them it came from. Then, Wes reared his head back, pulling away from where the two were still tangled together on the ground, and sunk his teeth into Leo's shoulder, just below where the pencil still protruded. Leo let out a howl and managed to break free but he hadn't gone more than two steps before Wes was on him, using his teeth to grab Leo's ankle and pull him back.

I stood there, paralyzed despite the pain, as I watched them rip at each other. Every nerve ending itched to jump in, to help Wes. He was fast, but Leo was agile and experienced, and what if something happened?

I wanted to do something, anything, to end it. But I couldn't think much past the burn in my arm. It was getting unbearable, and I had to bite back a groan. If I'd been able to make my mind and body work right, I'd have rushed Leo by now, or better yet, ran for my car. As it was, I was having a hard time staying on my feet, without swaying.

The burn traveled up my arm, into my shoulder. I couldn't feel my fingers in my left hand anymore. I gritted my teeth against the pain but some sound escaped my lips. It reminded me of a wolf's snarl.

Both wolves glanced in my direction, and Wes seemed to realize for the first time that I wasn't at the top of my game. Leo huffed out a breath, sounding satisfied.

"She's hurt," I heard him say.

Wes just glared down at Leo, who he had pinned against the asphalt.

"She needs you. I guess I'll have to take a rain check," Leo said.

Reluctantly, Wes removed his paws from Leo's chest, and stepped back. "This isn't over."

Leo stared intently at me before backing away. "If she insists on living in our world, I have no choice but to deal with her. With both of you."

"The campers were your work, then?"

"Yes. And Liliana was hers."

"You should consider it even."

"For this round, I do. But not for what she'll be if she

continues. Or what you already are. I can't let that happen."

"Is that what this is about? What I am?" Wes demanded.

"What you are is lazy, and unfocused. Content to settle. Neither of you deserve the power in your blood."

"What do you mean in *our* blood?"

Leo didn't answer. He cast a final, longing look at me and then turned and bolted into the trees.

Wes watched him go until he'd disappeared and then padded over to me. I had backed up and was leaning on my car now in an effort to stay on my feet.

"Tara?" he said, his eyes going from my face to the bloody mess that was my forearm.

The realization that Wes was safe made giving in to the pain a lot harder to resist. Black dots danced around my vision, this time closing in. My left shoulder slumped heavily and my knees began to buckle. I desperately just wanted to sit. "Yeah?" I managed.

Wes didn't answer. He backed up a few steps and then the air around us seemed to quiver and I blinked against what felt like a breeze. My blurred vision revealed nothing but empty space and I felt myself begin to panic as I realized Wes was gone. I blinked back the tears that burned my eyes.

When I refocused, Wes was standing in front of me—human again. The last of my strength slipped away. My knees gave out. Wes shot an arm out and grabbed me firmly around the waist, keeping me upright. With his other hand, he grabbed my wounded arm, and held it up for a closer look.

"What the hell? You're bit. Why didn't you say something? I thought it was just a scratch."

"Um, I'm bit. I'm saying something," I said, in a near whisper.

He looked at me and released my arm. It fell limply back to my side. "Give me your keys," he demanded.

"They're in the ignition," I mumbled. I felt the heat traveling again, this time across my chest and down my back. When it hit my heart, I could feel the rhythm increase. I gasped. "It ... burns," I managed to choke out. I squeezed my eyes shut.

Wes cursed. Wasting no more time, he scooped me up and carried me around to the passenger side of the car. Some aware part of my brain noticed he wasn't wearing a shirt and the delirium in me relished in how cool his skin felt against my burning body. And that the smooth skin of his chest was a stark contrast to the sleek coat of fur he'd worn moments ago. I pressed my palms to his skin until I felt myself being lowered away from him.

He set me in the passenger seat and belted me in. Then he came around and slid into the driver's seat, revving the car's engine. I heard him mutter something that sounded like "piece of crap" and then we were racing down the empty road.

The pain only got worse as Wes drove. Every little pothole and bump was like an extra sting. I wanted to yell about that, but when I tried, my voice only came out in a whisper, so I gave up. I watched the scenery pass with bleary eyes. I wondered vaguely where we were going, but the pain was bad enough that I didn't care. Wherever it was, they'd better have a way to make it stop.

Wes pulled the car up in front of Jack's in a flurry of dust and rocks. He wrenched the door open and all but flew around to my side. Somewhere between the car and the front door, I blacked out.

CHAPTER FIFTEEN

WHEN I came to, I could hear muted voices. They sounded far away, like a dream. I turned my head toward the sound and realized with some surprise that the movement didn't hurt. As a matter of fact, I couldn't feel much of anything, pain or otherwise. I glanced down at my arm and saw it was heavily bandaged. There was a small circular mark on the vein inside my elbow. They must have drugged me; I was pretty numb. It felt nice, especially after the blistering heat that had scorched me from the inside out.

I heard the voices again and tried to make out the words through the buzz in my ears. The door to my room was cracked open and the conversation drifted in from the hallway.

"She's going to be fine, Wes." Jack. I immediately recognized his baritone voice.

"Yeah, this time," Wes shot back.

I was shocked to hear the desperation in his words. He sounded ... bleak.

"What do you want me to do? I can't force her," Jack replied.

"I know, I know. But we have to convince her, somehow. She can't be left helpless. What if I hadn't been there?" There was a pause, and then he rushed on before Jack could respond. "I should've been there sooner. I don't know why I decided to meet her at home instead of meeting up the minute she left school."

Another pause, then, "Or driven her myself. That's what I'll do from now on."

"She's got to make the decision for herself," said Jack. Wes didn't reply and I could picture the stubborn set of his jaw as he tried to think of some way to force me to do whatever it is he wanted.

Jack spoke again and this time his voice was milder and unmistakably amused. "Trying to force her to train is not going to work. She's just as stubborn as you are."

"He's not going to let this go," Wes said, ignoring the last comment.

Fee's voice joined the conversation. "No, he's not. The question is, is he telling the truth."

"Liliana was part of it. He said so himself," said Wes.

"Maybe they were involved. We all knew Liliana was turning on us. She could've easily told him about you," said Jack.

"Yeah. I know but that doesn't explain how he knows about Tara. If he even really knows. He could've said it just to mess with me," said Wes.

"I don't know ... I'm going to call Vera, see if she can tell." That was Fee.

"We've got to convince her. She has to train. Otherwise, you might as well paint a target on her." The desperation returned to Wes's voice.

"We'll all try to convince her," Fee said, her tone placating. "One of us should check on her now. She should be awake soon, and I don't know if I've given her enough pain meds."

"I'll do it," Wes said quickly.

I heard footsteps, and then the door opened fully. Wes stood there, leaning on the frame. When his eyes met mine, and he saw I was awake, he left his post, and hurried forward. The relief and happiness that rocked through me was overwhelming, and I felt a big stupid grin spread across my face.

"You're awake," he said, taking my hand in his and peering down at me. "How are you feeling?"

"I'm not feeling much of anything," I admitted, in a croaky voice. "What did you give me?"

"Morphine. We had to. Jack had to stitch the wound closed." He looked pained as he said it. "You don't remember?"

"No." I glanced down at my left forearm covered in gauze and decided I didn't want to look just yet. "But I feel great now. Kind of loopy." I grinned, unable to help myself. I felt like an idiot in some sober part of my brain, but the drugged part just shrugged and grinned bigger.

Wes looked unsure how to respond. I think he was expecting to have to comfort and soothe me, like he had that first night, but I was so far from that reaction right now. Still, I tried to stay focused on the day's events. "So, are you going to tell me who Leo is?"

"What makes you think I know who he is?"

"He talked to you like he knew you. And besides, I heard you talking to Jack." Oops. I hadn't meant to admit that part. Dang these drugs.

Wes's eyes narrowed at that last part. "How much did you hear?"

I shrugged, which was kind of hard to do, considering I was still lying on my back. I suppressed a giggle at the awkwardness of the movement. "It doesn't matter. Are you going to tell me or not? And don't say 'or not' because Jack or Fee will just end up telling me, anyway."

Wes sighed. "Leo is adamantly against the message of The Cause. He speaks out against us every chance he gets, but mostly prefers to just silence the messenger, if you know what I mean."

"Huh. Sounds like a great guy. How do you know him personally?"

"What makes you think I do?"

I threw my hands up in frustration though it was kind of impossible to actually feel angry with this much pain medicine floating through me. "Here we go. Back to dodging my questions. Why are you always trying to keep things from me?" I demanded.

"I'm trying to protect you."

"No, that's *your version* of protecting me."

He rolled back on his heels. "And what would be your version?"

"Tell me everything you know. Anything less than full

disclosure could get me killed. If I had known who he was before I ran into him, maybe I—"

He cut me off. "What? Would've been able to kill him more easily?"

"No, but I wouldn't have gotten out of the car, that's for sure."

Wes looked thoughtful. "I was wondering about that. How did he manage to get you out?"

I told him how Leo and I had run into each other—literally.

"And since I didn't really know who it was, or that this was the Big Bad Wolf himself, I got out to see if he was okay."

Wes's eyes had gone wide near the beginning, right around the part where I'd hit Leo, but when I got to the bit about wanting to see if Leo was okay, they almost popped out of his skull.

He stared at me for a long moment after I was done and then finally shook his head. I waited for the lecture I could see coming. When he finally spoke, his words surprised me. "You're right. I should've told you everything. And I will. But you have to do something for me."

"Like a deal?" I asked, skeptical. I tried to raise my eyebrows but they were numb and I wasn't sure if it worked or if I just looked goofy.

"Exactly." He sounded way too cheerful. "A deal."

"What is it?"

"I'll tell you everything I know about Leo, from here on out, if you promise to let Jack train you."

I rolled my eyes. I had a feeling that's where this had been going. Then again, after today's fight, I couldn't deny that I needed help. Besides, I still needed to figure out a better weapon to carry. And a better way to carry it. Still, there was the matter of keeping it from my mom, and my friends. But at least this way, Wes could think it was his idea. "I don't know," I said, not wanting to seem too eager.

"Tara, you stabbed him with a pencil," he said, throwing a hand up. "You need some help, admit it."

I huffed out a breath, tempted to defend myself against that move. Then I remembered how well that had gone with the plunger handle conversation and decided to let it go. My fuzzy brain had no shot of winning an argument right now. And I didn't want to be mad at him, after almost—well, getting hurt like this. "Fine, but only until this thing with Leo is over. After that, the deal's off. I may or may not continue my training. It's my choice."

"Fair enough." Wes's eyes sparkled with his victory. A half smile formed on his lips.

At some point during the negotiation, he'd leaned closer, and I could feel his breath on my face. It mingled with his scent, an earthy, musky smell that scrambled my thoughts until the only coherent thing in my mind was him. All thoughts of training and blood disappeared. I found myself staring at his lips and wishing they were on mine.

I sighed. "You're pretty cute when you get your way." Oops, something else I hadn't meant to say out loud. Things just kept slipping out.

Wes' mouth curved in amusement but his eyes were serious and intense. "You're not so bad yourself. Drugged and tangled is a good look for you." He brought his hand up and brushed a lock of hair away from my face. The amusement disappeared as some new thought dawned on him; his expression turned sad. "Some bodyguard I turned out to be," he whispered. "If you hadn't been okay ..." He didn't finish and I realized some deeper part of me yearned to hear those unspoken words.

The problem with asking him? Stringing words together was kind of difficult at the moment. Instead, I reached out and grabbed his shirt and pulled his lips down to mine. I felt his shock for a brief instant, and then he relaxed, sinking closer and letting his fingers tangle in my hair. My hands were clasped around his neck, our lips firmly locked, when my phone rang.

Wes was the first to pull away. "You going to get that?" he asked, his voice husky.

"Do I have to?"

He chuckled.

The phone stopped ringing, and I shrugged. "Too late, it went to voice mail." I tried raising my head so that I could reach his lips again.

He inched back. "You're drugged, Tara," he said, giving me a scolding look.

"So?"

He sighed. "So, I'm not going to take advantage of you this way."

"I thought it was kind of the other way around," I mumbled, as he sat back.

He grinned down at me.

I sighed loudly. "Fine."

My disappointment seemed to amuse him. I glared at his crooked smile and pushed up onto my elbows. I grabbed my phone and reluctantly dialed my voice mail. I punched the numbers for my password and waited. As I listened, all of the amusement and laughter faded, replaced by panic and horror. Before the message ended, I was already struggling to stand.

"What is it?" Wes asked, as soon as I'd hung up.

"George was attacked," I whispered. I looked up at him. "That was his mom. He's in the hospital."

"Damn."

"I have to go see him." I tried pushing past him but he held me firmly in place, his hands on my shoulders.

"You're hopped up on painkillers, and you're hurt."

"I have to see him," I repeated, my voice gaining volume.

"Not until the medicine wears off." The finality in his tone left no room for argument. "What did the message say?"

"That some stray dog had attacked him for no reason when he got out of his car. It had to be Leo. He must've gone there right after he left us. I've got to do something, Wes." I struggled to get up again. This time Wes didn't need to lay a hand on me to send me slumping back to the pillow again.

Wes frowned. "I'll go."

I stayed down this time, slightly relieved by the suggestion. He didn't sound overjoyed with the idea, but it made me feel better, and I smiled at him, grateful.

"I'll make sure he's okay and call you from the hospital. Just stay here and do what Fee says. You aren't out of the woods yet as far as the venom, so take it easy, okay?"

"Okay," I agreed.

"And Tara? I'm sorry, for what I said the other day. About it being your fault, for killing Liliana. It's not your fault. None of it is."

"I know," I said. Any lingering anger over our argument was gone; I was too loopy to be anything but touched by his apology. "Thanks."

The darkness in his eyes lightened, making the gold flecks more pronounced. He stood up and looked down at me, still frowning. "I'll get Fee to come sit with you until I get back."

I tried to look insulted. "You don't trust me."

"Not even a little."

He left the room, and I could hear him calling out for Fee. Hushed voices followed, too far away for me to hear this time. I waited, impatiently, until I heard the muted sound of the front door clicking closed. Outside my window, I heard the distinct sound of an engine revving and then fading away. Fee came in a minute later.

"Wes told me about George. Jack went with him to see if they can pick up a trail," she said.

I nodded, comforted a little that they were taking it so seriously, but still distracted with thoughts of George. I could only hope he was okay. Broken up or not, I didn't think I could handle it if I was responsible for something bad happening to him. Is this what Leo had meant when he said he could do more than just kill me? If so, who would be next?

"Tara," Fee called gently, reading the panic in my expression. "It's going to be okay. Wes and Jack can handle this. We're going to find him, and we're going to stop him."

I nodded, wishing I could feel as sure as she sounded.

"How's the arm? Are you in any pain?"

"No, I'm pretty out of it. You must've given me a lot of pain medicine."

"I gave you a double dose of morphine," she admitted. "You were in a lot of pain when you got here. The venom had been in your system a long time and had already worked its way into your chest. I wasn't sure if I could push it out and trying was very painful for you."

"What do you mean 'push it out'?"

"Well, usually we can just give you a shot of the antivenin, near the spot of the bite. In your case, that wasn't enough. So I used my gift to expel it."

"You can do that?"

"It's not easy, and it's pretty painful for the patient, but yes."

"So, you have a gift for healing? Kind of like with Wes and the memory thing he can do."

Fee gave me a funny look, and then nodded. "Not everyone has extra abilities but those of us who do, it comes in handy."

"Is it something you can use on George?"

"Probably not. Humans don't get infected with the venom like we do. George's wounds would be tissue and organ damage, and my gifts won't repair that. I'm sorry," she added, when my face fell.

"It's fine. Thanks for healing me," I said, not wanting to sound ungrateful. Then something else occurred to me. "He's not going to turn, is he? I mean, can a Werewolf bite do that?"

She smiled. "No. A human can't be turned. Werewolves are born. It's in the blood, just like Hunters."

"Oh." I was relieved. "I almost forgot. If the offer still stands, I'd like to train with you and Jack."

"Wes told me. Of course we'll do it, Tara. We're happy to. Just get some rest so you'll be ready. Jack won't go easy on you," she warned.

I didn't disagree with her. Even though Jack seemed like the softie she claimed he was, his wolf self was still a hulking mass of fur. The mere mention of the word *rest* made me sleepier, but there was something else I still didn't understand. "Fee, what did Leo mean when he said Wes and I didn't deserve the power of our blood?"

Fee hesitated and some muddled part of my brain knew that this was important. "Well, we're not sure exactly, but it sounds as if Leo believes you to be very powerful."

"More powerful than other Hunters? Why would he think that? I don't even know how to properly stake something," I said.

"I don't know. But we'll figure it out," she said, patting my hand.

Her explanation seemed a little too simple and vague but my thoughts were hazy with the morphine, and I couldn't see her clearly through my drooping lids. I nodded, my head heavy against the pillow.

Fee saw this and told me she'd look in on me later, before quietly slipping out. With nothing but silence to distract me, I gave in and slept.

CHAPTER SIXTEEN

I woke up in my own bed, which was a little disturbing, since the last thing I remembered was passing out in the guest room at Fee's. The dull ache in my bandaged arm was evidence that the morphine had finally worn off. I looked around and tried to get a sense for how long I'd been out or how I'd gotten here. It was dark outside my window, and the clock on my nightstand read 9:18. Before I could figure out what to do next, the door creaked open, and my mom poked her head inside.

"You're awake."

"Hey, Mom," I said, uncertainly. "When did you get home?"

"About an hour ago. I didn't want to wake you." Her expression grew worried. "Are you getting sick again? You're not usually in bed this early."

"No, I guess I just didn't sleep much last night." Her concern didn't seem appeased by that explanation. "I'm fine, Mom," I added, in a firm voice.

She didn't look convinced, but she let it go. "All right, I'll be downstairs in the sunroom if you need me."

"Okay."

As soon as my door clicked shut, my bathroom door opened, and Wes stepped out.

"What the hell? You scared the crap out of me," I hissed,

130

glancing at the place where my mother had just stood and taking a deep breath to calm my racing pulse.

"Sorry. How're you feeling?"

"My head is clear but my arm aches a little. How did I get here?"

He sat lightly on the edge of my bed and looked down at me with concern etched across his features. "I brought you. By the time I got back from the hospital, it was getting pretty late. I didn't want your mom to worry, so I drove you home."

"I don't remember," I said, distractedly. I could smell him again and was having trouble keeping my thoughts organized, even without the morphine.

"You were sleeping," he admitted.

"The hospital," I said, suddenly remembering. I glanced at the closed door and lowered my voice. "How's George?"

"He's fine. Some cuts and scrapes but nothing major. *He* was able to escape back into his car," he said, giving me a pointed look.

I ignored that. "Good. Did you find a trail?"

"No. It disappeared on the other side of the trees that border his neighborhood. He probably had a car waiting and shifted so we couldn't track him."

I sat back and sighed. To his credit, Wes looked just as frustrated and tense as I felt. Still, Leo was out there, and anyone I cared about could be his next target. "I want to train. As soon as possible."

Wes nodded. "I've already spoken to Jack. You start tomorrow."

I nodded and let myself relax. I tried to take comfort in the fact that soon, I wouldn't have to rely on Wes and Jack to protect my loved ones.

"Are you sure you're feeling okay?" Wes asked. Small worry lines creased his forehead just above his brow.

"I'm fine," I said, distracted. Details were trickling back slowly. "Tell me about Leo."

"I don't know much more than I told you earlier. He's a known leader for the opposition. He hates the idea of Werewolves and Hunters working together. Always has. He's been fighting The

Cause since it first began, according to Fee and Jack. And apparently, he perceives you as a threat."

"He's never been caught?"

"No. He's always managed to slip away. I think he's got a gift for that. And most times, he's not even on the scene, anyway. He likes to sit back and direct the action."

"How do we stop him?" I squeezed my eyes shut. "I can't let him attack someone else."

"We've got to find him first. That's always been our problem. We'll get word on where he's holed up but by the time we get there, he's slipped away."

"We have to find him. Before he hurts someone else."

"I know."

We were both silent for a minute and I could tell Wes was lost in thoughts of hunting Leo down—and finding him. The morphine haze had worn off, and I remembered my conversation with Fee. "What did Leo mean about the power in our blood? I asked Fee but she didn't really answer me."

"I don't know," he said, quickly. Too quickly. His gaze flicked around the room. Everywhere but on me. "Probably just messing with us."

"It didn't seem like it. He was convinced that you and I were different, more powerful than others of our kind."

"Well, we're not. As evidenced by the fact that he almost killed you," he said. His tone was a little sharp, and I stiffened, ready to snap some retort. Wes sighed, long and loud, though and then said, "I'm sorry. I didn't mean ... You did great. I'm just angry at myself for letting it happen."

"It's not your fault," I said, but I could see he wasn't letting himself off the hook.

"It is, actually. If I'd met you at school, instead of waiting for you at home, it wouldn't have happened. He wouldn't have attacked."

"You don't know that."

"Okay, but if you hadn't gotten hurt, there's a chance I could've finished him." I opened my mouth to argue, but he went on. "Usually, age and experience are what tip the scales in a fight between our kind. But I'm faster and very strong. I have an advantage. I can fight better than most Weres twice my age."

"Is that why he ran off instead of staying to finish me off?"

"Yeah. Obviously he only picks fights he can easily win." He flashed a grim smile. "I wasn't so easy to beat."

If it had been anyone else, it would've sounded like bragging. But with Wes, I knew he was just stating a fact. One that I could personally attest to after seeing him in action. "Your mixed blood is your advantage, isn't it?"

His gaze sharpened but he didn't look as mad as I'd expected. "How did you know about that?" Actually, he looked on edge.

I hesitated, unsure of how much to admit to knowing. But in the end, the look on his face decided it. He was tense, and obviously nervous about my reaction. "Fee told me. At The Cause meeting the other day. She didn't know it was a secret, so don't be mad."

"What did she tell you?"

"About your parents. Who—and what—they were. And about you being a mix of them." I waited for his reaction. He looked relieved.

"And why would Fee tell you all of that?" he asked.

"I might have let her think I already knew," I said carefully.

He laughed. "I shouldn't even be surprised."

Some idea tickled at the back of my mind. Something about this conversation, and the one Wes had with Leo. "She said Werewolves call you Dirty Blood," I said slowly, letting the pieces form. "Is that what Leo meant earlier?" My jaw fell open as everything slid into place. "He doesn't think that I'm ...does he?"

"Like me? No," he said, his voice firm, absolute. "Like I said, he was trying to mess with us, throw us off, so that we wouldn't focus on finding him or ending this."

"Wow, yeah, I guess it was working for a second. That would be crazy, though, right?"

"Yeah. Crazy," he agreed. "Well, I'm going to go. Let you get some rest. I'll be nearby, though, keeping an eye out. Call me if you need anything."

"I will," I promised.

I waited, half hopeful that he would kiss me again, but he didn't. Instead, he stared down at me for a brief moment, his eyes unreadable, and then he rose to leave. I started to ask him how he'd get out without my mom seeing. Before I could, he was at the window and pulling it open.

"What are you—?"

"Lock this behind me, okay?" Without waiting for an answer, he pulled it open and disappeared through the opening.

I gasped and rushed over, peering into the darkness of my backyard. On the ground, just below me, was Wes. He glanced up at me and then jogged toward the trees, the shadows swallowing him up.

I closed and locked the window and returned to the warmth of my bed with every intention of going back to sleep. Instead, I lay there for hours, wide awake. Whether my body was tired enough to sleep didn't matter; my brain wouldn't shut off. I had to struggle against overwhelming worry and the urge to panic whenever I thought of Leo, and what he'd tried to do to George.

I couldn't shake the feeling that someone else I cared about would be next and that led to panic because I felt helpless to stop it. So, to keep from completely freaking out, I thought of the only other thing that could really hold my attention: Wes.

What was his deal?

I couldn't quite seem to figure him out. One minute he was concerned and caring, the next he was cold and distant. Then there were his half-truth answers—always holding something back. And just when I thought I had a handle on him, his mood would change. I wasn't sure how much more of it I could take.

Then again, there was no question that I'd fallen for him. Hard. So, what choice did I have?

CHAPTER SEVENTEEN

I managed to be up and ready for school early the next morning, which was definitely a first. Then again, I didn't usually get to nap—twice—in a day, so that probably helped. On the way out of my room, my booted toe hit something, and plastic crackled. I looked down and found a bag peeking out from under the edge of my bed. The green hoodie I'd bought at the mall last week. I'd totally forgotten about it. Smiling to myself, I put it on over my tee and zipped it up before heading downstairs.

I scanned the note my mother had left on the counter, telling me she'd be home late, finishing inventory. It made me think of Julie and George, and whoever might be next. Painful images of Angela or Sam, their skin marred by teeth marks, distracted me as I headed out the door and locked the deadbolt behind me. A glint of silver caught my eye, and I turned. An Aston Martin idled at the curb. Wes stood in front of it, leaning against the passenger door. The sun shone brightly on his hair, making it look more of a burnished bronze color and casting a golden glow around his face.

No magnetic force was needed; the desire to go to him and wrap my arms around him was pure physical attraction. I shoved my hands in my jacket pockets and walked over.

"What are you doing here?" I asked.

"Driving you to school." He turned and opened the passenger

door for me. "Consider it guard dog duty," he added, in a half smile.

Once inside, I found my seat already toasty warm, as was the rest of the car. Wes came around and got in, revving the powerful engine and easing us forward.

"How are you feeling?" he asked, as he steered us onto the street.

"Much better. My arm barely hurts anymore, and I think I got enough sleep to last me, like, three days."

"Don't be so sure. You start training today and Jack doesn't go easy, believe me."

"Yeah, the thought of having to fight him is a little intimidating," I admitted.

"He won't fight you today. He'll start with the basics."

"Well, when will we get to the fighting part? I don't exactly have time to start slow."

"It's not like you can learn this stuff overnight, Tara. It'll take time."

"Well, I don't have time. Can't you guys give me the accelerated version or something? I need to be able to defend myself and, more importantly, everyone else. Leo could try again any time. I need to be ready."

"If you try to go too fast, you could get hurt. Your muscles aren't used to battle yet. You need to condition them slowly, or they won't be ready, and you could seriously hurt yourself. Then you won't be able to protect anyone."

I knew he was right, but I was too impatient to want to hear it. "How do you know how my muscles will react? I'm sure it's not quite the same for Werewolves."

"No, it's not. But I'm not just a Werewolf, remember?"

"Right, Dirty Blood," I said. He gave me a hard look. "Sorry, does that term bother you?"

"Would 'white trash' bother you?"

"Point taken. So that's how you know about a Hunter's physical abilities."

"I have an idea, yes."

"And is that why you can move like that? Because you're

both?"

He seemed to be considering my question. "We think so," he said, slowly. "There's no precedent or comparative information but we think it's a matter of me getting the best of each race's attributes so the strength and speed are twice as much."

"Why didn't you tell me before?"

He kept his eyes on the road and for the first time ever, I thought I saw a hint of red color his cheeks. "It's complicated."

I waited, but he didn't say more. Maybe it was because he always seemed so sure of himself but it took me a moment to realize he was actually embarrassed. "It's not really that big of a deal," I said with a shrug, hoping to ease his discomfort.

This time he did turn to look at me, and his eyes flashed. "Actually, it is a big deal. Werewolves don't look kindly on it. It's a disgrace to our lineage. And Hunters, well, they don't really know what to do with me. It's kind of a mess. The only group that's ever really accepted me is The Cause. Then again, they look at it as the ultimate peacemaking tool."

"Well, if you think about it, it is a good way to bridge the gap. I mean, there probably aren't too many of you out there but—"

"None," he said, cutting me off in a grim voice. "I'm the only one."

"Is that why Leo hates you so much?"

He nodded, his mouth a hard line. "Probably. To him, I've betrayed our kind twice. Once just by being born and again by joining The Cause."

We rode in silence for a few minutes. I wasn't really sure what to say. I was starting to realize why his mixed genes were such a big deal. Clearly, it bothered and even embarrassed him to tell me. But I also felt like there was a lot about it that I still didn't understand. I glanced at him out of the corner of my eye. A tiny muscle in his jaw twitched with tension. New questions popped into my head, but I bit my tongue. I decided it was probably best to let it go for now. We were almost to school, anyway.

We got stuck in traffic; the long line of cars waiting to pull into the student lot was creating a traffic jam at the entrance so we had to stop for a while and wait for an opening into the drop-off lane.

While the car idled, a familiar face rolled up next to us.

Cindy Adams, in her family's Taurus, gawked openly at the Aston Martin's shiny silver paint and sleek lines. Her eyes settled on the darkly tinted windows and I could see her straining to see inside. When I realized she couldn't, I felt a smirk cross my face and before I could resist, I was pressing the automatic window button, letting the glass slide down a few inches.

"What are you doing?" Wes asked, eyeing the descending glass. He knew I wasn't a fan of the cold.

"It's kind of hot in here," I said, still watching Cindy. Her eyes were almost popping out of her head, trying to see over the tiny crack of the window. I knew she had to be dying to know who was inside. We didn't see a lot of flashy cars at our school. Most of the kids who could drive got their parents hand-me-downs, so nothing was brand new, much less luxury class. I hit the window controls again, letting it slide down another inch.

"I can turn the heat down," Wes said.

"It's okay. I want the fresh air," I lied.

Finally, I couldn't help myself any longer, and I pushed the control and sent the window all the way down, revealing my face. Cindy's expression registered surprise and then open envy as her eyes went from me to the car and then finally, to Wes. She stared at him for a full thirty seconds before she realized I was still watching her. I smiled with devious satisfaction as she tried—and failed—to smooth it over into a blank stare. The traffic moved, and we inched past her. I rolled up the window, still smiling to myself.

"Who was that?" Wes asked.

"Just some girl I know," I said. At his stern look I added, "Her name is Cindy Adams, and she's basically been president of the We-Hate-Tara club since sixth grade."

His eyes narrowed a fraction, like he was still trying to understand what was so great about letting her see me in the car. Did he not own a mirror? The second he pulled up to the curb, I grabbed my bag and hopped out before he could question me further.

"Two thirty?" he called.

"Two thirty," I confirmed. "See you then." I pushed the door shut and hurried toward the entrance.

"Holy Mother ..."

I looked up to find Sam blocking my way up the steps, but she wasn't watching me. She was watching the back end of the Aston Martin as it disappeared around the corner. I stopped and waited for her to turn her attention back. When she did, it was with both eyebrows raised.

"Was that the guy?" she asked.

"Yeah," I said, hesitantly.

She let out a whistle and a couple of sophomore guys stopped and grinned at Sam with eager faces that she ignored. "Wo-ow," she said, falling into step beside me. "He's a little bit gorgeous, with some yummy on the side. I thought you said that phone call was a bust."

"Well, it was. At first, anyway. But he came over yesterday and we hung out and ..." I let the sentence hang. Aside from the Hunter stuff, I had absolutely no idea what was going on between Wes and I, if anything.

"Hanging out is good," Sam said, easily accepting my explanation. Then again, with Sam, "hanging out" was as serious as it got. "Does George know?"

"They've met," I said, carefully.

She snickered. "How'd that go? Any violence?"

"It was touch and go." I let out a frustrated breath. "Seriously, though, George has no say anymore. He doesn't get to be mad or have an opinion. We're not together."

"Yeah, good luck telling him that."

"I know." The first bell rang, signaling we only had a few more minutes to get to class and Sam and I parted ways.

CHAPTER EIGHTEEN

WHEN we got to Jack's after school, an extra car sat in the driveway. Before I could ask Wes about it, Jack and Fee rounded the corner of the house accompanied by the aristocratic woman I'd seen at The Cause meeting. They were talking and laughing, though Jack's booming voice drowned out the women. Wes nudged me, veering toward the house.

"Oh, hey, you two," Fee called, coming toward us.

Wes grimaced but his expression cleared before he turned to face them. "What's up?"

"Oh, nothing, Vera was just reinforcing the wards," Fee said.

"Is everything okay?" Wes asked.

"Everything's fine," Vera assured him. "Just a routine checkup." She smiled at me. "Tara, I don't think we've officially been introduced."

Fee smiled apologetically at her and then gestured to me. "Yes, I almost forgot. Tara, this is Vera Gallagher. She's a member of The Cause. Vera, Tara Godfrey."

She smiled, a gesture that didn't quite reach her eyes, and extended her hand. "A pleasure to meet you, Tara. I've heard a lot about you."

I took her hand, shaking it slowly, trying to figure out the odd expression she'd worn a second ago. "Nice to meet you," I returned.

"Jack and Fee tell me that you're new to all this. No training at all, yet you managed to take down a Werewolf all by yourself. Impressive," she said.

"Thanks," I mumbled, wondering why it felt like an insult when her words were meant to be a compliment. "Good reflexes, I guess."

"Hmm." She frowned. "Have you been able to determine any more of your Hunter heritage?" she asked, her eyes sharp as they searched my face.

"Um, no, not really." I was starting to feel a little uncomfortable, like she was searching for something I hadn't given her permission to see.

The others finally seemed to catch on to Vera's scrutiny. Wes glanced at me and then back at Vera. Fee and Jack watched Vera like they expected something. An awkward moment passed.

"Well," said Vera, "let us know if we can help in any way."

The thickness in the air receded and everyone exhaled. I nodded. I wasn't sure what had just happened but I was glad it was over.

"Vera's a Hunter, Tara. If you need anything, she's here to help as well," said Fee.

"Thanks," I said, pretty sure I wouldn't be going to her for much of anything.

The three of them wandered away toward Vera's car. Wes led me inside.

"What was that about?" I asked once we were alone in the house. He didn't answer, just kept walking, into the living room. I followed. "Wes?"

He stopped in front of the bookcase, hands stuffed into his pockets and turned to face me. He looked just as confused as I was, and lost in thought. "Honestly, I don't know."

"But you have an idea."

"Vera's very ... intuitive. It's sort of a gift of hers. Sometimes, she just knows things, and other times, she picks up on a flash or an idea of something, with no real details as to the whole picture."

"Is that what just happened with me?"

"Maybe." He seemed guarded.

"Well? Can't you ask her?"

He shook his head. "Vera's also very traditional. She won't share anything she sees with anyone but Jack and Fee. Then, they'll decide together if it should be shared with the rest of us."

"If it's about me, I think I have a right to know."

"Vera doesn't necessarily see it that way." He had his back to me so I couldn't see his face. His voice was hard, and again I felt like I'd hit a wall of information he was holding back.

I sighed, knowing I wouldn't get anywhere, even if I pressed it. "Why Jack and Fee?"

"They're the leaders of The Cause, and they represent the Werewolf half of our group. Vera represents the Hunter side."

"So they're like the board of directors or something?"

"Sort of."

The front door opened and closed and Jack appeared in the doorway. "Training time. You ready?" he asked, looking at me.

"Ready," I said, glancing at Wes one last time before following Jack out.

CHAPTER NINETEEN

THE drive home from Jack's was awkward. Wes didn't say much and kept his eyes on the road. At first, I barely noticed, I was so preoccupied with the screaming muscles in my body. I vaguely remembered Fee telling me Jack was a hard teacher, but I hadn't really believed her. I mean, sure, Jack looked pretty intimidating, but once I'd gotten to know him, I'd realized he was just this big teddy bear. Or maybe puppy was the right word. But the minute the clock had started for our training session, it was like he became a whole different person. He was strict and no-nonsense and definitely pushed me way beyond the limits I thought I could handle.

In the two hours we'd spent together, I think I'd done more pushups and sit-ups than ever before in my life. I'd also run—for a ridiculously long time. We ran a trail through the woods, so I couldn't be sure the distance, but any time I stopped or even slowed my pace, Jack was behind me, barking an order to get moving. I was exhausted and sweaty and desperately wanting a shower and my bed, in no particular order.

We were a fair distance away from the house before Wes's clipped silence dawned on me—and before I felt like I was breathing normally enough to hold a conversation.

"What did you do while I was with Jack?" I asked.

"Cause business."

"Anything interesting?"

He glanced at me quickly and then back to the road again. "Vera needed me so she could finish reinforcing the wards."

"What are wards?"

"I guess you could call it a security system. Vera weaves a spell that spans the edge of Jack and Fee's property. It keeps unwanted guests out, and lets Jack and Fee know when someone—or something—crosses over it."

I guess it shouldn't have surprised me that Vera could do magic. And in a way, it didn't. She was exactly the sort of modern-day witch I would've pictured, but the fact that magic existed, on that level, never ceased to amaze me. "So why did she need you there?"

"The spell can be programmed to let certain individuals pass, but you have to present them properly. She was programming me in, so I wouldn't get zapped with a thousand volts of electricity next time I come over."

"Good idea. What about the rest of The Cause members? How will they get through?"

"Vera will be at the end of the drive to meet them and program them in as they arrive. Then, they'll be okay to come and go until she has to redo it."

"How long will that be?"

"A couple of months. It probably lasts longer, but with everything going on, we aren't taking any chances."

Somewhere during our talk of magic, his shoulders had relaxed, and his tone had become less strained, his words not as short as when we'd left the house. "Did you ask Vera if she saw something about me?"

Immediately, the tension returned. "No. I forgot."

He was lying. And poorly, at that. Usually when he kept something from me, he did a better job concealing it, so that I only suspected, without any real proof. But this one had been obvious. His eyes had shifted and he still wouldn't look at me. I wondered what Vera had seen. Was it something bad? Was it about Leo hurting someone else? Or me? Did he think I couldn't handle it?

"I thought we had a deal," I said. "Training in exchange for full disclosure."

He shook his head. "I promised I'd share everything I knew about Leo. And I have."

"You're still keeping something from me."

"But it's not about Leo," he said, as if that made it okay.

I clenched and then unclenched my teeth. "You would've made a fantastic lawyer."

He grinned, like it had been meant as a compliment.

I shook my head. "I'll find out, you know. Whatever it is you're keeping from me." He just stared at the road, so I went on. "The truth always comes out. And if something happens, or if someone gets hurt, and it could've been avoided if you'd just been honest with me, that would be hard to forgive."

"What if telling you would hurt someone?"

I might've argued that the truth was always better, and secrets always had a way of coming back to bite you, but the sincerity and quiet desperation in his tone stopped me. Whatever he was keeping, it was wearing on him. For a split second, it made me feel bad for him, but then I realized how dumb that was. If he'd just tell me, we could face it together, and he wouldn't have to feel all "world on my shoulders" about it. Besides, all of this overprotectiveness was reminding me of my mother.

I sighed. "I still deserve to know. Even if it hurts," I said.

"I'll keep that in mind."

CHAPTER TWENTY

"NO, don't point your toes, unless you want them broken. Keep your foot flat, leg straight. That's it," said Jack.

I breathed in, making sure to balance myself correctly, and then kicked hard against the pad in Jack's hand. His wrist barely budged from the hit, though I felt the vibrating impact all the way to my knee.

"Better," he said.

I blew out a breath. "Whatever," I grumbled. I was frustrated at my lack of progress.

Jack either didn't hear or, most likely, pretended not to. "Again."

My brow lifted. "Seriously?"

"Again," Jack repeated.

"Jack, I'm done. I'm out of breath and energy and our time's up."

Jack didn't bother checking his watch. "We've got five more minutes. And I'm in charge, not you. So I say when you're done. Besides, do you think your enemy is just going to stop attacking to let you catch your breath? Push through. Again."

I glared at him but fell into a fighter's stance. I balanced and then kicked out, almost missing the pad altogether.

Jack gave me a scolding look. "You know, tomorrow I'm going

to start fighting back. This is the easy part," he said, his voice gruff.

I opened my mouth to argue but he cut me off. Before I could react, his padded hand came up and whacked me across my cheek. My head jerked to the side and I froze in surprise. I turned back to him, glaring. "What the hell was that for?"

He grinned. "Motivation. Again."

With renewed energy, I kicked out and made contact, pleased to see that I drove him back a step this time. Okay, it was more like a quarter-step, but I'd take what I could get. Jack was like a wall. I kicked again, and again, each time with the same angry, determined energy.

After the fourth kick in a row—just as I was getting into the rhythm of my movements—Jack straightened and dropped the pads. "Good, okay, that's it for today."

I stared at him. "What? But I was on a roll."

"Time's up, like you said," he pointed out.

I put my hands on my hips. "So what? Let's keep going. I'm feeling better now."

"No."

"No?" I repeated.

He stepped over and leaned down until he was in my face, all traces of smiles and teasing gone. "You need to learn to fight just as good when you're not mad." Then he spun and headed for the house.

I watched him go, too dumbfounded by his response to argue further. The back door swung shut behind him and I wiped at the sweat on my forehead with the back of my hand. My arm muscle protested against the movement; everything felt like Jell-O. Then again, that was becoming routine for my body.

I'd been training with Jack for four days and my body hadn't made the adjustment yet. I was sore and stiff and because of that, I was afraid I'd be useless in an actual fight, if it came to that right now. Which was probably part of the reason I was so easily pissed off at Jack's teaching methods and my own lack of progress.

I collected the pads from where Jack had thrown them onto the grass, and returned them to the container marked "Padding." Jack had a room full of similar containers, all marked with different labels. I'd noticed the ones labeled "Weapons" the previous day when he'd asked me to retrieve this one. I was impatient to get to that one but Jack kept putting me off. So far, we were focusing only on hand-to-hand combat. Jack insisted this was more important; a weapon wasn't always guaranteed.

"He's tough but he's good," said a voice behind me.

I spun around. A tall man with dark hair stood leaning against a nearby tree. He looked familiar but I tensed, anyway.

"Sorry if I startled you. Miles Ducati. We met at the meeting last week."

"Oh, right. I thought you were going out of town or something."

"I did. I'm back. Just waiting for Jack to finish so we can talk business."

"Oh." I didn't really know what else to say. Something about this Miles guy put me on edge, like I could never tell if he was messing with me or being serious. I wandered over to where I'd set my water bottle and took a swig to fill the silence. I could feel Miles's eyes on me and it was a weird feeling. If he'd been ten years younger, I would've said he was checking me out; maybe he was. But there was something else behind his smile, something calculating. I started gathering up my things, expecting him to say something else but he didn't. "Well, I better get inside. Nice seeing you again," I called.

"And you," he said as I walked away.

I found Jack waiting for me at the back door, a grin tickling the edges of his mouth. "Still mad?"

My earlier aggravation with him returned, though not quite as strong. "No," I lied.

He laughed good-naturedly, the sound coming from deep in his chest. "Same time tomorrow?" he asked, completely transitioning out of his trainer role and back to friend.

"Yeah, same time," I muttered.

"Tell Wes to get you a heating pad for your shoulders," said Jack.

"What makes you think I need a heating pad?"

Jack laughed. "Because you're walking like you've got wooden limbs. Alternating hot and cold will help loosen your muscles before we start combat training."

"I'll tell him," I said, though I wasn't sure if I would. Things had been awkward between Wes and me the past few days. And even though he was still driving me to school in the mornings, picking me up every afternoon, we hadn't said much, and I wasn't even sure how to fix it. It made it almost worse that Wes acted like nothing had happened. His responses were all friendly and cool; there was a distance to him that I couldn't push through and couldn't figure out.

I finished helping Jack put away the box of training gear and then left him sorting through containers in his study-turned-stock room. I found Wes in the living room, locked in concentration and staring at a chessboard sitting between him and Fee. She looked much more relaxed than he did, and had a smug smile on her face to prove it.

"I'm telling you, it's checkmate," she said, cheerfully.

"It's not. It can't be. Give me another minute," he grumbled.

She laughed. "Take all the time you need but it won't do you any good. Your only hope against me is a full moon."

He glared at her and then caught sight of me in the doorway, his face going carefully blank. Fee turned and smiled. "Tara, how's training going?"

"Fine, I guess." I shrugged and instantly regretted the movement.

"She's doing great," said Jack, coming up behind me and laying a hand on my shoulder.

"He uses that word loosely, I think," I said, trying not to make a face at the soreness the weight of his hand triggered. "Then again, we haven't tried to kill each other yet."

Fee laughed. "Well, that is something."

"You're too hard on yourself," said Jack, settling into his usual chair and propping his feet on the coffee table. "You're two weeks old at something most Hunters would have been learning when they were babies."

Fee nodded. "Jack's right. You have to remember how new you are at this."

"Great, so I'm like the slow kid, the one who got held back in kindergarten," I muttered. I eyed the couch, torn between wanting to get off my feet and not sure if I could get back up again without help. I leaned harder on the doorway instead.

"I think you're doing a little better than that," Fee said.

At my sarcasm, Wes's lips inched up at the corners, giving off a ghost of a smile, and despite my body's exhaustion, my stomach fluttered. I pushed it away, refusing to notice. The past few days with Wes had been beyond frustrating. It had started the first day of my training with Jack. He'd been quiet and distant and closed off, and I'd yet to come up with a good theory as to why. Every time I asked him about it—or anything else—his answer was the same. "Cause business."

I'd even tried bringing up the kiss we'd shared when I'd been doped up on morphine, figuring it would at least throw him off enough to give a real reaction. And for a split second, his eyes had sparkled in amusement, and the wall had come down. Then, just as quickly, it returned, and his expression went carefully blank, and he made up some excuse to leave or make a phone call. A part of me wanted to just let it go and give up on whatever had been beginning between us; but the part that still fluttered when he smiled knew it was impossible to even try.

"You ready?" Wes asked, pulling me out of my thoughts.

"Yeah, sure."

"See you tomorrow, Tara," Jack called.

"Can't wait," I mumbled.

The last thing I heard before I closed the door was Jack's booming laughter.

CHAPTER TWENTY-ONE

WES dropped me at my front door and went to park around the corner. I let myself in and punched in the code for the alarm. The beeping turned shrill and the whole thing went haywire. I mumbled a few words I was glad no one was around to hear and then punched in a different set of numbers. It beeped once more and then fell silent. My mother had reset the password after Julie ... anyway, I kept forgetting and setting it off.

I went straight to my bathroom and turned on the shower. I cranked the water as hot as I could stand it and then leaned my head against the cold tile while the steam filled the space around me. Slowly, I felt my muscles begin to relax and loosen under the constant stream. I was enjoying the perks of a quickly healing body on days like this. Unfortunately, I was apparently so far out of shape that every new training session left me just as sore as the last, and my muscles couldn't keep up. Still, the soreness faded faster than it should.

The only wound that seemed to be healing at a normal human rate was the bite on my arm. I was careful to hold that arm out of the stream of water. The stitches would be ruined if they got wet. At least the oozing had stopped, thanks to the strange homemade salve Jack had given me. And it didn't ache nearly as bad anymore. Fee had said to keep applying the medicine and once the stitches fell out, the healing would speed up and close the wound, just like every other scratch on my body. In the meantime, I was careful to wear long sleeves.

When the hot water began to run cold, I finally shut off the knob and climbed out. I pulled on sweatpants and a long-sleeved Cat in the Hat pajama shirt. I opened the bathroom door to clear the steam off my mirror and ran a comb through my hair. When I was done, I heard my desk chair squeak. I walked out and found Wes at the computer, playing solitaire.

"Hey," I said, crossing to my bed and sinking onto it, carefully. My muscles weren't screaming quite as loudly now, but there was a collective exhale throughout my body as I sank onto the soft mattress.

"Hey." He glanced over and then went back to his game.

I sat there for a minute, feeling awkward in the silence. I pulled my phone out and scrolled through the names. The need for someone to talk to was something I was struggling with. I still felt torn about approaching my mom, knowing it could quite possibly do a lot more harm than good.

She'd finally cornered me early this morning and demanded to know what was going on. She'd used words like *distracted* and *absent* and *preoccupied*. I'd somehow managed to ease her concerns by telling her I was stressing about life stuff, like the breakup with George, and college, and normal teenage dilemmas. I think she bought it. For now.

And telling Sam or even Angela about any of it was not an option. Mostly, I just didn't want to put that kind of stress on the people I cared about. It wasn't fair to them. But the one person I wanted to talk to, the one person who understood everything that was going on, had no interest in speaking to me apparently. At least not about anything that mattered.

My phone rang in my hand. George. I still hadn't seen him or talked to him since his attack, and my concern won out. I decided to answer.

"Hello?"

"Tay, what's up?" He sounded like himself, maybe a little tired.

"How are you? Your mom called me about what happened." I felt Wes's eyes on me, but I stared down at the floor and focused on George's response.

"I'm okay. It wasn't as bad as she made it sound, I'm sure," he said.

In the background, I heard his mother say, "Eighteen stitches isn't bad?"

"George, that's a lot of stitches," I said. "Are you sure you're okay?"

"I'm good. Just been takin' it easy. Mom said I can go back to school tomorrow, though." There was a pause and then he said, "What's been up with you?"

"Not much, um, busy with ... helping my mom out at the store." A pang of guilt shot through me at the lie. Partly because it was George, and there was a time not so long ago that I'd never had to lie, and partly because I just really wanted to talk to someone right now.

He didn't press me for more detail, which meant he believed me. He cleared his throat, and I sensed a change in conversation coming. "So, are you going to the dance tonight?"

"I don't think so. I forgot about it."

"Do you want to go? I mean, you'd have to pick me up, but we could go together. Just as friends," he added, before I could answer.

"George ..."

"We can be friends, Tay."

"I know. I just have a lot going on right now, at home. Things are stressful," I said. Wes was looking at me again, I could feel it.

"Do you want to talk about it?" George asked, in a soft voice.

I hesitated. "Do you ever feel like you've been waiting your entire life for a specific moment when it'll all make sense?" He didn't answer. "Or like you're right on the edge of it all making sense, but you know you don't have all the pieces yet?" Wes's gaze was like pointed arrows.

"Tara, what's going on?" he asked. George's tone was worried.

I sighed. This wasn't going to work. No way could I tell him. He wouldn't even believe me if I did. "Nothing, never mind," I muttered. "Look, I've gotta go. I'm glad you're okay. I'll see you at school." I stole a glance and saw that Wes had gone back to his computer game. Obviously, all he'd cared about was making sure I keep the secret.

I hung up before George could argue and stared down at my phone. I continued to scroll through my list of contacts, knowing without looking that no one on that list was a realistic choice.

I sighed and tossed my phone aside, rolling onto my stomach to stare out the window.

"Can we talk?" I asked, hesitantly, a few minutes later. Wes turned to face me. He gave me a look that said he'd rather not, but he waited without protesting. "Look, I don't know what happened the other day, or why you've stopped talking to me, but it's getting old."

"Okay." He shrugged.

"Okay? That's it. You're not going to offer any kind of explanation?"

"No."

I bit my lip, trying to push down on my irritation. "I just want to make sure we're good. I don't want to be fighting with you when we should be fighting Leo."

Something in his eyes flickered when I mentioned the name and his expression softened. "I know," he said. "We're not fighting. I just have a lot on my mind right now and I think it's best if we keep things ... professional."

"Professional," I repeated, raising my eyebrows.

He nodded.

My eyes narrowed, and even though I was trying to stay calm, I could feel my temper getting the better of me. "So that's how you're going to play it? We need to be professional? Don't you think it's a little late for that? I mean, I don't know what I did to change your mind, but at least don't act like there was never anything going on."

My voice had risen a few octaves by the last part, but I didn't care. The whole situation was grating on me, and I was sick of trying to always smooth things over or decode his mysteriousness. He stared back at me but didn't answer, which only made me more frustrated. To my horror, tears gathered in my eyes, and I blinked them back, hoping he didn't notice. I knew they were angry tears but still ...

I blinked harder, but my eyes only became more watery, until his face blurred out of focus. I turned away, flopping over on my bed, hoping he'd take it as my temper and just go back to his computer game.

"Tara." Wes's voice had gone quiet, and I realized with a sinking feeling he must've noticed the tears.

"I'm done," I said, careful to keep any emotion out of my voice.

I heard the chair creak, and then the mattress sank a little behind me as he sat down. "Tara, I'm sorry. I didn't mean to make you upset," he said.

"Stop. Don't do that."

"Do what?" He looked genuinely confused, which actually made it worse.

"Be nice. You always do that when I finally get fed up and lose it over you being cold or distant or I realize you're keeping something from me. Between your mood swings and this stupid magnet thing between us, I can't keep up. I'm done."

"Tara, I'm sorry—"

I blinked a few more times, finally clearing my vision, and then whirled to look at him. "I said, I'm done. You don't have to apologize. You just have to leave me alone. You can get someone else to guard me, or I can handle it on my own. But with you, with this, I'm finished. Please. Leave."

I jumped up from my bed without waiting for a response, and stalked out of the room and down the stairs. I found my bag near the front door and pulled the *Draven* out and took it into the living room, opening it to a random page and settling on the couch. I stared at the words, but I had no idea what page I was on, or even what chapter. My chest felt heavy and tight; saying the words, telling him to leave, had actually been painful. The thought of removing him from my life left me breathless with a panic that overrode anything Leo could do to me. But I just couldn't take the back and forth anymore. Or the cryptic answers or the lies. He obviously didn't feel the same way about me, anyway, based on his hot and cold—lately, mostly cold—attitude toward me. Then there was the whole magnet issue; what if that was the only reason I felt something for him? What if it was science, based on some physiological response and not real outside of how our cells were programmed? Thinking about that only made me mad again. Being mad was easier; it lessened the ache in my chest.

I waited, but I didn't hear any noises from upstairs. Several minutes passed and still, silence. My curiosity got the better of me, and I set the book aside and crept back to the front entryway, peeking up the staircase. Nothing. I padded quietly up the stairs and peeked into my bedroom. There was Wes, playing solitaire at the computer. Anger speared through me. I couldn't believe he'd just gone back to his game, like nothing had happened, like I hadn't just told him to get out of my house.

He didn't want to leave? That was fine. I would.

I crept back down to the first floor. I went straight to the laundry room and shut the door behind me.

It took me a minute, but I managed to find my black skirt—still in the to-be-washed pile—and brought it up to my face. It didn't smell terrible; it would have to do. I found an off-the-shoulder blouse to go with it, luckily clean, and changed quickly. The only shoes I had downstairs were my ballet flats so I slipped those on and then used my fingers to try and arrange my hair into something that resembled combed in the bathroom mirror. The whole time, I kept glancing toward the stairs or the ceiling, but I still hadn't heard a single noise, and every moment that passed made me more determined to get out of here.

I grabbed my bag and coat and slipped out the sunroom door. There'd be no way to lock the house this way, but I wasn't worried about it. The kind of people that wanted in wouldn't be deterred by a lock, anyway. Wes was proof of that.

I was afraid the sound of my car's engine would alert Wes so the only advantage I had was time. If I could get out of the neighborhood before he got to his car, I had a chance of getting away before he saw which direction I went. So I blew out a breath and turned the key in the ignition, hitting the gas and throwing it into reverse at the same time. The car lurched backward, throwing me forward a little, and then back again as I hit the brakes. I slammed it into gear, stomped the pedal, and took off. I didn't glance back to see if Wes had come out yet. Instead, I concentrated on getting out of the neighborhood and onto a side road as fast as I could.

I felt like a getaway driver in some crime, the way I weaved around corners and turned this way and that, speeding down back roads and side roads and trying to lose a tail. Somehow, though, it must've worked because the Aston Martin did not appear in my rearview.

About twenty minutes into my aimless maze of turns, I ended up in front of my high school. Cars filled the parking spaces in the student lot and I remembered the dance. I checked the clock. It was pretty early still. Maybe I could find Sam or Angela and hang with them. And going stag wasn't the worst thing in the world. I hesitated briefly as I realized George would probably be in there, too, and ready to pounce the moment I walked in. But, right now, I don't think I'd mind so much. It would feel normal, and right now, normal would be nice. Besides, this part of my life seemed to somehow be fading away as my new Hunter life took over, and I was willing to deal with George if it meant getting my old life back, in some small way.

I parked my car in an open space near the back, hoping it would blend in, if Wes somehow got the idea to look for me here. Which, hopefully, he wouldn't. I used my emergency makeup kit I kept in the glove box to smooth over some of the redness in my cheeks, leftover from my temper and the chilly air, and again did what I could to smooth my almost-dry hair into looking like I'd actually brushed it. Then, I headed inside.

Just like any other high school dance, the theme was "crepe paper in the gym," so it was hard to be impressed. The smell of sweat and rubber soles still hung in the air from earlier in the day. But it was dark and someone had strung colored LED lanterns on a couple walls, so everything glowed a little, which at least made it harder to notice the dirty floors. On the dance floor, couples swayed to a cover band version of Taylor Swift's "Love Song." I recognized Sam the quickest, since her dress was by far the shortest, and she was surrounded by at least three guys who looked to be hanging on her every word. I rubbed my arms against a tiny chill and headed that way.

"Tara," she called, when she saw me. "You came." Her smile faltered a little when she saw my plain black skirt and eighties-throwback blouse, but she stepped away from her group of followers to talk to me. "I thought you weren't coming."

I shrugged. "Plans changed."

Her eyes narrowed. "Did something happen between you and that yummy-looking guy? Do we hate him now?"

"No, nothing happened," I said, putting emphasis on the *nothing* part.

Sam gave me an understanding look, still frowning. "Well, he's an idiot. Do you want me to have Eddie pay him a visit?" she asked, gesturing to the stockier of the boys still waiting for her to return.

"No, I'm good," I said, smiling a little. "Have you seen Angela?"

"She was dancing with what's-his-name earlier, but I haven't seen her since then."

"Well, I'm going to wander around and try to find her. I'll let you get back." I gestured to her groupies and she grinned.

"Duty calls."

I made my way through the crowd hovering near the food tables and decided to stick close to the wall, to scan the room easier. I went half the length of the gym without spotting her and sat down on the edge of the bleachers to wait, trying to decide if I should just leave. I'd seen several of my classmates but no one seemed interested in stopping to chat. Maybe coming alone made me look pathetic. Everyone just smiled politely and kept walking.

A high-pitched giggle floated by and I turned towards it in disgust. I knew that laugh anywhere and I was not in the mood today. I expected to find Cindy standing there but when I looked, the space beside me was empty. It took another giggle before I realized it was coming through the bleachers, behind me. Cindy must be back there with someone who didn't mind the threat of a good ol' STD. Gross.

I stood up to leave, but the sound of another laugh stopped me. This one was deeper, definitely male, and all too familiar. I froze and then turned slowly toward the sound. I had to bend down to peek through the slats in the bleachers to see them. It was darker and harder to make out faces all the way against the far wall, but there they were: Cindy Adams locking lips—and other body parts—with George.

Apparently, his wounds were healing nicely, thanks to all the attention her hands were giving his body.

I watched them in shock, disgusted but unable to look away since I couldn't believe what I was seeing. Cindy had her back to me, and her lips were stuck to George's so hard, it looked like she might be suctioning the life out of him. She pulled back, smiling and giggling a little. That was when George noticed me. His eyes widened and he pushed on Cindy's shoulders, trying to get a better look at me. I was surprised by the amount of pain I felt as his frozen expression transformed to one of instant regret.

Over these past few weeks, I'd missed our friendship, but other than that, it felt like my feelings for him had faded. I realized, though they might have diminished, those feelings weren't completely gone. The wrenching pain of betrayal washed over me. It must've shown in my face because George's expression softened; next to him, Cindy's eyes glinted with an evil satisfaction as she finally figured out what was happening.

That was it.

Time to get out of here.

I kept my eyes down, dodging dress shoes and hem lines. I heard George call my name once, but it was faint and it didn't come again. I made it to the parking lot without knocking anyone over and then ran for my car. The tears didn't start until I was safely inside but as soon as I'd shut the door, they welled up and overflowed onto my cheeks and all I could do was let them come.

CHAPTER TWENTY-TWO

WHEN the worst was over, and I could actually see well enough to drive, I left. I wasn't sure where to go, but I knew if I stayed here, someone would find me. If not George, then Sam or Angela—and I didn't want to face any of them. I'd texted my mother earlier that I'd decided to go to the dance after all and she'd told me to have fun and she'd see me at home. She was probably there now, which meant Wes was gone—finally. But I didn't want my mom to see me like this, either.

I weaved through some back roads for a while, still unable to decide on a destination. I came to the intersection that would either lead me home or back through my maze of turns. At the stop sign, I swiped my hand across my cheek and sniffled, trying to pick a direction.

The sound of a racing engine reached my ears, and I glanced up to my rearview. A car came speeding up behind me and screeched to a halt, inches from my bumper. I watched as the driver's side door opened, and a figure stepped out. I couldn't see him until he stepped into the glare of the car's headlights, but I already knew.

Wes strode up to my window and beat on it with the side of his fist, his eyes wild, his expression fierce. I hesitated, wondering how far I'd make it if I tried punching the gas. Not far, I was sure. I sighed and unlocked the door. Before I could even reach the handle, Wes had wrenched my door open and pulled me to my feet.

"What the hell were you thinking? Where have you been?" he demanded, his hands squeezing my shoulders. "Do you have any idea how stupid that was? Anything could've happened to you. What if I hadn't found you first?"

His questions were rhetorical, I think, but I attempted an answer, anyway. "I went to the dance," I said, trying to sound angry and sure of myself. "I told you, I'm done."

"Well, I don't care if you're done or over it or whatever. I have a job to do, and you're making it impossible!"

"Well, how about I make it easy for you? You're fired. Job over. Leave. Me. Alone." My voice broke a little at the end but he didn't seem to notice. His eyes were still wild and a little unfocused and even though he stood only inches from me, I don't think he really saw me. My words only seemed to make him angrier.

"Stop saying that." His fingers increased their pressure on my shoulders, and I winced. It probably wouldn't have hurt if my muscles weren't still sore from training, but just that small amount of pressure was enough to cause a shot of pain.

My reaction seemed to finally get through to him because he instantly released my arms and stepped back. He blinked a few times and seemed to really be noticing me for the first time.

"Sorry, I didn't mean to hurt you. I—are you okay?"

"I'm fine," I mumbled, swiping at my cheeks again and trying to figure out a way to just end the conversation so I could get out of here.

He must have finally noticed how shaken I looked because he stepped closer again, this time with concern. "Something happened. What is it?"

"I'd like to go home now," I said, keeping my eyes down.

His entire body sagged and the energy seemed to seep out of him all at once, like a deflated balloon. "Fair enough, but we need to talk."

I glanced up at him, warily. "About what?"

"Everything you said earlier. And other things."

"What things?"

"I'd rather talk about it at home."

"Well, I wouldn't. I—" I halted, midsentence, suddenly over-whelmed by the tingling shiver that ran up my spine and spilled over into my arms and legs. "Werewolf," I whispered, but Wes was already scanning the darkness for movement.

"Get in the car, Tara," said Wes. He stepped in front of me, blocking me from the coming danger. He continued to stare into the darkness of the trees that lined the road.

"No, I'm going to stay out here and help you," I argued.

"We're not staying. Now get in the car."

I started to move toward my car.

"No. My car," he said.

"I can't just leave it here."

"Yes, you can. We'll get it later."

A rustle of leaves sounded from somewhere in the forest, growing steadily louder.

"Dammit," Wes muttered. "You're driving."

"Me? Why?"

"Stop asking questions and just go. I'll be right behind you."

I didn't have time to question him further because in the next second, a dark gray wolf leapt through the trees, aiming straight for me. Wes jumped forward to meet it, changing to wolf form in midair.

Scraps of fabric rained down, but I barely noticed. I stared at the wolf that was Wes as he tackled the other one, watching them tumble, a tangle of teeth and fur. Wes was easily twice the size of the other Were, and his reddish-brown fur glinted in the moonlight. He came out easily on top and pinned the attacking Were with his paws. Then he looked over at me, and his eyes flashed.

"Go!" he said. "The keys are in the ignition. Don't go home. Follow the GPS."

I nodded mechanically and ran to his car. It was still running and the GPS system glowed on the dashboard, telling me to turn left. Through the windshield I could see Wes's sharp teeth as he snapped at the other wolf's throat. It managed to twist away and get free and it took off, racing for the car. Wes was on him in half a second and drove him back, out of my way. Snarling and grunting came in through the open car window, making the hairs on my arms stand on end. Every part of me itched to get into the fight.

I threw the car into reverse and backed up enough to maneuver the Aston Martin between my own car and the two wolves fighting it out on the other side of the road. I hesitated for only a second, hating
the thought of leaving Wes there, but then I punched the gas. As I passed, the attacking wolf twisted his head around and looked at me.

"Dirty Bloods," he spat. Then Wes's teeth made contact with his throat, and I looked away as I sped off.

I had no idea where the GPS was leading me but I followed, knowing its destination was the only place Wes would be able to find me. And no matter how angry I might be, I had to know he was okay. The directions it gave led me to a residential area not far from my house, behind a shopping center, mostly townhouses and small apartment buildings.

The computerized voice sent me to a small apartment on a side road that dead-ended at the parking lot. I could hear the buzz of the highway on the other side of a treed border.
I wasn't sure whether to go inside or who else might be there, so I parked the car and locked the doors, slouching in my seat to wait it out.

Chapter Twenty-Three

THE minutes ticked by. It was getting late. My mom would start to wonder about me soon. But I still had to know if Wes was okay. At a sudden tap at the window, I jumped and bit back a scream. Wes stood outside. His hair was disheveled and not in the carefully styled way I'd always seen on him. He wore baggy jeans and running shoes and a half-zipped windbreaker. He looked ... sloppy, compared to his usual look. I hated that I found it completely sexy.

I pushed the car door open and climbed out. "What happened?"

"Not here. Come on." He turned and headed for the apartment building, sidestepping the front entrance altogether and turning the corner that led around the back. A narrow sidewalk provided a path and I scrambled to keep up.

I searched for any sign of injury on him as I followed him around the building. I couldn't see any, though, and his movements were sure. I started to relax a little.

Around back was a wooden staircase that led up to a second-floor entrance. It creaked under our weight. Wes pulled a key out of his pocket and unlocked the door, stepping inside and holding it open for me to enter. I did, hesitantly. Wes closed and locked the door and then flipped a switch. An overhead light came on, flooding the space of a loft-style apartment. The living room and kitchen were open and flowed into each other. The sparse furniture made it feel spacious and bigger than it was. On the far left was a set of double French doors and tucked in the right corner was an open doorway, revealing a bedroom beyond.

Wes kicked off his shoes and headed for the fridge. He pulled out a bottle of water and gulped it down. His chest was bare underneath the windbreaker and I remembered the pieces of clothing that had been ripped away when he'd changed.

"Where did you get the clothes?" I asked, still standing near the front door.

"I keep a spare set in the woods near your house. I stopped off to change. Sorry it took so long."

"Is the wolf ...?"

"He's alive. But he won't be back for a while. I think I broke his leg. And he probably has a torn windpipe."

"You're okay?"

"I'm fine," he assured me, swallowing more water.

I wandered toward him and the bar that separated the living space from the kitchen. "Where are we?" I finally asked.

"My apartment."

My pulse sped up a little and my breath hitched. For a moment, I forgot all about the fact that Wes had just fought another Werewolf for me, or that I was mad at him, or that I'd caught George making out with my mortal enemy in the school gym. All I could think about was that this was Wes's apartment, his private space, and we were alone.

I realized Wes was giving me an odd look so I did my best to smooth my expression. "So, what now?"

Instead of answering, Wes set his water on the counter and came around to stand in front of me. He stared down at me for a long moment and then, slowly, his arms came around me so that his hands were tangled in my hair. He lowered his face until it was inches away from mine and then stopped, watching me with a question in his eyes. I held my breath and waited. When I didn't push him away, or move to stop him, he closed the distance and pressed his lips to mine.

Heat coursed through me, and I felt my muscles go deliciously soft. Wes's arms tightened around me and he stroked my hair, deepening the kiss. I could feel his body relaxing against me. It was satisfying to know he was affected, too, and I wrapped my arms around his neck, pulling him closer, not sure how long it would last and not wanting it to end. I could smell him again, woods and wind. His breath tasted tangy, and there was a hint of animal still in him that was both exciting and scary.

Eventually, he pulled away, but he kept his hands on my hair and face. He stared down at me with an intensity that took my breath away.

"You don't know how long I've been wanting to do that," he said, his voice gravelly.

"When can we do it again?"

He smiled at that, but it was sad. "Soon, I hope. I mean, if you still want to. There are some things I should tell you first." He took my hand and led me to the couch, pulling me down next to him. When he turned to face me again, the smile was gone, but the sadness still lingered.

"What is it?" I asked, a heaviness forming in my stomach.

Wes took a deep breath and I braced myself, knowing whatever it was, wasn't good news. "When you left, I tried to follow you, but you were already gone by the time I got to my car. I called Jack and Fee and had them search for a while, too. Mainly because they can sense you and I can't. Anyway, I kept driving around, looking for your car in parking lots and gas stations, but, of course, nothing. All I could think was that something horrible was happening to you ..." He squeezed his eyes shut against whatever mental image still tormented him. "Vera called. She said she'd 'seen' something. Just a flash, but it wasn't good."

"What was it?"

"It was you," he said in a grim voice. "Lying in the middle of that intersection, with that Werewolf from earlier standing over you. Your blood was everywhere. You weren't moving."

"Oh," I said, letting it sink in. I understood why Wes had made me leave without him.

"I didn't even know if I would get there in time," he said

quietly.

Neither of us said anything for a minute. He still looked pained, and I could tell he was berating himself for the whole thing.

"I'm sorry," I said.

He looked surprised. "For what?"

"If I hadn't snuck out, this wouldn't have happened."

"True. Well, not tonight, anyway. But eventually, yes, it would've. And it will again. That's the other thing I need to tell you."

"Okay," I said, trying to read the strange look he wore.

"Vera saw ... something else. She's been seeing it for a while now. It's about you." He stopped.

"Like that day at Jack's? The vision you wouldn't tell me about?"

He nodded. "It started as just a feeling, I guess. A feeling that someone new was coming. And then she started seeing images. They were blurry at first but got clearer as the time got closer. She said she didn't know when, but a girl was coming, and she would be a part of our group. An important part. A leader who would finally bring peace. She said the girl would be a Hunter but nothing like we'd ever seen before. The problem was she didn't know who the girl was or when she would come. So, we all sort of forgot about it. But the other day, when she met you at The Cause meeting ...she recognized you ..."

"As the girl from her vision," I finished for him, though my voice held more than a little skepticism.

"Yes."

I shook my head. "I think she has me mistaken for someone else."

"I thought so, too, at first. Or at least, I wanted to think so. But then I saw the face in Vera's visions."

"You saw them? How?"

Wes took a deep breath, held it, and then released it in a rush of words. "I read it, in her mind. I can read minds."

"You can read minds?" I repeated, full of disbelief. Then again, why shouldn't I believe it, after everything else I'd seen?

He nodded.

It took me a minute to understand where this might be going. "Like, anybody's mind?"

"Only on a full moon, but yes, anybody's mind. I don't know why. It's always been like that."

The admission brought on a whole new list of questions, but I tried to stick to the subject at hand. "Okay, so you saw her vision and recognized me?"

"Yes."

"And I'm supposed to be this big, bad leader?"

"Something like that."

"Huh. What does that even mean? Is that why they keep looking at me like they're waiting for me to turn water into wine or something?" He didn't answer. "Is this what you've been keeping from me this whole time?"

"Yes. Vera said it would scare you off to tell you everything. She insisted we needed to let you come into it naturally. So we all had to promise not to tell you. I'm sorry. I've wanted to, I just … didn't know how."

"It's easy. You just say it," I said, snapping the words.

"It's not easy, especially when you've been ordered to keep quiet. Jack is the alpha in our pack, and when he gives an order, you don't disobey."

"But you did. Just now." I wasn't feeling angry so much as stubborn. He could've told me any time. Instead, he kept it to himself and I looked like an idiot.

"And I could get kicked out of The Cause for it, too," he said. "It's a serious thing to disobey an alpha's order."

I didn't say anything. I couldn't think of anything *to* say. Of all the things he could've admitted to, this wasn't what I was expecting. Wes reached for my hand but I moved away. I needed time to think, to process what he was saying, and I couldn't do that with him touching me. I rose and wandered the room, not really pacing but unable to stay still.

I stopped in front of a massive bookshelf against the far wall. It held an even mix of books and music, and I scanned the titles of paperbacks, distracted. There was a wide range, from Westerns to documentaries. Even Mark Twain was represented.

"There's more," he said.

Of course there was. I didn't turn. "What is it?"

"The comment Leo made about our blood and its power, I think you guessed correctly. I think it's possible that you might be—" he broke off, and his voice dropped to a whisper, "like me."

I turned, wide eyed, to face him. "You mean dirty—" I stopped, knowing he didn't like that term. "One of each?" I shook my head. "But you said he was messing with us. That you don't trust anything he says."

"Not usually, but ..." He looked away, staring at some spot on the far wall.

"But?"

"He has it out for you, bad. It doesn't add up. I mean, you're new and not even sure how involved you want to be in this world. But he's convinced you're top priority and need to be taken out." I winced. "Sorry. But I just don't understand why else he could be so focused on you. Or how he found you in the first place."

"So because Leo wants me dead, Vera must be right—I'm some important Hunter leader come to rescue everyone?"

Wes sighed. "I can understand it's a lot to take in, but I also thought it was time to be honest with you. Earlier, when you were talking to George ... I just didn't want to keep lying anymore. I want it to be me who you talk to about this stuff."

"So do I," I said. I took a step toward him. His expression clouded, the way it did when he held something back. I stopped. "There's something else." He didn't answer and refused to meet my gaze. "More visions of death? Or some huge destiny?"

He stared down at the floor. "Destiny. That was the word she used, too."

"Who?"

He looked up at me. His eyes had darkened to a muddy brown. "Vera. She said you were my destiny."

"What do you mean?" I asked, trying to ignore the chest fluttering his words caused. Something invisible sprang to life, coating the air, thickening it. It made it harder to breathe.

"She told me she keeps seeing you and me, together, leading

The Cause, and finally bringing the two races together."

"Like, as a couple?" I asked. Without meaning to, I held my breath while I waited for him to answer. I felt hot and cold, excited and terrified.

"Yes."

"Oh." I tried to keep my voice even and resist the urge to jump up and down or something equally embarrassing. Suddenly, Vera's vision wasn't sounding so bad. Then I realized Wes didn't look nearly as overjoyed as I felt. "You don't want that?"

"It's not that." He smiled. "I want that very much," he added quietly.

Relief flooded through me so hard, I felt light headed. As if to prove his words, Wes rose and walked over to me. He tugged my hands free from where I'd clasped them around my arms and pulled me into him, wrapping his arms around me and stroking my hair.

"I owe you an apology, though," he said, his lips so close to my ear, I could feel his breath on my neck. "I was irritated at having my future decided for me by some vision. I was stubborn and unwilling to admit I was falling for you, even when I already knew I had. I kept trying to push you away, along with my feelings for you. It didn't work, obviously, but I am sorry because I ended up hurting you."

I pulled away and lifted my head so I could look up at him. "That's the reason for all the mood swings? Vera's visions?"

"Yes. I'm sorry."

I wanted to let him off the hook, I really did, but it still made me mad that he'd kept something so big from me. Whether I believed Vera's visions or not, it made all the pieces fit, at least about Wes's behavior these last few weeks. "You should've told me."

"I know."

"Vera can't, I mean, this pull we feel to each other—did she do that?"

"No." He shook his head. "She can't do something like that. The pull is real. If I'm right about you, it probably has to do with both of us being mixed."

"Like our body's sensors don't feel danger around the other?"

"Something like that."

I thought about that. It would be nice to believe it was all science. Then, maybe, I wouldn't have to feel like it was some sort of confusing, made-up attraction. I looked back at Wes. His eyes had lightened again, but his brows were creased with worry. Then I remembered the apology he'd offered. I'd yet to accept. "I forgive you."

He smiled, and his features smoothed into relief. "You seem to be taking all this vision stuff pretty well."

I shrugged. It wasn't that it didn't bother me; I was just too busy enjoying the upside, the part where Wes was my destiny. I didn't really want to think about the rest of it. Or whether I even believed it. "I guess I'm just glad to finally know what everyone's been keeping from me. Not that I really believe what Vera saw, but, if I did, well ...you can't mess with destiny," I said.

"I guess not," he agreed, bringing his hand up to brush a lock of hair out of my face. His gaze held mine, burning with intensity. The room seemed to blur and disappear until all that was left was him. His smell, his arms around me, his chiseled jaw. And those eyes. They'd gone dark again, a lovely shade of bark brown.

"Tara, I love you," he said.

"I love you, too" I whispered, breathless. Then, I put aside visions and war and peace, as I pressed my lips to his.

His kisses were gentle at first, like our mouths were getting to know one another. Then the heat began, winding its way through my insides. I pulled him tighter against me, needing to feel more of him. Everywhere our bodies touched, was heat. He deepened the kiss, drawing it out, and slipping his tongue into my mouth. I decided then and there that it didn't matter what Vera envisioned, from here on out. As long as I got to be with Wes, just like this.

I barely felt my feet touching the hardwood floor, or moving, for that matter, but somehow we ended up on the couch. His kisses were fast now, frenzied, reminding me of the animal that lived somewhere inside him. My breath came quicker, sucking in air between the pressure of his lips on mine. His hands left my hair and traveled down, coming to rest on my hips. I felt like I might explode.

That was the moment he suddenly eased back. His lips left mine, and he pulled away, removing his hands from my hips and bringing them back to my face. His expression was dark and intense; he'd never looked more gorgeous than this moment.

"Tara," he said.

I sighed, because with that one word, a semblance of reality hit. "My mom will be worried," I said.

He nodded, and reluctantly began to disentangle our limbs and get up from the couch. As soon as I realized what he was doing, I grabbed him and pulled him back down. His body fell back onto mine, and I held his shirt to keep him from trying it again. I had no intention of leaving.

"Tara, your mom," he warned, but he didn't move to get up again.

"Can't we just have one night with no one else dictating our destiny?"

He smiled and I grabbed for my phone. I sent a quick text to my mom, letting her know I was spending the night with Angela and then quickly powered it off so she couldn't argue. I knew it was risky; my mom could always call Angela's house to verify, but right now I didn't care. I was here, with Wes, alone, and he loved me.

CHAPTER TWENTY-FOUR

SPENDING the night with Wes was almost enough to make me forget about the other half of Vera's visions or Wes's suspicions about my mixed blood. Almost. My mind kept wandering back to it but before I even had a chance to voice my worries, I would feel Wes's eyes on me again, full of assurance and love, and my fears would fade.

Unfortunately, morning came too soon, and I knew I had to get home. I turned my phone on and was glad to see I only had one missed message. It was a text from my mother, a reply to the alibi I'd given her. I scanned it with a sinking feeling. It read: "Come home immediately." The weird thing was, the time stamp said it had been sent in the middle of the night.

"What is it?" Wes asked, noticing my expression.

"I don't know, but I think I better get home."

"Give me a minute," he said, before disappearing into the bathroom.

I listened to water running in the sink and tried to figure out what was so important that my mother had been up in the middle of the night texting me to come home. Especially when she hadn't left any other messages. If she'd somehow discovered I wasn't with Angela, she would've freaked out and there definitely would've been more of an attempt to contact me. Like police. And a county-wide manhunt.

I got dressed quickly, changing out of the oversized shirt Wes had given me to sleep in, and back into the clothes I'd worn last night. I wished I had something else to wear, but at least my mom hadn't seen me leave in them yesterday, so hopefully she wouldn't know I was doing some sort of walk of shame—not that anything had happened. There'd been a moment where I thought it might.

It was after I'd texted my mother. We'd been kissing and Wes's hand had found its way to my hip again, squeezing me there. My breath had caught a little and I waited but slowly his hand had inched back up to my face and hair and after a few more minutes, he'd pulled away to catch his breath, mumbling something about "protecting my virtue, as well as my life."

I'd snickered at that until I'd realized he was totally serious. I wasn't sure if I found it completely outdated and ridiculous, or endearing. Maybe a little of both.

"Do you think she knows I lied to her?" I asked worriedly once we were in the car. Wes was taking me to pick up my car from where we'd left it the night before.

"I don't know."

"Do you think something's wrong? What if Leo—"

"Not possible," he said, shaking his head. "The patrol schedule includes your house. I told Jack I'd found you, but I didn't tell him you didn't go home, so there would've been someone nearby all night."

"Okay, good." I blew out a breath, trying to feel reassured by his explanation. But the closer we got, the worse I felt.

By the time we got to my car, I was jittery and all nerves. "Can you come with me?" I asked.

"Absolutely. I'll follow you back and be nearby. Just call me when you're done."

"Okay," I agreed.

I got out and walked to my car, digging for my keys. I could hear Wes following me over. I unlocked my door and told myself it was no big deal, just my mother being her normal, OCD self. Wes put a hand on my arm, and I turned back to him. Without a word, he wrapped his arms around me and pressed his lips to my forehead, holding me that way until I relaxed. Finally, he pulled away to look at me. "See you in a bit."

I nodded and got in.

Wes followed me home, and I felt better seeing his car in my rearview the entire way. The text was probably no big deal, I told myself. My mom probably couldn't sleep and had seen how messy my room was and gotten ticked off. Or maybe she hadn't gotten my text before falling asleep and had woken up wondering where I was. Whatever it was, it was easily explained, and I felt better knowing that even if she was mad at me, she was safe.

I turned onto my street, parting ways with Wes as he continued farther down to park in his usual hiding place. I'd almost reached my driveway when I noticed a black Mercedes parked at the curb directly in front of my house. It looked strangely familiar. Probably some friend of a neighbor or something.

"Mom?" I called out, closing the door behind me and dropping my bag in the entryway. "I'm home."

No answer came and I wandered through the empty rooms, searching. My mother's muffled voice came from the den, and I hurried toward the sound.

"... still doesn't mean your visions are true," she said, her voice hard.

I stopped short in the doorway, spotting my mother, and feeling the impact of her words, at the same time. In the chair across from her sat Vera. Surprise and dread and panic coursed through me as they both rose to face me.

"Tara, come in here, please. We need to talk." My mother's eyes were puffy and glassy.

All the blood drained away from my face and I turned to glare at Vera. I couldn't believe this. Did she think her visions of me gave her the right to come here and dump it all on my mom, expecting her to accept it, just like that? Obviously, my mom was ... well, there was no telling what my mom was ...

"What are you doing here?" I demanded, my hands balling into fists at my sides.

"Tara," my mother said.

I ignored her and stared at Vera. "You had no right to come here," I said, through clenched teeth. "Or to tell her like this." I looked back at my mother again. "Mom, whatever she told you, I can explain. It's—"

"Tara, I called her," my mother said.

"What?" I took a step back and, for the first time since I'd walked in, really looked at my mother. She watched me with a strained expression; she almost seemed to be hugging herself, her hands cupped around each shoulder, her knuckles white with tension.

"You need to come in here and sit down," she said.

I complied, mainly because I was completely lost now, and tried to understand what was really going on. Vera still hadn't said anything, but she sat when I did. My mother remained standing, looking down at me with a tight frown.

"I was straightening up last night, after I got your text," she paused and her expression grew darker. "But we'll come back to that in a minute. Anyway, I was cleaning and putting things away, and I guess you forgot to hide it again before you left."

She gestured to the coffee table in front of me and I looked down. The *Draven* sat on top of the pile of magazines my mom usually kept there. Well, crap. Had I left it out? I couldn't remember.

"Where did you find this?" I blurted, without thinking.

My mother's eyes widened. "That's your response? No explanation, just wondering how I found out? Oh my goodness, I can't do this." She threw her hands up and wandered a few paces away, pressing her fingertips to her forehead.

Vera cleared her throat. "Elizabeth, may I?"

My mother waved a hand, without turning, in a gesture to go ahead.

Vera turned back to me and I purposely hardened my expression, still not convinced she wasn't to blame for all of this. "Tara, your mother found the *Draven* by accident. She wasn't snooping, from what I understand, if that makes any difference. And when she realized what it was, she called me."

"She called you?" I repeated, skeptical.

Vera nodded. "She and I knew each other many years ago. I didn't even know she lived here until last night when she called. It's no wonder I couldn't get a clear sense about you. Then again, it finally made sense, when I realized what you were ..." She trailed off, lost in her own thoughts and I tensed, sure she was going to go into something about a vision of destiny. I could NOT handle that right now.

After a few seconds, she blinked and gave a forced smile. "But I'm getting ahead of myself. The point is, your mother called me. Not the other way around, and she already had a pretty good idea of what was going on before I got here. I was actually able to reassure
her that you were not alone in all this and, in fact, being made quite safe."

"The Cause is not safe, Vera," my mother said, dryly. She was still standing across the room, arms folded, watching my expression with scrutiny.

The thing was, she was calm. In any other situation, my mother would've been flipping—
pacing the house, gulping coffee, cleaning out cupboards, yelling. But no, with this, she just stood there, like it was inconvenient but not unexpected news of epic proportions. That was my first clue.

"Okay, wait a minute," I said, putting up a hand when Vera tried to go on. I turned to my mother. "You mean to tell me, you knew that I was a Hunter?"

My mother and Vera shared a look, and then my mother wandered back toward where I sat, resignation heavy on her face. She stopped just behind the empty chair across from me. Her eyes met mine, her jaw set. "Yes. I knew."

"And you kept it from me, all this time?"

She sighed heavily, but her gaze didn't waver. "Yes."

I shook my head. "I don't believe this," I said, to no one in particular. Partly because I couldn't believe she'd been keeping it from me and partly because I felt like I should've seen it. It felt so obvious now, in this moment, with Vera sitting beside her, and the calmness with which she admitted it. Images flashed in my mind, bits and pieces really, but they all clicked into place for me—pieces of the puzzle. Her incessant worrying and annoying overprotectiveness, the elaborate locks and security systems ... Even her OCD cleaning habits made sense, a product of the stress of living on the run. I felt like an idiot. It made me angry at myself, which, in turn, made me angry at her.

"I think I deserve an explanation," I said.

She shot Vera a look. Vera nodded, and my mother's shoulders drooped slightly. I got the impression she was hoping for a way out of telling me the truth—again.

She came around and perched on the edge of the chair, back stiff, fingers fidgeting with each other. "All right, Tara. You do deserve the truth, so here it is." I watched in stony silence as she smoothed out an invisible wrinkle in her pants. "You should know that my life was a lot different before you came along. I was young, not much older than you, actually, and idealistic. Believe it or not, I was an activist for The Cause."

"You worked for The Cause?" I asked, eyebrows raised. Somehow I just couldn't picture my scaredy-cat mother as an outspoken politician.

She nodded. "It was something I believed in very strongly. And I wasn't afraid to speak out about it. But then, some things happened, right after you were born. It became more and more dangerous for your father and me—"

"Wait, so Dad knew? Does that mean he was a Hunter?"

"Yes, your father knew, but, Tara, I'm the Hunter," she said, giving me a meaningful look.

At her words, I felt the first trickle of unease over the thoughts I'd been pushing away since last night. "Then Dad was human?"

She didn't really answer, except to continue her story. It reminded me of when Wes had told me about his parents and the script he seemed to have to follow, just to get the words out. "When I met your father, he was already involved with The Cause. Their mission and the danger were exciting to me, and it pulled me in."

I tried to picture my mother being the type to welcome danger, to rush at it. The image wouldn't come. I kept listening.

"It wasn't until after you were born," she went on, "that the danger became real to me. Especially after word got out about you." She teared up, and I could see her struggling to keep herself composed, but I refused to give her a reprieve. I needed to hear what was next too badly to let her off the hook just yet.

"What do you mean, especially after word about me? Does that mean Dad knew what you were? What I was?"

She nodded. Her eyes were watery and threatened to spill over. "He knew because he was part of that world, too. He was a Werewolf, Tara."

Chapter Twenty-Five

I stared at her, more surprised than I should've been after what Wes had said, and Leo before him. In a way, I'd seen it coming; I'd just ignored it. I thought of what Wes had said about Vera's visions. "A Hunter, but unlike any we'd ever seen before ..."

I looked back at my mother just as the tears finally spilled over onto her cheeks. She sniffled once and impatiently brushed them away. "Sorry, I've never had to say all this out loud."

Despite my anger, I felt a rush of compassion. I was still angry. Definitely still angry, but she'd obviously done what she did to protect me. And she'd sacrificed everything, including her own family to do it. Whether I agreed with her decisions or not, I knew her heart had been in the right place. I tried to see it from her perspective, and realized I couldn't imagine the kind of pain she'd been in to have to make this kind of decision. She'd lost her husband, her sense of security, and done the only thing she thought she could do to protect the one thing she had left.

"I get it," I said finally.

My mother looked up at me; her red-rimmed eyes were wide with surprise. "You do?"

"Yeah, I mean, you did what you thought was best. And you kept me safe. So I get it. It doesn't mean I like it."

Her expression turned relieved. "I've been worried about how you would feel about me keeping this from you. Then, when Julie was killed ..."

"You knew it was a Werewolf," I said. I remembered her telling me to stay inside, how she'd been changing the alarm codes every other day.

"Yes." She reached for a tissue out of the box on the end table and dabbed around her eyes. Vera, who'd been silent through the entire exchange, sat still as stone. My fingers played absently with a loose strand in the hem of my skirt. No one said anything. It felt awkward.

My mother finished pulling herself together and set the tissue on the arm of her chair. She rose and wandered to the open space on the rug, to pace. She was obviously keyed up. It was frustrating that I didn't even know what to feel right now. I could be angry. That was easy. And I had good reason. She'd kept this from me my entire life. But I also felt bad for her, in a way. Whatever she'd been through had changed her. She was a completely different person than the one my father had known.

"So, now what?" I asked, breaking the silence.

She was still pacing, not even looking up as she talked. "Now we figure out what to do. I mean, obviously you have to break ties with The Cause, and then we should move—"

I cut her off. "Wait, what?"

She stopped and looked at me. "Tara, The Cause is dangerous. Add to that what Vera told me about Leo ... We can't stay here."

"Yes, we can. Jack has the group watching the house to keep us safe until we can find Leo and deal with him." I could feel my head spinning a little with anxiety and the speed of her planning.

She froze in place and narrowed her eyes at me. "Did you just say 'deal with him'? You can't deal with him. It's Leo. He'll kill everyone you know or have ever said hello to in the hallway at school. Then, and only then, will he come for you. He's strong and he's powerful and he's patient. Not to mention completely crazy. You cannot *deal with him*. We need to leave." By the time she was finished, her hands had fallen to her sides and were balled into fists.

"You sound like you know him."

"All too well," she agreed. She went back to her pacing. I waited for her to say more, but she didn't.

I felt angry heat rise on the back of my neck, spreading to my cheeks. She was treating me like I was still the helpless baby she'd run away with, incapable of doing anything to protect myself.

"Well?" I demanded. "Are you going to tell me how you know him? Or are you just going to keep lying to me?"

She glanced over at me, and something in my expression made her stop. Her shoulders drooped. "He's your uncle, Tara. That's how I know him." I stared at her, mouth agape. Not the answer I'd been expecting. She went on. "He's your father's brother. When I ran away with you, I changed our last names, even got new paperwork. Your grandmother helped with that. Our real last name, your father's last name, is DeLuca. So, yes, I know Leo. And he apparently knew about you, too. We can't run, not if he's already found us."

"Okay, so we're related? I know family can be annoying, but they don't usually try to outright murder each other."

My mother wasn't amused. "He's been searching, Tara. Don't you see that? He's obviously been looking for us all these years, and now that he's found us ... This is not a joke."

"You don't think I know that? I've been the one dealing with it these past few weeks. Not you. So don't talk to me like I don't know the stakes, Mother."

"That will change. I'm going to deal with it."

"Why? Why do you think you can do a better job of dealing with it than I can?"

"There's a lot you don't understand, Tara. And I can't take the time to explain it all to you right now. There's too much to do and we don't have much time. We're past the point of leaving, I think." She didn't even give me a chance to respond. Instead, she turned to Vera. "Make the call. I don't have time for anything else at the moment."

"I'll call right now," Vera said, rising from her chair and pulling a tiny phone from her pocket. She strode out into the hall as she held it to her ear.

"Make what call?" I asked.

"Jack and Fee. Vera suggested I meet them and let them continue to help protecting the house. With my knowledge this time," she added.

"So we're not leaving?"

She sighed. "There's no time. But I will have to call your grandmother and figure out something, long-term. When was the last time you saw Leo?"

My head spun. My mother was like a windstorm ever changing in its direction. She'd been so set on moving, but now she'd changed her mind. My mother was nothing if not practical. Leaving outweighed the risk of staying.

Right now, I didn't care about *why*. We weren't leaving, running to some far off city to hide out, with no Cause and no Wes. We would stay, and we would fight. Though I wasn't sure if the last part fit into my mother's plan or not.

"Tara? When was the last time?" she prompted.

"Monday, on the way home from school, I sort of ran into him." No need to worry her further with the details, like almost dying from being bitten.

She nodded, absently, her eyes darting around, not really settling in any one place. "Vera said something about that. Said he told you that you didn't deserve the power of your blood," she said.

"He's talking about me being a Dirty Blood, isn't he?"

Her jaw hardened. "Where did you hear that word?"

I shrugged. "Some friends told me. *They* were honest with me about my history," I said, my voice taking on an edge to match hers. I could afford to be angry again, now that I knew we were staying.

Her mouth tightened. "Uh-huh, and does this friend have a name? Or something to do with the reason you were out all night?" I opened my mouth to argue, but she put her hand up to stop me. "And don't say you were with Angela because I know you weren't. She called right after I found the *Draven*."

"Did you say anything to her?"

"Of course not." My mother gave me a scolding look. "Give me some credit, Tara. I've been doing this a lot longer than you have."

"Right. You've been lying to your own daughter. Angela

should be a piece of cake," I muttered.

I expected a reaction but none came. My mother continued to stand, expressionless, obviously waiting for me to answer the question. I thought about lying, but I knew Vera would rat me out eventually. I could faintly hear her talking from down the hall. She wasn't going anywhere anytime soon. I sighed. "His name is Wes. He's part of The Cause." Then I realized something. "You might have known his parents, actually. They were in The Cause, too. Sebastian and Audrey St. John."

My mother blanched and seemed to stop breathing. "Wesley St. John? You've been seeing *him*?" She stared at me like she'd never seen me before and then shook her head, hard. "The only other mixed blood on the face of the earth, and you somehow found him. Great."

I bit my tongue to keep from muttering some nasty retort about not so much finding him as him *saving* me, more than once, which is more than I could say for her. I was really trying to hold it together. "I take it you knew them."

"Yes. They were killed the same night as your father."

I stiffened. "But you said he died in a house fire."

"It wasn't a lie. Entirely. There was a fire the night of the attack. They used flamethrowers to break the windows and draw us outside."

"So you lied. Again." My fingers let go of the loose thread they'd been fidgeting with, and my hands balled into fists. I was losing hold of my temper. She kept dropping bombs, and adding my dad to the list of lies pushed me over the edge. It seemed disrespectful, somehow, to his memory that I'd believed he'd died in a normal—okay, well, normal compared to the truth—house fire. How was I supposed to trust anything she said now?

"Tara, there's just a lot that you don't understand about this. You need to tell me exactly what happened when you saw Leo. Everything he said and did."

I crossed my arms over my chest, my hands still fisted. "No."

She blinked. "What?"

"Why should I? You haven't told me a single bit of truth my entire life until now, and you seem to think you can just sit me down and offer up an excuse or two, and I'll accept it and forgive you and get on with my day? Well, it's not going to be that easy." I stood up and headed for the door.

"You're no match for him, Tara," called my mother. When I didn't stop, she added, "He's responsible for the attack that killed your father."

That got my attention. I turned to glare at her, too angry to even feel surprised by her last admission. I held her gaze for a long time before saying, "You know, I think I liked it better figuring it out on my own."

"You need my help. You've never even been trained to fight."

"And whose fault is that?" I shot back. I marched down the hall and straight out the front door, slamming it for effect. Admittedly, I was pretty sure I hadn't slammed a door at my mom since I was eleven, but it seemed like the thing to do right now. I stomped down the stone sidewalk, toward the street, and then stopped short at the sight of Wes coming toward me from the side yard.

He caught sight of my face and increased his speed. "What's wrong?"

"My mother—" I stopped, unsure how to explain, where to begin. I could feel frustrated tears forming at the corners of my eyes and blinked them back.

"She knew you weren't at Angela's?" he asked, trying to figure out the reason for my distress.

"Yeah, for starters," I muttered. Behind me, the front door opened. I didn't turn around.

"Tara, we need to finish this," my mother called. She was attempting to hide the anger in her voice, probably hoping to reel me back with kindness. It wasn't working.

I turned on my heel and marched back to where she'd stopped on the front step. I didn't look back to see if Wes was following. "And how would you suggest we do that?" I demanded.

My mother sighed. "For one thing, you could calm down so we can talk." Her gaze darted left to right and then back to me. "And it would be best if we did it inside."

"You care what the neighbors think? Really? What about what

I think? Or doesn't that matter to you at all?" I said, my voice rising. I knew I was probably making a scene, but I was too angry to care. Every time I looked at her, I felt betrayed.

My mom seemed to realize there was no hope of calming me down with the current line of conversation, so she switched tactics. "I'm Elizabeth, Tara's mother. You must be Wesley," she said, sticking her hand out.

Wes shook her hand, looking completely confused, but unwilling to ask. "Yes, ma'am. Nice to finally meet you."

"Tara tells me you've been helping her figure things out. Thank you."

"You're welcome," he said quietly.

"But you won't have to trouble yourself any longer. I'll be taking it from here."

"What?" I demanded.

"Tara, The Cause is dangerous, and so is associating with any of its members. I can't allow it," my mother said. "It would risk everything we've worked for, all these years."

"No, it would risk everything *you've* worked for. I had no say in any of it, remember?"

"Tara, I'm not going to argue with you. This is the way it's going to be."

"But you're meeting with Jack and Fee. You said you'd let them help."

"And I will. But you should keep your distance."

"So, I just go back to pretending I'm human?"

"No, but I'll educate you myself about what it means to be a Hunter."

"Well, I'm not just a Hunter, am I?"

My mother blinked, momentarily at a loss for words. Beside me, Wes cleared his throat, and I froze. I'd almost forgotten he was standing there and, too late, I realized this was probably not the best way to tell him that his suspicions had been correct. He'd spent his entire life defending his mixed blood, and his own life, because of it. He didn't see it as a good thing. I wasn't sure how he would feel knowing I was the same.

"Tara?" Wes asked quietly.

I stared down at the ground, some of the anger draining out of me. "My mom has informed me that she's a Hunter and my dad was a Werewolf."

"What?" he asked, though I'm sure he'd heard me.

"I'm a Dirty Bl—"

"Don't say that word," my mother hissed.

Wes didn't say anything and, finally, I made myself look up at him. His expression was unreadable. "This is a good thing," I whispered to him. "You're not the only one anymore. We can help each other." I reached for his hand.

For a second his expression softened and I thought it was going to be okay. But then, my mother cut in.

"Tara, I'm not asking anymore. House. Now. Goodbye, Wes."

I would've argued, but Wes stopped me. "It's okay. Go. We'll talk later," he said quietly. Reluctantly, he let go of my hand.

Behind me, I could hear my mother tapping her foot against the porch step. "I'll call you," I told him. He just nodded.

When he was gone, I turned back to find my mom still standing on the front steps. She had her arms folded in front of her and was absently rubbing them from the chill. She was watching me with a mixture of relief and determination.

"I'm sorry," she began, when I got close.

"I really don't want to talk about it," I said. "Any of it." I walked past her, into the house, and headed for the stairs. "I'll be in my room."

When I was on the second floor, out of sight, I stopped and leaned back against the wall, listening. I wasn't sure if my mom was really going to leave me alone up here, and I wanted to call Wes. A second later, I heard the front door click closed and my mother's footsteps faded down the hall.

I sank down on my bed and pulled out my phone, excited to see a text message already waiting. I opened it and felt the disappointment wash through me. It was from George, apologizing over and over for what I'd seen between him and Cindy. I let out a frustrated sigh, not bothering to respond. With everything else that had happened in the past few hours, I'd all but forgotten about the scene at the dance. I didn't have the energy to respond to it.

I dialed Wes's number and waited. From below, my mother's voice trickled up to me. Her tone sounded harsh but it was too muffled for me to make out what she was saying.

"Hello?"

"Hey," I said. "I'm sorry about that."

"What happened exactly?"

"My mom found the *Draven* and called Vera. Apparently they go way back. Vera came over and saw my pictures everywhere and confessed everything to my mom. They were waiting for me when I got here."

"What did she say?"

"Everything." I sighed and lay back on my bed, staring up at the ceiling. "The short version? My dad was a Werewolf, they were on the council, they fell in love, and I was conceived."

"So you really are ..."

"One of each? Yeah."

Silence.

"Is that okay?"

"It's not great. I mean, it puts you in more danger. Not just from Leo, but in general, forever. You'll always be a target."

"I know. She knows Leo."

"How?"

I took a deep breath. "He's the one responsible for the attack on the council." When he didn't respond right away, I pressed on, wanting to get it all out there. "And he's my uncle. My dad's brother." It felt weird to say it out loud.

A long pause and then, "Do you want me to come over?"

Footsteps sounded on the stairs. I silently cursed her timing. I really wanted to talk about this, make sure he was okay. His parents were dead because of Leo, just like my father. "Uh, maybe later. Gotta go." I clicked the phone shut just as my door opened.

My mother stood there, glaring at me. "Who were you talking to?"

"Wes."

She stepped into the room and held out her hand. "Give me your phone."

"Why?"

"Because I don't want you talking to him. I thought I made that clear already."

"You mentioned it. I don't agree."

"And I'm in charge. Hand it over."

I handed her the phone. "It doesn't matter. Vera's vision—"

"Is wrong. Besides, he might think he has feelings for you, but it's only because Vera claimed he would. Suggestive thinking. And picking up on your feelings for him probably didn't help, either."

"I didn't tell him about my feelings for him until yesterday," I argued.

"You didn't have to tell him, Tara. He obviously read it in your mind."

I opened my mouth and then shut it again. I did remember Wes telling me about that, in his apartment, but discussions of visions and destiny had distracted me from it. "He can only do it during a full moon," I said, remembering his words.

"Tara, check the calendar. From what Vera said, you've seen a full moon since the two of you met." She pocketed my phone and walked out.

I went to my desk, more curious than anything else, and pulled out my day planner. The cycles of the moon were clearly marked and I flipped back to February, searching for the last full moon phase. When I found it, I just stared, replaying the day over and over.

CHAPTER TWENTY-SIX

IT was the day Wes had first come to my house. The day after I'd killed Liliana. Then a new thought hit me; it was the day I'd first noticed how gorgeous he was. He'd been able to hear every single thought in my head. And he hadn't bothered to tell me.

I paced my room as little bits and pieces of that day came back. In particular, I remembered the moment we'd stood outside Jack's house, and Wes's eerily accurate response about waiting a minute, and they'd answer. I'd forgotten all about it in the chaos of everything else. Now, it made sense. He had heard my thoughts.

It was a little embarrassing, knowing he'd heard everything. Okay, it was a lot embarrassing. But mostly, it pissed me off. Maybe because I was already pissed off—at my mother, at Vera, and at what the circumstances of my life had somehow become. But, it was an invasion that I hadn't been prepared for, from the only person I trusted, and I desperately wanted to confront him about it.

I waited until nightfall, after my mother had finally gone to sleep, which was only after I'd pretended to be for over an hour. I crept into the hall and stood outside her door, listening to the even breaths that signaled sleep. Then I padded downstairs and took the cordless from the kitchen, and slid to the floor in the darkened laundry room. I dialed Wes's number and waited.

"Hello?" His voice was muffled by sleep.

"It's me. Did I wake you?"

He became instantly alert. "It's fine. What's up? Is everything okay?"

"Everything's fine. I need to ask you something."

"What is it?"

"It's about your mind-reading thing. Can you, um, turn it off?"

"No. Why?"

"Because I was looking at the calendar, and I realized the date of the last full moon."

A pause. Then, "Oh."

With that one word, my temper flared. "Oh? That's it? You're still not going to admit that you heard every single thought in my head that first day?"

Wes sighed, deeply, like he'd known this was coming. "Most wolves can do memory manipulation on some level. It's what helps keep them a secret from humans, and normally the ability only works on humans. On the full moon, the ability is always strongest. For whatever reason, it means I can read minds—humans, Werewolves, Hunters, doesn't matter. I don't have a choice and I can't turn it off."

"So you heard everything I was thinking that day?"

"Not everything. I somehow missed the plunger handles you decided to carry."

"Not funny."

"And while we're on the subject, I know you were wondering, and yes, I was checking you out. It had nothing to do with the scratches."

His voice sounded gravelly at being woken up. That, combined with his latest confession, made it hard to be angry right now. I missed him. "Why didn't you tell me?"

"It's hard to explain."

"Try."

"Vera didn't want me to. She thought it would scare you away, just like the visions. And honestly, I didn't want to scare you away for my own reasons. Selfish reasons. I liked being around you, and I didn't want that to end if you were offended by my eavesdropping." Another pause, then, "Are you mad?"

"Why would I be mad? Just one more thing to add to the list of things that was kept from me."

He was quiet for a minute, probably trying to figure out how to handle me without making it worse. "It's not like I tried to hear you. I don't have a choice. I hear everyone. Do you know how annoying it is to be able to hear a million voices at once? I'm lucky it's only one day a month. It's enough to give me a headache for three days afterward."

I stayed stubbornly silent.

"I've heard you before that, too. Once." He paused, waiting for a reaction.

"When?"

"It was a couple of months ago. At Moe's. I was in the back, praying the place would stay empty, to keep the volume in my head to a minimum. You came in with Sam and set up at a table by the door. I almost left after that—after hearing Sam's thoughts. Hers are the type I try to avoid. But yours were different. They were kind, without being a pushover, and fun without being shallow. And surprisingly deep. It was fascinating, the way you interacted with Sam, despite being total opposites, and the affection you had for her."

I knew the day he meant, because it was one of the few that Angela had missed. "It was a girls' day. Angela had to stay home and babysit her sister," I said.

"I thought about going to talk to you, even with the dilemma of being able to hear you properly over everyone's thoughts shouting inside my head."

"Why didn't you?"

"For your safety," he said quietly.

His answer should've comforted me, or at least made sense. Instead, the entire story only broke my heart; I wasn't even sure why. "Don't," I said. "Don't do that. You're always doing that."

"Doing what? Keeping you safe?"

"Yes. It's irritating and annoying and ridiculous and ... just like what my mother did." My voice rose on the last part and I hastily lowered it again. "My mother thinks me not seeing you is the best way to protect me. She took my phone."

He didn't answer for a long time.

"Are you still there?"

"I'm here. I—I can't go against your mother, Tara."

"What?" I was pretty sure I hadn't heard him right. I hoped I hadn't heard him right.

"Jack came by after he left your house to lecture me about it. I've been thinking about it since he left, and I just can't. What if you snuck around to see me and something happened?"

"Then you'd be there to prevent it."

"She would blame me. And she wouldn't be wrong."

This time it was me who didn't answer.

"It's more than that, though. Jack sort of ordered me to stay away unless your mother changes her mind."

"What do you mean 'ordered'?"

"He's the alpha, and ... I don't really have a choice here."

"I can't believe Jack would do that," I said, shaking my head.

"I think it was Vera's idea."

"But Vera's the one who said—"

"I know, but she also wants to give your mom time to come around to it all. She envisions more than just us as a couple, you know."

I remembered the flip side to what Vera had seen. Me, a leader, bringing peace to the two races. Ending the war. I shook it off; I couldn't think about that right now.

"I don't care what Jack, or Vera, or my mother think," I said, stubbornly.

"I can't go against an alpha's order. Not again."

I stayed quiet and chewed on my lip.

"Tara, don't be mad," he whispered.

"I'm not mad, I'm just ... I'm sick of being treated like an invalid. No one gives me a say in what would make me safe. Not even you. And I can't live like that."

"I can't NOT protect you, Tara."

"So what are you saying?"

"I'm saying we should take a break. At least until we deal with Leo. Then, maybe your mom will change her mind."

"You're breaking up with me?" My eyes filled with tears. They spilled over onto my cheeks before I could even attempt to blink them back. I should've known, after the night we'd spent together, that he'd go cold again.

"Tara, it's not like that."

"Then what's it like?"

The kitchen light came on, and I held my breath. Soft footsteps padded closer, and a cabinet opened. The sink came on.

"I'm sorry, Tara. I'll talk to you later, okay?" said Wes, in a strained voice.

Before I could answer, he hung up with a click that echoed all the way into my bones. I sat there, numb inside and out, long after the kitchen light had shut off and my mother had returned to bed.

CHAPTER TWENTY-SEVEN

IT was a tensely silent car ride to school on Monday. My mom insisted on driving me, part of the whole "protecting me herself" initiative. I'd spent all of Sunday either arguing with her about the new schedule she seemed determined to implement or sneaking off to try calling Wes again. He hadn't picked up, though, and on the last try, the recorded voice had informed me his mailbox was full.

I didn't want to believe that he meant what he'd said to me on our last phone call, but after two days without any contact from him, I knew it was for real. We were over and there was nothing I could do about it because my mother had basically put me under house arrest until further notice.

She'd informed me that I would be driven to school and picked up, by her, and I'd be spending my afternoons with her at the flower shop, doing school-assigned homework or learning about Hunter history. There would be no further contact with anyone associated with The Cause, and until she felt she could trust me, I was grounded from even going out with my human friends.

Arguing did no good; neither did threats. She'd even called a security company to have the alarm system upgraded so that it would alert her remotely if I tried to leave without permission.

They were scheduled to come tomorrow. In the meantime, I would've gladly snuck away for a few hours but there was only one person I wanted to sneak away with—and he wasn't speaking to me.

So, with no other choice, I let her drive me to school and tried to pretend everything didn't completely suck. I stared out the window, feeling more alone than I ever had.

"How's Angela doing? I haven't seen her or Sam lately." My mom tried to keep her voice casual, and I suspected she was just desperate for a way to ease the tension between us. I wasn't ready for that yet.

I remained silent and shifted in my seat, letting her know with my body language that I had no intention of responding. She took the hint and didn't speak again.

My mom let me out at the curb and I hustled away before anyone could notice I was getting dropped off by my mother. Besides that, I welcomed school if it got me away from her for a few hours. But that thought was followed by a big, fat "never mind." As soon as I was in the doors, George rushed toward me. I suppressed a groan and tried to keep going, but he was too quick.

"Tay, I'm so glad I caught you. I texted you all weekend." He ran a hand through his sandy hair, looking nervous. The first glimpse I'd seen of the old George in a long while. "Look, I'm really sorry, Tay. Cindy said she wanted to talk to me, and that she knew something about you. I shouldn't have believed her, but you sounded upset on the phone, and I miss you, and I just wanted to believe her, I guess ..."

He trailed off, waiting for me to say something, let him off the hook. I didn't. "I know you hate Cindy," he went on. "And I don't even really like her, either. I just, I don't know. She kissed me and I didn't see it coming. I was already pushing her away when you saw us. I'm sorry."

I shrugged, only mildly affected by the pleading look he wore. "I appreciate the apology, George, but it's not a big deal. We aren't together anymore, and you're free to see whomever you want."

"But I don't want to be free, I want to be with you," he argued.

I fought an urge to smile at the way his words had come out.

His expression lightened, though, so I must've given something away.

"I know I messed up. A lot. But I'm going to fix it, and I don't care how long it takes. So just get used to it because I'm going to win you back, eventually."

"George—"

"Don't say anything. Not right now. Just think about it." He sounded determined.

I sighed, unwilling to argue with one more person today. "Okay. But I gotta go."

As if on cue, the first bell rang.

"I'll see you around, Tay," he said, his eyes sparkling.

I didn't answer, and he disappeared into the rush of kids scrambling to get to class. I had to run the last leg, but I managed to get to class just as the tardy bell rang. I dropped my books onto the desk and flopped into my seat.

A high-pitched giggle floated by, and I felt something inside me straining against the leash of my temper. I glanced over and found Cindy beaming at me through an overly thick layer of mascara.

"Tara, I'm so glad you're here. I've been meaning to ask you, does George always talk in his sleep, or just sometimes? I was curious, you know, from one girlfriend to another. Oh, I mean, ex-girlfriend to girlfriend."

Missy, the short brunette in front of her snickered and that was the last thing I heard. Without even realizing I was doing it, my arm swung out and my fist made contact with Cindy's face. Her head snapped to the side from the impact and the rest of the room went completely still. When Cindy finally swung back to look at me, I saw that a red, swollen lump was already forming on her cheek.

"You little bitch," she spat, struggling to get to her feet in the aisle between us.

Apparently, I'd hit her just hard enough to royally piss her off. I jumped up, too, and planted my feet firmly on the linoleum. I vaguely heard voices chanting mine and Cindy's names but it didn't really register. All I wanted was to lay Cindy flat on the floor and shut her up. A part of me knew this was all a product of everything going on in my own head, with my own problems, but I couldn't stop. The dam had broken.

I took the time to cock my arm back, putting momentum behind the punch. This time, when I hit her, her whole body was driven sideways by the blow. She stumbled back, half sitting and half lying in her desk seat. Her hair covered her face, but through the light strands, I could see red liquid seeping from her nose. Blood dripped onto her cashmere sweater.

A hand grabbed my arm, and I whirled, jerking myself free. I had to stop myself from swinging out against my attacker and was glad I did. Mr. Knowles stared back at me, wary but determined to hold his ground.

"Miss Godfrey, there is absolutely no fighting in my classroom. Principal's office. Now." He spoke with authority, but he made no move to grab me again.

Without a word, I grabbed my bag and slid past him on my way out the door.

It wasn't until I was halfway down the deserted hallway that reality set in and I realized what I'd done. I stopped and leaned back against the wall, already dreading how this was going to end. The principal would call my mother, of course. And she'd have to pick me up early. Which meant, I'd spend even more time at the flower shop, with her. And what if they suspended me?

I'd never been in trouble for fighting before, but I knew that was school procedure. That meant spending days at a time, with no break, with my mother.

I pushed off from the wall and changed directions, heading back the way I came. I ducked underneath the window of Mr. Knowles classroom so he wouldn't notice my detour, and hurried on. The double doors at the end of the hall led to a small courtyard where the seniors were allowed to eat lunch. Hopefully, no one would be out there this early. Ditching was something else I'd never done before. Might as well break the rules all at once.

I pushed open the doors and stepped into the low-walled courtyard, weaving around the plastic tables and chairs. Luckily, no one was out here yet, so I hurried to the concrete wall that edged the area and hopped up. It was only four feet or so, and on the other side was a small grassy area that led to woods. If I could make it there without being spotted from a window, I was home free. I looped my bag over my shoulder to secure it and set off for the trees.

I made it to the edge of the woods without being stopped and ducked around an old oak to catch my breath; I had no idea truancy was so nerve-wracking. I spotted a couple of sad-looking plastic lawn chairs, probably dragged here by a senior couple wanting to be alone, and I sank into one of them while I considered my options.

That was when I felt the tingles.

CHAPTER TWENTY-EIGHT

THEY started on the back of my neck and traveled down my arms and legs. My head jerked back and forth, searching into the shadows of the trees. In the distance, behind me, a car horn honked and I jumped. My head jerked toward the sound. I kicked myself for letting my guard down, even for a second, and turned back. Out of the corner of my eye, something moved.

The tingling heightened to an unpleasant humming inside my skin. My muscles strained against the itch it created and my mind went blank of all thoughts but this: find the source and make it stop.

A low growl emanated from somewhere nearby, but the sound echoed, thrown off by the open space at my back. A blur of gray flew by, and I glanced up just in time to roll out of the chair, barely getting clear of the sharp teeth dropping at me from above. I rolled to my knees and then my feet, dodging the teeth as they came at me again.

"Leo," I said, through a mixture of fear and anger. A small, rational voice in the back of my mind was whispering that I never should've ditched school and come out here alone. But the Hunter side, the part of me whose muscles strained and raged for a fight—this fight—ignored it.

Instead of immediately attacking, Leo stepped back and began slowly circling me. "I see your sidekick isn't with you today."

I felt a small pang at the mention of Wes, but I brushed it aside and kept my tone light. "He should be here anytime," I lied, continuing to circle and looking for an opening. I wasn't overconfident like I'd been the last time we met, but I was more sure of my moves, and I had two goals: to kill Leo and stay away from those teeth. And if Leo thought help was on its way, so much the better.

"Well, then, I'd better be quick," he murmured.

We lunged at the same time. I angled my shoulders and neck so that I was out of biting range and landed a hard blow to his ribs. He stumbled back but landed firmly on his feet. I wasted no time in a second swing. This one missed, and it threw me off balance so that I had to twist my upper body hard to avoid his teeth. My muscles protested against that particular maneuver, but as soon as I straightened, the discomfort disappeared.

Leo lunged at me again and I sidestepped him at the last second. I could see he was in more of a hurry this time, unwilling to prolong the fight any more than necessary. I wondered briefly where Wes might be right now and then dismissed it. I had to stay focused. This might be my only chance to end this.

I glanced around for anything I could use as a weapon. There wasn't much out here; dead leaves littered the ground, along with a few small branches, none of them big enough or thick enough to penetrate Were flesh, and the lawn chairs. I let Leo maneuver me closer and, keeping my eyes on him, I grabbed a chair and brought it down hard over my knee. There was a sharp crack as the cheap plastic gave way and snapped in two. Leo lunged again and I used the piece in my right hand to block him while shoving the other piece into his open mouth. He backed off, thrashing around to loosen the plastic that had wedged into his left fang. With Leo distracted, I pulled at the chair's legs, separating them from the seat. When I'd freed them, I held one in each hand and rushed at Leo, arms raised.

The plastic was still lodged in his teeth but at my attack, he stopped pushing at it with his paws and brought one up to swipe at me, claws extended. I hit it aside with one hand and brought the jagged end of the chair leg down with the other. I hit him behind his shoulder and realized quickly that my weapon was too thick to penetrate. Instead, I ripped it across his back and then danced out of the way. A second later a thin red line appeared.

At the sight of his blood, the humming under my skin intensified and my muscles tensed in anticipation. Unable to control my need to fight, I leapt forward, forgetting to keep clear of the claws that reached up to meet me. They swiped across my arm from elbow to wrist and left two thin red lines that burned where the skin broke. I cursed myself for being careless and fell back.

I circled, cautious but determined. Leo finished pulling the plastic free from his fang and tossed it aside with his mouth. His eyes closed to slits and his lips pulled back over his teeth. He crouched low and I could feel him about to spring when, behind me, a familiar voice called out.

"Hello, Leo. Starting the party without me?"

Despite the fact that I was in full-blown Hunter mode, and despite the fact that all my conscious brain wanted was to kill this Werewolf, my heart sped at the sound of that voice. I forced myself not to turn.

"Took you longer than I thought," Leo said.

Wes came up next to me and pressed his palm lightly against my back. That surprised me. I assumed he'd be in wolf form already. "Tara, go back inside," he said quietly.

"No way, we can take him down together. Now's our chance," I hissed.

"Tara, go inside," he repeated, an edge in his voice.

Temper boiled up inside me. I kept my feet firmly planted. I'd been miserable without him the past couple of days, wanting nothing more than to see his face, feel his touch. Now that I could, it was more of the same. He was still ordering me around and deciding what was best for me, without consulting *me*. "No," I said.

"Tara—" he started to argue.

"If you're here, then it must be to watch. This is my fight, and I'm not going inside. There's a seat over there," I said, nodding to the remaining lawn chair.

Beside me, Wes's jaw clenched hard enough for me to hear him grinding his teeth. I knew he probably wanted to snatch me up and carry me back to the school, but we both knew better than to take our attention off Leo.

Leo watched our exchange with amusement. "Give the girl what she wants, Wes. We were just starting to have fun."

Movement behind Leo caught my eye. A wolf was moving steadily toward us through the trees. I didn't recognize it but that didn't mean anything. Then, another came into view, several yards away from the first. Then, another. Leo didn't turn, but his ears were flicking, taking in the soft crunch of leaves as they moved closer. When I looked up again, there were a total of six wolves facing us.

Wes's hand on my back pressed harder, and I felt the rest of him stiffen. I knew then, that these wolves were not friendly and that Wes was seriously debating how to handle things. I sensed the change in Leo before Wes did, though, and I shifted, letting Wes's hand on my back fall away.

"All this indecision. Maybe I can help," Leo said. And with that, he lunged, aiming straight for me. Behind him, the wolves rushed at us.

I braced myself, but Leo never made it that far. Wes took a running leap and in midair, he transformed. Torn pieces of fabric that used to be his clothes rained down around me. A growl tore from his throat, a menacing, spine-chilling sound that seemed to rip through me and out the other side.

The other wolves were on me then. They came in, two at a time. I managed to smack them away with the pieces of jagged plastic in my hands, but that's about it. I couldn't get enough of an opening to do any damage. And I could feel two of them circling around behind me. I knew I didn't have much time.

Off to my left, a keening howl cut through the growling and snarling of the fight. Before it had died away, two more wolves broke through the heavy brush and hurled themselves at the two closing in behind me. One of them sailed straight over my head, and the other whipped around me, its thick tail brushing my hip as it passed. I recognized him, based on sheer size. Jack.

The two wolves in front of me rushed forward, probably knowing they had minimal time remaining to make their kill. I batted them away again, managing to draw blood on one of their noses with my plastic weapon. It yelped and jumped away but the other came again. Its claws raked over the same spot on my arm that Leo had scratched, and I jumped back, cradling my arm and wincing.

The wolf crouched and I knew it was coming again, but then a figure—a human one—appeared beside us. Cord didn't even look at me. She stared at the wolf with an expression of concentration and determination and swung up with her stake, sinking it into the wolf's heart with a disgusting squish sound. The wolf stilled and then began to crumple. Cord slid her stake free and stepped back just before the wolf thudded to the ground. She glanced at me briefly, a look of disgust on her face, and then ran to the next wolf, intercepting him before he could step in my direction. Her stake dripped with blood and the tip glinted.

I searched for Wes and found him circling a snarling Leo. I saw a thin line of red just above Wes's eye and then he was moving again, too quickly for me to actually see him clearly. The two growls blurred into one as they rolled and snapped at each other. A second later, I heard a yelp and then Leo was pinned underneath Wes's massive paws. Wes snarled and snapped his teeth at Leo's throat but Leo was quick and used his back paws to rake his claws across Wes's underside. Wes flinched and that was all the time Leo needed to wriggle free. When he rolled to the side I saw a small red wound on his throat covering a longer, more jagged scar—the remains of his last fight with Wes.

I sensed movement beside me and whirled, ready to defend against an attacker, but it was Jack. He was breathing heavily but looked unharmed.

"Are you okay?" he asked.

"Yeah. Just scratched but I'll be fine. Thanks."

He dipped his head in a nod, his eyes on Wes and Leo.

"How'd you find me?" I asked.

"We patrol the grounds while you're at school," he said. "I don't know how he got through."

I remembered my mother saying something about working with Jack. "Is that Fee I saw? Is she okay?"

"She's fine. Stole all my action. I'd love to jump in and help Wes, but Leo's quick, and I don't want to get in the way," he said.

Fee came up beside me, her tail swishing along my arm. "You should get back inside," she said.

"Not yet." I shook my head. "Not until ..."

Neither of them argued. They stayed next to me, though, while we watched.

Leo pressed his claws into Wes's side, making him release his hold. They separated and circled again and Leo finally noticed that his band of followers were no longer providing backup. I knew he was getting ready to run.

"Another time," said Leo.

"No time like the present," said Wes, stalking toward Leo. I could see he wasn't going to let him go so easily this time.

"You don't deserve your strength. There's only one who does," he said, a harsh growl lacing his words. And then he was running, heading for the trees.

As soon as he took off, Jack and Fee raced after him. The tingling under my skin receded and then disappeared.

I spotted Cord, standing over the dead wolves and talking on her phone. She saw me watching her and turned her back. I watched the trees until Leo was gone and then I turned to Wes, surprised he'd stayed behind. He was still in his wolf form and he was standing rigidly still, staring at the trees where Leo, Jack, and Fee had gone.

I watched him, a little curious. The only other time I'd seen him as a wolf was a little foggy to me. It was strange to see him like this but not in a bad way. And it was nice to be able to look at him, in this form, without the disgusting crawly feeling under my skin. I remembered I was still holding the plastic pieces and dropped them on the ground. He didn't turn at the noise.

"Wes," I finally called.

Reluctantly, it seemed, he turned to face me. I took a step toward him, still staring. Even like this, there was something commanding about him.

"He's gone," I said.

"I know."

"You can change back if you want," I added.

"I'm going to help Cord clean up. You should get to class."

"Right." His words brought me back to reality and I realized I'd almost forgotten that I was at school. I tried to think of something to say; the silence suddenly felt awkward. "I called you."

"I know."

"Why didn't you call me back?"

"There was nothing else to say."

"There's plenty to say."

"Like what?"

"Like, how could you just walk away like that?"

"I'm not walking away. It's just a break, Tara." He sounded tired.

"You're being ridiculous."

He didn't answer and I felt myself panicking. "What about Vera's visions? About the future, and me and you being leaders together? You're giving up on that, too? Or it wasn't true to begin with?"

"It's as true as it can be for something that hasn't happened yet. For now, being apart is what's best for you."

"Really? After what happened today, with Leo attacking me, you really think so?" I felt kind of low about using Leo as a reason for Wes not to leave me, but I was desperate.

"I'm not going to be far, at least not until Leo's dealt with. But we can't be together. It'll just create more problems and it's not fair to you."

"Right, none of it's fair or safe or right. Heaven forbid I should have a say in my own life," I snapped.

He looked away. "Goodbye, Tara," he said, his voice strained.

I opened my mouth to argue but he turned and sprinted away before I could.

I stood there for a while, hollow and numb. Cord still had her back to me, even though I knew she'd heard everything. Finally, I turned back to the school.

CHAPTER TWENTY-NINE

I made it through the doors and down the hall without passing anyone I knew. Everyone was still in class. I didn't know which one, though, or how long I'd been gone. It felt like hours.

At my locker, I stopped and leaned my forehead against the metal door, squeezing my eyes shut and trying to clear my mind of the image of Wes leaving—twice. I still had to go to the principal's office for punching Cindy and deal with my mother when she found out.

"Tara?"

I spun around and found George standing there. "Hey, George," I mumbled.

His curious expression clouded over with concern the second our eyes met. "Are you okay?"

Tears stung and threatened to spill over. I nodded, not trusting my voice.

"What's wrong?"

"I just ..."

The look on his face tugged at me. Tears ran over onto my cheeks. George rushed forward and put his arms around me, pulling me close. "It's okay, Tay. I'm here," he murmured.

He didn't ask me any more questions, just held me and let me cry. When the fabric of his shirt was soaked through, and my sniffling had somewhat subsided, I pulled away, realizing it probably wasn't a good idea to let George have his arms around me. Standing this close, I recognized the scent of his cologne that clung to him like a second skin. It was heavy and musky and so completely George and it filled my mind with too many memories of being held by him, exactly like this.

"Sorry," I mumbled, wiping my cheeks with my sleeve. "It's been a rough day."

"You can talk to me, Tay. You know that, right?"

Just like the other night when I'd talked to him on the phone, I thought about it. It would feel so good to unload on someone, and there was a time I'd been able to tell George anything. It was tempting. But I knew better. "I'll be fine. I've gotta get to the principal's office before Mr. Knowles realizes I'm lurking in the halls."

"Principal's office? Why?"

"I sort of punched Cindy. In the face. Twice."

George's eyes widened and his brows shot up, disappearing into his sandy hair. "Seriously?"

I nodded.

"Wow, Tay. That's … impressive." A grin tugged at the edges of his mouth. "I guess it has been a rough day." His smile disappeared, and he suddenly looked nervous. "Is this about what happened? I mean, you're not going to punch me, are you?"

"No, I think I'm done punching people for today," I assured him.

"Good."

"So, I'll see you later," I said.

"Yeah, you better get going," he said. "Good luck."

I moved to go around him but he reached out a hand to stop me. When I looked up at him, I found him eyeing my arm, with a weird expression.

"What is that on your shirt? Is that blood on your arm?"

I looked down and realized I'd completely forgotten about the scratches from Leo. My shirtsleeve was ripped open where his claws had raked my skin, revealing the raised, bloody slashes underneath. At the reminder, I realized I did feel a dull sting from the wound.

"Oh," was all I said out loud. I was trying to figure out how to explain this when George cut in.

"Did Cindy do that to you?" he asked.

"Uh, yeah, I guess," I lied. "I didn't really notice it before."

"You should stop off at the nurse and get that checked out."

"I will."

"Do you want me to walk you there?"

I hesitated. His concern for me was sweet and reminiscent of the George I'd fallen for. It made me want to do whatever I could to keep this version of him around, but I didn't really have any intention of letting the nurse see my wound—or anyone else, for that matter.

"No, I'm good," I said. "Thanks, George."

"Yeah, okay. Well, call me if you need anything. You know I'm here for you," he said, his voice heavy with meaning.

I gave him a tight smile and walked away.

As soon as I was out of sight, I ducked into the bathroom and cleaned my arm as best I could. I had a change of clothes in my gym locker, but my mother would be sure to notice it and ask, so I put my hoodie on instead to cover the damage. The wound burned a little but it was more of an annoying throb than anything else. At least I could manage it on my own.

Inevitably, washing the blood away made me think of the fight—and Wes. A dull pang had developed in my chest and the more I thought of him, the sharper it got. I tried to think of something else. I couldn't really accept that it was over. If I did, I was afraid I'd crumble into pieces, and until Leo was dealt with, I couldn't let that happen. The people I loved were depending on me, whether they knew it or not.

Presenting myself at the principal's office wasn't nearly as bad as I thought it would be. Probably because I wasn't a repeat offender. The kid who went in before me was—I recognized him from a couple of classes, always slouched over in the back of the room—and Principal Sellers' raised voice could be heard all the way into the waiting room while that kid was in there. So, when they came out and Principal Sellers gestured that it was my turn to enter, I shuffled slowly into his office, feeling like a criminal.

I took a seat in one of the hard-backed chairs in front of his desk and waited. My fingers fidgeted nervously with the shoulder strap on my bag. I stared down at a brown stain on the carpet.

Principal Sellers rounded the desk and stared at me over a mess of paper coffee cups and thick files held down by what looked like homemade paper weights. He was picking at his stubbled chin. "Miss Godfrey, I'm surprised to see you here, especially for the reason that brings you. Do you want to tell me what happened?"

I suppressed a sigh. "What do you want to know?" I asked. I really just wanted to get this done and get to the really scary part— my mother.

"I want to know why you punched her," he said.

"If I tell you, will you change your mind about calling my mother?"

"No."

"Okay, well, then I'd rather not get into it."

"And why is that?"

"Because it's not like my reason will sound good enough to warrant hitting her. So, it doesn't really matter why, does it? She made a stupid comment, like she always does, and I snapped."

"That's it?" he asked, clearly skeptical that I didn't want to say more or try to tell my side of the story.

"That's it," I assured him.

He eyed me for a minute, probably waiting to see if I was really finished. But I really was. I didn't feel like giving excuses, not to him. It wouldn't change the situation, and it wouldn't help fix any of my real problems. Not that punching Cindy wasn't a real problem; I did feel bad, sort of. But when compared to Leo or my mother or Wes ...

"Okay, well." Principal Sellers cleared his throat and stood. "You mother should be here soon." He must've caught my grimace because he added, "We'd already called her before you got here. You can go wait for her in the front office. You'll be suspended from school for the next three days, which is school policy for a first offense. Mrs. Fletcher will give you the paperwork."

I nodded and followed him back out the door.

"I do hope this is an isolated incident, Miss Godfrey," he said as I passed by him on my way out.

"Me, too," I mumbled.

Mrs. Fletcher, the gray-haired office assistant, handed me some official-looking papers as I passed her desk. She tried giving me a disapproving look to go with it, but I ignored her and found an empty chair to await the firestorm otherwise known as my mother.

CHAPTER THIRTY

AN hour ticked by, and I could feel my muscles getting sore and stiff. The cotton of my jacket chafed against the scrapes on my arm, and Mrs. Fletcher gave me a dirty look every time I shifted in the chair. Finally, Stacey, one of Julie's friends and my mother's new employee, showed up to get me. She had her bright blond hair pulled back in a harsh ponytail and her eyes were rimmed in red.

"Hey," she said, smiling a watery smile.

"Hi," I said.

Stacey was halfway through her junior year of college, so in a way, I felt like she was more my age than a grown-up. And even though I didn't really know her (I'd met her a couple of times when she'd been in the store to see Julie), the fact that she didn't give me the same disapproving glower that an adult would made me instantly glad it was her instead of my mother.

"Where's my mom?" I asked, gathering my stuff and following her out of the office.

"She said she would close up and see you at home," she answered, holding the door open and then falling into step beside me.

"Oh, okay," I said, kind of shocked my mother had opted for work instead of guarding me like a prisoner.

"Did you want her to be the one to get you?" Stacey asked,

giving me a sideways glance, eyebrows raised.

"No, it's fine," I said quickly.

Stacey smiled knowingly and led the way to her second-hand Mazda parked at the curb. As soon as we were on the road, I waited for her to start questioning me about what happened, but she stayed quiet. Maybe it was my preoccupation with my own problems, but it took me a minute to realize Stacey was just as distracted.

"Everything okay?" I asked hesitantly. I knew what happened to Julie had to be rough, but I wasn't sure I was the best person to reassure her.

"Hmm? Yeah, just thinking about something that happened at the shop earlier," she said. "Actually maybe you can help. This guy came in, around your mom's age, and asked to see her. Wouldn't give his name, just said he was an old friend. But when she saw him, her expression turned all weird."

"Who was it?"

"I don't know. She asked me to come get you and basically kicked me out the door."

"What did they talk about?" I asked, not sure why I suddenly felt so uneasy.

"They didn't. At least not in front of me. It was this awkward, tense silence," she said with a shrug.

"What do you think it was about?"

"No idea. She locked up behind me, too. She's never closed the store in the middle of the day like that before. Weird, right?"

"Weird," I agreed.

"Do you have any idea who the guy could be?" she asked.

"What did he look like?"

"Forty-ish, brown hair and beard with streaks of gray ..." She squinted in concentration. "That's about all I remember."

"I don't know," I said, shaking my head. "Doesn't sound familiar." I tried thinking of people my mother knew who might fit Stacey's description but the list was short. Mom didn't really have a lot of friends and the ones she did were middle-aged neighbors, all female, who she used to call on to keep an eye on me, when I was home alone. I briefly wondered if it could've been another

Hunter or member of The Cause, but dismissed it. The only one she said she knew of in the entire area was Vera, and even that connection was made recently. Besides, based on Stacey's recollection, he didn't sound like any of the group I'd met.

"Well, at least you're off the hook for a little longer about the fighting," she said, breaking into my thoughts.

"Yeah, thanks for that," I agreed. My stomach growled loud enough for Stacey to glance over.

"You hungry? I can hit a drive-thru if you want."

"That would be great. There's probably not a whole lot at home," I said. Plus, I wanted to prolong the ride as long as possible. The rest of the afternoon stretched out in front of me, empty and alone, in my house. It didn't sound like fun. We hit up McDonald's and then took back roads home.

"I'm really sorry, about Julie," I said, glancing over at Stacey and then away. I didn't want to make her upset again.

"Thanks. Her funeral was Friday. Your mom said a lot of really nice things." Stacey pulled in behind my car, and I gathered my stuff, reaching for the door handle. "Hey, good luck later," she said with a sympathetic smile.

I thanked her and got out, slowly making my way toward the front door. I dug for my house key while gripping the paper bag that held my lunch. The sound of Stacey's whining engine disappeared behind me. I felt my fingers close around my key ring, somewhere in the depths of my bag. I stepped up to the front door and was hit by a solid wave of tingling.

It ran up my arms and down my back, leaving goosebumps in its wake. Every muscle in my body went taut and I strained my ears against the sunny silence in my yard. A sliver of panic curled its way up my spine as I realized my front door was already cracked open.

I reached out and pushed it wider, staying where I was on the front step as I scanned the entryway for signs of movement. Cheery sunlight filtered through behind me, the contrast somehow giving the whole place an ominous feel. The front hall was empty and untouched but beyond that, I could see overturned furniture in the den. I hesitated only a second before I crashed through the debris and pushed forward into the house, dropping my bags as I went.

The lack of windows in the den made the shadows heavier but I didn't bother flipping the switch. It was a safe bet nothing would happen, since I could already see the shards jutting from the fixture where the bulb had been smashed. I kept waiting for someone—or something—to jump out at me, but the room was empty. The access door to the garage was hanging open and I peeked in and froze. My mother's car was parked inside, the engine still creaking with warmth.

Panic rose and suddenly I didn't care who or what heard me.

"Mom!" I yelled, turning and racing for the hallway that led to the rest of the house. The living room and kitchen were trashed. All of the furniture had been overturned and anything breakable had been smashed to pieces. I kept going, not even slowing to take note of the damage that had once been my TV or the dining room table that was split in two. One thought dominated any fear I might have felt and drowned out all rational thought as I turned the corner and ran for the stairs.

"Mom!" I screamed. Still, no answer.

The pounding of my feet on the stairs echoed against the walls. At the top, I stopped just inside my bedroom and stared. Clothes littered the floor; my computer had been ripped from the wall and thrown across the room. My mattress had been slashed and my comforter shredded. I halted my inspection when I realized the room was empty and continued on to my mother's room.

I threw open the door and stopped. This room was also empty and trashed but something else entirely had already caught my attention. Across the room, a piece of paper was pinned to the wall. A lump rose in my throat and I slowed to a walk as I crossed to it, dreading its message. It was handwritten in elegant cursive and addressed to me. It read: "I'm willing to trade. I'll be in touch."

I stared at it, a tight fist just beginning to wrap itself around my heart. Downstairs, the sliding glass door slammed shut and I jumped, jerking into motion. I raced back down the stairs and wrenched the door open, stepping into the yard, scanning for movement. Nothing. A car engine revved, and I bolted toward the front. I didn't bother with the locked gate, instead using the momentum of my body to swing over the fence. I landed with bent knees on the front lawn and ran for the curb. Red taillights in the distance faded around a corner, taking the tingling feeling with it.

My knees threatened to buckle, and for a second, I was tempted to give in to the despair and fear that gripped me, squeezing harder and harder inside my chest. I could barely breathe from the pressure and I doubled over, trying to get enough air. I had to think. I had to clear my thoughts enough to figure out what to do. The answer was easy. Wes. It was the only coherent thought I could form. I straightened and felt my pockets for my phone. They were empty.

Then I remembered: my mother had my phone.

I raced back through the front door and into the kitchen, yanking open the junk drawer next to the sink where my mother liked to think I didn't know she hid things. Batteries and flashlights fell as I rummaged roughly through the drawer's contents, until my fingers closed over my phone. I gripped it with white knuckles, like a lifeline, and messed up twice before I found the right buttons to dial Wes.

It rang four times, which felt like four hundred, and then his voice mail came on. It wasn't until I heard the recorded message that I remembered he wasn't taking my calls. Panic seized me harder, and I couldn't think. I sucked in a gulp of air and pushed the panic away as best I could, finally remembering there was someone else I could call.

He answered on the second ring. "Hey, Tara. What's up?"

"Jack, I need you to come get me. Right now." I still felt out of breath and talking made it worse so my voice came out whispery and faint. It must've been enough to get Jack's attention, though.

"What happened?"

"He was here. He took her."

I could hear him calling to Fee in the background and then his voice came back on. "Where are you?"

"My house."

"Dammit, Tara's home early." His voice was muffled and I assumed he was talking to Fee. Then he came back on. "Okay, who was there? Leo?"

"Yes."

"Did you see him?"

"No."

"Who did he take?"

"My mom."

"Shit." On his end of the phone, a car door slammed. Then another. Then an engine revved and I could hear him muttering stuff to Fee again. "Okay, we're on our way. You need to get someplace safe until we're there. Can you do that?"

"Um ..."

"The woods," I heard Fee saying. "Tell her to go to the woods behind the house and stay put until we get there."

"Did you hear that?" Jack asked.

"Yeah," I said, squeezing my eyes shut in a futile attempt to block out the panic and fear. "Yeah, okay, I'll do that."

"Okay, I've got to make some calls so I need to hang up now, but I'll be there in a few minutes. You gonna be okay?" Jack asked.

"Yeah," I said, my voice near a whisper again.

Jack hesitated and I knew he wasn't convinced, but he didn't have a choice. "See you in a few," he said finally.

We disconnected but I kept my phone in my hands and got to my feet, heading for the back door and the woods beyond. I managed to find a decent place to sit—using an old tree stump for a chair—and dropped heavily onto it. The problem with waiting is it gives you plenty of time to think about things you shouldn't, things that only make the panic and fear worse. In this case, it was guilt, over the way I'd treated my mom the past few days and all the nasty things I'd said to her about everything being her fault. I'd acted like a kid throwing a temper tantrum when she'd really just been protecting me, the best way she knew how. And now, she'd been taken because of me.

Heavy tears filled my eyes and wasted no time in spilling over onto my cheeks. My vision blurred and sobs racked my shoulders so badly that I'm pretty sure I wouldn't have been able to feel a

Werewolf, even if one had walked right by me. Mostly, the tears were a result of my fear for my mother but a few were for Wes, too. He hadn't even picked up the phone. When I'd needed him the most, he hadn't bothered. It made me angry, and it hurt, which made me even angrier. I cried harder.

I needed to get myself together before Jack and Fee found me. Crying and falling apart wouldn't help get my mother back. Neither would being mad at Wes. I had to do something, take action, and I couldn't do that if I was a wreck. So I did my best to push aside the agonizing worry and wiped the tears from my face with my sleeve, determined to do whatever I needed to rescue my mother.

When Jack got there, the tingling came first. I tensed up, worrying an enemy Werewolf had found me, but when I heard the extra heavy crunching of leaves under human feet, I realized who it was and stood up as Jack came into view. He strode toward me, scrutinizing my face as he got close. I hurried over to him and he surprised me by reaching out and pulling me against him in a suffocating hug. The embrace lasted only a second, which was good because I couldn't breathe against the bulk of his chest, and then he let go of me, looking slightly awkward about it.

"Come on. The truck's waiting out front," he said.

I fell into step beside him, which was tricky, since I had to take two steps for every one of his. "Where's Fee?" I asked.

"In the house, checking it out and packing some things for you."

"What things?"

"Clothes, whatever you'll need. You're not staying here until Leo is dealt with. We don't have the manpower to fight him and guard your house."

"And you think dealing with Leo will take a while?" I asked, dreading his answer, and what that might mean for my mother.

"I don't know, but we have to be prepared."

Fee was already at the truck when we rounded the side of the house. She slung my blue duffel bag into the back and then turned to wrap her arms around me. "You okay?" she asked.

"Yeah, I think so."

She gave me a quick squeeze and then released, nudging me toward the open truck door. "Get in, we need to hurry back to meet the others."

I wedged myself between Jack and Fee, and we left. I couldn't say we were necessarily speeding, because I wasn't sure this truck was capable of it, but Jack definitely didn't brake for corners or stop signs, so it was a jarring ride.

"Who are we meeting?" I asked, when we'd made it out of my neighborhood and onto the main road.

"Miles, Cord, Bailey, and Derek. Vera's farther out so it'll take her a little longer. The rest are all on assignment so they can't get here in time, but we put the word out and they'll be here tomorrow, if we need them," said Fee.

"What about—did you call Wes?" I asked, hating that I even wanted to know.

Jack and Fee exchanged a look. "He's cleaning up the mess from earlier. Did you want us to?" she asked, gently.

"I don't know. I guess not," I said.

Nobody said anything after that. I had to concentrate on staying upright in my seat, as Jack sped around the back roads and curves like he was on a race track.

There were a couple cars out front when we arrived. It made me feel a little better knowing we had help. I knew they were doing it for Jack and Fee, not for me, but I didn't care. Whatever it took to get my mom back.

Derek met us at the door.

"Where are the others?" Jack asked.

"Kitchen. Bailey's already pissed because he knows you're going to sideline him."

Jack grunted. "What else is new?"

Derek eyed me as I passed him, but he didn't say anything as he shut the door behind me and followed me down the hall. Jack waited until we were all together in the kitchen, then he turned to me.

"Tell us what happened."

I didn't answer right away; the abruptness of the question threw me off, along with everyone's eyes swiveling to me. "He took her," I said.

"How do you know?"

"I got home from school and the house was trashed and I sensed a Werewolf. I wasn't really that worried until I found my mom's car in the garage, which meant she'd come home. I ran through the house looking for her, but all I found was a note in her room. I heard the back door shut and I ran down but he was already gone."

"What note?" Jack asked.

"It was on the wall in my mom's room. I guess I forgot to tell you about it," I said.

"Here, I grabbed it," said Fee, holding up a piece of paper. She handed it to Jack.

"Yeah, so obviously it was Leo," I went on while Jack read. "He loves leaving me cryptic little notes."

Jack looked up at that, his eyebrows wrinkling in confusion. "This isn't from Leo."

"What are you talking about?"

"This note is from your mother," he said.

"What? No, it was from Leo. It said something about trading her for me," I said.

"This one is different. I found it in your room when I was packing your stuff," said Fee. "I would've showed you but I assumed you'd already seen it."

"You need to read it." Jack handed me the letter.

I took the crumpled paper and unfolded it. It said: "Tara, I don't have much time, but I want you to know that I love you and everything I've done is to protect you. I know you don't understand, but this is my choice. I've gone with Leo willingly. He agreed to leave you alone if I do. Please don't come after me. This is my decision. Find Vera. Call Grandma. They will help you stay safe. I love you, forever. Mom."

When I was done, my hands fell limply to my sides and I stared at Jack, without really seeing him. I felt the paper slip out of my fingers as the others passed it around.

"Tara?" Fee called gently after a moment of silence.

I shook my head vigorously from side to side. "I don't

understand. How could she just...?"

Fee tilted her head to the side in a sympathetic expression and led me from the room by my elbow, up the stairs and into the same guest room where I'd woken up on morphine. She nodded to my duffel bag, which was sitting on the bed already. "You should get cleaned up. Take a few minutes for yourself," she said.

That brought me out of my haze. "No, I'm fine," I argued. "We need to make a plan, go get her back."

"And we will, but you need to take a few deep breaths first. You won't be any good to us, or your mother, if you fall apart in the middle of the mission. Besides, we're still waiting on Cord to get here. So take a shower. You'll feel better."

Something in her tone made me glance down and I stared in surprise. My shirt was ripped along my rib cage, and my jeans had dirt and grass stains on the knees. I could only imagine what my hair looked like. "I jumped the fence," I explained.

Fee's lips curved. "I don't doubt it. See you downstairs."

After the door shut, I went to my bag and unzipped it, curious to see what clothes Fee had managed to grab for me; my room, and its contents, had been pretty destroyed. There wasn't much in the bag: a pair of faded gray sweatpants I'd forgotten I owned, a pink thermal tee, and a pair of black leggings that I'd borrowed from Sam and never returned.

I showered quickly, antsy to get going and search for my mother, but knowing deep down that Fee was right. If I was going to fall apart, I better get it over with now, or at least be sure it wouldn't happen later.

I just couldn't believe my mother had gone willingly. I thought about the possibility that Leo had made her write the note but I wasn't so sure. There was a small part of me that got angry thinking about the line she'd written, how she was doing this to protect me. It seemed everyone else knew better than I did what was best for my safety, even if it meant putting themselves in more danger to do it.

Which only made me think of Wes again, and how he hadn't answered his phone.

My anger turned to a sadness that left a physical pain in my chest as I shut off the steaming water and stepped out. My mom was out there somewhere, a prisoner, all because of me. I towel-dried my hair, threw on the thermal shirt and sweatpants, and ripped a brush through my wet tangles. I pulled my hair into a loose ponytail as I hurried down the stairs.

Everyone else was already assembled in the living room when I got there. Miles sat behind Jack, in the chair by the window. It reminded me of Wes sitting there, playing chess with Fee. I shook the image away. Bailey sat in the chair beside him looking sullen. Derek was in the chair I'd sat in that first day I'd come. His back was to me. When I walked in, he glanced at me once, and then turned back to Jack.

Fee was on the couch, wringing her hands, and looking just as stressed as I was. Cord came in behind me, her heavy boots clomping on the hardwood, and leaned against the railing near the stairs. Jack was in his usual chair by the fire. Instead of his usual pose, which included his feet propped up on the coffee table, he was leaning forward on the edge of the cushion, his elbows propped on his knees. Worry lines creased his forehead and he was staring intently into the flames.

A harsh rap on the door cut the silence and I turned to answer it. Cord rushed past me, glaring in disapproval, and threw open the door. Vera stood there, looking sleek and businesslike in a black pant suit. She strode past Cord and me without a word and went straight to where Fee sat. Fee rose to greet her with a relieved expression and took Vera's hand in hers.

"Any visions?" Fee asked quickly.

Vera shook her head. "Not yet, but I had to keep it closed off while I drove. Let's do it together, to keep it focused on what we're looking for."

Fee nodded and they sank onto the cushions together, hands still joined. They bowed their heads and Vera's lips began moving in some sort of silent chant. I glanced around the room for some clue as to what they were doing but everyone else just sat and watched them expectantly.

"What's she doing?" I asked Cord. I was hesitant to speak to her considering the way she always glared at me like I had some communicable disease, but she was the only one close enough to whisper to.

"Trying to see your mom," she said, her tone letting me know the answer should've been obvious.

I tried to be patient while I waited for Vera to finish but I kept shifting my weight from one foot to the other; my body itched to *move*, to take specific action in searching for my mother. Inevitably, my mind wandered to her, where she was, if she was okay, if I would ever find her. From there, my mind drifted to images: her smile, the color of her hair, her perfume.

My fault. My mind kept sending me back to that. This was my fault.

Whether I agreed with her twisted and faulty reasoning of doing it to protect me or not ... the fact was, it was still my fault. The familiar pang in my chest sharpened and I shifted again, needing movement.

Finally both women looked up and opened their eyes, immediately focusing on me.

"I can't see where she is," Vera said, sounding frustrated. "Not completely. Something's blocking me. But she's alive and unharmed, at least."

I had no idea how she knew this, but my heart soared at the news.

"I sensed a closed-in feeling," she continued. "Underground, maybe. But that's all I could get." She frowned. Her gaze flickered over me and away.

"What do you mean 'you sense it'?" I asked.

"Vera's visions can sometimes be focused to a specific person or event," Fee explained. "It's unpredictable at best and doesn't always work, even with a great deal of focused energy."

"So what are we supposed to do? She could be anywhere," Derek said.

"We'll use our contacts," Jack said. "Someone has to have heard something."

"All right, I can ask around," Derek replied slowly, obviously unconvinced.

No one moved from their spots, and I wanted to yell at them

to get going already.

"It may be slow going, but it's all we've got for now," Jack said, picking up on everyone's hesitation.

"In the meantime, I'll keep trying to get a better read on her," Vera added.

"Fine, then let's get moving," Cord snapped. For once, I didn't mind her impatience.

"We need to stay in pairs," said Jack. "Cord, you and Miles—"

"I'll go with Tara," Miles interrupted, rising from his chair by the window. I'd almost forgotten he was here, he'd been so quiet.

"Okay, then," Jack said, nodding once. Beside me, Cord snorted.

Miles turned to me and I shifted under his unreadable gaze. I wanted to argue but Jack continued.

"Cord and Derek, you two stick together. Fee and I will go together, and Bailey—"

"Yeah, yeah. I'll be here to hold down the fort, blah, blah, blah," said Bailey.

Derek grinned.

Jack's mouth tightened. "I need you to stay with Vera in case she gets any more information on Elizabeth. If she does, you can take her wherever the vision leads."

Bailey did a small fist pump in the air, a grin spreading across his face.

"But don't forget to call us so we can meet you," Jack added sternly.

"Jack, do you think it's a good idea, letting him help like that?" Fee asked, giving Bailey a motherly frown.

Bailey's grin disappeared and his face fell.

"No. But we're short-handed. Wes is still out on that tip we got earlier. I don't have a choice."

Fee sighed and nodded and Bailey's smile reappeared, a little smaller.

Miles rose and stepped over Derek's sprawled feet, coming to stand in front of me. "Ready, then?"

I nodded and pushed off the doorframe, not excited to be paired with Miles but willing to make do if it meant action.

Everyone shuffled to their feet and readied to leave. Cord and Derek huddled together in the entryway, making hushed plans about where they would go, whose car they would take. Jack and Fee disappeared into the weapons room in the back of the house, and Vera rose, saying something about making some tea as she headed for the kitchen.

"We can take my car," Miles said, placing his palm on my back and leading us to the door.

"Don't we need to wait for Jack and Fee to give us weapons?" I asked, sidestepping so that his hand dropped away.

"I have a stash in my trunk. We should get moving. I have an informant in Lake Anna who might be able to tell us something."
I moved to follow him and he pulled the door open, ready to follow me out. I took a step and then pulled up short, realizing someone was blocking my exit. My pulse sped when I saw who it was.

Chapter Thirty-One

"WHAT the hell is going on?" Wes demanded, glaring past me at Miles.

"What are you doing here?" I asked.

His gaze flickered to me and then around to the rest of the faces. He pushed past me and stepped up to Miles. "What do you think you're doing?"

"Leo took Tara's mother. I'm helping Tara find her," Miles answered evenly.

"She's not going with you," said Wes. Without waiting for an answer, he rounded on Derek and Cord. "Where's Jack?"

"In the weapons room," Derek answered, eyeing Wes warily. Cord just looked bored.

Wes stalked off in search of Jack. I stood in the open doorway, staring after him, trying to figure out what to do next.

Cord and Derek shot me a glance and then went back to their planning. Miles was still holding the door open, watching me expectantly. Raised voices were coming from the weapons room.

"Um, I guess we should wait," I said, stepping back into the entryway.

Miles just nodded and closed the door, leaning down so that his mouth was closer to my ear than it needed to be. "I'll be in the kitchen."

As soon as he disappeared around the corner, the door at the end of the hall opened and Wes came out, his face grim but determined. He stopped in front of me, his gaze searching my face, and his expression softened slightly.

"Are you okay?" he asked quietly.

"I guess," I answered.

He turned back to Jack who'd come up behind him and began talking about strategy and weapons. My head cleared enough to remember why we were here *and* why Wes wasn't here until a moment ago.

"... So she'll need some way to protect herself," Wes said.

"I know, I just haven't had time to train her on the metal tips," Jack said.

"Well, give her something," Wes said impatiently. "We need to get going."

"Wait a minute," I interrupted. "You think I'm going with you?"

Behind us, the rest of the group fell silent, watching our exchange.

"Of course," he said.

I shook my head. "Unbelievable. Of course you do. Well, sorry to disappoint, but you missed the pairing off, and I'm going with Miles."

Miles, who'd wandered back in from the kitchen at the sound of our voices, raised his eyebrows but didn't contradict me.

Wes stared at me. "Tara—"

"Don't." I made my voice as cold as possible and glared at him for as long as I could, without letting myself be sucked in. Then I turned to Jack. "Miles has weapons stashed in his trunk. We're leaving, but we'll check in soon."

Jack nodded slowly. "Fine, but Miles, I haven't trained her on the silver tips yet, so don't give her those."

"That's all I have," Miles admitted.

"I have something else." Jack crossed to the bookshelf and pushed a small black button I'd never noticed before. When he did, the bookshelf slid aside with a wooden groan, revealing what looked like a large walk-in closet. He flipped a switch and the space lit up. Rows of weapons lined the wall, covering every inch of space. Long wooden stakes with gleaming metal tips and crossbows were mixed in with rifles and handguns of all shapes and sizes. Jack grabbed a small handgun and two plain, rough stakes and handed them to me. "Take these."

I took the stakes and stuffed them into my boots like I'd seen Cord do. I hesitated over the gun. "I don't know about that."

"Take it," Jack said. "It's probably not enough to make a kill, but it'll slow them down long enough to get a stake in the right place."

I looked over at Miles, still unconvinced. I'd never even held a gun before, much less fired one.

Miles nodded at me. "I'll show you how to use it."

I took the gun from Jack's outstretched hand. It felt lighter than I'd expected and ice cold against my clammy palm. I held it, feeling awkward, careful to keep my fingers far away from the trigger.

"Safety's on," Jack said. "Here. Extra magazines." He handed those to Miles, who slid them into his inner pocket.

"Ready, then?" Miles asked me. I nodded and turned to go, avoiding Wes's burning gaze.

"Check in every hour," Jack added.

"Tara," Wes began, stepping forward. "I'm sorry. I just want to help."

"Feel free," I said, without stopping on my way to the door. "Call if you find anything."

"Tara, just listen—" he began.

"No, you listen," I said, whirling on him angrily. "I tried to call you. Before, when it first happened. You were the first person I thought of. So I called you, freaking out. But you didn't answer. Because you thought it was best for me if you stayed away. And don't say you were protecting me—I am so sick of everyone saying that, without any regard for what I want." I turned so that my angry stare briefly included Jack, for his part. "So, until I get an equal say, stay away from me. I don't need your idea of protection. Miles will do just fine."

Wes listened in stony silence, giving no reaction—until I

mentioned Miles. Then, his expression darkened and something flashed in his eyes. "Don't go with him," he said, in a low voice.

I felt myself hesitating. I wrenched my gaze from his, before I changed my mind. "Let's go, Miles," I said.

CHAPTER THIRTY-TWO

"WHERE are we going exactly?" I asked, as we climbed into Miles's car.

"Lake Anna. An informant for The Cause lives there. He may have heard something." Miles revved the engine and put the car into gear, easing us forward. A hand slammed down on the hood and Miles stomped on the brake. Wes stood in the way, his hard expression illuminated by the car's headlights, and making him look even more dangerous. Slowly, he came around to my side and wrenched open the door to the backseat. He slid inside and slammed the door shut again behind him.

"Odd number. Jack said I could tag along with you guys," he said.

"I thought I made myself clear," I said, turning in my seat.

"You want to argue, take it up with Jack, but we're wasting time."

I looked to Miles, waiting for him to demand that Wes get out, but he just nodded at Wes evenly and eased the car into gear again.

"You're not going to say anything?" I asked him.

"He's right, we shouldn't be wasting time. Besides, we need to work together if you want your mother back."

I slumped back into my seat, arms folded, biting my lip. Miles was right. My love life wasn't a priority right now. My mother was. I'd have to put aside my feelings until this was over.

Dirt and gravel flew up behind us as Miles picked up speed down the driveway. At the intersection for the main road, the tires spun and then caught as we turned onto the asphalt.

"What's your first stop?" Wes asked.

Miles's eyes flicked to Wes by way of the rearview. "Our informant in Lake Anna," he answered after a beat.

"Fleck? He turned on us," said Wes.

"He's sworn allegiance again."

"Right, like he did the last three times. His information isn't even remotely reliable."

Miles's expression tightened. "What would you suggest?"

"Donovan Harding."

"You think he knows something?"

"He's a better gamble than Fleck."

"Not by much," argued Miles. "He's too new."

"But he wasn't for their side, even before. He's always been neutral."

"That's my point. How would he know anything about Leo?"

"He knows Benny."

Miles considered that. "All right," he finally agreed. "We'll try him first." He took a left at the light, putting us on Route 1, heading back to town.

"Who's Donovan Harding?" I asked, directing my attention to Miles.

Wes answered before Miles could. "A recent addition to The Cause. It's taken years of coaxing to get him to commit, though. He's always proclaimed himself Switzerland in all of this, saying he didn't want to put his family in danger by officially picking a side."

"So what makes you think he'd rat Leo out? Wouldn't that put his family in danger if Leo ever found out?"

"Exactly," said Miles, glancing at Wes in the mirror again. Wes didn't answer.

We rode in silence for a while. I felt Miles's gaze wandering to me a couple of times, which gave me the same creepy vibe I'd gotten the day we'd met in Jack's backyard, like he was sizing me up. But I wasn't going to make a big deal since that would wind up leaving me with Wes; and I was determined not to cave on where I stood with that. Things had to change if he expected me to forgive him. For those reasons, the air inside the car felt thick.

I pressed the automatic window button and rolled it all the way down. I rested my head on my arms and closed my eyes against the brisk breeze that hit my face. I realized the sun had slid to the other side of the sky and glanced over at the clock. It was midafternoon. Time was slipping away, and I had to fight the urge to panic with every minute that passed without news of my mother.

"We're almost there," said Miles, a few minutes later. He blew through the yellow light to make the turn and wound through the neighborhood. He halted at the curb hard enough to push me against the seat belt before thumping back again. Across the street was a small one-story house with a black minivan parked in the driveway. I recognized the house.

"This is it?" I asked in disbelief.

"Yes, why?" Miles asked.

"I know the kid who lives here. He goes to my school. Mason..."

"Harding," Wes finished for me. "I know. Donovan's his father."

"They're Werewolves," I realized. "Wow." I shook my head. There were probably other kids at school who were a part of this world, living a lie, just like me. Strange that I'd never felt it before. Or maybe I had, passing the tingles off as being cold.

"You or me?" Miles asked Wes.

"Both. It'll be more intimidating, if it comes to that," Wes said.

Miles nodded in understanding and looked at me. "We'll be back in a minute."

"What? No, I'm coming with you guys," I said, unbuckling my seat belt.

"Not a good idea," said Miles.

"You can't," said Wes, at the same time.

"Why not?" I demanded.

Wes ran a hand through his hair, making it stick up haphazardly, and ruining the carefully mussed look he always wore. "Look, Donovan's priority is to protect his family. Information is one thing. Housing Enemy Number One is another. If you show up at his door, it could freak him out enough to keep him from talking to us."

I glanced at Miles, but he nodded in agreement.

I sighed. "Fine." Miles got out and went around to rummage in the trunk, for a weapon, I assumed.

Wes slid out and shut his door. He turned, leaning down into my open window. Gently, he raised his hand and brushed his fingers over my cheek. His eyes burned into mine and my pulse sped. "Tara, do you think I want to leave you alone right now? Even for a second? I don't. Having you out of my sight is going to be just as hard for me as it is for you. Why do you think I came with you, knowing how much you didn't want me here? If I could bring you inside right now, I would, but it won't work. Not if you want to find your mom. So give me five minutes, okay? Can you do that?"

"Okay," I whispered. I couldn't bring myself to argue with him.

"Let me see the gun." I reached into my jacket pocket and handed it to him. He took it and pointed it at the windshield. He pulled the chamber back and inspected it, and then let it click shut again. "Okay, it's loaded. Here, this is the safety. It's on right now, so if you try to shoot, nothing will happen. If you need to use it, press this button first. Then, just aim and pull the trigger, okay?" He handed it back to me and showed me the tiny black button.

"Okay," I agreed reluctantly. I took the weapon and held it gingerly, careful to keep it pointed away. It felt awkward in my hands.

"I'll be right back," he promised. He straightened and fell into step beside Miles, moving toward the Harding residence.

Miles rang the bell and a moment later, a man answered. He was tall and broad shouldered, and he immediately reminded me of an older version of Mason. His expression, upon seeing Wes, wasn't pleasant. They exchanged a few words, and then the man stepped back and Wes and Miles disappeared inside.

I faced forward again and scanned the empty street, focusing on movement rather than detail. I didn't see anything but my breath came quicker and my mind was on alert for any tingly feelings. Several minutes passed. A high-pitched beep broke the silence, and I jumped and clutched at the gun handle. I willed myself to relax and reached for my cell phone with my free hand. A text sent from my mother's phone lit up the screen and my breath caught. I opened the text with shaky fingers and read the message. "No fun without you. Wish you were here. Love, Leo."

I stared at the screen until the light faded to black and the words disappeared. A dull aching was growing, at my temples. I knew Leo was only trying to get to me, with his vague and ominous messages. The problem was, it was working. The hand that held the gun squeezed tighter on the handle, in fear and impatience.

With my other hand, I illuminated the screen once more to check the time. Wes had thirty seconds left or I was going in. Part of me hoped he didn't come out in time so I could go looking for a fight. Anger was mixing with the anxiety, and my muscles were itching to move, preferably with force.

Just as I was about to go looking, the front door opened and Wes appeared, Miles in tow. Behind them, Donovan stood in the doorway, a deep scowl on his face. Watching him, I felt the hair on the back of my neck stand on end. Wes pulled open his car door and climbed inside. With the gust of cold air came the tingling, and I kept my eyes trained on the man at the door. He didn't move, just watched with a frown as Miles got in and started the car. When we pulled away, the man finally closed the door.

I watched the house grow smaller and smaller behind us through the car's side mirror, my muscles only relaxing when it finally disappeared. "How'd it go?" I asked.

"We have to go see someone else," said Wes.

I didn't answer, and Miles glanced over at me, his brow wrinkling slightly at my expression. "Everything okay?" he asked.

"I got another message from Leo."

His gaze swiveled from the road to my face. "What kind of message?"

"A text. It came from my mom's phone."

"What did it say?" Wes asked, his tone sharp. He shifted in his seat and leaned forward.

I hit the button to illuminate the screen on my phone so he could read it over my shoulder. "'No fun without you. Wish you were here,'" I recited, for Miles's benefit. I managed to say it with a little bit of sarcasm, but I couldn't help but feel the threat in them, too. I had no doubt this was a game, one where Leo made the rules and all of the moves—so far.

"He's messing with your head," Miles said. "Just remember what Vera said. She's not hurt. We know that, at least."

"We know more than that," I said pointedly. "I can't believe she thought he'd leave me alone if she did this."

"What are you talking about?" Wes asked, still hovering just behind me.

He was close enough to touch, and I purposely kept my face forward, staring at the road ahead. "My mom left a note. Fee found it in my room when they came to get me. She says she went with Leo to protect me. That he promised to leave me alone if she went willingly." I shook my head. "And she believed him."

"I'm sure she had her reasons," said Wes.

"Like what?"

"I don't know, but I think you should at least give her a chance to explain."

"Right, I forgot, you're on her side," I snapped. He didn't answer. "And you?" I said, glaring at Miles. "Do you think she should be able to sacrifice herself for me, without my permission?"

"That depends," he said carefully.

"On what?" I demanded.

"On if it would really work. And without your permission, obviously it hasn't. But ... would you sacrifice yourself for her?"

"In a second."

"It's the same concept," he said.

Behind me, Wes snorted.

I ignored him. "Where are we going?"

Miles shot a glance in the rearview, apparently realizing by whatever Wes's expression was that he wasn't going to answer. "A guy we know. Not exactly elite society, and a Werewolf, so this should be interesting."

"Will he try to attack?" I asked.

This time, Wes did answer. "He'll be curious about you, but he's not the violent type, so just stay close and try not to talk too much. Either way, in this neighborhood, we can't leave you in the car."

I didn't ask why because, frankly, I was just glad to be in on the action this time. By now, we had woven through downtown and come out the other side. This part of town wasn't so great. On one side of the road were run-down, three-story apartment buildings with darkened side streets; on the other was the river. Through my open window, I could hear the rushing of water over rock.

The smell of garbage hung in the air. Miles turned onto one of the side streets and parked along the curb behind a rusted-out Nissan. It was by far the best-looking car on the block. Up ahead at the corner, a group of guys in baggy sweatshirts huddled in a group, swigging from bottles. Sirens sounded in the distance and then faded away.

I reached down and grabbed the gun again—this time without any prodding from Wes. I started to reach for the door handle but Wes's voice stopped me.

"Stay close to me, and don't talk to anyone, even if they talk to you. And pull your hood up."

"Why?"

"Just do it. Put the gun in your pocket but keep your hand on it. Ready?"

I yanked my hair free of its ponytail so I my hood would stay in place and adjusted my grip on the gun. I slipped it into my left pocket and got out. I found Wes watching me. Something in his expression settled the raging in my head, and I heard myself say, "Ready."

"Let's go."

I followed Wes from the car and fell into step between him and Miles on the sidewalk across the street. Following Wes's lead, I kept my head down as we passed the group of guys on the opposite corner. They were laughing loudly at something one of them had said. I could tell the moment they spotted us. The laughter died, and their voices got louder.

"Hey," one of them called. "Is that Miguel over there? What's up, Miguel?"

"That's not Miguel," said another. "He's serving his last three days this weekend."

"Who is it then, JR?" said a third.

"Keep walking," Wes whispered. "Don't look up."

Miles slowed his pace and fell back, walking behind us. I did as Wes said and kept my head down, peeking out the edges of my hood at the group of guys as we passed them.

"Hey, I'm talking to you," the first speaker yelled after us, with an edge in his voice now.

Wes picked up the pace, and we ducked around the corner of a building and out of sight. I exhaled in relief as we hurried out of earshot. I knew there was no reason to be scared—I could have taken on the entire group myself. But that didn't mean I would feel good about it after.

We were well into the alley and the light was dimmer here, the sun blocked by the walls. Either that, or it just refused to shine in a neighborhood like this. A thick layer of grime covered the brick walls of the surrounding buildings, broken up by graffiti in bright reds and greens. Most of it was curse words, some spelled wrong. There were no windows until the second floor and those were all boarded up. The ones above were yellowed and blurred with age.

We reached the end and Wes stopped. Miles was still close behind; I saw him glance back down the alley before turning to look at Wes.

"They're following," said Miles.

"I know," said Wes.

Wes headed for the entrance. Miles and I followed. Inside, the way was split in two. A narrow hallway lit by a single hanging bulb ran the length of the building. To my right, a set of scuffed linoleum stairs wound out of sight. Wes walked to a weathered door halfway down the hall and knocked. I joined him, and we waited in silence. A minute later, it opened a crack, pulled tight against the still-fastened chain. Immediately, my skin tingled and my anxiety peaked.

A pair of green eyes, obviously female, stared out at us. Her face was browned by either a tan or birth, I couldn't tell which, and I saw strands of jet-black hair sticking out from underneath the blue ski cap she wore. Goosebumps rose on my arms.

"What?" she snapped.

"I need to see Benny," Wes said, unconcerned with her cold welcome.

"Who are you?"

"Tell him Wes is here."

"Who's she?" the girl asked, eyeing me.

"She's with me." Wes's voice took on an edge of impatience.

She scowled and slammed the door with a thud. Once the door closed, the tingling faded by a few inches, but it didn't disappear. I had a feeling it wouldn't unless I left—or ended the source of it. Wes exchanged a quick look with Miles, who'd hung back out of sight during the exchange, and then Miles slid silently back outside.

"She's a wolf," I whispered.

"I know." The words were matter-of-fact, but his tone was just the opposite. I could hear the stress it was causing him to bring me here. For a split second, I thought about taking his hand or making some small reassuring gesture, but a voice inside my head responded with a resounding "bad idea, Tara," and I stopped myself. It had to be all or nothing, and I couldn't let Wes think I'd settle for anything else.

The chain behind the door scraped against wood, and the door swung open. This time, a man stood on the threshold. He had dirty blond hair that looked like it hadn't seen a shampoo bottle since the '90s, a smudged T-shirt that read "Virginia Is for Lovers," and a faded pair of blue jeans that hung way too low on his hips, considering he wore his boxers so loose on the waistline. He was grinning from ear to ear.

"Wes, get in here, you asshole," he said, motioning us inside with a swoop of his arm. "What the hell are you doing here at this time of night? Don't you know what could happen to your pretty little car down here?"

Wes stepped forward. "Benny, it's the middle of the day and you and I both know my car is fine where I parked it unless you say it isn't."

"Day, night, can't tell the difference anymore, except once a month." Benny wiggled his eyebrows, and his eyes flicked to me. He stopped and stared. "What's this?" he asked, though his tone was far more curious than angry.

Wes sidestepped, blocking me from Benny, his body language sending a message. "This is Tara. She's with me."

Benny glanced back and forth between us with interest. Then he grinned, and the tingling along my arms increased at the sight of it; it wasn't an unfriendly smile, but it was definitely one I didn't trust. "Interesting. So are you trying to restart your father's council, or you just couldn't get a date with your own kind?" He laughed at his own joke and then moved on when he saw Wes's expression darken. "Well, either way, come in. It's been awhile. We can get caught up."

He led us into the living room, which consisted of a couch and two armchairs, all sagging in the middle, and all a nice shade of dirt brown. At least I hoped *dirt* was the color and not the condition of the furniture. I perched softly on the cushion and settled in slowly; I had a high suspicion a cloud of dust might rise up around me if I sat too hard. Wes sat next to me, and I was careful not to touch him. Benny might be laughing, but underneath the curiosity was disapproval when he'd looked at me. I couldn't afford to ruin this lead before seeing where it took us.

Benny sank into one of the armchairs, which seemed to sag a little more than the other, and leaned forward to grab a glass off the grimy coffee table. He sipped generously on whatever honey-colored liquid was inside and then held it out to us.

"You want?"

"No," Wes answered.

I shook my head and then glanced around. There was no sign of the dark-haired girl who'd answered the door, which put me on edge since there weren't many places she could be in this tiny apartment. My guess was behind one of the doors that lined the too-short hallway, just off the living room. Both were closed and no sound came from behind either.

"So, aren't you going to tell me about your date?" Benny asked, gesturing toward me with his cup. He downed another swig.

"This is Tara. I'm sure you've heard the name," Wes answered. His tone was casual, but I could still hear the edge behind it.

"Should I have?" Benny took another gulp.

"Depends on who you hang with these days."

"I don't hang with anybody. They're all so boring. Nobody likes to party anymore." Benny's voice was almost a whine. "But, then again," he added, perking up, "nobody could party like you."

I clamped my jaw shut so it wouldn't hang open in shock, or worse, speak out loud. Wes, a partier? No way.

"Benny, I didn't come here to party. I need some information," Wes said.

"Like what?" Benny leaned back and emptied the remaining contents of his glass.

"Like the kidnapping of a human woman earlier tonight."

"Why would I know anything about that? Or care?"

Wes's jaw tightened. "Don't play games with me, Benny. I'm not in a good mood."

"When are you ever in a good mood, anymore? You used to be in a good mood all the time when you hung out with me."

"I'm serious. Tell me what you know."

Benny's eyes were wide with feigned innocence—and glassy with alcohol. "I don't know anything about it."

"Funny, I heard different."

"From who?" Benny leaned forward, setting the glass down with a sharp thud.

"Doesn't matter." Wes shook his head. "I'd have come to you, anyway. We both know if it's dirty or crooked, you've got your nose in it."

Benny tried for a smile and wagged his eyebrows. "You're right. The dirtier, the better. Just ask—"

"Benny." Wes shot him a warning look.

Benny's shoulders sagged and for a minute I thought he was

going to give in. Then he turned and glared at me. "What does she have to do with this?" He jerked a thumb in my direction.

"Don't worry about it. Who did the kidnapping?"

"I don't know." His tone was flippant, like a stubborn child.

Wes didn't answer, except to stare stonily back at Benny.

"Look, I don't know what you heard, but they lied. Do I look like someone who has connections?" He finished by gesturing to the apartment around him.

Wes snorted. "You've always looked like this, and you've always had connections, so don't try to play me. Just tell me who did the kidnapping. Last chance."

Benny didn't answer. From where I sat, I could feel the muscles gathering and tensing in Wes's arms and legs. Still, he waited.

Benny shifted in his chair and after trying, and failing, to hold out under Wes's heavy gaze, his grin faded, and his voice became a low whine. "C'mon, Wes, I can't tell you what I don't know. Look, why don't we all just have a drink and—"

Wes didn't let him finish. In a blink, he was over the coffee table and on Benny. He grabbed Benny by the shirt and hauled him out of the chair, throwing him against the wall. The sound of Benny's head cracking the plaster made a muted thud. Small chips of drywall broke loose, and I watched the dust and debris float to the floor, stunned by how quick Wes had moved.

"Tell me what you know," Wes growled, his face inches from Benny's.

Everything happened fast after that. Wes's shoulders started shaking and Benny's face transformed from a look of surprise to a violent scowl. I reached down and grabbed for one of the wooden stakes in my boot just as the dark-haired girl appeared from the hall. I saw her expression change from confusion to rage as she surveyed the scene. She turned with her lips curled back in a wordless growl and ran at me. She took three strides and launched herself over the furniture, transforming into a shiny black wolf in midair.

"Kat!" Benny shouted.

I sidestepped at the last second, and just barely missed her extended claws. They hit carpet instead, leaving holes and exposed threads where they grabbed. Her head whipped around and when her eyes found mine, her lips curled back, revealing gleaming fangs. I backed up a few more steps, toward the kitchen, hoping for a more open space to move in. Out of the corner of my eye, Wes and Benny were barely hanging onto their human forms. Wes still held Benny pinned to the wall and both of them shook and quivered with the effort of staying human.

"Not enough room, Benny," Wes warned.

Then Kat was coming at me again. I gripped the stake in my hand and fell into a crouch, sidestepping again, looking for an opening. She led her attacks with her teeth, and there wasn't really room to maneuver around them so I was forced to sidestep or retreat. The problem was, there wasn't really room for that, either. About three seconds later, my back hit the fridge, and I realized I had nowhere else to go.

I was barely managing to hold her gnashing fangs away from my face with fistfuls of her fur. Her green eyes bored into mine with malice and her stale breath hit my face in angry, exerted puffs. I could feel my grip slipping and I knew when it did, I probably wouldn't move fast enough to get out of her way before she bit me. After that, I'd be no good to the rescue mission. I couldn't let that happen.

Gathering all my strength, I pushed as hard as I could one-handed against her weight, concentrating mainly on keeping her teeth out of my flesh. With the other hand, I dove into my pocket for the gun and ran my fingers over it. I felt a small click against the metal and prayed it was the safety. Then, I curved my hand around the cold metal and whipped it out. I shoved it hard against her shoulder and pulled the trigger.

The momentum from the shot shoved me harder against the fridge; the handle dug into my back, and I winced. A ringing in my ears began, echoing the blast like a sonic boom.

Kat staggered back and swayed, her expression full of disbelief. "You shot me." She staggered again, almost fell, but managed to catch herself on the wall. She leaned against it and slid down, panting hard and eyeing me.

I didn't answer her right away; I was surprised to see fear in her expression. I hesitated, an idea forming. I turned back to Wes. There was no way I could voice what I was thinking. He would just have to figure it out.

I turned back to Kat with as fierce a look as I could muster and stared her down. "It hurts, doesn't it?" I said, with what I hoped was a thick layer of malice in my voice. Then I turned and locked eyes with Benny. "Let him change, Wes," I said in a smooth voice, almost teasing. It took a minute for Benny to respond. He kept looking from me to Kat and back at me again, his body frozen still. I stared at him while he took it in and made sure to keep my expression hard, my breathing even, while I watched his gaze flicker from her to me.

"You shot her," Benny said.

"You want me to let him change?" Wes asked, the doubt clear in his voice.

I had no idea if Wes could see the bluff I was going for, but it didn't matter. If he didn't, and Benny changed, I'd follow through. The feel of the gun in my hand made me confident enough, under the circumstances.

"Yes," I answered, turning my voice to a whine and doing my best to achieve a pout. "Kat doesn't want to play anymore." To prove my point, I didn't even bother glancing at her as I said her name. I kept my eyes on Benny and smiled at him. "Do you want to play, Benny?"

"What the hell ..." Benny said.

"If that's what you want," Wes said. Abruptly, he let go of Benny's shirt and stepped back. "What's it going to be, Benny? You can tell me what I want to know, or you can *play* with Tara."

Benny looked back and forth between us, clearly trying to decide whether Wes was serious. Then his gaze flickered to Kat, who lay hunched over in the corner, whimpering. Blood seeped out of her shoulder and onto the carpet, leaving a bright red stain.

"What are you?" he asked, turning back to me.

I tilted my head to the side, still in character, but inside I was confused. There was almost a note of awe in his voice. "I think you know I'm a Hunter," I said.

Benny's brows knitted in confusion. "Not like any I've seen. You feel ... different."

I shrugged. "I'm just better."

Benny looked back at Wes again, as if for confirmation. Like me, Wes just shrugged. A second later, Benny's shoulders sagged, and I knew it was over.

"Okay, here's what I know," he began. "There's a guy—name's DeLuca. He's been coming around, asking if I know you." He nodded to Wes. "Asking me how long I've known you and have I met your little girlfriend over here. Just wanted information on you. I didn't know much—I mean, we haven't hung out for a long time. But he paid well and he was one of us. Said he just wanted to look you up, so I told him a little bit." He glanced nervously at Wes again. "Just past stuff, nothing recent or personal or anything," he added.

"Then what?" Wes asked.

"He kept coming back, and one night he brought Kat with him. Said she was new around here and could I be a friend to her. He said all I had to do was find him an empty place nearby, something untraceable where he couldn't be bothered. So I did it. But I don't know anything about a kidnapping, okay? I swear. That's all I know."

"Where's the place?" Wes asked.

Benny hesitated.

"Benny," Wes prompted.

"He said he'd kill us if I told anyone," Benny whined.

"And if you don't tell us—" Wes shot a pointed look to where I stood.

"Fine." Benny sighed. "It's a warehouse. 700 Gordon Road."

Wes dug out his cell and dialed a number. "Jack. I need Fee to babysit ... Uh-huh. I'm at Benny's ... That's fine. We'll wait ..." He gave our address and ended the call. Then he turned to Kat, eyeing her wound. "You want some help with that?"

Kat whimpered.

Wes took a step towards her.

I glared at her and stayed where I was; this time my wariness had nothing to do with the role I was playing. "Why doesn't she change back?" I grumbled.

"She'll heal faster this way," Wes said, eyeing Kat. When she didn't move, he gave an exasperated sigh. "Come here and let me pull it out." Wes walked over to where she huddled against the wall, still in her wolf form. He reached down and gently took her paw in his hand, holding it still. Kat yelped and jerked away.

A quick knock sounded on the front door, and I felt myself jump. I shot a glance at Benny, hoping he hadn't noticed, but he looked more spooked than I did. He didn't move to answer it, instead watching Wes and I like a deer in headlights. Wes let go of Kat's paw and rose.

"Is it Jack?" I asked, walking toward it.

"No, it's too soon. They were going to get Vera first."

I stepped up and pressed my face to the peephole and exhaled. "Miles," I said. I unhooked the chain latch and pulled the door open, letting him in.

"How'd it go?" he asked, quickly taking in the scene.

"How'd it go? What the hell? You were supposed to be right outside," said Wes.

"I was outside," said Miles, his tone unruffled.

"And you're going to tell me that you couldn't hear the noise she was making, trying to get at Tara?" Wes demanded, gesturing to Kat.

"Of course I could. I ended up having to deal with our friends on the corner," said Miles.

"That should've taken all of thirty seconds," Wes shot back.

"They were feisty."

Wes glared at him, shook his head, and went back to Kat.

"Tara, keep an eye on Benny while I get this bullet out, will you?" Wes called, already reaching for Kat's paw again.

"Sure," I said, leveling my gaze back on Benny, who'd sunk back into his chair and was curled up, watching us nervously.

Miles wandered over to where I still stood in the kitchen and stopped in front of me. I glanced up at him and then back to Benny.

"What?" I asked.

"You can put the safety back on now," he said.

I looked down and saw, with horror, that my fingers were still curled lightly around the trigger. Immediately, I let go and clicked the safety on. Then, I slipped it into my pocket and let my hands fall to my side. I leaned my head back against the fridge, while still keeping eyes on Benny.

"Did he give us a lead?" Miles asked.

"An address," I told him. "We're waiting on Jack and the others before we go check it out. From her spot against the wall, Kat howled. I looked over to see Wes holding a bullet between his bloody fingers. Kat's howl died out and fell into a whimper. She caught me looking at her and tried to glare, but I could see her relief.

"Change back so we can bandage you up," Wes told her. He stepped back to give her some space.

After a second of hesitation, her shoulders shook and the outline of her fur blurred, and then she was a girl again. Wes went into the bedroom and came back with a blanket. He wrapped it around her, tucking it under her arms to keep her wounded shoulder exposed.

"Benny, do you have any bandages?" Wes asked.

"In the bathroom," came Benny's whiny response.

"Miles, go get them and bring them here," Wes said, kneeling down to inspect the human version of Kat's wound.

Miles complied without a word. He disappeared into the bathroom and I could hear him rummaging through cabinets. A minute later, he returned with gauze and a tube of antibiotic ointment. He set them next to Wes and returned to his spot next to me, against the wall.

"Tara, I need you to help me hold her," Wes called.

"What about Benny?" I asked.

"Miles isn't going to let us be attacked with our backs turned, right, Miles?"

Miles rolled his eyes and then nodded for me to help Wes.

"Sterilizing it isn't going to feel good," Wes said to Kat. "And I don't want a surprise fist to the face."

As soon as I got close, Kat's head shot up, and she glared at me, baring her teeth in a menacing scowl. "You try to kill me and then offer to help put me back together?" she hissed.

"You started it," I shot back.

"You can let her help or you can bleed out," Wes said flatly. "Hold her arms," he told me, without waiting for her to answer.

I came around and pinned her arms behind her back, police style. It probably hurt her wound worse to do it that way, but I wasn't taking any chances by having her teeth near my face. Even in her human form, I got the impression she would really love to take a bite out of me.

Wes poured alcohol over the hole and Kat's arms pulled against my hold. She made a sound like she was biting back a scream, and then it was over. I let go of her arms and Wes patched her up as best he could with the limited supplies.

"It'll take a day or two, but you'll be fine," Wes told her.

She eyed me. "Good, then you and I can have a little rematch," she said in a nasty voice.

I opened my mouth to respond, but Wes beat me to it. His hand shot out and wrapped around her throat like a vise, pinning her to the wall. He brought his face down so it was inches from hers and leaned in, his lips to her ear.

"You touch her, and I'll make you wish you were dead. And that's just in the first few minutes."

Kat's face turned from red to purple before Wes finally let go. When he did, she coughed and gasped for air, rubbing her throat. Benny hadn't spoken during the exchange, though I'd been watching him carefully the entire time. His body had quivered at the edges when Wes had grabbed Kat. Still, he didn't make a move to intervene.

There was a knock on the door, and Wes went to answer it. Jack and Fee walked in with Vera right behind them. An excited-looking Bailey trailed in after her. Behind them, Cord and Derek squeezed in, and closed the door. The tiny apartment was suddenly shoebox-sized and everyone seemed uncomfortable with the close quarters. The tingling in my skin skyrocketed and my muscles ached against being so close to so many Weres at once, friendly or not. But then, the bodies shifted, as Bailey and Cord helped Kat into the bedroom, and I had to stop and simply stare at

Vera. My surprise must've shown on my face because she walked over to me with an amused look.

She wore her hair pulled back in her usual silver braid but she'd traded her business suit from earlier for leather pants and knee high boots that managed to look elegant and dangerous all at the same time. Whatever she wore as a top was covered by a wool trench coat. She smiled at my expression and then abruptly turned. "Benny, we meet again."

Benny scooted to the edge of his chair, like he wanted to get up, and then changed his mind. "Vera," he said.

Vera clucked her tongue. "I told you there would be problems for you if I had to meet you like this again."

"I didn't—I mean—I told them what they wanted to know," stammered Benny. He was on edge, his eyes flicking from face to face.

I watched the exchange, impressed and surprised. I mean, Benny hadn't exactly been a badass with Wes and me, but he hadn't been a spineless tool, either. What had happened the last time he'd met Vera?

"Benny, Benny, Benny," said Vera, pacing the carpet in front Benny. "This isn't good for you. Not at all."

"If his information is good, he gets a pass. I gave him my word," Wes said.

Vera frowned. She seemed to be debating whether that should save Benny. "Fine. Call us when you know."

Wes walked over and stood in front of me, obscuring my view of Benny. "Hey," he said. "How're you doing?" His forehead creased as he studied my face, and I realized it was the first time he'd looked at me since we'd arrived.

"I'm fine. I just want to get going to that address Benny gave us." That was an understatement. I itched to be on our way from the second Benny uttered the words.

Wes nodded in understanding. "We're going now. I just wanted to make sure you're hanging in there." He lowered his voice to just above a whisper. "You were great with Kat, though I almost had a heart attack when I realized I couldn't help you without risking Benny changing. And then with Benny—you were brilliant there, too."

My heart warmed with the compliment. "So you like my big bad Hunter act?" I teased.

His lips curved at the corners. "It suits you."

Something about the way his eyes bored into mine cut off my reply. His expression held a mixture of affection, relief, and … hunger. I suppressed a shiver.

"Wes," Jack called, "you ready?"

Wes reluctantly turned away, and I felt my shoulders sag as the tension in my muscles relaxed under his averted gaze. The others were talking and planning, but I could barely focus. I was still trying to calm my racing pulse. This was ridiculous. Here I was, in the middle of a crisis—I'd just put a bullet in a Werewolf—and all I could think about was the way Wes's eyes smoldered and how his stare weakened my knees. I was supposed to be mad at him, a fact I easily forgot and was struggling, even now, to remember. I shook myself and tuned in to the conversation I was missing, determined to focus.

Wes and Jack huddled in a corner, but the apartment was way too small for their voices not to carry.

"If we split up, we'd have a better chance of surprise," Wes said.

"I don't want to leave anyone exposed, though. Leo's too smart not to see us coming. We've got to be careful," said Jack.

"Doesn't matter. We have to do it," said Wes.

"He's right," Benny said, sounding more like himself again. "DeLuca's smart. Maybe smarter than you guys. What's the big deal about one human lady, anyway?"

Wes shot him a look, which Benny ignored. Then Vera cleared her throat and raised her brow and he shut up.

"We should discuss this outside," said Wes.

Jack agreed and after a quick goodbye, we all filed out the front door to the patch of dead grass that served as a courtyard. Fee and Vera stayed behind to watch Benny and Kat. Jack gave them instructions that if they didn't hear from us once an hour, get out and get home.

I made it as far as the front stoop when I heard my name.

"Tara," Vera called.

I turned and stepped back into the dim hallway. Vera waited at the apartment door, her arms crossed lightly in front of her. I was struck again at how dangerous she looked compared to our previous encounters. Our gazes locked, and she seemed about to speak. Then her gaze flickered to something behind me and she sighed. "Be careful."

I nodded, confused.

"That's all." She stepped back and shut the door with a soft click and I rejoined the group outside.

"What was that about?" Bailey asked me as I reached the edge of our loose circle.

I shrugged. "I don't know. She creeps me out," I admitted.

Bailey grinned. "Me, too."

"Okay, so we've got an address. This is what's going to happen," said Jack, his voice low but full of authority. "It's in the middle of a busy industrial area so we Weres can't change until we're close. Real close. Which means, the Hunters are going in first. Even so, we're waiting until dark." Wes started to argue but Jack cut him off with a look. "The Hunters can scout the area and let us know when it's clear. Then we can join you and change before going in. We'll work in pairs, so we know everyone's accounted for."

"I'll go with Tara," Wes said quickly.

"You can't," said Jack. "Hunters are going in first. She can go with Miles."

"Miles? Are you serious? He almost got her killed at Benny's," Wes hissed.

Jack flashed Miles a look. "I heard. He and I will speak later. In the meantime, we'll compromise. Tara, you go with Cord. Miles can stay with Wes."

"Fine by me," Wes said heatedly.

Miles shrugged. Cord glared at Jack, but she didn't argue.

"I'll go with Derek," continued Jack.

"What about me?" Bailey asked.

Jack blinked at him, as if noticing him for the first time. "Bailey—"

"Yeah, yeah, stay here," Bailey said, rolling his eyes.

"Actually, you can stay in the car," said Jack.

"Same diff," muttered Bailey.

"No, it's not," Jack said firmly. "One of us might need medical attention and if no one else has made it back, you being there will make a big difference." Jack's gaze flicked to me and Bailey must've caught that because he didn't argue anymore. "Okay, so we won't know how many of them there are until we get in there. I also don't know the layout so we'll have to play that by ear." Jack let out a heavy sigh. "I wish we knew what to expect."

"Whatever, we've got this. Can we just get moving?" Cord tapped her boot against the blacktop and for the second time today, I agreed with her. At least about wanting to get moving.

"We'll take a drive by it, see what we see," said Jack. "But we're not going in until dark."

Wes muttered something I didn't catch. Jack shot him a look, but didn't say anything, and we all headed back into the alley, toward the street. Wes stayed up ahead, next to Jack, talking in hushed tones. Miles followed behind, looking unconcerned. Derek and Cord walked side by side, a few yards ahead of me. I found myself hanging back, giving them space, and Bailey matched his pace to mine.

"So, I heard you took on Kat by yourself," he whispered. "Impressive."

"Um, thanks," I said.

"No, she shot Kat. Not the same as taking her on," Cord said.

"She still stopped her," Bailey argued.

"Real Hunters don't need guns."

"Give her a break, Cord, she's still new," said Bailey.

I smiled at Bailey. I appreciated him sticking up for me, especially since I wasn't quite sure what I could say without making Cord hate me even more, if that were possible.

We rounded the building, and I spotted Derek's SUV parked at the curb. Derek pressed the unlock button on his key ring and the locks clicked open. Jack went to the passenger side, and Bailey and Cord followed, already climbing in the back.

"Meet back at the house," said Jack.

Wes nodded and joined me on the sidewalk.

"Let's get going," said Miles.

No one spoke on the ride over and I found myself fidgeting with my phone, actually hoping for another text from Leo, something that would give us some clue about what to expect. None came, and Miles slowed as we pulled onto Gordon. Up ahead, Derek's SUV crept along, hugging the curb at a snail's pace. Large, steel buildings lined the road, most of them with chain-link fences enclosing one side. Even through the car's closed windows, I could hear the hum of machinery.

I searched for the letters that marked the addresses and counted up. We reached seven-hundred at the same time the road dead-ended. Painted white letters advertised the building as Red Shipping Co. The lot was gravel and empty of cars. Trees lined the back, and the chain-link fence leaned precariously towards the street. A second-floor window was broken and boarded. The front entrance was made up of a large garage door that looked rusted permanently shut, and another small door beside it with dirty glass panes. No lights. Everything about it seemed empty. Was my mother in there?

Just ahead, Derek curved around and pulled a wide U-turn before finally heading back the way we'd come. Miles followed and I strained against it. We shouldn't be leaving. She could be in there.

Wes seemed to understand my impatience. "Our chances are better if we wait till dark," he said. I didn't answer.

Chapter Thirty-Three

BACK at Jack's, everyone seemed to spring into motion simultaneously, heading off in various directions, with a clear-cut task. I found myself alone before I'd even reached the front door. I dragged my feet, feeling useless and hating the idea of sitting here, with nothing to do, until dark. It was only late afternoon, the sun still visible through the treetops lining the house. I ended up out back, staring down at the remains of the bonfire from the meeting the week before.

"Thirsty?" a voice asked.

I jumped and then made myself relax. "Hey, Miles." He held out a bottle of water for me. "Thanks." I gulped it, mainly because it was something to do. I was edgy enough without Miles standing so close to me.

"Do you want to talk about it?" he asked.

I shifted, unsure how to respond. "Not really." I glanced at him and then away again, sighing in frustration. "I want to do something. I can't stand sitting around."

"I know what you mean. But Jack's right. Chances are better if we wait."

"I know."

"I have something for you," he said. He waited until I looked over at him, and then motioned for me to follow. He led me around front to his car and popped the trunk.

"What is it?" I asked.

A second later, he straightened and handed me a stake. It was tipped with metal. "Don't tell Jack," he said, with a wink.

I glanced back, half expecting to see Wes storming up, but the yard was empty. I stuffed the stake into my boot. "Thanks."

"Just be careful when you use it. Metal or steel against a Werewolf is pretty powerful. It can hit you hard if you're not careful."

"What do you mean?" I asked.

His answer was cut short.

"Tara." Cord was coming toward us, and Miles hastily pushed his trunk closed. Cord glared, but no more than usual. "I need to talk to you," she said, looking at me.

"Okay. I'll see you later," I told Miles. Then I hurried to catch up with Cord, who was already disappearing around the corner of the house. "What's up?" I asked.

She reached the edge of the backyard and stopped, whirling on me. Her blond hair glinted in the filtering light, and her expression was that of a murderous angel. "Look, I don't want to be paired with you. I wouldn't even be doing this stupid mission for you, except that hopefully I'll get to kill some Weres. So here's the deal. Stay behind me, stay quiet, and stay alive. Got it?"

I blinked at her, and nodded. "Got it."

She huffed and started to walk away.

"What is your deal with me, anyway? What did I do to you?" I asked.

She marched back to where I stood, hands on her hips. "They think you're going to lead them to peace. They think you're different and special just because you're mixed. I think you're a spoiled brat who got an easy life. Too easy. Especially if you want to survive in this world. You're green and you're a liability. It's a waste of time."

"You think I asked for this? For any of this?" I could feel myself getting worked up at her judgmental attitude.

"I don't know. I don't really care. Just do what I say tonight."

With that, she stalked off.

I let her go, still trying to figure her out.

CHAPTER THIRTY FOUR

IT seemed as if the sun took extra long to finally disappear behind the horizon. When the last rays of light faded, I was watching, tense and ready, from the back steps. Finally, the pink light turned gray, and the shadows grew long enough to be considered evening. I turned and hurried inside. The entire house was rich with the smell of chocolate. I followed it and found Fee in the kitchen. She had flour up to her elbows and streaked across her face.

"I thought you were at Benny's?" I asked.

"Vera stayed. She can handle it. Besides, we need the numbers."

I nodded. In the last hour, a dozen or so cars had pulled in. I hadn't paid much attention to the newcomers and they'd left me alone, too. Most stayed huddled inside the house while Jack filled them in on the plan. I was grateful for their help, all the while hoping we wouldn't need it. "Is it time?" I asked.

Fee looked up from her oven timer and wiped her hands on her apron. "Almost."

"What are you making?"

"Brownies." She smiled a tight smile and shrugged. "When I'm stressed, I bake."

"I'm going to go find Jack. See if he's ready," I said.

"Tara, wait," she said. I stopped and turned, impatient. "I just wanted you to know, I called your grandmother."

"Why?"

"Your mother's letter made it sound like she'd want her to know. Vera said it would be a good idea if things—well, if things don't go our way."

I swallowed a melon-sized lump in my throat. "What did she say?"

"She was already on her way. Said she'd be here waiting for us when we got back, if she stayed on schedule."

"She was already coming?" I asked.

"Apparently your mother called her right before she, well, before Leo came to collect her. Your grandmother tried to talk her out of it, but she wouldn't listen, so she'd already hopped a plane."

"Wow." Just knowing that made me feel better. Grandma would know what to do. But Fee said she wouldn't be here until after the fight. "Thanks, Fee. I appreciate that."

"You go find Jack," she said, waving me out and running sink water over her powdery white hands. "I'm going to pack some of this food up to bring with us."

To my relief, Jack and the others were already out front, loading up various cars with armloads of weaponry. Derek's SUV was open and he and Wes were shoving boxes of medical supplies in the cargo area. Bailey stood by, watching, a sullen look on his face.

"Left behind again?" I asked, coming up beside him.

"As usual. Which is dumb. I've gone on missions before. Jack's just being—"

"Overprotective?" I finished.

He sighed. "Yeah."

"I know. I hate when they do that."

"At least I get to stay in the car, though, instead of wandering around here," he said, though it didn't sound like that cheered him up very much.

"Right," I agreed.

Jack slammed the last trunk closed and turned to face the loosely assembled group. I wondered if this was the part where he gave some inspiring speech about sticking together, or being safe, or brave, but all he said was, "Let's go."

It worked for me.

Everyone broke into groups and slid into various cars. I hesitated, unsure where to go. Wes jogged over to me. "Ride with me?" he asked.

I glanced around for Miles, not sure if my nerves could handle a car ride alone with Wes right now. Not on top of everything else. But Miles was nowhere in sight and his car was empty, so I nodded, and then smiled a goodbye at Bailey.

"See you after," he said.

I buckled up and held my hands to the vents, telling myself the only reason I'd agreed to ride with Wes was for the blessed seat warmer that was currently heating my underside.

"You have your stakes, right?" he asked, pulling the car into line with the caravan in front of us.

"In my boots."

"And the gun?"

"In my pocket."

"Good." He was tense. I could hear it in that one word, and see it in the set of his jaw. "Tara, I'm really sorry you thought I broke up with you. It really isn't like that."

"I can't talk about this right now," I said. "Not with what we're about to do."

"I understand."

We fell silent, and didn't speak again until we'd parked the car a few blocks from the warehouse. Wes reached for the door handle, his eyes on mine.

"It's going to be okay, right?" I asked.

He reached out and took my hand in his. "It's going to be okay," he said, sounding way more convinced than I felt.

CHAPTER THIRTY-FIVE

IT was completely dark by the time we walked the two blocks to the industrial district, Wes's hand wrapped firmly around mine. We found the others and huddled on the sidewalk.

"All right, then," said Jack. "Everyone knows what they have to do. If something goes wrong ..." He hesitated, and I could see everyone shifting their gaze toward me and then away again.

"It won't," said Wes.

"We get it, Tara's the priority here," said Cord impatiently. "Can we go kick some traitor ass now?"

Jack nodded, and we split off into our pairings. Cord looked just as unhappy as I was, but we fell into step together. Wes and Miles walked with us as far as the nearest corner and then we parted ways. Wes watched me reluctantly, but he didn't say anything and then they were out of sight.

Cord led the way, taking us in through the alley that separated this warehouse from the next. When we reached the end, Cord stopped and peeked around the corner that would take us to the battered side door I'd seen earlier. I listened for other noises, either inside or out, but there was only silence.

Cord reached into her pocket and held something out. "Here," she snapped, shoving a key into my hand.

"What's this?"

"An extra key for Derek's car. If you find your mom and can get away, then go. Don't wait for the rest of us—just get her back to Jack's. Got it?"

"I'm not leaving without you guys," I argued.

"Whatever. If you can get away, and we're tied up, then you go. Jack's orders." Her tone made it clear she didn't really care if I complied, but at least she'd done her part. I took the key and stuffed it into my pocket. "Let's go," she said.

I reached down to my boot and lifted a plain wooden stake out before following her around the corner. I left the metal tipped stake that Miles had given me inside my other boot. I wasn't sure what the deal was with metal, but I figured I'd use it as a last resort.

We crept closer, staying in the shadows, searching for movement. No streetlights shone and neither did any light from inside the warehouse. The silence was eerie and deafening. Even our muffled footsteps seemed too loud. When we came to the edge of the building, Cord stopped. Only a few steps of open space separated us from our destination. We waited, watching and listening. Finally satisfied that the coast was clear, Cord pulled out her phone and typed a text to Jack and the others, letting them know to join us. She hit send and shoved the phone into the front of her jeans, then waved me forward.

She led me to the side entrance, to the left of the large bay door. She gingerly put her hand to the knob. The door gave way easily, swinging open with a creak that seemed to echo through the entire neighborhood. We exchanged an uneasy look and then stepped inside. Again, I waited a few seconds to let my vision adjust, and dim images finally blurred into focus. With the shapes came a tingling sensation so strong, I jerked and bumped into Cord. She glanced back at me with a hard look, but I could see she understood what was happening. Every single hair on my body stood on end, and the tingling began pricking at me so hard, it hurt. In front of me, a few stray strands of Cord's flowing blond hair broke away and flew out behind her, giving the illusion of static electricity. I knew the only reason for this kind of reaction was Weres—a lot of Weres.

Cord gestured for me to turn so my back stayed against the wall and I could see all sides of the garage at once. The inside was huge, and empty from what I could tell. Across the room, metal stairs led to a catwalk that wrapped around the back and sides of the building, extending further into the blackness than I could see.

Cord took a few steps to the side and gestured for me to follow. When we'd gone halfway around the room, a door banged shut somewhere on the second floor, and we froze. Silence followed and after several seconds of listening—and barely breathing—we started forward again.

That was when the howls began. Muffled at first, they came from every direction, echoing so that I didn't even know where to look as I whipped my head back and forth toward the noise. Then came the sound of doors being wrenched open and the howls morphed into snarls and menacing growls as dozens of wolves poured out of the open doors on the catwalk, heading for the stairs. Every single pair of glowing eyes was focused on Cord and me as they rushed for the first floor.

Cord didn't even hesitate; she ran to the center of the room and planted her feet, producing a metal tipped stake in one hand and curling the other into a fist.

It took me slightly longer, as I couldn't seem to look away from the sheer number of rushing wolves. Then, my muscles tightened and tensed as the Hunter side of me took over and readied itself for the coming fight. I repositioned the stake in my hand and stepped up next to Cord.

The first few wolves reached the bottom of the stairs just as the door behind me crashed open against the wall. Jack and Derek rushed in. I didn't even have time to turn and look for Wes before the first wolf was on me. It hit fast with all the momentum it carried from running, and jumped on me, knocking me to the floor. Its claws dug into my shoulders as it pressed its weight down fully, knocking the wind out of me. I managed to hang onto my stake, though, and jammed it into the wolf's side just before it dove for my throat with its teeth. It jerked in pain as the wood penetrated through its flesh. I yanked my stake back out and shoved the wolf hard to my left, sending it rolling away.

In less than a second, it had righted itself and fell into a crouch, teeth bared, ready to come at me again. Another one was in front of me, also crouched and ready to spring. I took an automatic step back, trying to keep them both in my sights.

They rushed at the same time and all I could do was step out of the way at the last second. When I did, the wolves barely avoided running into each other, which probably would've been funny if another two wolves hadn't cropped up on my left, circling around behind me. I took another step and turned, in an attempt to keep all of them in sight. Out of the corner of my eye, I saw two figures rush through the door: one human and one wolf. Miles and Wes? It was too dark to tell. They threw themselves into the fight without pause.

By now, Larry and Moe had recovered from the near Three Stooges collision and had realized they were a part of a four-wolf attack now instead of two. The foursome stalked toward me, confident and determined. Larry or Moe—I wasn't sure which—came at me first, trying to pin me under his paws like he had the first time. His massive paws caught me around the shoulders, and I felt the sting of claws rake across my upper arms, but I managed to stay on my feet and push him back. Simultaneously, one of the others lunged toward my rib cage, and I didn't have any hands free to stop him, so all three of us went tumbling.

I could hear the sounds of teeth gnashing and braced myself for the white-hot pain of fangs sinking into my flesh. Somehow, maybe because they couldn't get out of each other's way, I managed to keep their teeth out of me. I twisted and turned against their weight, trying to slide out from under their dog pile.

Somewhere in the darkened room, I heard a distinct click, and dim lighting flickered on overhead. I didn't even let my muscles pause as my sight adjusted. I slammed a fist into the closest wolf's face, right between the eyes, and his whole body went slack for a second, a small whimper escaping his throat. I pushed him out of the way and slammed my stake into the belly of the other wolf who was trying to hold me down by sitting on me. He jerked in surprise and scrambled away, so I yanked the stake free and watched him retreat.

I took the opportunity to look up and see how the others were doing. Cord was still in the center of the room, a blur of blond hair, as she whipped her body around in impossible positions while somehow managing to stay on her feet and stake a Werewolf at every turn of her torso. Behind her, Derek the wolf covered any gaps and sank his teeth into any wolf that got too close to her but had somehow been spared the pointy end of her stake. Still, the number of charging Weres was daunting. For every one they downed, two more appeared in its place.

"This is insane! They were waiting for us!" yelled Derek.

Jack yelled something back that I couldn't hear and then rammed his head against an oncoming Were.

A blur of fur flew out in front of me then, taking my attention away the battle scene. Wes lunged and planted himself firmly in front of me as a particularly nasty-looking wolf cut a path straight for where I sat on the floor. Wes caught him with his teeth and hurtled him aside, a growl emanating from deep within his throat as he jumped toward my newest attacker and they rolled away in a blur of fur. That was enough for me to refocus, and I hastily jumped up and readied myself for another wave of wolves as they ran at me, full force. The solitary thought in my head: this is bad. Really bad.

I caught a leg of the first wolf as it reached me, yanking and hearing the satisfying crack of bone. The wolf went down in a shrieking howl. Two more were right behind it, but I didn't move fast enough. The first lowered its head and slammed into me. I felt my feet leave the ground for a split second and then my back thudded against the concrete wall a few feet behind. I grunted, and my stake clattered to the floor and rolled away. My vision blurred and I blinked, disoriented; my breath came in painful gasps, but there was no time to recover fully as the wolf was holding me up with its claw and snapping its teeth at my face. I grabbed it by the scruff of coarse hair ringing its neck in a desperate attempt to hold it off, pulling as hard as I could. I was able to hold it steady, barely keeping it out of reach of my throat, but it wasn't enough to pull him off.

Panic slammed into me and just like that very first night with

Liliana, I realized my death was inevitable, only seconds away. I struggled to keep my hold on the wolf and pulled with everything I had. It didn't budge. I squeezed my eyes shut and waited for its teeth to tear my skin. Stale breath puffed through its nostrils into my face. Then, all at once, the weight of the wolf disappeared, and so did the stench.

My eyes popped open wide and I looked up into the face of a boy I'd never seen before. He stared down at me for a brief moment, and then spun around, lunging at an approaching wolf, and artfully staking it right through the heart. He kept going, wading through the furry bodies without looking back. His hair hung down over his forehead and his skin was deeply tanned. Even in the chaos, I knew I'd never seen him before.

I thought about going after him to find out who he was, but then my attention was diverted by a petite redhead near the door, pulling a wolf off and stomping on it with her heel before staking it and moving on with a satisfied smirk. Walking through the door were three more strangers, all with metal-tipped stakes, all dangerous looking and undaunted by the scene before them. They jumped into the fight without the slightest hesitation or surprise. Had other members of The Cause arrived? Hunters I'd never met before? I thought Fee said everyone else was out on assignment ...

Miles shoved his way in front of me, blocking my view of the newcomers as he fought off a Were that was already bleeding profusely from his ears and nose.

"Who are they?" I asked, almost yelling to be heard above the growling background that hummed like white noise.

"Who?" he asked, without looking up. He swung out with a fist and connected with the side of the wolf's head. The wolf shook it off but came at him more slowly this time.

I pointed. "Over by the door. They just got here."

In a movement almost too quick to see, Miles's stake shot out and sank deep into the wounded wolf's rib cage. He yanked it free, and the wolf fell without a sound. Miles turned to glance at the Hunters streaming through the door. He stared for a minute and then shook his head. "I don't know them."

Any reply I would've made was cut off as a fresh group of

Weres approached. Miles melted back into the chaos of the fight, drawing them away. I knew I should've gone after them, but at that moment, a familiar silhouette darkened the doorway, and I froze. The figure scanned the room and stopped when she spotted me. Her petite shoulders visibly relaxed. She strode into the mayhem, cutting a path directly for me.

"Grandma?" I whispered.

Behind her, several more Hunters streamed through the doorway and jumped right into the fighting, stakes raised high. I watched Grandma weave her way through and around the fighting, and it dawned on me that it was really her; she was really here, right now, in the middle of all this. I broke into a run, trying to get to her, to protect her. Before I could, a wolf appeared in front of her, blocking her path, and crouched to attack.

"No!" I yelled, knowing I wouldn't reach her in time.

The wolf sprang at her and Grandma didn't budge an inch. Her hand shot out and locked around the wolf's throat, pulling it up short, inches from her face. It made a gagging sound and twisted, trying to free itself. Grandma didn't give it time. Her other hand shot out, and a stake sunk into the wolf's chest. It sagged, like a deflated balloon, and then dropped to the ground in front of her. I was close enough to see her expression now. There wasn't a trace of fear in it. Annoyance, maybe. Fear, no. She smiled at me, as I hurried over.

"Grandma, what are you—I mean, how did you do that?" I asked, breathlessly.

"Same way you can, dear. Now, listen. As much as I'd love to sit and catch up, there really isn't time right now." When I just stared, she said, "Fee told you I was coming, right?"

"Yes, but what are you doing *here*?" I asked, waving an arm.

"I'm here to help get your mother out, and I brought some friends with me."

"These Hunters are with you?"

"Yes. They should be enough to hold Leo's Weres back. Let's you and I go find your mother."

"Okay." I took a step and then stopped to look at her again. "Some of the Weres are on our side. Do your people know that?"

"Of course, dear. Now, come on, let's get moving. I have a few words for Leo."

I wanted to ask what they were, and how she knew about him. I wanted to ask a thousand things, but right now wasn't the time. Instead, I led the way, weaving through gnashing teeth and swinging stakes, heading for the stairs at the other end of the warehouse. The second floor was lined with a row of heavy metal doors. My bet was that Leo had to be hiding in one of those rooms up there, and wherever he was, my mother wouldn't be far.

We made it to the stairs and I hurried up, only having to kick aside three wolves in the process. The last one didn't go down as easy as the others, and I realized we were going to have to fight it off. Then, Jack appeared and charged, shoving it out of our way and changing the focus of its attention.

"Go!" he shouted, swiping at the other wolf with extended claws. I had no doubt Jack would be okay. He was easily three times the size of the other wolf and the other wolf seemed to realize this as we hurried out of sight.

At the top, I hesitated, glancing left and then right. "Which way do you think?"

"What about there?" Grandma pointed down a narrow hallway that curved out of sight. The tiniest hint of light shone from around its corner, making the metal walkway gleam with promise.

"Let's go," I said.

We hurried forward and then pulled up short to look around the corner. The walkway ended a few feet away at a single closed door. Light peeked out from the bottom, casting a shadow on some movement inside.

"Stay behind me," Grandma whispered. "Ready?"

I nodded, and we crept forward. We reached the door, and Grandma paused with her hand on the knob, listening. No sounds came from inside, and my heart pounded in my chest loud enough I was afraid they'd hear it downstairs. Grandma nodded at me, a fierce determination in her eyes, and then pushed the door wide.

I blinked once against the glare of the fluorescent lighting. In the center of the room was my mother, her hands high over her head, held by a thick rope, a gag stuffed in her mouth. Her eyes went wide at the sight of us, and she began vigorously shaking her head. Grandma rushed over to her, and I stepped fully into the room. Something moved on my right, but I wasn't fast enough. A hand—human and fisted—shot out and connected with my right temple, and I felt my knees buckle.

My vision blurred and all I could hear was a ringing sound shrill in my ears. I slid to the floor as everything went dark.

CHAPTER THIRTY-SIX

A stinging slap across my face jarred me into consciousness. My head swung to the side and my eyes stung with sharp tears. A bass drum throbbed a beat between my temples. I struggled to focus on my latest attacker. My grandmother stared back at me. She was crouched down in front of me, her brows and forehead crinkled with worry. My jaw dropped.

"Did you just slap me?"

"I did." She nodded, looking a little relieved.

"Why?"

"To wake you up. We need to find a way out of here and we can't do that if you're unconscious." She rose and began wandering along the wall, running her hands over it.

I stared at her back, still shocked. "But ... you slapped me," was all I could say.

"Would you rather I leave you here to sleep it off while I escape alone?" she asked without turning.

She was closely inspecting a pipe that ran down the wall, across from where I sat. We were in a dimly lit room the size of a large closet, and we were alone.

"Where's Mom?" I asked, slowly pulling myself to my feet, and rubbing a lump that was making my head thud with every blink.

"I don't know. Back where we found her, I imagine. It was a

trap, obviously. Though I'm sure they didn't expect me to be with you. They had a serious fight on their hands, too, let me tell you. They might've got me in here, but I was conscious the entire time." She gave up on the pipe and turned back to me, a gleam in her eye. "Which means, I know exactly how to get us out of here." She frowned. "But it also means that Leonard will be along sooner rather than later."

"Mom said he's my uncle," I said.

She came over to me and pulled me in for a quick hug. "A story for another time, hon. We need to get moving."

I didn't even feel surprised that she'd just confirmed it as truth. I was sort of numb to surprises by now.

She walked toward the door and I followed, not sure what we were going to accomplish. It was metal and sealed tight. Grandma banged on it and stepped back. I started to tell her that wasn't going to yield results but a second later it swung open. A man with wiry muscles and a graying beard stood on the other side, flanked by four wolves. He didn't come any closer, but he regarded Grandma with a dangerous glint. There was a fierce energy about him.

"Leonard," Grandma said, her small hands fisting at her sides.

"Edie, what a surprise. Was there a family reunion no one told me about?"

Grandma took a step and Leo clicked his tongue at her. "This is close enough." Then his eyes flicked to me, and his expression hardened. "Tara and I have ... business. Then we'll talk."

Grandma sidestepped, blocking me from Leo's view. "You and me first," she said.

Something thudded behind Leo and he turned. One of the wolves flanking him, the one farthest in the back, dropped to the floor and lay still. Grandma took advantage of the distraction and launched herself at Leo. He turned back just in time and jumped out of the way, sending Grandma's fist into a waiting Werewolf. Antsy to jump in and help, I reached down to my boot and came up empty. I felt my pocket, where the gun had been. Nothing.

Our weapons were gone.

A commotion began with the remaining two guard wolves,

and I strained to see beyond Grandma and the wolf that was snapping at her. Someone—or something—let out a yelp. A human hand clamped down on my ponytail, dragging me backward down a side hallway.

"Keep your mouth shut and your mother and grandmother *might* survive," Leo hissed in my ear.

I didn't answer. I was too busy trying not to lose my footing as he pulled me out of sight. We rounded another corner, and the catwalk became more of a platform that across to the other side of the warehouse. I used the railing to keep from falling as Leo continued to pull me along by my hair. Below me, I could hear the sounds of the fight, a growling, grunting hum of bodies in motion. My shoes caught on the lip of metal that signaled we'd reached the other side, and Leo turned and shoved me into a room. My shoulder thudded into the wall, and I was pretty sure a handful of hair came loose from my scalp.

He crossed quickly to the other side and, using the hand not still clutching my ponytail, he began punching numbers into a wall-mounted keypad that hung next to another door. I knew I had only a few seconds while Leo was distracted, and still in human form. I could only hope that would give me an advantage since there were absolutely no weapons to be had. As hard as I could, I jabbed my shoulder into Leo's rib cage.

He let out a surprised, "Ow," and his grip on my hair loosened. I jabbed again with my elbow and his hand came free. I scrambled away and managed to dodge Leo's fist, already sailing through the air, aimed at my face.

He was fast, even as a human, and his next hit landed against my shoulder, driving me back and throwing me off balance. He would've been on me then, but Jack appeared in the doorway, shoving his way in and sinking his teeth into Leo's ankle. Leo's knees buckled and he collapsed to the floor.

"Jack," I said. My muscles went weak with relief.

The second Leo went down, Jack was on him, teeth heading straight for Leo's throat. Leo managed to push him aside and then rolled away, his body blurring and fading around the edges. By the time he rolled to his feet, Leo was a wolf. I stepped back as far as I could, my back hitting the wall near the locked door. This room was getting smaller and smaller. Then, another wolf appeared in the doorway, its russet fur heaving up and down with labored breaths.

Wes watched Jack and Leo and then looked over at me. "Can you get around them?"

"I don't know. But you need to find my mother. And Grandma."

"I'm right here, hon. Oh." Grandma appeared behind Wes and stopped short at the sight of the two Werewolves snapping and clawing at each other in the tiny space.

"Go find my mother. I'll be fine with Jack," I said, not really seeing a way to maneuver safely around them.

Grandma nodded, but Wes hesitated. I stared at him, eyes pleading, and Grandma took it all in. "Come on, let's go get my daughter. Then, we'll come back to watch Jack finish off this useless sack," she said. When Wes still didn't move, she tugged at him, and he reluctantly turned and followed her.

I watched for an opening, a way around Leo and Jack. I couldn't really attempt it, though, even past Jack. He was too caught up in the fight and could just as easily snap at me as Leo if I tried to push past him. They came at each other, over and over, neither one really gaining ground. There wasn't really any ground to gain. It was an even match, in age and experience, and I wondered if it would come down to stamina. But Jack was ferocious. I had no doubt he could beat Leo.

I shrank away as a claw—I couldn't tell whose—swiped dangerously close to where I stood. The wall gave way and opened inward and I had to catch myself from falling. I turned. The door that Leo had been working on yawned open into the darkness beyond. I didn't even glance back as I stepped through, and pushed it shut behind me. It banged closed with an echo. I couldn't see my hand in front of my face. The sounds of the fight behind me were muffled; there was no way to tell who was hurting whom. I wondered if I should go back. What if Jack needed me? What if my mother wasn't where we'd left her?

I heard the click of the switch at the same time an overhead fluorescent flickered to life. I blinked, and saw that I wasn't alone. Miles was leaning against the far wall, about twenty feet away, just next to a short set of stairs, with EXIT painted in peeling letters. His hands were in his pockets. He had a jagged-looking cut on his jaw that was already beginning to heal.

"Where are we?" I asked.

He shrugged. "Attic, I think. The roof's up there."

A muffled snarl came through the door behind me. "Jack and Leo," I explained.

Miles cocked his head to the side. "You're so much more resourceful than he gives you credit for. It's probably the only reason you're still alive. Well, that and dumb luck."

Another snarl, louder than before. I winced. "I should go help Jack."

"Not enough room," he said, shaking his head. "They'd shred you. Both of them."

I sighed. "I have to do something. I can't just hide out here all night."

He pushed off from the wall and strode over to me. He stopped and bent his head down, so that his face hovered an inch from mine. "Yes, you can. Stay with me."

I tried taking a step back, uncomfortable with our closeness, and the way he looked at me. But my back was already against the wall. I looked away. His lips hovered over my cheek, instead. "You should be out there fighting, too."

"You don't want to stay with me?"

His hot breath blew in my face, and my stomach twisted. "Miles—"

The door behind us was wrenched open, and I fell backwards. Miles's hand reached out and caught me, inches before Leo's sharpened teeth did. I whirled to face him and took an automatic step back, bumping into Miles. He didn't move out of the way. My skin crawled.

"What the hell?" Leo growled. "Why is she still alive?" He was looking at Miles.

"We were talking," said Miles. There was no trace of fear or anxiety in his voice. He sounded annoyed and bored.

"I told you, she's not going to turn," Leo said.

"She might, if she understood what we're offering," said Miles.

Something about the easy way he answered, the familiarity with which they spoke to each other, triggered alarm in me. I tried to step away. Miles hand clamped down on my wrist, holding me in place. I looked past Leo, for Jack. He wasn't there.

"What are you doing, Miles?" I whispered.

"Giving you a choice," he said.

I twisted around so I could see his face, which I instantly regretted. He was close. We were nose to nose. "What choice?" I kept my voice as even as I could, but I knew I sounded freaked. "Why are you talking to him like that? He's the enemy."

"He's *your* enemy," said Miles. He smiled down at me, and I suppose he meant it to be friendly and inviting, but it wasn't. It was creepy and calculating, and I began to realize ...

"You're working with him?"

Miles looked past me, back to Leo, and his smile twisted into a grimace. "Don't have a choice, do I, dear old Dad?"

"Shut up. You're telling her too much," said Leo. "Kill. Her. Now."

I tensed, but Miles seemed utterly relaxed. He was looking at me again. I swallowed. "He's your dad? As in, you're my cousin?" I asked.

"I always wanted a big family," he said. His free hand went around my waist, holding me still inside the circle of his arm. He leaned in, inching his lips toward mine, and I had to struggle not to gag. He stopped and hovered with his lips just a breath from mine. His eyes were still open and he was watching my reaction. I couldn't help the horror that must've shown on my face. He frowned and eased back. "No? Not going for it, huh?"

"No," I said on an exhale. Had he really just been about to kiss me?

"Ah, well. Shame. I'd hoped we could work together. You have so much potential. But ..." He looked back at Leo. "You win again." Then his hands released me and he shoved me back through the door, straight for Leo.

I stumbled and then sidestepped Leo back into the tiny room.

Leo regarded me with a look I couldn't read. Probably because I didn't speak crazy. There was blood on the floor at his feet, but I tried to ignore that. Where was Jack? Maybe I didn't want to know.

A furry form appeared in the doorway and I almost cried. "Jack!"

"Tara?" He was panting and there was a shallow cut on his leg. "I didn't know where you'd gone. I was looking for you. Leo said you ran …" He trailed off and glared at Leo.

Leo looked seriously pissed. "One more minute, dammit. You couldn't stay gone one more minute?"

Jack answered by launching himself at Leo, jaw wide, teeth bared. A growl erupted as the two slammed into each other, and then the wall. I looked back at Miles. He stood, blocking the doorway to the attic. I inched to the left. Maybe he wouldn't notice, and I could slip out. Get help for Jack.

Miles watched the fight with a look of mild interest for several seconds and then abruptly turned his gaze back on me again. I froze, halfway to the door.

He looked angry. "Always someone there at just the right moment, isn't there? No wonder Leo was so set on killing you, instead of trying it my way." He shook his head.

I blinked at him.

Without another word, he reached inside his jacket and pulled out a gun, leveling it straight at my chest. It looked a lot like the gun I'd used on Kat. Then, he fired. I didn't even have time to duck or swerve. Just stand there and wait for the pain.

In that exact moment, Leo's claws took a swipe at Jack and he swerved and jumped out of the way, putting him directly between me and the gun. Miles slammed the door and disappeared as Jack went down.

CHAPTER THIRTY-SEVEN

"NO!" I rushed forward, reaching Jack just as he hit the floor. His eyes were open but glazed. Bright red liquid was already pooling on the floor underneath him.

"Jack," I said, choking back a sob.

"Tara. I ..." His words were garbled with the sound of liquid in his chest. A small trickle of blood escaped his mouth.

"Finally, that boy does something right," Leo said.

My head snapped up. "You. Shut. Up."

"He actually thought he could turn you," he said, ignoring me. He was getting worked up now, spitting when he spoke, saliva pooling at the corners of his mouth.

I squared my shoulders. "I'll never join your side. I'm a Hunter, not a Werewolf."

"You've got enough of both in you," he said, his eyes gleaming wildly as he spoke.

Beside me, Jack's breaths were coming in labored wheezes. I wanted to do something to help him, but I had no idea what. And Leo was advancing. I cast one last glance at Jack and then rose, stepping over him, to face Leo. This was what I could do. I just hoped Jack could hang on long enough.

"Not a freaking chance," I said, letting the anger and fury wash over me and wipe out the fear that gnawed at my gut.

"I figured you'd say that. We'll do it my way, then." Leo surged forward, teeth bared, in a jerky move meant to take me by surprise.

I blocked him and angled my body away, giving him a shove from behind, so that his momentum took him into the wall behind me. His shoulder took the brunt of it, but it wasn't hard enough to slow him down by any means. The space wasn't big enough to do that. He turned to come at me again, but now I'd caught him off guard. I swung out and punched him—hard—in the face, sending his whole body jerking to the side. I watched in satisfaction for a split second. Then I swung out again, same hand, before he could recover.

He managed to duck under at the last second and came up, teeth first. Fangs caught my wrist and scraped away my skin. I pulled free and backed up a step, quick to get out of range and recover from the sting. I had to get out of this room. There was no space to maneuver, and I didn't stand a chance against those teeth if I stayed. My wrist began heating up, and I knew I had to be quick.

I whirled and ran for the door, my feet pounding hard on the metal floor of the hallway. I made it several feet down the catwalk before I turned, knowing he'd be right on my heels.

He came at me again, but I managed to knock him away, his rear end knocking up against the metal railing behind him. This space was just as small, but a long stretch of metal hallway behind me would at least allow me to sidestep or retreat if necessary. I was completely realistic about my chances. I knew it was entirely possible I'd have to run. But then I thought about Jack, lying bloody and half-conscious in the other room, and I knew running was out of the question. If I did, he'd die.

With that thought, I steeled myself against doubt and focused on Leo, letting the Hunter in me completely take over my muscles and senses. As soon as I gave into it, I forgot all about the wound on my wrist. I felt no pain, nothing but anger and the hunger to see Leo without a heartbeat.

Leo felt the same. I could see it in his eyes. They were wild and fierce, locked on his goal. Me. His determination might've even been greater than mine. He seemed almost desperate about it, the way saliva pooled at his open jowls and his growl had become a cross between a howl and a whine. I hoped that meant he would make a mistake soon. I wanted this over. Still, some long-dormant Hunter part of me had awakened—as it did in every fight—and provided me with what I hoped was enough energy and supernatural strength to continue. That part of me wanted to draw this out.

Leo lunged again and, this time, I didn't step out of the way. Just before he reached me, my right hand shot forward and caught him around the throat, squeezing tightly and stopping him in his tracks much like I'd seen Grandma do earlier. He choked in surprise and his body went still for a minute, probably from the shock of being caught.

Then he was moving again, and I could feel the force of his contracting muscles as he tried to shake my grip. I only squeezed tighter, cutting off his windpipe. He choked again and his yellow eyes went wide. I needed a weapon. There was no way I could end this without one. My stakes were long gone, but there had to be something around here.

Leo twisted and snarled against my hold, though it came out guttural and more like a cough. I glanced around quickly, looking for anything nearby that I could use, but there was nothing.

Then Leo jerked his head hard to the side and took a step back, forcing me to move with him or let go. It was just far enough to make me loosen my grip. A furry paw swung out at me and I didn't see it in time. It connected; the claws scraped across my cheek, hard enough to drive my head sideways, as though I'd been slapped. I felt my grip on his throat give way, and he stepped easily out of it as I struggled to right myself and get my bearings.

I leaned into the railing, grabbing it with one hand, to steady myself. My cheek burned and I dabbed at it gently with my fingertips, already feeling the raised welts left behind.

I blinked to clear my eyes of the tears, and stepped back, trying to get a feel for Leo and what would come next. I didn't really have time to brace myself before he sprang again, sailing through the air, covering the entire distance between us in a single leap. His paws hit my shoulders, sending me flying. My back hit the metal railing with a painful thud.

We were further down the catwalk now, and this side of things was in a lot worse shape than anywhere else in the building. The welded rods that made up the railing were corroded and rusting. The joints that joined them were crumbling in places, and when I hit, I felt a tiny amount of give. I pushed off, afraid it would snap and send me plummeting to the first floor. Even my quick-healing muscles wouldn't forgive that.

But Leo was on me before I could get clear, shoving me back against the railing and snapping his teeth at my throat. I managed to hold his head away, using fistfuls of his fur to pull him back, but with both of us pressing on the crumbling railing, I could feel it buckling under the stress. Putting all my weight into it, I leaned and shoved as hard as I could against him, but he didn't budge.

Something behind me creaked and then snapped. Whatever had been holding me up gave way, and I fell with a thud onto my back, my left shoulder hanging off the edge of the catwalk. Leo went down with me, his weight actually helping to hold me on the floor instead of wobbling over the edge. I was almost afraid to push him off, since the momentum might be all I needed to complete the fall.

Maybe it was because of that thought, but my grip on him faltered a little, and his teeth snapped closer, scraping along the skin on my neck, and leaving a burning in its wake. I cringed but tried to push harder against his snapping jaws. Something about the singeing heat in my neck seemed to awaken the same pain in my wrist, and both of the wounds burned to life. I strained away from Leo's fangs, craning my neck as far from him as I could. When I did, something metal and gleaming caught my eye, just behind Leo's head.

A jagged piece of railing stuck out awkwardly from where the rest of the rods had given way and fallen to the first floor. It was rusted and crumbly, and I wasn't completely sure how loose it was, or if it was even within reach, but it was all I had. Using my entire right forearm to brace against Leo's weight, I let go and reached for the metal rod with my left hand. I was just able to grasp it with my fingers, but had to move closer and get more of my body over the edge of the catwalk. I was half on, half off. If this didn't work right, I was going over for sure. My fingers closed tightly around the rod and I yanked and twisted until it was free. The strain of it was causing my grip on Leo to lessen, and I could feel him pressing closer to me.

"It's almost over," he rasped. "Stop fighting it."

His hot breath blew in my face like a cloud and I gagged at the mangy animal stench. Saliva dripped from his jowls to my shirt. He strained closer. My stomach rolled.

I brought the metal rod around and up, arcing toward Leo's chest, just as his teeth broke through my flesh.

I vaguely felt the slide of the metal as it entered and sank deep inside through muscle and tissue and into what was hopefully, his heart. Then all I could really feel was the burning of Leo's teeth as it lit like wildfire through my veins. My vision blurred until all I saw were dozens of pairs of Leo's wild, yellow eyes.

That was when the vibrations began. It started in my hand—the one still holding the tip of the rod. The metal gleamed and glowed, heating under my palm like I'd shoved it into an oven. Smoke hissed and rose from the point of entry, and I wasn't sure if it came from the metal or from Leo's flesh. When he began howling, I knew it was his flesh. I jerked my hand free of the metal, and the heat faded some, replaced with a vibrating shock that shot up my arm and into my chest. My insides echoed with it, and I began to shake.

It took me a minute to realize Leo had stopped moving and was slumped over, completely pinning me underneath him. The vibrations were shaking me so hard now; this was what it must feel like to have a seizure. Leo's lifeless body shook with me. I squirmed against him, but I was afraid of making the wrong move and toppling over the edge. The vibrations finally ebbed enough to gain some sort of control over my limbs. Now, everything just burned.

As the fire spread through me, I began caring less and less about being pinned. My vision blurred and a voice inside me screamed and wailed against the flames that were boiling my blood. I brought my left hand up and gingerly touched my fingertips to the wound on my neck. I could feel the torn skin and yanked my hand away. It was covered in blood.

I thought I heard someone calling my name but it was muffled and unrecognizable. Maybe they couldn't see me, pinned underneath Leo's body like this. Maybe they'd never find me ...

It all happened in slow motion. Slender hands reached out and grabbed at the matted fur on Leo's back, dragging him off me with a strength that didn't seem to fit the slim arms that wielded it. I tried following the arms to the face that went with it, but everything blurred to red and black dancing dots. The hands returned, and grabbed the fabric of my jacket, pulling me away from the edge of the walkway.

I tilted my head and saw Leo lying beside me, twisted and awkward. His eyes were open but glazed, unseeing. Dried saliva coated the sides of his mouth and mixed with blood that still oozed from his throat. It dripped onto the metal flooring underneath him, and then further below to the first floor. The metal rod stuck out of his chest, a large ring of red staining the fur around it. I felt a small wave of relief and satisfaction, and then I shifted away.

My rescuer's face was bending over me. Maybe close enough to see now. I blinked and the edging of red receded and brought the face into focus. My mother.

"Tara? It's me. It's over, honey. Are you okay?" she asked. Her voice was strained. Her eyes flicked back and forth between my face and my arm.

"Yeah," I managed, though it came out more like a sigh. I was breathing heavy against the pain and any attempt to talk only seemed to make it worse. "Are you sure Leo's dead?"

"Positive. You used metal," she said, surprised. "Did it—are you sure you're okay?"

The burn traveled all the way through to my vocal cords; everything hurt. I remembered what had happened the last time I'd been hurt like this. "I'm—going to—pass out," I whispered.

"Okay. I'm getting us to the car. I'll take us home."

"No, not home. Not yet. Jack."

"I know." Her expression clouded. "We found him when we

went looking for you. Wes is with him now."

"Is he—"

"He's alive. Barely. Fee might be able to help." Her face clouded over. "I don't know if we caught it in time," she whispered.

I just nodded. Was she talking about Jack? Or me?

My mom smiled. "Tara, you did it. Leo can't hurt us anymore."

"Good." I tried to smile back, but my face felt tight for some reason. "Mom. It hurts."

"I know, those scratches look pretty deep," she said.

I felt a fresh wave of fire wash over me, licking at every single nerve ending. My body jerked and my head rolled to the side. Out of the corner of my eye, I saw my mom's eyes widen, and her hand went to her throat.

"Oh! I didn't see! You're bit—I thought it was just the scratches." She glanced up. "Wes!"

A second later, I heard heavy footsteps and the metal underneath my back vibrated. "What's wrong?"

"She's bit," said my mom, a hint of panic creeping into her voice.

He hurried closer, and I knew the moment he bent over me. I could smell him. A wild, animal version of woods and wind. But his hands on me let me know he was definitely human again. "Are you sure? I thought you said she was fine," he said. "You said it was just scratches."

"I didn't see at first," she said, her voice breaking. "Look."

I could hear everything they were saying, but it hurt too much to turn toward them. I lay there, feeling like a science experiment while Wes peered down at my neck. I didn't need to see his expression to know it was bad.

Wes cursed and then crouched lower and scooped me up in his arms. I bit my lip to keep from crying out. "Jack's already being loaded into Derek's Suburban, and my car's too small for her to lie in," he said.

He began making his way toward the stairs and my mother followed. I could hear her lighter steps hurrying to keep up with Wes's heavier, longer ones. I struggled to keep silent against the pain and squeezed my eyes shut with the effort.

"I'll ask Edie if they have a vehicle," my mother said.

I felt the shift of descending the stairs. I must've made some sort of noise because Wes whispered, "Sorry, almost there." At the bottom, Wes hurried forward, careful to keep me still.

"Edie!" he called out, picking up the pace. "Edie!"

"Oh my goodness," I heard her say. "Is she all right?"

"He bit her on the neck. It's not good," Wes said, his voice grim.

"What can we do?" I heard Grandma ask.

"Fee can help her better than anyone," he said. "We need to get her there."

"But she's going to be working on Jack," said my mother.

"She'll have to do both," Wes answered. "Edie, do you have a car?"

"Yes, yes, of course. Come on, this way. Quickly," she said.

We began moving again.

"Sophie," Grandma called as we walked, "tell everyone to finish cleaning up here and meet us at the address I gave you. I'm taking the Hummer."

Hummer? Grandma drove a Hummer?

"Since when do you drive a Hummer, Mom?" my mother said.

"There's a lot about me that might surprise you, Elizabeth. You've had your head in the sand a long time."

I felt the jostling of Wes climbing into the car, still with me in his arms. I winced, biting my lip harder against the scream that wanted to escape. He settled us in and wrapped his arms securely around me. Someone pressed a towel against my neck and held pressure to the wound. A second later, I felt the car lurch forward. The roar of the engine was dull in my ears, against the roar of the fire inside me. A moan escaped my lips after the fiftieth pothole in three seconds, and Wes's hands stroked and soothed my heated skin.

"It's going to be okay," he murmured, sounding way more confident than I felt at this moment. I kept my eyes squeezed shut and managed a nod.

"Did you get a head count for your people, Wes?" Grandma

asked from the driver's seat.

"Yeah. Everyone was accounted for but Miles. Derek got bit but it wasn't bad, and Fee treated it before we left."

"Miles?" my mother asked.

"Yeah, Miles Ducati," said Wes. "He's a Hunter. Did some side work for Jack a few times and then got accepted a few months back. Tall, dark hair. Did you see him at all?"

"No, I didn't. Maybe he's back at the house already."

"Miles." I knew the word came out muffled and weak, but I had to try. They didn't know, and they needed to. Before he hurt someone else. "He ... shot." I broke off, knowing if I opened my mouth again, any words I formed would be accompanied by a manic scream.

"No, Tara, Jack was shot. Miles is missing," said Wes.

I felt myself shaking my head, trying to tell him what I meant. Then the fire peaked and everything went black.

Chapter Thirty-Eight

THE sky was beginning to lighten around the edges. A hint of pink lined the horizon, just barely showing through the treetops that were visible through the second-story window opposite my bed. That was what I saw first when my eyes opened, and I knew I was back in the spare room at Fee's. Apparently, this room was now reserved for nursing Tara back to health. Nearby, a chair scraped against the floor, and I craned my neck. My mother leaned forward. Our eyes met, and she gave me a tentative smile.

"Hey," she said, brushing my hair back from my face.

"Hey." My throat felt like the Sahara. She held a straw to my lips, and I sucked water in through dry lips.

She set the empty glass aside. "How are you feeling?"

"Alive," I said with undeniable relief.

She nodded. "It was touchy. For a while, I wasn't sure ..."

I didn't answer. I couldn't reassure her, even now, when I hadn't been sure, either. "And Jack?" Panic twisted in my chest.

"Alive." She hesitated, then said, "It was a bad wound, though, Tara. He's going to have a long recovery, and he probably won't ever be able to move like he used to. The bullet tore a lot of muscle and metal isn't easy to heal from."

I nodded, still relieved more than anything else. If Jack had died from a bullet meant for me ... "Fee's pretty amazing," I said.

"She is. But then again, so are you." She shifted in her chair. "Which is why I want to apologize."

My eyebrows shot up, but I didn't interrupt.

"I gave myself up to Leo because I thought it would protect you." She took a deep breath, and let it out. Her cheeks reddened. "Obviously, it wasn't my best idea. But, I should've given you more credit. In the end, you saved yourself. You're not helpless, and I'm going to try to stop treating you like you are."

"The operative word here is 'try,' isn't it?"

"Rome wasn't built in a day."

"Right."

"But, I am still your mother, and things are going to change. I need to know where you are, at all times."

"How's that different from before?" I joked. She didn't smile, and I felt a hard knot form in my empty stomach.

"This isn't over, Tara. We know it was Miles who shot Jack, and we know it was meant for you. Jack told us," she explained when I looked back at her questioningly. She twisted her fingers together and looked away, out the window. "There's a school just a couple of hours from here. It's for Hunters, and it's well protected."

"You're sending me away?"

"Your grandmother and I agree that it's the best place for you right now, at least until we can resolve the ... situation."

"Do I have a choice?" I asked through clenched teeth.

"Don't think of it as me forcing you. Think of it as a chance to learn from the best. Wood Point Academy has the best instructors available. You could continue your training and be around other Hunters."

"But I'm not just a Hunter, remember?"

Her jaw hardened. I knew she was waiting for me to call myself Dirty Blood, and I knew she'd lose it if I did. She rose and paced in front of my bed, wrapping her hands around herself as she moved. "Either way, you need proper training," she said. She stopped and looked at me. "What were you thinking, using that metal rod against Leo, anyway?"

I shrugged, a little confused. "It was all I had. My stakes were gone."

"Well, you got lucky. Your new trainers will show you how to properly use metal against Werewolves."

"Jack's my trainer," I said, stubbornly. What was the big deal with metal, anyway?

"Jack's going to be out of commission for a while. Maybe permanently. Grandma pulled strings to get you in, and it's the safest place for you right now. I won't deny I made a mistake with Leo, but I also won't let you talk me out of making it right."

My shoulders sagged. I knew her mind was made up. Between her and Grandma, I didn't stand a chance of talking my way out of this. "Grandma." Suddenly, I felt selfish for taking so long to remember her. "She's okay, right?"

"She's fine. She's at our house, making arrangements to send her people home."

"How long is she staying?" I asked.

"Until she leaves."

"What does that mean?"

"It means, she hasn't told me yet," she said, rolling her eyes. "And I wouldn't be surprised if she settles in for a while. She's pretty excited that I'm going to let you train."

I knew Grandma must be excited if she was going to stay with us. She and my mother usually had a fifteen-minute maximum on civility while in the same room. "I can't believe she's a Hunter, too. I mean, she really knew what she was doing. She was pretty scary."

My mom laughed, and I closed my eyes and just let myself enjoy the simple sound of it. Who knew I'd ever feel this overwhelmingly happy to hear my mother laugh? Especially when I was technically mad at her, all over again. But even being angry at her didn't diminish my happiness and utter relief that she'd made it out of all this unharmed.

"Tara? You okay?"

When I opened my eyes, she was staring down at me, her brows knitted together.

"I'm fine, Mom. Just glad everyone's okay. Glad you're okay," I said. "And I'm sorry about fighting with you before ..."

She smiled, big enough to let me know that we didn't need to go there. She reached out and took my hand, squeezing it. "Me, too. And I really think you'll like Wood Point. Everyone there is a Hunter, too, so you don't have to pretend, not like you do here. You'll make friends and meet new people."

There was a specific gleam in her eye that made me wonder if she wanted me to forget all the friends I had, or just a specific one. I cleared my throat, almost afraid to ask. "So, have you seen Wes? Is he here?"

She nodded, pressing her lips together in a tight frown. "He's been here the entire time. I just kicked him out a few minutes ago to get cleaned up. The shower's been a highly coveted space for the past couple of hours." She paused and then said, "Do you want to see him?"

I ignored her reaction and her tone, both of which made it obvious that she wanted me to say no. "Yes." I sighed, unsure of what I would even say to him. But I did remember how he'd held me in his arms the entire way home. If my skin hadn't burned so badly, it probably would've felt nice. Okay, better than nice.

"I'll send him in," she said, leaning over and dropping a kiss on my forehead.

"Mom," I called, when she reached the door. I waited until she turned. "I love you."

She smiled. "Love you, too, honey. Everything's going to be okay."

The door clicked shut behind her, and I settled back against the pillow, amazed at how tired I still felt, even after being unconscious most of the night. You'd think blacking out would give your body the ultimate rest, but apparently not. My phone beeped, and I rolled over, trying to find it underneath all the blankets. I lifted the covers and realized all I wore was a nightgown—no pockets. The sound continued. I eyed my jacket. It was draped over the chair a few feet away. The phone was in my pocket, and no way could I reach it from here. I sat up slowly, feeling dizzy from the small exertion. A stiff pain shot up my spine, making it throb. Even my arms protested against the use of muscle. Ugh. I felt ... hung over.

My phone beeped again. I sighed. I pulled the covers back to my waist and eased toward my jacket. I managed to snag the edge of it and pull. As I did, my phone fell out of the pocket and thudded onto the floor. I eyed it viciously, debating on how badly I really wanted it.

The door swung open. Wes poked his head in. "You're awake."

I'd never heard so much relief uttered in two words before. He came in and closed the door with a click. I felt a pull to go to him that was so strong, it took my breath away. I watched his face as he lowered himself into the chair beside me. His eyes were bloodshot and exhausted, his jaw tight with tension. His hair was still wet from the shower and dripped onto the back of his plain white shirt. He smelled like rain-drenched woods. I forgot all about my beeping phone, along with anything else that might divert my attention.

He eyed me with scrutiny, like he didn't yet believe that I was going to recover. His gaze flickered from my face back to the gauze on my neck. I waited for him to say something. Instead, he held out a cup, half full of a mysterious green liquid.

"What's this?" I smelled it hesitantly and made a face. "It smells like old cheese."

He gave me a look like he agreed. "Fee sent it for you. It'll boost your energy. And keep you from needing any more morphine. Drink up."

He paused, obviously waiting for me to comply. I held my breath and threw my head back, taking the contents in one shot and trying not to let it hit my taste buds. At least I wasn't dopey like the last time.

"Ugh," I muttered, handing the empty cup back to him.

He smiled, though it didn't reach his eyes. "I can see you're feeling more like yourself every minute." His amusement faded, and his brow creased. "How *are* you feeling?"

"My neck still hurts, and I'm sorer than a week's worth of training with Jack, but I think I'm okay. Mom says I will be, anyway." At the mention of Jack, Wes's expression clouded further. "How is he? Mom said it was pretty bad."

"Fee's still with him, doing what she can, but he's not great. Punctured a lung. Some of the damage was irreversible. She says he's going to have a long recovery."

I shuddered, remembering the sight of him on the ground next to me, bloody and struggling to breathe. "I thought—I mean, I was really scared for him," I whispered.

Wes leaned forward, his expression a mixture of sadness and longing. "I was really scared for you," he admitted. "When we found you, with Leo ... I only left you because Jack seemed worse. Your mom said all you had were scratches, so I ..." He trailed off and squeezed his eyes shut.

I lifted my hand to my face tentatively. I'd completely forgotten about the scratches. I traced my cheekbone, feeling raised welts and rough scabs, and wondered if it looked as bad as it felt.

"They'll heal in another day or two," he said. I nodded, and caught sight of gauze wrapped around my wrist. "We almost didn't see that one. It wasn't nearly as bad as your neck, but it needed treatment and Fee almost missed it. Bailey was the one to notice it, actually."

"Tell him thanks," I said, feeling awkward. The way he was speaking, his tone, all of it was... not cold, but not like him. Distant. "And Derek? How is he? You said he got hurt."

He gave me an odd look. "You remember that?" I nodded. "I wasn't sure if you could hear me."

"I could hear just fine. It was responding that got complicated."

He didn't reply. The silence was uncomfortable, like there wasn't really anything left to talk about, except ... us.

"So, what now?" I asked, my fingers fidgeting with the edge of my blanket.

"Now we find Miles."

His answer didn't surprise me, but I felt a sinking disappointment, anyway. It was always about the business end first. "Mom said Jack told you about the bullet being meant for me," was all I said.

"Yeah." He ran a hand through his hair, sending tiny drops of water flying. "I suspected something was up when he didn't show up here afterward. Then Jack woke up enough to talk and told us what happened. We're launching a search, but I don't think we'll find him. He's probably long gone by now. Traitor."

"He's Leo's son."

His eyes widened. "What? How do you know that?"

"He told me." I suppressed a shudder and tried not to think about the weird almost-kiss, and Miles's hot breath on my cheek.

"He was probably messing with you. There's no way he could be Leo's son. He's a Hunter. I've seen enough to know that, at least."

"I don't know. Miles seemed pretty serious. And Leo got mad that he'd told, said he was telling me too much. Then, he seemed sort of proud of Miles, for firing the gun."

"Miles was really aiming for you, wasn't he?"

"Yeah. Apparently, Miles argued with Leo about not killing me. About letting me choose. I think they wanted me to turn and join their side. I told him no, so I guess Miles changed his mind and decided to do it Leo's way."

Wes jumped up, pacing the room and shaking his head. "I knew he wasn't to be trusted. I've been telling Jack this entire time. He's
too new, and we don't know a thing about him. But Jack vouched for him, said he'd done enough side jobs and he was in."

"What kind of side jobs?"

"He claimed to have gone undercover for a few weeks. He disappeared and none of us heard from him so we just had to assume it was legit. Then, he shows up out of nowhere and has an address for a possible hideout or base for Leo's operation. We get there and there's like two Weres in the whole place. Both are known supporters of Leo, but Leo himself is nowhere to be found. I told Jack then that it felt wrong but he was just happy for the info, small as it was. When I find him, I swear, I'll kill him. Very slowly." He stopped pacing, but his hands were fisted at his sides, and his eyes were unfocused, like he was picturing it.

"I think we need to prepare for that. Seeing him, again, I mean."

"I know. He's obviously just as crazy as Leo. It's only a matter of time before he tries something else." He sat next to me again, not really looking at me. "I should talk to the others; get everyone back here that's out on assignment, so we can figure out what to do about stepping up security." He was already moving toward the door, distracted with thoughts of strategy and manhunts.

Disappointment stabbed at me again, piercing my chest with a painful prick. Protecting me was not the same as being with me, and from what I could hear, protecting me would always be first on his agenda. It wasn't enough.

"I'm leaving," I said. I forced the words out quickly, picturing my fingers ripping off a sticky Band-Aid.

He froze, his hand on the knob. His shoulders stiffened and he turned around and walked slowly back toward the chair. "What do you mean?"

"My mom is sending me to a school. Wood Point Academy. She said it's safer there, while you deal with Miles."

He sank into the chair and gazed back at me. Pain flashed in his expression, and then he blinked and it was gone, replaced by resignation. "It's a good idea. You'll be safe there."

I stared down at the blanket, wondering if that was the extent of his reaction. "You won't be there," I said quietly.

"We'll make it work."

My head came up; my eyes found his. I felt the pull again, and I ached to reach for his hand. "Why?" The word slipped out before I could stop it, and I realized how rude it had sounded, but a small part of me—the part that struggled to remain unaffected by the magnetic force that drew us together—didn't care. "I mean, I thought you'd made your decision. You said it was too dangerous to be together. You broke up with me."

He sighed. "I never said we were breaking up, Tara. I said it was a break. I wanted to make things right with your mother first. And deal with Leo."

I felt myself caving and had to look away to remember what it was that I'd promised myself. What it was that still needed fixing. "And what about the danger?"

"Let's just say I have a feeling you're going to put yourself into plenty of danger, with or without me. I sort of drove myself crazy trying to keep you out of it, and in the end, it didn't do much good." A hint of a smile appeared at the corners of his mouth. "I figure it's better to let you be a part of things than leave you to try to deal with it on your own."

"So, now we're back to protecting me as a hobby? I don't want you to be with me just because you feel some responsibility, or because of some vision of destiny."

Wes got out of the chair and sank onto the edge of the bed, his eyes boring into mine with enough heat to rival the bite on my neck. It was the look that always made me feel like it went all the way through me, to my deepest self. The quiet tone of his voice held the same level of intensity and I knew whatever he was going to say, I wouldn't have the willpower to refute.

"I've been running around for days, trying to be everywhere at once. Protect you, find Leo, and keep you away from danger. But I'm not willing to lose you in the process. Responsibility and visions have nothing to do with it, Tara. You are my destiny."

Something in my stomach flip-flopped. The words were everything I'd wanted to hear since that very first night in the alley. Those words made things like visions and danger and invisible magnets seem like no big deal.

I tried to form some response worthy of what his words meant to me, but my vocal cords felt numb and useless. "And you're mine," was all I managed, and even that was a choked whisper.

I blinked to clear away unshed tears, and then Wes was reaching for me, pulling me to him, pressing his lips to mine. His hands brushed gently at the scratches on my face. His fingertips left trails of heat in their wake, but nothing like the pain and anguish of the bites.

This heat was delicious and dangerous all at once, and I pressed myself harder against him, not wanting it to end. And already feeling a pang of sadness that it would. His hands tangled in my hair, and I slipped mine under his shirt, pressing my palms to his back, wondering if my touch left trails of lovely heat on his skin, as well.

When he began to pull away, I wrapped my arms around his neck and held tighter. I didn't want it to end, not yet. Then I'd have to think about the fact that it still made me angry that he always put my safety ahead of anything else, including our relationship, or that I wasn't completely sure I trusted this strange magnetic pull that always drew me to him, or that there was another Dirty Blood, after all, and he was gunning for me. The list was endless.

I didn't know exactly what waited outside these walls, and outside this moment, but I knew it might never feel this good again.

Thank you for reading!
Cold Blood, Dirty Blood #2, is available now!

About the Author

HEATHER HILDENBRAND was born and raised in a small town in northern Virginia where she was homeschooled through high school. (She's only slightly socially awkward as a result.) She writes romance of all kinds with plenty of abs and angst. Her most frequent hobbies are riding motorcycles and avoiding killer slugs.

Get a complete list of Heather's titles on her website: www.heatherhildenbrand.com.

Other titles by Heather Hildenbrand:

GODDESS ASCENDING: In order to save her family and the one she loves, she'll have to ascend—if the darkness doesn't get to her first.

REMEMBRANCE: She's the cure that could save him... if only she could remember how. "Witches, Werewolves, and WTF?!"

A RISK WORTH TAKING: A New Adult Contemporary Romance with southern charm and a hippie farmer capable of swoon and heartbreak in the same breath.

IMITATION: A Young Adult SciFi Romance with life or death choices and a conspiracy so deep, even a motorcycle-riding bodyguard can't pull you out.

O FACE: Is Summerville's most eligible bachelor hot enough to melt the ice princess herself?

Printed in Great
Britain
by Amazon